House of Hate

House of Hate

Percy Janes

Introduction by Margaret Laurence
General Editor: Malcolm Ross

New Canadian Library No. 124

McClelland and Stewart Limited

New Canadian Library No. 124

McClelland and Stewart Limited

Copyright © 1970 by Percy Janes
Introduction © McClelland and Stewart Limited 1976

All rights reserved

This book was originally published by
McClelland and Stewart Limited in 1970

0-7710-9224-5

The Canadian Publishers
McClelland and Stewart Limited
25 Hollinger Road, Toronto

Printed and bound in Canada

The characters and events in this novel are fictitious.
Any resemblance they have to people and events
in life is purely coincidental

CONTENTS

PART ONE

1. SAUL STONE / 9
2. GERTRUDE YEOVIL / 14
3. SAUL AND GERTRUDE / 19
4. ANK / 32
5. FLINKSY / 56
6. RACER / 75
7. CRAWFIE / 101
8. JUJU / 136
9. FUDGE / 165

PART TWO

1. FAMILY REUNION / 185
2. ANK / 198
3. RACER / 212
4. CRAWFIE / 233
5. HILDA / 250
6. FUDGE / 266
7. SAUL AND GERTRUDE / 302
8. SAUL / 314

this book is dedicated to my sister

Introduction

House Of Hate is an apt title for this novel, for it is placed within the confines of the Stone family, and by remaining within these claustrophic limits the book gains its true strength. In the harsh and bitter character of Saul Stone, and in the varied characters of Saul's wife and children, Percy Janes gives us a complex and totally convincing picture of a family perpetually at war with itself.

We get almost no sense of the outer community, although the Newfoundland background, setting and history are all integral to the novel's effectiveness. True, the paper mill, which is as dark and satanic as any of Blake's, looms constantly in the background, meaning both livelihood and slavery to many of the townspeople, and we are aware of the town itself as a presence, with its stratified class system, its religious animosities, its petty-mindedness. But the townsfolk are mainly introduced in general group terms (one or another of the Stone sons is often said to be going out with a bunch of the "b'ys"), with the exception of those individuals who marry into the Stone family and become part of its domestic war. Most of the events of the novel take place within the ugly and sprawling house, just as the Stone family itself is held spiritually and mentally there, in unwilling bondage to one another.

Juju, the narrator, is the only Stone to leave Milltown for any length of time, except for Racer, who is forced to be away for six years during World War II. Juju is also the only one to obtain a university education. But we are told little about his wanderings in the years between Part One and Part Two, when he returns home for a year at the age of forty. We *are* told that he "came to realize that in these exotic places I had been seeking to prove to myself my passionate childhood conviction that all the world was not like Milltown." And yet the frightening thought occurs that perhaps "this whole world was essentially a Milltown in which I should find no home nor any place of refuge this side of the grave." In his travels, Juju may have carried only one suitcase, but he has plainly carried his entire family with him in his mind. Juju does not hold back on details of his own life – it is simply that anything not directly relevant to the theme of the warring family is not included. In fact, Juju does explain precisely those details of his adult life which relate to his having been "chilled in childhood," namely his inability to form a lasting personal relationship with a woman, and his dread of fathering children.

The angry and warped relationships of several generations of the Stone family is Janes' theme, and he never loses sight of it, never for an instant allows himself to digress. Initially, it may seem to the reader that this singlemindedness narrows the novel's scope, but I don't think this is so. The Stone family *is* narrow, its members living largely unto themselves, unable (except for Juju) to leave one another but also unable to leave one another alone, in the colloquial sense – forever quarrelling, criticizing, planning elaborate revenges for some slight, real or imagined. The shape of the novel thus has the effect of powerfully conveying the stultifying and tortured atmosphere throughout the years within the Stone house.

The focus and originator of the tensions within the family is, of course, Saul Stone himself, one of the most terrifying and yet tragic father figures in all Canadian literature, and we have had some very strong ones, as any quick glance through the Canadian fiction of this century will show. Saul, with his famine Irish Protestant background, knows only work. He is a compulsive worker and cannot permit himself even those few hours of leisure which his job at the mill might allow. His own obsession with work is something he forces on his wife and children as well. He is, furthermore, illiterate and believes his family looks down on him because of it, although it is many many years before Juju gains this crucial insight into his father's character. It is typical of Saul that he should throw his vast energies and frustrations into attempting to build a concrete wall around his house. Not only is he locked tightly into himself, but he also would like to shut the world out entirely. This is a man so enraged and embittered by his early life that he can express only one emotion – anger. Whether it is in bickering with Gertrude, his wife, or in beating the others in the interminable family card games, or in physically beating his sons, Saul Stone trusts only aggression. This is not to say that the only emotion he ever feels is anger. Far from it. His early courtship with Gertrude has had some tenderness, insofar as Saul's clenched nature would allow. And when his son Racer takes off for World War II, the Old Man (as he is known to them all) would clearly like to make amends for the brutal beating he gave the boy not very long before. But he cannot make any gesture which would involve the lowering of his terrible pride or the giving of anything of himself. Instead, he hands the boy a twenty-dollar bill. He is not a verbal man; he is not capable of self-analysis. But in his inchoate way he seems almost to be thinking at this moment that money has value whereas he, Saul, does not. He is a religious man, forcing the entire family out to church twice every Sunday (with Sunday School as well for the children). But his religion seems more related to those Old Testament prophets who believed in a God of Wrath than it does to any gentler aspects of Christianity. Indeed, within his own house, Saul takes on the as-

dustjacket of the original edition, the publishers predicted that *House Of Hate* "in time will be regarded as a classic of its kind." That was a bold claim, but in this case, I believe, a justified one.

Margaret Laurence
Lakefield, Ontario

HOUSE OF HATE

PART ONE

CHAPTER

1

SAUL STONE

Hate is the child of fear, and Saul Stone had been afraid of one thing or another all his life.

Mostly it was hunger, the certainty of not having enough food for today and the dread of having nothing at all for tomorrow. In his origins there was no great fault of character to blame for this chronic insufficiency; it was the misfortune of time and place rather than the result of human improvidence or bad judgment. Many times I heard him tell the tale of how both his father and his grandfather had survived with their families through several famine years on a diet of one potato per person per day. Their home was little more than a mud hut and their means of subsistence no more than a medium-sized potato garden in a remote corner of county Wexford. Such an existence, however, could not go on indefinitely, and with their number increasing every year or two, the original Stone family at last found itself driven by hunger and blind hope to join the swelling crowd that yearly abandoned their meagre holdings and drifted into the big city hoping for work or charity or relief of any kind whatsoever.

So they came to Dublin, and were out of the frying pan and into the fire, for in my grandfather's time, in the late years of the nineteenth century, Dublin was generally no more prosperous than the counties that fed it. Potato famine depressed the entire country, and as for the industry of Dublin, that was little more at this time than a number of petty enterprises profiteering from the fact that there were a hundred men clamouring for each job available in factory, shop, or office.

The Stone men found no work, nor were they as well-off or comfortable in a lousy, swarming, rackety tenement lodging as they had been on their farm; yet they all voted to a man against returning to that dreaded isolation. Instead, like thousands upon thousands of Irishmen at this time, they took the great resolution. They would emigrate. Hunger and despair were not the only prods behind them. Religion played a part too, since they were, as a family, a stubbornly indestructible island of Protestantism in an ever-pressing Roman Catholic ocean. Perhaps by emigrating they would find relief from this pressure as well.

A truly heroic effort of labour and economy enabled the family – all nine of them – to save the few pounds needed for steerage tickets on a shipping speculator's hulk bound from Liverpool to the United States. Boston was their goal and their dream, the city that like New York had already provided so many of their countrymen with work and bread and a measure of freedom and self-respect.

They never reached Boston. After a long voyage of incredible misery and hardship ("There was no room even to sit down. They stood up the whole time, and swalleyed their food like dogs," I often heard my father say), the ship ran into a storm just when land first came in sight, and the old tub simply could not take it. She literally came apart at the seams; her planks and timbers were dispersed and swallowed up like the pieces of an old shack under an avalanche.

None of the men below decks survived, and only a few of the women, who were hauled up on ropes and flung into dinghies so long as anything at all could be done against the raging sea. Hannah Stone, the mother, had no choice but to go in one of the boats, though she knew that all the rest of her family would be lost. But not quite all. She was once again pregnant, and so one child at least might be saved.

That was how our father, Saul Stone, came to the Island of Newfoundland – a child in the womb of a stricken widow. And there he was born, in Raggedy Cove, Conception Bay, in the year 1892.

Newfoundland: a large island but not a fruitful one, and in its geographical features not an hospitable one. An isolated, self-enclosed triangle, each of its coastlines like a graph gone mad, and the interior a wilderness, in its primitive state more suited to the violence of the hunter than to the patient, coaxing arts of agricultural man. And around this harsh land nothing but salt water, the all-encompassing ocean – another hunting ground for man in search of his daily bread.

While millions of emigrants went on safely to the waiting riches of the United States and thousands to the fertile plains of Canada, a dark and vicious fate brought this woman and her child to the shores of this great wedge of rock, tip-tilted against a continent, seemingly sliced off from it by a sardonic nature, and then tumbled out into the Atlantic as if by some mighty overflowing or tidal wave from the St. Lawrence River.

Raggedy Cove was aptly named, being in fact a ragged V cut into the coastline of solid rock. It composed no more than a few shelterless houses that stood deep in the mouth of the cove and backed onto a stretch of grey rocky barrens sparsely dotted with fir trees and blueberry bushes. Here the child Saul grew up and here, from the time when he could turn a fish or trench a potato, he knew one thing only: work.

Bodily labour was the condition and the law of his existence, and the boy accepted this as long as there was some kind of living to be drawn from the sea or scratched from the gritty soil. When that was no longer the case he bundled up the one change of clothes he owned and set out to try his luck in the nearby town of Carbonear. All he could find in the way of work was a berth on a fishing schooner bound for Labrador, and so his thirteenth and fourteenth years saw him spending long summers gutting cod on that solemn coast, and longer winters at home again trying to make his boy's share of the voyage last him and his mother until a few more dollars could somehow be earned.

The spring when he was fifteen he bulled his way into a place on a sealing vessel, but there he found conditions even worse than what he had heard his mother tell of the voyage from Liverpool to Newfoundland. One spring of being ice-bound, fog-bound, and above all, man-bound was enough. A man, Saul reasoned, was not a dog (even a poor workin'-man), and no matter what he agreed to on a wharf in St. John's, when his sixteen hours of toil were done he should have room in the vessel to turn around, without the fellow next to him spitting in his face or ramming an elbow into his eye.

Certainly it was not fear of hard work out on the ice that made him complain, for after pocketing their sealing wages he and a buddy lit out for Canada – "just fer divilment," as he afterwards used to tell it – and ended up in the Sydney coal mines, where again a strong back was all that counted in giving the boss satisfaction. That was all right, until his friend met a girl and got married, but after that they lost touch and Saul felt so lonely and out of place that he gave up his job and returned to Newfoundland for good.

Not to Raggedy Cove, however. Though he continued to send a few dollars now and then to his mother, he settled in St. John's, the capital city of the island, and stuck it out for some years, even though the only job he could find was driving a baker's cart for eight dollars and fifty cents a week. The thick Irish atmosphere of the city answered to his own blood, and people had no trouble understanding his talk or accepting his ways, as they had often had up there in Canada. The only trouble was he seemed unable to get ahead in life. Other young men he knew were not only building but feathering their nests while he continued living in a boarding-house and never put a cent in the bank from one month's end to the next. This pattern of frustration and a precarious existence on the outer edge of things seemed to be a web from which he could not thrash a way out, no matter which way he turned or how desperately he tried.

The Great War came, and he at once offered himself for the navy but was refused on the technical grounds that his mother was dependent on him for support. He therefore had to stand by and see the few friends he had made in St. John's set out on their voyage to the Old Country and adventure across the ocean, leaving him to shuffle his loaves of bread and slide his pans of cakes up and down the steep hills of the city from early Monday morning to late Saturday night. It was his loneliest and heaviest hour.

Dawn came first in the form of a rumour that out on the west coast of the island a big English company was going to put up a paper mill, a gigantic enterprise that would cost millions and offer work to thousands. For months the rumours flew thick and fast, and then one day it all became gloriously official. The Right Honourable Sir Edward P. Morris, Prime Minister of Newfoundland, appeared on the Court House steps facing Water Street in company with a real English lord and announced to a cheering crowd that the contract had been signed and work would begin almost immediately.

There and then Saul Stone made up his mind: if he couldn't be a soldier, at least he would throw off this womanish baker's trade, and at the same time start earning some real money. The fact that his wages had shot up to thirteen dollars a week since the war started did not deter him for a moment once he had worked out his week's notice. Prices had shot up correspondingly, but apart from all that he had a feeling that this was his now-or-never chance.

He suffered gladly the forty-hour trip on the old narrow-gauge Reid Railway and arrived on the mill-site one spring morning with earnest hopes of good wages and a decent living in his heart. For once he was not disappointed. The first time he applied for work the foreman looked him over, front and back, checked his certificate of exemption from military service, and put him to work as a blacksmith's helper on the vast and seemingly never-to-be-ended operation known as Construction.

CHAPTER

2

GERTRUDE YEOVIL

Gertrude Yeovil's forebears came out to Newfoundland as fishing servants. After heaving about for generations on the chill and foggy Banks and being sailed back to their homes in the West Country of England with hardly a day on land; after many bad summers and few good ones in the trade; after a succession of greedy masters on the fishing station and poor winters at home – following all this cumulative discontent, a few of these broad-boned, mild-spoken fishermen determined to evade the laws against settlement in Newfoundland and to make the island their new home.

Of course they could not remain in St. John's or at any place within a few miles of the eastern seaboard, where the master or the Governor's men might pick them up and force them back into bondage; therefore, on escaping from the vessel, they struck inland in a south-westerly direction and after a few days' rigorous travel came to their haven in Placentia Bay on the south coast of the island. Here they would be safe from interference by the English and depredations from the French, who had once lorded it in this spacious bay, but had long since been expelled from all of Newfoundland except for certain fishing rights along the shore.

Haystack was the inexplicable name by which the Yeovils' home became known – inexplicable because in the course of an entire summer hardly enough grass grew there to feed a few goats, and there was never any hay at all. Fishing, not farming, was still the main business of their lives. Until the ice came, lobster, cod, and herring kept the men healthily busy or at least enabled them and their families to survive.

Other families came to Haystack, and during the long winters the men hauled wood by day, and by night they saw to it with the zeal and energy of comparative leisure that their families increased and multiplied. Perhaps it was this – the burden and drag of too numerous offspring – that kept the Yeovils from ever succeeding as independent fishermen.

When they had been in Haystack for two generations, they, like most of their fellows, found themselves in the hands, and on the books, of the local merchant, and from then onwards this crude wholesaler and primitive capitalist ruled their economic lives. They gave him all their fish, receiving due payment at his leisure and pleasure; but no money passed. He paid them in his own profit-making goods, so that after a while they never really knew the value or even the price of anything, eventually reaching a state where they did not care much one way or the other.

In the fall they received from him their barrel of flour, cellar of potatoes, a cask of oil for their lamps, and a few other staples that would at least give them some chance of not perishing until the spring of another year. Until then it was chiefly a matter of the wife and mother stretching the food, scrimping and cutting corners and coddling up her small store of food into meals bulky enough to keep the men going and the youngsters from tormenting her beyond human endurance.

That was how Gertrude Yeovil remembered it from her childhood. When she was an old woman she could still hear herself and her eleven brothers and sisters clamouring at their mother for "bread-and-lassie, bread-and-lassie," and could still see her harassed mother pitifully yet half-reluctantly drawing a loaf of bread from the oven, cutting twelve small slices, spreading a dab of the viscous blackstrap molasses over each and having them snatched from under her hands before she could even finish warning the children to eat it slowly because there would be nothing else before dinner time.

Gertrude also remembered going to school in a dress made out of a dyed flour sack, with the trade-mark still showing across her hips; but the social and educational part of this mortification did not last long, for at the age of eleven she was plucked out of school and put to work in the merchant's lobster canning factory where all hands wore a stiff apron made from a material known as brin bag. During four years she put up with this labour at a wage of ten cents an hour, which again was paid out to her father in goods, her legs being in a perpetual ache from the twelve hours of standing each day, and her hands forever torn and bleeding from the jagged pieces of lobster shell and the edges of the cans. Then she risked – and lost – her reputation by stowing away on a freighting schooner going to St. John's. No man from her own family was a member of the crew, but the master of the schooner turned out to be a decent man who, when he found the shivering, starving girl just as they were rounding Cape Race, fed and protected her for the rest of the voyage and agreed to take her back with him on the return trip to Haystack.

On reaching St. John's, he was appalled by the passion of the Yeovil girl's refusal to return; in fact, he saw clearly that to take her back he would have to tie her down in some part of the vessel, and that went against the grain. He demanded her reasons. Gertrude would give none, though she saw only too clearly her mother's fierce frown of disapproval (in Gertrude's private phrase, she was "strict as the Bible") and the long silence that would be part of the punishment if she did venture to go back home. The rest of her punishment she saw in terms of the Methodist minister being informed of her sin, his preaching at and praying over her in open church while she sat there between Ma and Dad, forced to repent her shame in public as well as in the suffocating atmosphere of piety at home. No. The unknown perils of the big city were easier to face than such an ordeal.

Worn down by her tenacity, the captain finally placed

Gertrude in the home of a St. John's acquaintance of his, a respectable widow who ran a boarding house on Duckworth Street for transient fishermen, sealers, loggers, and railwaymen. The girl was contented enough with this while it lasted, though it was all hard work and poor pay; but then winter came again, all the men boarders went off home or to their camps, and the widow simply could not find enough work in the house to keep herself and a girl busy. Yet she was reluctant to put such a fundamentally sensible girl out on the streets.

Fate stepped in in the form of an advertisement in the *Evening Telegram* which said that a general maid was wanted at Government House to live in and be employed on a permanent basis. Gertrude was still too shy and nervous to go up to the big greystone house on Military Road for an interview herself, but through the widow and a friend it was all arranged, so that within a matter of days she found herself installed in a new situation amid people and surroundings that she had only dreamed about in the most remote and fanciful way up to this time in her life.

The years went by like comets and she learned to accept, even to like, the grim old city of St. John's, or as much of it as she came to know during her weekly half-day off and with the severe limitations of a female in her social position at such a point in the island's history. These were her most impressionable years, and friends noticed that her manner gradually took on ease and confidence. Even her speech changed somewhat. The drawling, word-champing dialect that came to her naturally from dim origins in Somerset, with modifications added by the isolation and local conditions of Haystack, now became overlaid with the colonial Irish spoken by nearly everyone in St. John's. All in all, she came gradually to think of the place as a second home, and often spoke of it as such in later years.

Then the coming of the Great War changed everything for her, as it did for everyone throughout the island. First of all, her young man suddenly went off to England. So did the butler at Government House, his place being taken by an older man whom the entire domestic staff correctly branded as a tyrant, a crook, and an old billy-goat; the blackout came down over the city; wickedness mushroomed in all its most frightening forms; winter nights were like eternity; and if you ventured out in the daytime, there was hardly a young man around to flick your skirt at or torment a little while he walked you up to the back door of the House just before dark.

The whole situation began to get on Gertrude's nerves. She was not excited or moved by the sudden and traditional wartime importance that Britain's oldest colony had taken on for Britain, in contrast to the obscurity and neglect from which the island suffered in time of peace. She resolved on a change; so plucking up her courage, she gave notice and at the same time persuaded a friend who worked in the Church of England Bishop's Palace to do likewise. They would leave this gloomy old city together. What was the use of staying, with everything sky-high in price, so that your wages would hardly keep you in stockings, much less allow you to save the scattered dollar, with the chances of catching a husband about as good as fishing for lobster in January?

One day she and her friend jumped aboard the westbound train and gaily, if also apprehensively, set out for a new life. The idea of returning to Haystack never entered Gertrude's mind as a serious possibility. Of course, she thought of the family there when the train passed through Come-by-Chance, the station she would get off at in order to make connections for the Cove, as the Yeovils' home was always called among themselves. She even felt a pang of sentimental regret while the train was pulling out, but it was not long before her spirits rose again at the prospect of better wages and a freer, brighter kind of life away from all the restrictions and fog and regulations of the eastern city. The two young women left the train at the site of the big new mill on the west coast, a clanging, thriving place where Gertrude had no difficulty at all in finding a job as kitchen maid at a place called The Company Inn.

CHAPTER

3

SAUL AND GERTRUDE

The Company Inn was a ramshackle frame building flung up without regard to design or expense or anything else. It was intended to house all the management personnel, engineers, and other high-ups who had suddenly and numerously appeared on the scene until there was time to put up a proper hotel in a good location.

In Gertrude Yeovil's department things were haphazard too; the kitchen stove was always going out of order and each time it did so she appealed in a fuss and in vain to the janitor. These crises were only to be got over by the head housekeeper asking the manager of the Inn to send for a mechanic or a blacksmith or somebody from the mill to come and repair the stove once and for all.

One morning, when things were a little worse than usual and Gertrude was all in a fluster because the meat would not brown and she had thirty-seven men to get dinner for by one o'clock, she heard a rap on the door and turned from the maddening stove to see the doorway filled by a shabby, rusty-looking young man who hung back diffidently from the threshold and seemed as if he might stand there forever without explaining his presence if she did not stir him up. Impatiently she asked what it was he wanted. Not a meal, she hoped, because they had nothing to give away until after the regular dinner was done, and that would be never in God's world by the look of things at that moment.

The young stranger stiffened on being treated in this

way. He was by nature so dark that he seemed always to be standing in shadow, yet now his face grew darker as it was overspread by a scowl of pride. He stepped into the kitchen, slowly removing his cap as he entered. He had come about the stove, and was therefore suddenly welcomed by Gertrude instead of being shooed away as an extra annoyance. Gertrude had almost to arch her back in order to see his face properly when he came closer; at the same time she inhaled with relish the strong odour of maleness that emanated from his person – a pungency of sweat and leather, tobacco and iron and unwashed clothes that had always been for her the smell of a real man.

His features were good too, though sharply cut inward from temple to chin, and he had thick hair black as tar that lay neatly across the right side of his head in a shallow wave. When he moved toward the stove and stood with his back to her, she noticed with a pang how thin he was; his shoulder blades stuck out through a threadbare jacket like stirring wings. He seemed strong enough for all that. His long-boned fingers handled the heavy cast-iron pieces of the stove as casually as Gertrude would handle knives and forks, and when he had to shift the stove in order to examine the back he did not need any help at all. It was his eyes, however, that captured her attention and gave her a thrill. They were ice-blue in colour and glowed in that sombre face beneath a Neanderthal ridge of bone like far-distant stars. They gave her the cold shivers, but made her no less impudent in watching him and studying him as he was explaining the trouble with the stove. Loose dampers – they were the chief defect, causing most of the heat to come out into the room when it should have been warming the oven. Gertrude was again impatient over his technical talk. All she cared about was whether he could fix the thing. Well, new dampers were needed and they would have to be sent away for, unless they could be cast down in the foundry. That would take a few days at least, but for the present those cracks and holes could be plugged with a proper asbestos cement that would hold in the heat as long as she did not remove the dampers. The young man then went back to the mill to fetch the cement.

The moment he had gone, Gertrude rushed over to the mirror she kept above the sink for emergency purposes and observed with horror that there was a smudge of soot on her forehead and that her crinkly auburn hair was, in the language of that time, like a birch broom in the fits. A dash to her room for a clean apron, after she had washed and tidied herself, made Gertrude feel at least decent by the time the workman had come back to finish his job.

When it was all done and her meat sizzling and bleeding nicely in the oven, she felt grateful to him and suddenly apologetic about the way she had received him on his first appearance. He answered her gentle words with a grim smile and the remark that she was the first person in the world who had ever taken him for a bum. Gertrude saw at once that she must look sharp to win back ground already lost in his estimation. She assured him with her most deprecating smile that she had meant no harm; it was just that they got dozens of loafers hanging around the kitchen door coming on toward dinner time, even though there was plenty of work on construction. She hurried on to ask him whether he had steady work at the mill and how he found conditions in general. Yes, he had a steady job. That was all right, but there was not much for him to do in the evenings or at the weekend. He had no people in this place; in fact, he had nobody at all except his mother, and she was still out on the east coast. Then he had to stay in a boarding-house, Gertrude assumed, pressing her advantage in having made him talk at all by keeping the conversation on himself. What did they feed him in such a place? she wondered, and did not hesitate to survey his gaunt frame with frank womanly concern. The young man complained that he got a lot of beans and that creeping stuff they called spaghetti. Worms, he and the other men called it. Gertrude tut-tutted in sympathy.

Then she had an excellent idea that came out so spontaneously it might not have occurred to her until that very instant. She invited him to stay at the Inn for his dinner that day and have a proper meal for a change. At this her guest thrust out one arm in an awkward, self-deprecating gesture and muttered an inarticulate objection, but Gertrude understood him at once, and for answer took him into the servants' dining-room where he would not feel out of place in any way. There she soon had him dealing ravenously with the kind of food he understood – thick slabs of roast beef, whole potatoes, and salty cabbage all covered in a viscous, blood-flavoured gravy. After his second helping he slowed down a little and seemed to become more approachable and even relaxed. He told her straight out that that was the best meal he had ever had since leaving St. John's, and thanked her with old-fashioned fullness of courtesy, calling her "missis" several times, obviously gratified by more than the food.

Gertrude felt it was time to ask him his name. It was Stone, Saul Stone, and the old Bible name caused Gertrude to smile again because such names were so common in her own family. When she introduced herself and told him to call her Gertie like everyone else, she passed on to her next query. Why wasn't he in the army? Gertrude made no bones about her curiosity, but the question brought another scowl to Saul Stone's face followed by a reluctant explanation. He had offered to join up, the same as any *man* would; the only trouble was the authorities had turned him down because he was his mother's only support and therefore exempt from service. Saul drew his creased and greasy exemption paper from his inside pocket, at the same time assuring Gertie that there was nothing wrong with him, nothing in the way of what they called disability. Here he was less reluctant to talk, even urgent in his defensive pride. Gertrude had to assure him she had meant no offence, and she then admonished him in motherly fashion not to be so *takey*.

Half mollified, he still grumbled that if a man was not

wearing khaki people seemed to take it for granted that he was some kind of a cowardly hangashore, a slacker. To calm him down still further, Gertrude quickly served him with two cups of barky tea (she knew he would like it good and strong) and topped off his dinner with a plate of blueberry pudding and cream. Finally she offered him a drink of rum from the kitchen supply; she was not in the least put out when he refused that; in truth, her reaction was one of approval when he informed her that he rarely used liquor and never at all during a working day.

While Gertrude was busying herself with getting things ready for all the men who came to their dinner at one o'clock, Saul Stone sat back and used his few precious minutes of rest in reflecting that here was a woman who certainly knew how to treat a man. One of the old-fashioned Newfoundland breed, she clearly had no foolishness about her and she was pleasant to look at too; not tall, and not "done up," with a pale face shaped like a broad shield, smiling mouth, and an almost perpendicular forehead that gave her a look of earnestness to offset the mischief in those dancing tawny eyes. She had a large chin coming forward at the base and pleasantly rounding off a salient jaw line. As for her figure, buxom was the only word to describe Gertrude Yeovil, and even that could give only an impression of her utterly feminine plumpness, the dramatic flare of her hips, and all the obvious though never blatant pleasure she took in her own womanhood.

She managed to spend a little more time with Saul before he went back to his afternoon's work and to give him a thick packet of meat and pickle sandwiches, in case he got hungry before his tea time. When he demurred and wondered if she might get into trouble over such a thing, she urged him to take the food, and welcome he was to it. According to her, they threw out enough at the Inn, every week, to feed a regiment for the same length of time. A shocking wasteful place it was! Again Saul nodded his thanks on accepting the extra food, and again Gertrude had to smile at his reserve and the economy he used even with words. To keep him a moment longer, she asked how soon he thought the new pieces for the stove would be ready. Oh, a few days, he thought, maybe a week. Didn't he find it lonesome out there on the west coast, after the town? Gertrude lingered with him at the doorway as long as she dared. She was lonesome herself. She missed the crowds, all the racket in the streets, and above all the parades and the military ceremonies at Government House. At last when she could share memories with him no longer, at the peril of losing her place, she invited him to come back any time, no matter if the pieces were not ready. If he liked he could come back again as soon as he got tired of that creeping spaghetti.

He did come back, soon, and without any excuse beyond his own inclination. Two evenings after their first meeting, he was waiting round at the back door of the Inn a good hour before she would be free. Spotting him as soon as he appeared, Gertrude did her best not to keep him waiting for more than the unavoidable hour, and even took some of her working time to tidy herself after the day's final clean-up in her kitchen. She noticed at once and with pleasure that he was nicely dressed, though without a tie – because, as he explained later, he could not stand anything tight round his neck, unless he was going to church or to a funeral or something like that. Again, he simply was not used to it. Gertrude smiled and privately thought that he looked quite nice indeed for a man out on his own and with nobody to look after him. She herself was wearing her second-best and was fully conscious of showing herself to advantage in the tight-waisted, square-bosomed, truly graceful costume that was modelled from a picture of the Princess Alexandra.

On that first evening they did nothing much beyond going for a walk, but this was an old-time Newfoundland walk: a trek of several miles over rough ground and a similar test of endurance all the way back by a different route. Gertrude did not mind. Nor did she mind having to do most of the talking, for Saul still had to be coaxed into conversation and seemed to regard his words as valuable coins not to be lightly thrown away. As they were returning to the Inn, she teased him a little about being so glum and asked him if he were worried about anything, or if he had any trouble of that kind. Then he must be in love, Gertrude accused him with a full-throated laugh and another teasing look.

Saul only tossed his head as though to be tolerant with a woman's foolishness, but Gertrude kept on at him in a slightly more serious tone. He seemed kind of *down*, somehow – that was what she meant; perhaps it was that hole he lived in, or the newness and strangeness of the whole place for everyone thus far. On her asking him whether he liked it at all, he answered with convincing, almost explosive force that it was better than Raggedy Cove, by Jesus, a sight better! She hushed up his swearing and continued her efforts to make him talk by asking if he were ever homesick and ever felt any longing to head back east. It was no again to that. He would stay where he was as long as there was regular work and they treated a man decently, as it seemed he was being treated in the forge. Gertrude was glad of this answer, for she too preferred to take her chances out here; she found it exciting to watch the mill and the town growing almost daily and people flocking in from poorer places as if it were the Promised Land. Besides, she felt people could draw their breath out here and had a real chance to live. It was not at all like sooty, slummy St. John's or the slavish poverty of places like Haystack.

That was all that happened on their first evening together, Saul coming only a little closer when he said a respectful goodnight and leaving her with a more or less wordless understanding that he would come back to see her on her next evening off, and this Gertrude accepted in the belief that once the ice of his reserve was broken he would soon show himself a more likely lover. Already she felt as sure of him as that.

And indeed he did prove himself, at their next few meetings, quite punctual and reliable, even eager to please her in his awkward, pathetic way. The first time he kissed her goodnight he needed only a little encouragement. Then one Sunday evening when the air was dry and mild, they went deeper into the surrounding woods than ever before. She began to tease him again, and suddenly he flung her down and took her body by storm. He needed no encouragement then, and recognized no resistance. The passion in those pale and blazing eyes was not to be denied.

Afterwards, Gertrude made little fuss, though in fact it was her first time going all the way. Most of the girls she knew jumped the gun where sex was concerned, and most of them got their man. More than one she had known in St. John's, and out here too, had provoked a rape in order to hook him. At least she would never have to reproach herself with that. Now her feeling of the difference in things was chiefly expressed by her taking his arm in a more settled and proprietary way than formerly, on the long walk back home, signifying that there was an understanding between them which anyone they knew might hereafter take account of.

Their ease with each other soon reached the point where Saul was telling her all about his bodily complaints. He "found" his stomach, it seemed, and could get no satisfaction in his diet or regularity in his bowels. Gertrude assured him that he would never be much better until he got away from that boarding-house and the everlasting beans and spaghetti. Often at this point he nodded his head and, turning to face her, belched volcanically. Gas. That was his main trouble, apparently, and he told her all about it in the solemn style of one giving evidence in an important case. Gertrude added sympathetically that his trouble might also come from not being able to chew properly. He would have to get his teeth soon, before they....

Gertrude chopped off her words at that point, but Saul perfectly understood what she had intended to say. He stopped on the woodland path they were following. Their eyes met. Although he stumbled and muttered over his proposal, he did manage to get out that he had been *talking to* her now for a nice while. A lot had passed between them, and so if she was willing, *he* was. And – well, what about it? Gertrude smiled and accepted this form as perhaps the best he could do; she stretched up for a kiss and whispered yes, she was his for life, if he was sure he really wanted her. They kissed once more, and without further talk on that subject resumed their stroll in a close embrace and with a new sense of something more than physical closeness. They were a young couple taking refuge in each other from a strange and often hostile world.

Their engagement period was brief and uneventful except for one or two odd incidents that made Gertrude anxious about the wisdom of her choice. About a month before her wedding was to take place, she heard, as an item of backstairs gossip, that a fellow named Saul Stone had nearly killed a man down in the mill with a shovel; and when she tackled him with the rumour that same evening, he was at first quite evasive. She demanded to know what in the world such violence was all about. In fact, she was frightened, yet bent on learning the truth. Saul muttered savagely while assuring her that the whole thing was nothing to make such a fuss over. At last, after more prodding on Gertrude's part, he came out with the kernel of the story: the man he had attacked had mentioned her name.

Surely that was no crime! Gertrude was still puzzled, and remained so until Saul came out reluctantly and bitterly with his next bit of information. The man, in mentioning her name, had smiled. From the way Saul said this and the look that came with it, Gertrude at last understood, and she defended herself hotly against the implied charge. It was clear that when Saul had said "smiled" he meant "leered": the man had attacked her reputation. With full justification Gertrude now assured Saul that, even though he was not the only young man she had walked out with in this place, there had never been anything out of the way in her behaviour, except with himself, and that of course could be known only to themselves. She kept on talking (inwardly cursing those loose-mouthed, untrustworthy men she had previously known) until Saul was nodding vigorously in assent, assuring her that he had never believed it all in the first place. He just would not allow anyone to talk and act as that bloody liar had acted when speaking about him or any person belonging to him. Besides, he knew he was the very first one with her, and nothing could change that.

These assurances calmed Gertrude at last and swung her mind to another aspect of the matter. She felt flattered as well as alarmed over all this: it was a good thing to have such a single-minded, passionate protector, as long as he did not get into any more fights or really serious trouble. On the whole it would be best if they got married quite soon, and then nobody could say anything of *that* kind to damage her name or to upset Saul, and put him into the rigid passion that this foolish incident had induced. Gertrude's thoughts in the matter of an early wedding were given a rude jolt forward after she missed one monthly, then another, and finally knew for certain that, as she accounted it to herself, she was already Saul Stone's wife in everything but name.

During the time of preparations for the wedding, another incident occurred that might have caused anxiety to a woman less pliable or more dogmatic than Gertrude Yeovil. She happened to ask him what church they were going to be married in. Why, in the Church of England – naturally. In *his* church. Saul showed surprise at her even asking such a thing, and when she mentioned that in that case she would have to turn, he hardly understood her at all. Gertrude explained that she was Methodist, but to Saul that made not a particle of difference in any way. He insisted roughly and peremptorily that they had to be married as he saw fit. Just to tease him a little more she said casually, whimsically, that after all there was the possibility of him turning to her. At that he straightened up fiercely to his full height and said in the most emphatic of tones that he had no use for a turncoat. It was of no use at all for Gertrude to point out that if she married into his religion she was a turncoat, for to Saul that was a different thing altogether: it was only right and proper for the woman to turn to the man. As he was laying down the law in this fashion, he began to tremble with impatience, perhaps with anger, and when Gertrude saw him make that familiar cutting gesture, she now recognized a danger signal. She expressed only one more thought which was simply to the effect that she did not know what her Ma would have to say about the whole thing. How she kept on! Saul complained. It was not as if she had been a Catholic. Before leaving the subject, as she judged it best to do, Gertrude could not resist the temptation to ask him what he would have done if she *had* been a Roman – just supposing, of course. Saul drew apart from her, gave her an indignant stare, and answered in unmistakable terms that in such a case he would never have had anything to do with her at all.

Though hurt by this remark, Gertrude felt no resentment based on religion because she did not in the least care which religion they were married in as long as it was done soon, according to the laws of God and man. Of more genuine concern to her was the question of where they were going to live when they had become man and wife. After talking it over with Saul she was relieved to find that on this matter they were in complete agreement. The new townsite was not for them. Too fancy and too dear. Only the "big fellows" from the mill could afford to rent or buy a house in there. Saul and Gertrude gladly acknowledged themselves as below that class of people.

To Gertrude's delight it turned out that Saul had already bought a small block of land up on the heights to the east of the townsite. And never once had he mentioned it to her in all their time together! Exclaiming over this, Gertrude drew from him his slow, rueful smile and the remark that he had to give her a nice little surprise once in a while, he supposed, seeing they were still a courting couple. He had certainly managed to do that now, for the beauty of it all was that Gertrude herself would have chosen just this area in which to build a home. In some important ways, at least, she felt she had picked a dependable man and a sensible one too. Nothing would do but that they must walk up, and he would show her the place that very evening.

They climbed steadily away from the mill and the harbour, Gertrude panting and puffing as she tried to keep up with her man's vigorous and enormous strides. Once she stopped and turned to let the breeze play on her overheated face and to survey the scene below. She wondered what they were going to call the whole place once the mill was finished and it became a regular town. Saul had heard it was going to be called Milltown. Gertrude did not like that name and when Saul, who thought it was appropriate enough, asked her why, she said it was a shame to put a dull name like that on such a pretty place. She thought it should have a more pleasant or fancy name, like some of the places on the east coast or over around her home, towns like Harbour Grace or Heart's Delight, areas such as Fortune Bay. Saul only laughed at her for having queer women's notions at times.

But Gertrude did like the piece of land he had bought. They stood in the centre of it, her body leaning trustfully against his, and talked dreamily of their future on this spot, side by side. It would be so good for Saul to come home to a properly cooked meal in the evening, and above all so pleasant for Gertrude to have nobody to boss her around in her own kitchen. Saul appreciated all that, though what he saw most clearly was the beauty of privacy and, above all, independence. He was forever reminding her that when you were independent you could "tell 'em all to kiss your arse." Gertrude laughed jubilantly as he repeated this now. It reminded her too of how careful he must be with his money, since he was only a labourer, paying his board, living all on his own – not able to manage like a woman, she meant; and yet he had still been able to save enough to buy the land.

Saul admitted to not wasting much. That had been bred into him or knocked into him as far back as he could remember. His achievement was all the more remarkable in that he had also been sending something to his mother ever since starting work in the mill.

That brought Gertrude to another point she wanted clearly settled before they set up house together. She approached it obliquely, asking in a soft voice whether they would really be all to themselves up there. At first Saul did not understand what she was driving at, so she came right out and asked him whether it was likely his mother would want to come out and live with them once they were settled. On this point Saul set her mind at rest instantly and without the slightest doubt: his mother would never leave Raggedy Cove. That was as sure as fate, and would remain so.

Gertrude tried not to sound too pleased while she broached the only remaining point of great importance, which was the question of where they were going to live right after they were married. Saul had thought of that too. He reckoned they could stay at his boarding house and Gertrude could help out the missis there as part payment for their keep. (He would not hear of Gertrude continuing at the Inn as a married woman, as *his* wife.) And then, in the spring of the year, they could start putting up their own place on their own ground, and before the cold weather came again they would be in their own home. That was the best he could do, he told her, studying her face and asking whether it suited her. Indeed it did suit her, she answered him with a grateful sigh. Indeed it did.

CHAPTER

4

ANK

That was how our family came to live up on the Humber Heights in Milltown. Here in this ruggedly beautiful haven of the Bay of Islands, a spot where every prospect pleases, we were all born and raised and met our various fates.

It was indeed a pretty place, with its great oval harbour lying at the town's feet. Throughout each summer day, it changed colour from pale turquoise at dawn to deep, steely midnight blue. The only break in this oval was on the east side where the Humber River flashed and thundered down through its own deep valley and brought fresh water to meet the salt just a few hundred yards down from our doorstep. And all this beauty – harbour, river, and town – was ringed and cradled in the rear by an unbroken range of blunted sierras, fir-clothed on their inner slopes, turning the air at their summits into a misty indigo haze in the late afternoon light. Only here and there on these slopes was there an outcropping slab of rock, whitish limestone or gleaming granite, as though even here nature were spasmodically showing her teeth.

By the time I came to know it as the place where I belonged, the town itself was divided into three parts. There was the central residential area or townsite, built on the only level ground available and running right back through the east and west valleys until the newer houses butted up against the mountains. Then there was the West Side, a ragged hilly area flanking the townsite from that direction as our own Humber Heights flanked and overlooked it from the east. There was also Shacktown, a section of the west side where the very pooor lived, and beyond that Crow Gulch which was the dumping ground for bums, bootleggers, and other less-mentionable outcasts. The focal point of all these divisions was the mill, now a vast amorphous pile covering acres and acres, from the peninsula of bark that kept creeping out into the harbour back to the enormous pyramids of pulpwood that lay on the landward side of the mill. These were constantly built up and renewed by huge phallic conveyors slowly but relentlessly bearing their sperm of logs to the very top and then dropping them onto the precious pile that activated the mill, giving life to the whole town. Work in the mill never stopped, night or day, Sunday or Monday. Always there came from that immensely sprawling paper factory a hiss of steam and belch of smoke and hum of power, plus periodic waves of the nose-tickling, throat-clutching sulphur dioxide gas which was one of the many by-products and which we up on the Heights received in full blast and flavour when the wind was in the north-west.

We did not live on a street. The straggling stony lane, rising up from the beach to our house and beyond, pulled crazily from one side to the other by the staggered line of houses, was known simply as The Hill. Our home was a one-storey frame house of matchless ugliness, built on land so steep that in our basement there was head clearance of ten feet on the lower side, while on the upper there was hardly room to push a shovel between the sill and the ground. This gave the building a towering, up-ended look and made one feel, as do so many of the terribly exposed houses throughout Newfoundland, that a good stiff offshore breeze would tumble the whole place right down into the salt water.

Brown was the permanent outside colour of this monstrous great box, a matt brown like that of unsweetened chocolate. Inside, there were the usual wooden partitions covered with wallpapers that varied only in the degree of their hideousness. For many years we had no heat in the whole house except from the huge wood-and-coal stove in the kitchen, and so it was to this room that most of the activity and life of our family was drawn – from the chilly August evenings to the first real warmth of summer that generally came about the time school closed late in the month of June. It was not an especially large kitchen, but it was saved from claustrophobic inadequacy by two large windows that commanded a view of the entire harbour right out to the narrow channel that allowed the company's ships escape from the bay, and brought the outside world to Milltown in the form of passenger ships and paper boats that came and went from spring to fall, until the ice closed in for the long months of winter.

It was a good thing we had this spatial relief from the pressures of our family life in the kitchen, for during those early years we Stones were a smarmy, gregarious, quarrelling lot, from our father, Saul, down through Mom and all the five children of whom I was the youngest, the baby of the family. To us, Dad was a remote, pasty-faced source of survival and odd bits of cash and other less pleasant things; Mom a robust figure moving rapidly in her moods from jollity to sadness, to anxiety, and then back again to the cheerful ribaldry that seems to have been characteristic of her in those spring-time years of our family life.

Outside the home both had honourable reputations in working-class Milltown circles, and on the hill our mother was kindly known to one and all as Big Gert. Her capacious bosom was balanced by two massively rounded projections of flesh extending backward from her shoulders, which stood out with extra prominence, I always observed, whenever she dressed up to go down over the hill. A mighty belly and all the rest were in proportion, except for her comically spindly legs, and her face had a fullness that blurred any individual feature though it could never hide the liquid vivacity of those taffy-brown eyes. Touch her body where you would, it was as if you had prodded a sponge. Two hundred and twenty pounds was her normal weight, and within this mass of flesh she lived and moved as comfortably as some great gentle bird who has built around herself an ample, cushioning nest that will endure a lifetime.

By the time I was ten and my oldest brother was fourteen, I began to see us all as a family unit. Of course memory goes back beyond that, but it was then that I became clearly conscious of the hierarchy within our family, and of my own unconsidered position within that hierarchy. My brother's name was Henry, which we in our rapid, incisive way had soon declined from Henry to Hank to Anky to Ank, by which flat monosyllable he was always known to family and friends. Ank was a square-cut, stubby fellow, stubby in physique, in beard, and even in his finger ends. He showed in his blocky shoulders and heavy features the brute strength that reinforced his natural position among us as eldest son and deputy father. When we all went swimming together – all of us boys – we always referred to him as the whale, to myself as the pinfish, and to the others as salmon or cod or eel, according to the fancy of the moment.

Ank was always relied on by Mom to settle our brawls and knock us into some kind of order and peace and quiet each weekday about five-thirty, before Dad came home. That was a kind of family deadline and the point that in our minds marked off ease and joy from sober attention to behaviour and duty. Each evening Ank would round us all up from various parts of the hill and herd us into the house and over to the kitchen sink where Flinksy, our only sister, would give the younger boys the vigorous scrub with Sunlight soap and cold water that served to keep us clean above the neckline day by day until our great family scouring in the washtub on Saturday night.

After the evening wash we would fidget around, picking at the pots and pans on the stove and getting on Mom's nerves to the point where she would passionately wish for the thousandth time that "the cats had the youngsters." She would then be obliged to call once more on Ank for moral and physical support. She was big, but all together we were too many for her. That was the way it always went, day after day, with Mom getting more and more anxious as the clock ticked on toward six o'clock and Dad was due any minute. Quite often she would spill or break something at the stove, or Flinksy would do so while setting the table, at which times her exasperation would draw from our mother the one great exclamation that seemed to sum up and express all the irritations of her domestic life.

"Shit!" she would cry with explosive passion as another cup shattered on the floor. "Curse it, can't ye leave me in peace till I gets the tea? Ank, make 'em stand sound, will you?"

"Aw, they needs a good lash in d'arse, the whole bloody lot of 'em," Ank would growl in the local *patois* which our family speech had hammered down from the Irish and West Country of our heritage and the gobbled syntax of unlettered Newfoundlanders.

We would all laugh at Mom, and also at Ank, knowing but still not fully recognizing his authority, until he became really angry and the taut, glassy scar tissue over his left eye, where Crawfie had once thrown a pair of scissors at him, began to glow scarlet with the pressure of his wrath. Then we heeded him.

Although we were only four boys and one girl, we always sounded like a roaring crowd and were in fact a crowd that even Ank found hard to control. Not until there came that long, slow tramp in the lane running into our house, and that firm proprietary tread on the back steps, was our brawling quite stilled and our mingled laughter and vituperation cut off as though by the stroke of a sword. Dad was home.

He would stand in the doorway scowling at our sudden silence, so tall and spare and sombre his figure that I once gained the tribute of a laugh from all the rest of the family by comparing him to a lighthouse with the light gone out. His mouth sagged as though tiny weights had been suspended from the corners and blackish runnels of tobacco juice extended and deepened its whole parabolic line. At the parting of his hair, as on the opposite side, there were deep receding V's of bare flesh, bringing the central mat of his hair forward to a sharp point which added to the effect of Mephistophelean acuteness made by his whole countenance. For a long moment he would stand blocking the light in the doorway, an alien in his own house, while Mom relieved him of his lunch can and scurried to take up the meal and have it steaming on the table by the time he had washed his hands in the sink.

Our tea, as we always called our evening meal, was like a solemn mass compared with the free and easy midday dinner we had all enjoyed when the Old Man was at work in the mill. He seldom uttered a word at the table except complaints, but these came readily enough to his tongue on any pretext whatsoever. Quite often before we had even begun eating he would take up his fork and, stabbing it into one piece of food or another, break out with his customary snarl.

"Gert! Gert! Them spuds is not biled. Hard as rocks. The peas is like goatshit. What's dis – harse meat? Can't I get one decent meal when I comes home from work?"

And Mom would come rushing out of the pantry with her perpetual anxious frown and her tut-tut-tut of annoyance. "Will you quit bawlin', Saul? There's nutting wrong with the spuds or anything else. Ank, ent them spuds soft enough to your likin'? Ent they?"

Ank would briefly lift his head from his plate and mutter that they seemed all right to him. After this there usually came from Mom the old refrain of fourteen years' frustration. " 'Tis some job to please you! You'll have to get your teet', Saul. How many times am I after tellin' you? But it's all no good. I could talk till I'm blue in the face, and you'd still just sit there mumblin' and grumblin' like a . . . like a ole nannygoat."

Thus she would go on and on, overwhelming him with a torrent of words until in self-defence he would finally attack his meal without any further complaints, except to say that it was all cold as ice in the bargain. Usually he added to his case against her by pushing away his plate while about one-quarter of the large meal remained on it.

"Give us a cup o' tea, fer Christ sake," he then called out in a surly tone, as though doubting whether he could get such a simple thing as tea without having it botched up in some way.

This was the moment some of us were waiting for, chiefly Racer, Crawfie, and myself. Having finished our own portions we were now faced with the problem of how to snatch the remains off Dad's plate and gulp them down without so much noise and racket that we would either be sent away from the table or suddenly brought to order by a clip from the Old Man's heavy hand right across the chops. Usually Racer and I won out, Racer by his superior strength at this time and I by alertness, whereupon Crawfie would set up a howl and keep on howling until Mom brought him a little something extra from the pantry and thereby staved off another "fuss," as she always termed Dad's explosions of anger against his family.

After tea the evening routine contained no more peace or harmony than the hours from breakfast to tea-time. Most nights there was a dispute between Mom and Flinksy over who would do the dishes and who would make the bread, iron the clothes and in general tidy up and get things ready for the cup of tea that was our daily ritual at bedtime. Dad paused only briefly for a smoke after tea, then plunged into his mania, like some madman whose days were numbered.

His mania was work – general and incessant improvements around the house which he, with a devilish inventiveness, was continually devising in and out of season, and by which he very nearly drove us boys to despair. In spite of the drag and dehydration of long days in the inferno of the blacksmith's shop at the mill, he seemed always ready for an evening's toil inside or outside the house. Mixing cement was his favourite pastime. We had already replaced the wooden shores under the house with concrete posts, then put a concrete wall around three sides of the basement, floored the lower part with concrete, and finally erected huge pillars to support the twin gates at the end of our drive.

Now he had got the morbid idea of putting an eight-foot-high concrete wall along the lower side of the drive so as to prevent our ground from crumbling and dribbling down onto the property of our neighbours and piling up against their shack. It was a big job, needing first of all a wide trench to be dug well below the frost line and the entire length of the drive; and so almost any evening we were to be seen shortly after tea – all of the boys except Racer – out there in the mud, Crawfie fumbling with the heavy wheelbarrow, myself demanding to know why all the rush whenever the Old Man swore at me and feverishly demanded more speed in my light labours, and Ank now and then spitting fiercely on both hands and rubbing them together as he once more laid into the task with pick and shovel.

Meanwhile Racer was usually to be seen escaping out the front door dressed in the best clothes in the house that would fit him and precociously bound for one of his legendary dates. Most often he waited until Dad's back was turned, but just as often Crawfie spied him in his finery and called out, "Hey, mister, give us a nickel?" Racer would give him a murderous look and take off down the hill like a desperate fugitive. Resigning ourselves to his absence, we would then settle down to slavery until it was dark, time for our cup of tea, and the final racket of getting to bed.

That was the way it went from Monday to Friday, but Saturdays were a kind of holiday, though this day too had its perils. After our communal bath, we had to line up and have our heads combed out for Sunday. Mom would sit by the kitchen window and, holding each of us in turn by the chin, would press forward heavily along the scalp with a fine-tooth comb and then eagerly examine our scalps for nits and lice and other foreign bodies that might be seen and talked of by anyone close to us. Whatever she found would be triumphantly squashed against the comb with a little sensual click and a tiny spurt of blood and guts from under her thumbnail.

The other peril of Saturday nights was the cutting of our nails. Until we achieved co-ordination and self-determination, Mom always did this too, and her weapon was a large pair of sewing scissors with which she would swoop and slash away in an off-hand, absent-minded style that always made me dread the whole operation. There was no escaping her grip and her bulk, and it was little short of a miracle that we all grew up with ten complete fingers and toes. A thing that further troubled me was the entire absence from her operations of what I later learned to call the aesthetic element. She always left great wedges of nail in the corners or else she chopped straight across and so close to the quick that your finger curled up at the end. But when I protested against the look and feel of the thing, she only laughed and called me a queer little monkey and never made any change in her methods.

The occasion of all this cleaning and paring – Sunday – was in some ways worse than a weekday. It nearly always began with a fuss. Soon after breakfast there was Dad in his undershirt seated at the kitchen table with a pan of hot water in front of him and a straight razor in hand, ready for the painful process of his bi-weekly shave. Hardly had he made the first scrape when Mom would come walking across the floor in the ordinary course of her work, shaking the whole house with the weight of her tread.

"Jesus Christ!" Dad would exclaim. "Jesus Christ – makin' me say so of a Sunday morning. Can't you sit still for five minutes till I'm finished me shave?"

"I got to do me work too, haven't I?"

"I'll cut me t'roat, woman, if you keeps on like that."

"Too bad about you."

"Keep *still*, I'm sayin'."

"Oh, all right, all right. Don't be bawlin'. They can hear you all over the hill."

"I don't give a damn if they hears me on the West Side.

I'm not goin' to cut meself to pieces just 'cause you goes and shakes the whole place like a t'understarm."

"I'll go and make the beds, then. But hurry on, or else we'll all be late."

At last the shave would be accomplished by Dad, the mess would be cleaned up by Mom, and off to church we would go, driven in a small herd by the glare of the Old Man's eye and the oppressive consciousness of his presence directly behind us. On Sundays he always wore his heavy grey overcoat which he had owned so long it went in and out of style; there was usually a large drop hanging from his nose; and whenever we looked behind to see just how close he was, we were always amused by the sight of Mom clutching at his arm and scurrying along a pace or so behind him while she continually begged him not to walk so fast.

The boredom of that dolefully chanted, half-Latinized, and wholly incomprehensible Matins was exceeded only by the boredom of Sunday School in the afternoon and then Evensong, to which again we were all driven, or sent, under the threat of punishment not in hell but right there and then on earth, and with the Old Man's razor strap. The only scrap of Sabbath compensation we had came at the end of Evensong, when like a pack of unleashed hounds we would burst out of our own church and race one another up to the Salvation Army Citadel on the Heights, where there was lively music and all sorts of interesting things like violent personal testimony to the mercy of the Lord Jesus, and the awful, sometimes hilarious spectacle of seeing a new sinner or an old backslider being actually saved from everlasting damnation.

On Monday, of course, it all started again – the weekly routine of work in school and more work at home. Wherever we turned there was work, and it was only to be expected that the major burden of all this toil should fall on Ank as the eldest and strongest among the boys. For years he laboured without murmur or protest, giving his strength freely and proudly to each heavy task, but as time wore on we, his brothers, sensed a gradual change in him. At night, when he came to his cot in the same room where Racer, Crawfie, and I slept in the other bed, he would begin to mutter curses between his large carious teeth.

"By Christ," was the refrain of his vows, "it got to stop. The teacher gives me hell 'cause I haven't got all me homework done, and the Old Man gives me double hell if I'm not out there every night slavin' away in that goddam Panama Canal he's tryin' to dig."

The first radical change came when Ank left school to go to work and help out with the family budget. In Milltown conditions were not as good as they had been throughout the early days of the mill's operation. Some two or three years before this change in Ank's life we had heard echoes of something called the Crash, and now we too were suffering like the outside world from the effects of the Depression. Ank did not mind leaving school, as he had already passed his fourteenth year without achieving Grade VIII, and in any case he was even then entirely permeated by the local conviction that money, and not learning, made a full man. So, although the mill was on short time and there had recently been a general cut in wages, he was very glad to find a job loading the gigantic rolls of newsprint from wharf to ship on the company's waterside premises.

From this time dated Ank's revolt against what amounted to the Old Man's feudal domination. He was still the workhorse among us boys, but rebellion was rising in him like a brute beast that has been prodded once too often with a thorny stick. He took to dropping in at the beer parlour with his wages on Saturday night, although he did not spend much money there and was always scrupulous about giving Mom one half of his wages for board. What mattered to Ank was the principle of his new status. He was now earning his own money and therefore felt he should be his own man and not a bloody ox, as he partially expressed it. But to our father, ideas and principles meant nothing unless *he* had formulated them, and certainly he was not a man to be influenced by revolutionary ideas coming from one of his own youngsters. The terms of conflict between him and Ank were clearly defined.

"All I wants is a little bit o' time to meself," was Ank's frequent plea.

"Time to yerself!" came the mocking reply. "Lard Jesus, I never had any time to meself. All I ever done was work. What in the hell's flames do you expect – a bed o' roses?"

"No. I expects a bit o' time off once in a while," Ank repeated stubbornly.

"Why should any o' ye be entitled to what I never had?"

"T'ings is diff'rent now."

"Far's I'm concerned, t'ings is just the same as always. Now you shut yer gob and get to work."

It always ended that way, until one evening Ank broke out into open revolt. We were out there toiling on the Great Wall of China as usual; even Racer had been roped into a pair of overalls and put to work before he had a chance to escape. But despite this full complement of labour, things were not going at all well. The chief cause was the Old Man's feverish haste to complete a job once he had begun it, for he would never take the time to see that a corner was properly square or a form adequately braced before sloshing a batch of our hand-mixed concrete into it. "Whatever you goes at, you makes a *arse* of it," was Mom's perennial comment on his pointless haste.

On this occasion the disaster turned into a frightful mess. Dad had just given Racer and Crawfie orders to pour a large mix into the first section of the long form while he went on to plumb the next section. They obeyed, and when the weight of the rising concrete came against the form, the whole thing came unstuck and collapsed with a rending noise of yielding nails and splitting wood, sending the whole batch down into our neighbour's yard in one great horrible, wasteful splash. Then the form that Dad was working on also went askew, dragged out of position by the collapse of the first form. He gave one look and sprang toward Ank, his milky eyes blood-flecked with rage. "Didn't I tell you to drive stakes in the ground behind them supports?"

"No," Ank replied. "You said nails in the wood. Drive in nails, you said."

"No such of a goddam t'ing! Now the whole batch is spiled. *Look*."

"I'm lookin'. And I'm sayin', you said nails."

"Don't *arg*."

"It's true."

"And none o' yer goddam lip. I don't want none o' that needer. What did I say, nails or stakes?" Dad glared the question at the rest of us. Moving out of arm's reach we all supported Ank, while Ank himself, head thrust down between his shoulders and hands still gripping a shovel, obstinately and desperately stood his ground. "There's needer one o' ye I can trust, not one," Dad yelled disgustedly. "And *you*," he turned again on Ank, "you're the one I blames the most, 'cause you're old enough to have more sense."

"I done what I was told," Ank replied doggedly. To settle the argument the Old Man suddenly gave him a swipe over the ear. We saw Ank began to tremble and grip his shovel more tightly, and during one tense moment we gazed at one another, Racer, Crawfie, and I, thinking he was going to let the Old Man have it. For the present, however, a crisis was postponed. The crash and all the shouting had brought Mom out onto the back steps, and just as the tension was becoming intolerable, she broke it by calling out in her usual tone of strain and anxiety.

"Dad! What's ye bawlin' about now? Oh!" Seeing the mess around Ank's feet, she said, "Ye went and wasted the cement, did ye?"

"No," the Old Man gritted, "I'm flooring over this yard with concrete. Get on back in the house."

"But ye looked like ye was fightin' again."

Ignoring her, Dad turned balefully toward Ank, but whether it was Mom's intervention, or the brief cooling interval between his being struck and the idea of active retaliation that made Ank hesitate, he offered no violence. Fear of the Old Man came into Ank's eyes, his head sank a little lower, and he threw down the shovel with a half-articulate oath signifying that the Old Man could clean up the horrible mess himself. Then he escaped into the house. We all realized that a crisis had been reached and a new stage in his relations with the Old Man. He was not pursued and driven back to work at the toe of his boot. The rest of us had to scrape up all the concrete and do everything that was necessary to make things ready for the next night's work. Darkness did not necessarily bring an end to labour, as then the Old Man would quite often drag out a light on an extension cord by which we would continue until bedtime.

A year or two passed by in much the same manner, with Dad continuing in his tireless, frenzied way to improve our old dwelling inside and out. On the hill we already had a name for being fancy ("Dem Stones, dey t'inks der big," was a common saying), and when we had dug a well under the house and put a hand pump in the pantry, so that we would no longer have to carry water by turns from the communal tap at the foot of the hill, we were almost considered as traitors to our class. Fierce delight in the neighbours' envy, and a crowing defiance, was our father's reaction to this criticism of his endless striving toward all modern conveniences in the home. So the burden of our labour increased, but nevertheless Ank had gained a point by his revolt, and after long bickering on Dad's part, nagging of Dad on Mom's part, and sullen, ominous silence from Ank himself, it was finally agreed that Ank was to have one night a week off, besides Sunday.

That was all right for a while, until Ank suddenly acquired a girl friend in addition to his taste for beer and a certain amount of independence. Then the sparks began to fly and the curses started to echo once more in our restless home. Soon Ank had the boldness to bring his sweetheart

Mavis into the house on Sunday evenings after church; they would sit in the front room making signs to each other and whispering, while in the adjoining kitchen Dad would be snoring away on his couch (a square-cut piece about as soft as iron, covered with coarse canvas stolen from the mill and painted the same muddy brown as the outside of our house), having fallen asleep listening to the news on our ancient American Bosch radio.

Soon the devil would get into Ank and he would draw Mavis closer and begin to sandpaper her cheek with his gritty stubble of beard; he would keep on and on until the inevitable happened – Mavis bursting into a series of giggles, or perhaps crying out in real pain as Ank pressed deeper and deeper into her flesh. The next thing was Dad menacing them as he stood in the doorway between kitchen and front room. "Looka here, can't I close me two eyes a minute without all this racket? Hey?"

"We wasn't makin' any racket," Ank would protest while Mavis froze into an agony of shyness and embarrassment.

"'Tis lies you wasn't. I couldn't hear me ears."

"We was only talkin', sir. No more than that."

"Why don't ye go out for a walk? Such a nice evening."

Dad would for once make some effort to soften his tone, perhaps in honour of the guest in the house. Mavis was not yet familiar enough to be treated as he might treat one of his own children. Their spooning ended or spoiled for the evening, Ank and Mavis generally went off to her place and left us in something like peace for an hour or so until he returned and we were all once more assembled around the table for our cup-of-tea-going-to-bed, at which time Dad often made up for any softening of tone he might earlier have allowed himself toward the young lovers.

"Mark my words," was his customary opening gambit. "Ye can go cattin' around all ye likes, any one o' ye," here his eye lingered on Ank and then on the romantic-minded Racer, "but if ye goes to work and gets some ole bag in trouble, young as ye are, or if ye gets any of 'em a-tall knocked up, don't go comin' to me lookin' for money to get ye out o' the scrape."

"Hush, Dad! Hush up," Mom often reproved him, while Flinksy blushed and Crawfie glanced at me with a smirk as though anticipating these delights which he and I so far only vaguely understood. Racer frequently gave Ank a wink and a grin in an attempt at manly comradeship, but Ank always seemed too preoccupied and self-absorbed to take up the cue. He just stared back at the Old Man as the latter fumed on: "I'm only sayin', just in case. That's all. They can go to gaol before I lanches out a red cent to pay for any o' their bastards."

"Goddam it!" Ank exploded, "who's askin' you to pay, if anything *did* happen?"

"They better not. They better not, if they knows what's good for 'em."

So the position of everyone on this delicate subject was made clear and I, along with the others, was coming to accept the Old Man's fuss over it as so much more hot air, when one day only a few weeks after this conversation, Crawfie rushed up to me with the shining eyes of one who bears great news. "Hear about Ank?" he demanded breathlessly.

"No. What?"

"He got her fixed."

"Who?"

"Mavis, b'y! Mavis."

"What's that?"

"Ank got her up the stump. Now he *got* to get married."

This consequence and the whole situation were clarified for me only when Racer, from whom Crawfie had got the momentous news, joined us in conclave and explained that Mavis was going to have a kid for Ank, and they had to get hitched before it began to show.

We all waited for the bombshell of Ank's announcement to explode inside the house, but in his extremity Ank took the wise course of confiding in Mom first instead of butting heads with the Old Man over the question of his marriage. Being eager to keep the peace, Mom put quite a lot of time and thought into softening up the Old Man on the point of Ank's right to more independence than he then enjoyed, without of course saying anything at all about a baby. Even so, the Old Man's first remark to Ank in front of us all was not exactly a genial one.

"Married!" he cried. "Lard Jesus, ye're not hardly dry behind the ears yet."

"I s'pose I got as much right as anyone else," Ank sputtered in his trip-hammer growl, and frowned fiercely at the table.

"Too young – that's the t'ing."

"I'm almost twenty. No younger, or not much, than you and Mom when ye got married."

"That's true enough for you, Ank b'y," Mom entered the fray. She turned to Dad again: "What've you got against him gettin' married, really?"

"He'll be spilin' his chances."

"Christ!" said Ank. "Me chances o' what?"

"Gettin' ahead."

"Look out now!" Mom cried rhetorically. "You done all right, I daresay, in the last twenty years, and you had no more than a job when we started out, same as Ank now."

"Them days was diff'rent, altogedder diff'rent."

"There you goes again!" Ank lost his temper and banged his fist on the table. "The old days! A man could only work full time then, just like I been doin' for over a year meself – and slavin' away all night too. What in the hell are you talkin' about?"

"You better have a bit o' respect and mind yer tongue, or else I'll show you what I'm talkin' about."

"Come on then, by Jesus, come on!" Ank shot up from his chair, flames dancing in his eyes and little bullets of spit flying from his mouth along with the bitter words. "I'm sick and tired of all this bullshit about how good a man was in the old days, compared to now. So come on and show me, and we'll find out once and f'r all." And it might well have come to blows ending in parricide had not Mom rushed over from her place at the foot of the table and stationed herself in front of Ank, who was now braced for battle and whose eye never left the Old Man's as he spoke a little more quietly. "Look out, Mom. I means it."

"Yes, I know you means it, my son. But don't ye go fightin'. For *my* sake, Ank?"

We all watched in tense expectation while Ank continued to tremble without backing up an inch. Dad also stood his ground but did not offer the first blow, even though Ank had no shovel in his hands this time. The deadlock was broken by Mom using her tremendous weight to ease Ank imperceptibly backward until he and Dad were out of striking range. Then we all drew breath again and realized with various degrees of disappointment and relief that Ank was not going to get a "lickin'" after all.

Personally I felt a vague wonder at Ank having gone so far in defiance as an actual challenge to the Old Man without being "floundered" by him, permanently. I sensed a slight change in the balance of power that governed my own life, and from this time onward was a little less paralyzed by the fear that was the governing principle of our entire family existence.

The real showdown between Ank and Dad came not through an exchange of blows but during one of our passionate, soul-baring games of cards. Like most Newfoundland children, we could all play cards before we could read, and this perilous pastime, which among us was more battle than game, was the only thing our family as a whole could turn to by way of indoor recreation. When the weather was too bad for outside work and we had for once used up all our repairing materials on the inside, we sometimes gathered around the kitchen table for a full-scale six-hander. Auction, or one hundred and twenty, was our game, a very simplified form of whist and bridge with three on a side, all cards in circulation for each hand, and no mercy shown. Flinksy generally sat out when we were casting jacks for partners because she was afraid of being linked as partner with Dad in the coming struggle. And then if she made a mistake! Nor would Mom ever play partners with him, though her reasons took in more ground than did Flinksy's, her chief joy in these games being to oppose him and get the better of him by hook or by crook for once in their never-ending personal duel.

On one occasion the sides were Mom, Ank, and myself against Dad, Racer, and Crawfie, with Ank sitting on the Old Man's left, or under the gun as we boys termed it. No more than a few hands were needed to hot up the game and the family temper. Each time Dad won several tricks in a row, he would neglect to pull them in one by one; instead he let the cards pile up in the middle of the table in a colourful confusion of triumph, and on his last trick would bang down his trump on the table with a knuckle-crushing thump and a defiant shout of, "There! Beat that if ye kin. Beat that and look pleasant."

If, as usual, nobody was able to beat it, his two huge hands arched out over the pile of cards and swept them all toward him like the hands of a miser gathering in his gold. On and on he would rave: "Ye wouldn't play cards fer brewse! Ha-ha! I can still trim ye, f'r all ye t'inks ye're so smart." His lip curled half in scorn, half in triumph, and all in gloating. "And that's all by meself. What would I do if I had any partners, instead o' *them* two? I'd soonder have a couple o' cats playin' wit me." His eye fell on Racer and Crawfie who could not accept this as humour and took refuge in looking at each other sheepishly, sharing their misery and disgust. Mom could not stand Dad's repeated triumphs.

"Where in the name o' goodness do you get all the cards?"

"Ha-ha! I jigs 'em," Dad always replied.

"You never jug nutting."

"You saw me" – indignantly – "when I went twenty. One card I had, the lone jack. I jug all the rest."

"'Tis lies you did! You jackarse."

"Where did I get 'em then, fer God's sake?"

"I half believes you keeps cards and then plays 'em when they comes trumps."

"How bad-minded are you? Ye all saw me. What did I go on?" All of us had to admit it was only the jack. "Besides," he reasoned, "how would I know what to keep till I knows what's goin' to be trumps? Talk sense, Gert."

It really was amazing what luck he had; his cards kept coming as he wished them, and each time he put us in the hole he would give the unfortunately placed Ank a sudden shove with the heel of his hand and jeer in his face contemptuously for two or three minutes at a time. I was just as close as Ank to Dad, on his right, but up to this time I was still considered too young, and too small, to bear much responsibility if our side lost.

Consequently, Ank bore as usual the brunt of the rivalry between our parents, as well as his present load of torment from the Old Man's maddening victories. Ank stood it for as long as he could without Mom having to close down the game on some pretext other than the impending "fuss"; but his fuming patience was finally rewarded and his chance for revenge came when the Old Man once again bid twenty on the jack of spades, slapping the card down face up to vindicate his last such triumph and to prove his continued boldness.

This time Ank, who was dealing, had among his own spades the five (top card in our game, with the jack coming next), but instead of taking Dad's twenty he slyly let him go, and then prepared to smash him. This he did right off the bat by whisting his five, thus calling for trumps all round. When the Old Man saw that five he threw in all his cards along with the jack and on the instant turned sulky, while the rest of us watched Ank clean up the whole hand and put the other side ignominiously in the hole. On his last trick a roar of laughter went up from our side. "Ha-ha!" Mom called out derisively, "you never jug nutting that time, old man."

"That's not playin' cards, fer God's sake," Dad complained.

"Why not?" Ank demanded hotly, his face sobering dangerously. "Why ent it playin' cards? I got a right to whist if I wants to."

"You seen what I had."

"You had no business showin' it."

"That's true enough," Mom declared. "Well done, Ank b'y. He's laughin' on the other side of his mug now."

On the next hand the cards were more evenly divided, so that for the last trick Dad held the eight of trumps, which Ank, however, unexpectedly topped with the nine and thereby put the other side in the hole again.

"I t'ought the trumps was all gone except my eight." This again was a complaint from Dad.

"You t'ought wrong then," Ank snapped.

"I had 'em counted."

"Well, you counted wrong too."

"What did you put on my eece when I whist it?"

"I put the t'ree."

"You done no such of a t'ing!" A pause, an awful silence. "You reneged!" Dad brought the accusation against Ank with a kind of solemn horror.

"No sirree! I trumped your eece with the t'ree o' diamonds." But Dad would not believe it. He pulled the mass of discards toward him and turned up a handful representing the trick that had been won by his ace of diamonds. The three was not among them.

"There you are! Where's yer t'ree o' diamonds? It ought to be right next to the eece, accardin' to what you claims."

"It musta got mixed up with the other cards."

"That's a damn poor excuse. Well, if you're goin' *cheatin'*, I won't play no more."

"I wasn't cheatin'." Anger now vibrated in Ank's voice again.

"Prove it!" the Old Man challenged him. There being no way for Ank to do that with certainty, the argument raged on, threatening to blaze up at any moment into another crisis, until Mom thought of a possible way to end the monotonous to-and-fro of Dad and Ank's recriminations.

"I knows what we'll do," she cut in. "Listen!" We all turned toward her questioningly. She met us firmly. "We'll ask Juju." Now all eyes shifted to me. I straightened up, felt myself flush, and tried to look responsible.

"Yes, yes," Dad protested, "ask Juju. Sure signs, he's on yere side."

"Aw, what do he know about it?" Ank brushed aside the suggestion of my being appealed to. "Don't go draggin' him into it, pore little bugger."

"Yes, what's you pickin' on Juju for?" Flinksy asked unexpectedly.

"Because he *notices* everything, that's why. Just like a little ferret, he is. Now Juju, did Ank put the t'ree on Dad's eece?"

In this minor crisis of my life I gulped two or three times and hesitated fearfully, even though I was determined to bear witness to the truth: Ank *had* played the disputed three of diamonds, and in his greedy haste to win all the tricks Dad had not checked carefully enough on the number of trumps already gone by the time he came to whist his eight. So to Mom's question I now nodded affirmatively and with unmistakable emphasis.

Instantly I was showered with abuse. "He don't know the diff'rence, I tell ye," the Old Man wound up his tirade at me and at Mom for her suggestion.

"He *do* know the diff'rence, as well as you or me. You just can't take your own medicine, that's all," Mom countered warmly.

"Like I said, you're bound to hold with the young fella when he's on yere side. Stands to reason."

"All right, then," Ank came back at him, "if you t'inks *we're* all a bunch o' liars, ask somebody on your side." This brought the argument to a temporary halt, and now Racer and Crawfie were on the spot. At the two of them Dad glared with a mixture of hope and doubt and menace in his eyes.

"Go on," Mom further challenged him. "Ask 'em. Then you'll be satisfied."

I could see now that Dad hardly dared put the question to Racer and Crawfie, but finally he did put it, and they, directing their eyes and obviously all their support as well toward Ank, swore that he was in the right. Before the Old Man could further express his rage, Ank forestalled it. "There you are! If you wants proof, now you got it, I hope. Go on. Ask 'em again! They're on your side. Ask Flinksy. She's not even playin' a-tall."

On the theory that a watcher can often see more than those involved in the game, Flinksy was accordingly consulted and her reply was diffident but firm: Ank was being falsely accused. Far from allowing himself to be swayed by this unanimity, the Old Man crankily refused to accept our decision; he could not bear to be beaten. After we had all given opinion against him, he just sat there for a while at the head of the table, his eyes passing slowly from one to another of us as though we bore the brand of Judas, while in the silence Ank fumed and fretted and waited for him to admit – just for once – having made a mistake. Suddenly Dad got up from the table looking aggrieved, then stretched out on his couch, turned his face to the wall, and would not budge or utter a word until we had all had our cup of tea and gone to bed.

After this episode we were all aware of a further change in Dad's attitude toward Ank, who now had time off occasionally to work on a place of his own on the hill. The crisis of Ank's fight for freedom had been passed, not through the game of cards itself but in the secondary or symbolic meaning that these contests of will and skill in our family always bore.

During those tense moments when we were all being questioned about the trumps, I was not the only one who had noticed a wavering and something like a retreat in our father's eyes. Was it a momentary realization that though he might still be able to handle each one of us individually, he could not stand out indefinitely against the whole family? Whatever his secret thoughts, there came about a gradual relaxation in his severity toward our eldest brother. No word was spoken to ratify this, nor any overt act performed in recognition of Ank's new status; in fact, the Old Man went on grumbling about him as much as ever, but the psychological relationship between them was now one small step nearer to equality, or at least a sense of equality. No doubt Mom's informing Dad about this time of Mavis's condition had also some effect in leading him or forcing him to accept the inevitable. Instead of flying into another epic rage, he treated us all to a long and lurid I-told-ye-so lecture and to ghastly detailed predictions of what misery lay in store for Ank if he kept on like that.

And yet, after all this ranting and raving, it was agreed between our parents and Ank and Mavis that, since their own house was not yet finished and would be too cold to live in during the winter, somehow room would be found for the young couple to move in with us until the warm weather came around again in May or June.

CHAPTER

5

FLINKSY

By right of seniority our sister Hilda was next in line for the position and authority of deputy parent. Although Ank was in the house for a time after his marriage, his position and the way in which we all regarded him were quite altered, since he now had a wife and would soon have a family of his own. He was in a separate category altogether. Nevertheless we were all far from being willing to transfer the feelings we admittedly had for Ank, the prestige he commanded, to Flinksy. She was only a girl, and in this family of arrogant, overbearing males that counted for little or nothing.

Power in our group was largely a matter of physical domination and brute force. Least of all did Mom champion her only daughter in these early years; for whatever deep and mysterious female reasons, she seemed to regard Flinksy with distrust and something very like scorn, giving the impression that her chief duty toward a growing girl was to check up on her and keep her down. And Flinksy may have had abundant reasons for proclaiming that although she was the only girl among us she was also the black sheep of the family. She grew up touchy as a boil.

There seems to have been no particular reason why this arbitrary and perhaps cruel attitude was taken toward the poor girl. My own memories of her are chiefly memories of kindness and a quickness of sympathy that I did not find in my parents or any of my brothers, for while looking up to Ank as a child I also felt that he shared something of the omnipotence and therefore also the remoteness that invested our father. Racer I could not cling to, and Crawfie was too near my own age and helplessness to serve my need. So it came about that Flinksy and I adopted each other, in a manner of speaking, within the family and became chums and mutual champions in many a lonely hour and frightful crisis of these childhood years.

Often on Sunday nights in winter, when Flinksy had been let off from church to mind the house and I was left at home with her because I was too young for Evensong, or because it was too cold for me to go out, she and I would celebrate having the kitchen all to ourselves by first tidying everything up just to our liking, then building up the fire, and finally settling in to our favourite game of Restaurant. This consisted simply of telling what foods we would have in one gigantic, orgiastic meal, if we had heaps of money and nothing to spend it on but nice things to eat. In our part of Milltown the nearest thing we had to a restaurant was the Chinese fish-and-chip place down over the hill, but this was quite sufficient as a launching pad for our greedy imaginings, and most nights we would realize our game more vividly by each making out a private list of what we would order if we suddenly found ourselves transported by magic to a lusciously real restaurant in New York, say, or Hollywood, or Montreal. These long lists frequently began with chicken, a rare treat for us, and ended with things we had read or vaguely heard about, like chocolate-coated walnuts or cherries dipped in cream and sprinkled with sugar or coconut. The only item that never appeared on our orders was fish. Flinksy and I would always laugh gleefully and appreciatively into each other's eyes when we exchanged lists and found so many of the same luxuries on each one.

We had some compensation for fancy's delayed but inevitable fall to earth after all these saliva-stirring flights, for if there was enough butter and sugar and cocoa in the pantry for Flinksy to risk it, she would sometimes make a pan of home-made candy or fudge which we generally attacked while it was still cooking and so hot that we had to dance the chunks about from one hand to the other before tossing them into our mouths.

No matter what blunders or disasters took place during the mixing or cooking, that fudge always tasted delicious, so delicious that on many of these Sunday nights Flinksy had to restrain me or outwit me if there was to be any scrap at all left to share with the rest of the boys when they came home from church.

Once in a while Crawfie stayed home with us too, and then in addition to Restaurant we would play Beauty Parlour and Concert. Beauty Parlour was nothing more than Flinksy waving our hair with an old pair of curling irons Mom had long since given up using, and then dressing us up in odd bits of girl's clothing to put us in the proper style for performance in the Concert. For some reason we thought performers on the concert stage were exclusively female. First Crawfie would be stood up on a chair and, holding up the frills of his apron and vigorously nodding his frizzled head, would attempt a familiar song such as "Seeing Nellie Home" or "The Star of Logy Bay"; then came my turn in a similar vein, but my renditions were no more successful than Crawfie's – no matter how much Flinksy tried to encourage or support me. Neither Crawfie nor I could get through "The Ode to Newfoundland," even without hopeless wandering off key and continual flatting. "Ye got no more choon!" cried Flinksy regretfully, but she herself and all the others could never rise much above a monotone. Music was never able to charm or soften such a dismally tuneless crowd.

If these Sunday evenings were warm and pleasant, Monday never failed to bring its cold shock of reality as usual, with all hands except Mom off to work or school and all dreams and fancies banished if not forgotten for another week. Things went on like this for two or three lightning years, until we boys suddenly became aware one day that a change had come over Flinksy. She was always a dumpy little girl, compact of figure, broad-faced like Mom, and healthy as a horse; now two little bumps about the size of apricots appeared on her chest, and we were told we would have to be more careful where and how we hit her in our frequent rough-house recreations. For explanation of the whole thing, Racer came to Crawfie and me one day and told us that from now on Flinksy would have the rags on once a month, like all other women – even Mom – and that she was going to be cranky and queer in her ways around that time for the rest of her life. I was no wiser for all this, but as Flinksy's behaviour toward me showed no substantial change, I accepted the odd explanation as just one more of those numerous mysteries that would become clear when I was grown up.

One thing we all noticed immediately was that Flinksy began to take an abrupt and passionate interest in the subject of looks. Loud and frequent were her complaints of injustice over the fact that all of the boys had curly or wavy hair while hers was as straight as a ruler, and many were the hours she spent with a glass trying to coax or train her brittle hair into some kind of a wave; but as the change never lasted much longer than the time it took for her hair to dry, she was often in despair over the whole business. Any sort of professional hair-do being out of the question, she would spend more hours with the glass propped on the kitchen window-sill, sticking cheap wire curlers into her head. Endless hours were spent too on the squeezing out of blackheads, a process so endless that every time Flinksy went at it Mom would finally be driven to an extremity of impatience and the rudest of interference. Usually she wound up by snatching the glass out of Flinksy's reach, scolding her in a tone of disgust: "For the love o' mercy, maid, stop foolin' with yourself. You spends days squeezin' and pimpin', fussin' and frettin' over your face, and you don't look none the better for it after all. Look at you now! Face like a biled lobster. I'd be ashamed to stick me head outside the door, if I was you."

"Big cow," came Flinksy's accusing retort.

"Mind y'mout'! And go and do your work."

"I done it all."

" 'Tis not done. 'Tis only half done."

"It's all I'm able to do." At which Mom would march away, carrying the glass, with a toss of her head showing even greater disgust than before.

"God help the man that gets her!" she would then exclaim to the world in general. Flinksy's usual reaction to this insult was a sharp intake of breath on the word "oh" to signify that she would hope to do as well as certain other people in marriage when the time for that arrived.

But if her own attempts at home-made beauty and glamour were frequently crushed, she remained none the less generous in her appreciation of good looks in others. Here the focus of her wonder and admiration was Racer; the girls were already starting to notice him, she informed us, and one of them had already declared that he ought to be in the movies. What really astonished us boys, though, was Flinksy's claim that Dad was not bad looking either. The Old Man good looking! The idea was grotesque. Yet Flinksy assured us in all seriousness that if he got his teeth and really dressed up for once, with a white shirt and all, he would be quite handsome. We simply could not accept such an opinion on any terms. "And his eyes!" Flinksy always added as her final argument. "Don't ye notice them? They're so *blue*. They goes right through me."

The most devastating thing that happened to Flinksy, once she had surmounted and was beginning to accept her puberty, was that about this time she was plucked out of school. This crime was committed in her thirteenth year, when she was in Grade V; the reason given was that she was needed to help Mom around the house. Of course there was also the saving that would be made from her school fees and the fact that being at home she would not have to have as many or as expensive clothes as would be required if she continued at school. Once installed at home she became the household drudge, working seven days and five or six nights a week without pay and with never a word of praise or appreciation to lighten her burdens.

Nor was any thought given to her future. It was taken for granted that she would marry some day, and for that she was getting all the training she needed. Girls must have domestic skill as men must have bodily strength – this was our assumption and our law. Therefore in Flinksy's life it was cook, wash, mend, scrub, clean, bake and sweep and patch until each day became a long blur of dreary tasks only half completed before she was summoned to some new domestic emergency that Mom was not able to cope with all alone.

After our tea, while Dad was out in the privy and we boys were enjoying the interval before getting to work outside the house, Flinksy's bondage was most apparent and her chronic depression in those years was at its most acute. "Must be great to be a man," she often said, wearily and wistfully, watching all of us from Ank down to myself as we sprawled over the furniture observing her at work and for the moment savouring our superiority over all females whatsoever. She would be still gazing at us in envy when Mom's ponderous tread jerked her back to duty and their usual evening struggle over the division of labour, starting with this bit of dialogue: "After you finishes the dishes you can make the bread. Did you hear me? Stop *gawkin'*, Hilda. We haven't got all night."

"I hates makin' bread."

"There now! Just listen to her. S'posin' *I* said that. How would we all keep goin'?"

"I don't know, and I don't care."

"I 'lows I'll have to tell Dad on you yet. Then you'll care."

"I don't care if you goes and tells him right now – right this minute."

"What ails you lately, Flinks? Hey?"

"I wish I was dead."

Whereas we boys had only the single great conflict in our lives (the struggle with the Old Man), Flinksy had also this continual running battle with Mom and furthermore a constant need to defend herself from all her brothers. Crawfie in particular was a menace to her in a physical sense, as he had a habit of doubling up his forefinger and punching her sharply on her shoulders and upper arms. At every blow she would contract her features in pain and then relieve herself by an oath against Crawfie, against her sex, and against her dismal fate in general. More humiliation stemmed from the circumstance that she received no pay for her drudgery, no fixed allowance that would permit her some show of dignity and independence; she was forced to nag and natter at Mom and beg from the older boys if she were to have any pin-money at all.

For years after he went to work, Ank gave her half a dollar every payday. As to clothes, that was the sorest subject of all and again a source of triple torment to Flinksy, whose square-cut figure was hard to fit and who had no confidence in either Mom or herself when it came to choosing her clothes. In her agony she would sometimes turn to us for an opinion only to be told that the coat she had just bought was like a dyed brin bag or her new Easter bonnet like a pisspot turned up side down. Tears would soon flow, and she would vow never to wear the coat or hat in public – people would only laugh at her; but Mom always defeated her at this point by declaring that Flinksy would in that case have to return the purchase herself and ask for the money back. This Flinksy was much too shy to do, and since it was unthinkable that anything any of us had paid for should not be used, she had to wear the offending article for two or three years at least, until she had got the good out of it, no matter what self-consciousness or ridicule she might suffer during that time.

Half-way through the Great Depression all the mill

workers had to take another cut in pay – a dark but inescapable fact that had a direct bearing on Flinksy's immediate fate. It was decided by Mom and Dad that, being already out of school anyway, she must go to work. The only question was, what could she do? Obviously there was only one answer, and that was that Flinksy would have to go out in service. The wives of the biggies in the townsite were always looking for strong and hearty young girls to act as maids, so there would be no difficulty in finding her a place; then if she did not actually contribute to the family budget, our house would at least be relieved of the expense of keeping her. Somehow Mom would have to manage all her own work and other family cares without her. It was stated to be a matter of necessity.

The only difficulty in this plan was that Flinksy herself would not hear of it. In a passion of tears and fears, she swore she would never go out in service, and when the violence of her protest caused Mom at least to try to reason with her ("It's no disgrace," "Girls does it every day") the only coherent explanation Flinksy could give was that she was mortally afraid of going out like that among strangers. This was not good enough for either Mom or Dad, the latter seeming to settle the matter once and for all by pronouncing that she had to go, and that was all of it. He didn't want to hear another goddam word on the subject till she was on the job. As the day of Flinksy's departure drew nearer, her misery became greater and greater.

Then she surprised us all by her first genuine show of character, when before the fatal day she went out entirely on her own and found a job that paid nine dollars a week instead of the six she would have received as a servant girl. Her new position was unassailable because she would now be bringing a bit of cash into the house every week by paying her board, and also sparing the household expenses in that she would be able to save up and buy her own things as they were needed or according to her power of economizing. Mom said that Flinksy did not know and would probably never learn how to manage her money, and so the best thing would be for Mom to take charge of everything and pass out the cash in accordance with Flinksy's needs, tempered by Mom's experience and wisdom.

This plan never succeeded either. The job itself was nothing more than clerking in the town's chief commercial establishment, the Company Store, situated in the townsite about two miles from our house. Once Flinksy had got over her first-job nervousness, she began to enjoy the daily contact with the public, her great fear in the beginning centring around the arithmetical calculations that were part of her daily routine. Many evenings she spent feverishly working on fractions, which she had never arrived at in school. She appealed to Ank to explain how you found the cost of $2\frac{1}{2}$ lbs. of cod tongues at 15 cents per lb. or (one of her nightmares), a quarter of a yard of calico at $37\frac{1}{2}$ cents a yard. Somehow she got through it all without fatal mishap and once she had accepted the additional embarrassment of walking alone four times a day through the town, where she always felt out of place, she soon settled comfortably into her new status of wage-earner and semi-independent young woman. Mom enjoyed Flinksy's job too, for through Flinksy's public position she could find out and pass on all the particulars about who was buying fancy things when they couldn't afford them, who was expecting again, whose man was still on the booze, and, finally, what the minister's wife ordered each week for her Sunday dinner.

It was only to be expected that after a year or two Flinksy would have saved enough to buy some new clothes, and the natural consequence of being in style, or at least not altogether drab and shabby, was that she should start going out in the evening a little more. This was the period during which she was given the name Flinksy ("Wild One"), as pathetically undeserved a nickname as ever a soberminded young puritan female was saddled with; but in our fiercely critical and self-righteous family, any little outburst of sociability or romance was always pounced on and rudely labelled by one or other of us as a major fault of character.

Her womanly enjoyment of life came out too in her burgeoning malice toward other women; she would laugh chubbily and appreciatively at Racer's comments on one of her girl friends who used to come to our house dressed in garments that were considered old fashioned. "Them round stockin's," Racer often complained with reference to this girl's coarse seamless hose, "they makes her legs look like a couple o' fence posts, for God's sake." And Flinksy would burst out laughing and keep on as long as Racer found things to criticize in this unfortunate, unstylish young woman.

Hell broke loose in our home over Flinksy's very first taste of the honey of admiration and romance. It started one evening about five-thirty when, instead of Dad's usual weary tramp in the lane, we heard a quickened step and saw him crashing into the kitchen looking darker and more menacing than any of us could remember ever seeing him before.

"Where is she?" he barked, without a previous word to any of the family. He always referred to our sister as "she" or "her," never calling her Hilda or even Flinksy.

"What ails you now?" asked Mom in mingled disgust and dread.

"You'll soon find out! Where is she?"

"She's not home from work yet. Come on and have your tea. She'll be home directly." At this very moment we were all paralyzed by the sight of Flinksy coming through the door and the Old Man at once turning on her in his fury.

"Where was you last night? Hey?"

"I was only down over the hill same as usual."

"Where to? Don't you tell me no lies now. Did you go in any place?"

"Nowhere special."

"*That's* a bloody lie, to start with." By this time Flinksy had turned a deep scarlet in the face, she was trembling all over, and had backed away toward the front room door.

The accusing yell of the Old Man came down on her more heavily. "You was seen talkin' to that Ben Swersky."

"Ben Swersky? I only spoke to *him* for a minute. I s'pose that's no crime, is it?"

"In his store," the Old Man insisted. "Right inside of his store, with blinds drawed and the door closed too."

"What about it if I was?" Flinksy flared up momentarily in self-justification. "Ben is just as good as anybody else."

"A Jew! Bloody Christ-killer. That's all the like of him is. You must be pretty hard up, by Jesus, if you got to go chasin' around after them kind. Wastin' yer money in there too, prob'ly."

"Benny is all right. And I wasn't *chasin'* after him. We were only talkin' for a little while, that's all."

"What odds if she do speak to Ben Swersky?" Mom tried her usual pacifist tactics. "Come on and have your tea."

"You shut up. I'll have me tea when I'm goddam good and ready. I got more to say on this yet."

"Look out now," Mom countered. "Mind you don't piss yourself."

"I blames you as much as her."

"Oh yes. Yes. Cert'n'y. 'Tis always *me*. You makes me sick!"

"She's a girl, so *you* ought to be lookin' out to her."

"I told you a thousand times: I can't do nutting wit 'em – her nor any o' the rest. They're gone right crazy."

"Crazy or not, I'm tellin' you right now, once and f'rall." He swung around on the half-defiant Flinksy again, "If I ketches you again so much as lookin' at that Swersky fella, I'll give you a lickin' you wunt forget in a hurry. I'll redden yer arse so's you wunt be able to sit down for a munt. Pay heed to me now! Curse it, if I let you alone I daresay next t'ing you'd be runnin' around with them Chinks or the niggers offa the boats, or God knows who else. Before I knows it I'd be draggin' you up out o' Crow Gulch."

"I'll speak to who I likes!" cried Flinksy in desperation, and this word was the match that set off the Old Man's inflammable temper. With an obscene oath he sprang at her, his fist raised high – but she had already opened the door and jumped inside the front room to escape his wrath. Having missed with his hand, he swung at her with his boot, barely grazing her behind. With a scream of mortification and hurt pride rather than physical pain, Flinksy fled to her bedroom and locked the door. For a while we thought the Old Man would smash it in, but this time (perhaps restrained by thoughts of economy), he cooled himself down by railing at her for some time longer, and then returned to the kitchen to finish off his tongue-bangin' on Mom and his other children.

"That goes for the rest o' ye too," his eye lingered as he spoke on each one of us in turn as though he were once again brooding on the poor man's bitter bargain of a few minutes' lustful pleasure in exchange for a lifetime of torment and expense for having begotten us. "She's gettin' too big for her drars, and so are ye all. Gone mad, fer Christsake. But I'm not puttin' up wit it all any more. Ye'll mind what I tells ye. Or else ye'll suffer for it."

All that evening we could hear Flinksy crying in her room, and for a good many evenings afterward she remained in the house toiling away like an unwilling martyr, silently resentful of the ban and the insult that had been put upon her. In our private discussions of this fuss, what puzzled us boys was how the Old Man had found out about Flinksy's little visit to Benny at all; none of us, not even Crawfie, would have told if we had seen or heard of anything going on in his clothing store. We would have mercilessly teased and baited her, but never would we have squealed about such a thing to the Old Man.

For a long time we were left with the mystery, until Mom unwittingly solved it one day by remarking that the chief product of the mill was not paper but gossip. "The men, they spends their whole blessèd time down there just chewin' the fat" – that was her way of putting it. We realized that some passer-by on the night of Flinksy's visit must have seen her and then shot off his mouth at work to the Old Man.

As for the attractions of Ben Swersky, they consisted chiefly of the report of his having once said that Hilda Stone was the nicest-looking girl on the hill, a statement not too wide of the truth for a girl like Flinksy to cherish it secretly and to desire some personal acquaintance with the man who had made it. At this time she looked more pleasant than pretty; she might have been positively attractive if that aggrieved look had not already become stamped on her youthful face.

In the absence of a sister and in her continued martyrdom, Flinksy turned to me as the nearest thing she could find to a family confidant. There was never enough free time in her life for the making of close friendships among the other young people in our neighbourhood, but often, close to tears, she used to tell me how some of the other young girls whom she did know seemed to be their Daddy's darlings and undisputed favourites in their homes, whereas she was always picked on for the very reason that she *was* a girl. Some of the bolder girls were starting to use make-up too. What would happen to her, she asked me with dreadful wonder in her eyes, if she started that, even away from the house, and the Old Man ever found out about it? Paint and powder were whore's bait in our scale of moral and social values. Flinksy's first smoke came within my knowledge too, with all its overtones of guilt and fear in addition to the sputtered question as to how anybody could really enjoy such a rank taste and go and spend good money on cigarettes.

Although she confided in me, and I relied on her to some extent as protector in a violent and bewildering household, it was to be expected that her ripening womanhood should eventually draw her away from me and into an almost total preoccupation with the hunt for a man. This I could not be plainly told, and was still too young and too sickeningly tossed on the seas of puberty to understand for myself. I merely felt and recognized a change from the time that Rome appeared on the scene.

His real name was Fletcher Robinson, but from his first appearance as Flinksy's potential boy friend, we dubbed him Rome or Romeo and thereafter laughingly refused to call him by any other name. He was too shy for protest, and Flinksy was too glad of a steady to insist on dignity and respect in our attitude toward him. At this time Rome was a day labourer just recently come to Milltown from Lark Harbour some distance out in the Bay of Islands. His speech was slow as cold molasses and his manner deliberate as time; but if we ridiculed his bayman's ways we also respected his capacity for hard work, and on the whole received him in our home with patronizing goodwill. The trouble may have been simply that because we boys were all taller than he we could not take him quite seriously as a romantic figure and our sister's suitor.

Flinksy saw him differently. Though short, he was tall enough for her, his body tough and close-knit as spliced rope, and his gentle smile promised a tenderness she had never known. Above all he was a Protestant, so if they did become serious there was no insuperable obstacle to their romance ending in permanency. There could be no talk of turncoats, Judas, invincible ignorance, or eternal damnation. Rome was a reliable man in other ways as well. Whenever Flinksy had to work late at the store in the evening, there he was long before she quit, waiting outside the staff entrance to walk her home, always indulgent and receptive if she had had a hard day and needed to relieve her pent feelings by abusing the manager of her department and the other clerks at her counter. It was Rome's faithfulness that won her heart and made up for his want of ardour and dash.

Naturally there were rocky places and hills and valleys on their pathway to love. Not long after Flinksy started going with Rome, Mom began to complain that she could no longer get any good out of her at all; the girl wouldn't do a tap o' work in the house; she wouldn't even wash out her own drawers, as Mom put it, unless somebody drove her to the task; she expected to be waited on hand and foot just like she thought she was one of the biggies in town, or God knows what. Further trouble came from the more reasonable accusation that Flinksy now wasted every cent of her wages on clothes and otherwise dolling herself up, on one or two occasions even keeping back part of the money for her board and thus getting so far behind in her accounts with Mom that the latter eventually claimed Flinksy would have to fork out all her earnings for at least six months if they were ever to be square with each other again.

Dad's chief complaint about Flinksy's love life was in connection with our front room. Although the place was hardly ever used, except for special visitors like the minister or somebody who came to do business, it was typical of the Old Man that he should find something to complain about in Flinksy and Rome using it almost every night for spooning and courting, and he always insisted that the kitchen door be left ajar until the hour came for Rome to be leaving. He was much stricter in every way than he had been with Ank and Mavis. Spying on Flinksy and Rome, Crawfie and I frequently witnessed the scene about half-past ten when Dad came through the door into the front room and spoke to Rome. "Now then, b'y, it's gettin' late. All hands got to be to work in the morning. Or are ye two goin' to put in the whole night here?"

"Yes sir," Rome replied, in his nervousness meaning, "No sir," at once straightening up and moving some distance away from Flinksy on the sofa.

"I got nutting *agen* you, mind, and you're welcome in this house long as you acts right and long as I got anything to say about it. But there's reason in all things, see Rome? And I daresay your own people wouldn't want *you* up all hours o' the night."

At this point in Dad's moderate protest, Rome would silently rise and began to fumble about for his cap, while

Flinksy just sat there for a moment or two, half-petrified with shame. As I watched her through a crack in the hall door, I could almost feel the heat of the blood rising and overspreading her whole face. Finally she and Rome would get as far as the front door of the house, but most nights that was not the end of the trouble, for quite often Dad would feel himself obliged to go out again and say a few more words before Flinksy had murmured her final good-nights and gone off to her room in a despairing huff.

Her whole personal and private life was poisoned by this coldly maintained supervision and the cramping curfew. Being now a young woman of nineteen, Flinksy felt that she should be shown a little more consideration in the running of her own affairs, yet when she and Rome stayed out on the front verandah after he had walked her home on a summer night, there was trouble about this too. "Ye got no business out there a-tall," the Old Man declared more than once when Flinksy got up the nerve to protest again. "Ye're not doin' anything me and y'mudder shouldn't see, are ye?"

"No, we're not *doing anything*," Flinksy snapped with rising spirit.

"And don't mock me eeder, if you knows what's good for you. And ye can do it in the front room, same as before."

"We're entitled to be by ourselves once in a while around here, I s'pose."

"I don't want ye smudgin' around out there on the verandah. Makin' a show o' this place and givin' it a bad name. Ye'll have me name all over the town," he added with a grimace of disgust.

Though at times she sank further into despair, Flinksy would not be turned away from Rome; her will was set on him to the point where only his failing her privately and intimately could have altered her determination to keep him. From the person who might have been expected to help her in the various crises of young love – from Mom – she received no sympathy or co-operation whatever. Many times Flinksy bitterly appealed to her and to the rest of us as well against the Old Man's attitude.

"That bad-mindedness!" she cried. "That's what I hates. That dirt. Do he think me and Rome don't know how to act respectable, no matter where we are or if we're by ourselves or not? He thinks everybody is just like himself. Mom, can't you talk to him and get him to leave us alone?"

"You knows now how he is. I can't do nutting with him either."

"Rome don't say much, but he thinks all the more."

"Then let un ask for your hand and be done with it." Mom smiled suddenly, and as she went on her ribald strain broadened and deepened the smile into one of her famous house-rattling belly laughs. "Then ye'll be more on yere own, like. Oh yes," she insisted as we all joined in the laughter on this point which by now had become a standing joke among us, "Rome got to do it proper. He got to come to Dad and ask for your hand reg'lar, or else I'll never consider ye engaged, that's what I won't." It was the idea and the picture of the extremely gauche and inhibited Rome getting through such an ordeal as this interview with the Old Man that gave us all so much amusement. Flinksy sniffed defensively and blushed self-consciously as she always did when the subject of marriage was brought up.

"I guess Rome could do it good as anyone, if he took a notion."

"And I got to be there too," Mom said firmly. "I got to see it all with me own two eyes."

"You have not," Flinksy scolded her. "It's always between the groom and fi-ancy's father – a thing like that."

Somehow the young couple arranged that momentous interview to exclude Mom and bypass the rest of us nosey parkers who took a friendly but impertinent interest in Flinksy's love life. All we ever knew for sure was that it went off in an extremely short time and therefore with an economy of words that we could readily imagine, considering the two people involved. So the engagement of Rome Robinson and our sister became an established fact.

For a time Flinksy irritated Mom by the hours she spent contemplating her ring (a symbol that obviously was cherished far beyond its assurance of one man's desire for her), but in general Mom's feeling came through mainly as relief at getting her girl safely married to a decent, hardworking fellow who would not be likely to neglect her or to take her away from Milltown.

Mavis, Ank's wife, of all people, was called in to give advice on a subject that Flinksy would never have discussed at this time of her life with Mom: when to do it, and when to keep your legs crossed, or what to use if you did not want to become a mother too soon and unexpectedly. Before Mavis and Flinksy went off to their secret and smiling conference, Ank, who was now living in his own place and had come along to our house just for the visit, expressed himself without invitation on the forthcoming union.

"Married!" he ejaculated at Flinksy and spat, his voice harsher than usual from the weight of disillusion and scorn it carried. "Christ, what do ye want to get married for?" Now he glared at Mavis like an angry bull while she crimsoned from neck to scalp and told him to shut up and mind what he was doing with the baby. It seemed that Ank's twelve months of being a husband had not been a realization of love's young dream.

"Stay like you are, b'y," he warned Rome when the latter arrived at the house that evening and found that Flinksy was still closeted with Mavis. "You don't know when you're well off."

This ungallant attitude on the part of Ank was not, however, shared by all of us, even though we continued to torment Flinksy over things like what would happen if Rome forgot to give the ring to the Best Man, or if she fainted away going up the aisle, or if something even more grotesquely embarrassing happened during the ceremony. As for the Old Man, he silently accepted the responsibilities and shouldered the expenses of father-of-the-bride, just as Mom undertook to arrange all the details of the reception and so forth, within our means as common people, with no more than the traditional amount of bustle and agitation.

I remember clearly Flinksy's wedding day just before Christmas in the year 1938. I had been away to St. John's for some months but came back for the holidays and the big event. It took place on an inauspicious wintry day with no sky visible through the thickly swirling snow and everything around us, from hills to harbour, fast locked in heavy ice. There was no brightness anywhere except the lurking gleam of triumph and imminent liberation on Flinksy's face. Nothing could quite smother that, not even a sty that came out on her left eye just two days before the wedding and almost drove her to self-surgery by remaining unglamorously inflamed and prominent right up to and all during the ceremony.

In the church Dad played his role with grim self-consciousness, wearing his own wedding suit which still fitted him without any audible stretching or straining when he moved. Both Flinksy and Rome were pale but steadfast throughout their ordeal. Even Mom for once was totally serious, breaking down toward the end of the service and shedding a few tears, which surprised us all a little on account of the way she always used to be going on at Flinksy before she was married.

Without any sentimentality there was a brief season of kindly feeling in our house during this double festivity of Christmas and a wedding in the family. Dad offered to rent Rome and Flinksy the room occupied by Ank and Mavis after their marriage, but Rome's refusal, whether it came entirely from himself or not, was quietly and politely firm. What were Flinksy's secret thoughts and feelings about the offer I never knew until years later. She and Rome went to live in what was little more than a painted-up old shack just a little way down the hill and on the other side from our own place.

CHAPTER

6

RACER

Raymond, or Racer, was the nearest our family came to producing a Golden Boy. Crawfie and I gave him the nickname Racer after he had competed in one of the school road races and come in eleventh out of twelve; but there was also some genuine appropriateness in the name because he was the one among us all who seemed most likely to forge ahead and win some coveted prize in the race of life. Racer it was to whom everybody looked for any distinction that our family name might come to bear. Was he Mom's undisputed favourite as a result of all these hopes placed in him, or were these hopes born of the fact that as a boy he was the object of her most unbridled and discriminating love?

Certainly his appearance from boyhood on suggested that merit alone was the reason for all this confidence we placed in his future, a confidence not diffidently shared by Racer himself. Eyes of Havana blue, a complexion fresh as apples at dawn, and golden glints in his thatch of auburn hair – these were the points that charmed one and all in our tight little social group, where for both men and women the Anglo-Saxon type was a heavily preferred ideal. Dark men were deep men suggesting Romanism and unnamed evils. Racer had litheness in his body as well as charm in his looks. He always stood lightly on the balls of his feet and when he walked seemed almost to be dancing. Expectation shone out of his azure eyes, and because he expected, people gave, whether it was money or favours or love that seemed to be asked of them.

If in the early years of our family life I did not enthusiastically share the general admiration for Racer, I was in some degree overborne by it and could hardly make my resistance felt when as time went on I and all the other boys in the family came to be identified in Milltown as Racer Stone's brother. Yet I always kept my doubts about him. They started one Christmas when I was still very young, but old enough to share in the gift-giving which at this time was still our custom and obligation within our own group. By careful saving and with some help from Mom, I had gathered a little store of money from which I had spent enough to buy Racer a cheap pair of socks. These I wrapped in white tissue paper and with some pride and pleasure handed to him on Christmas Eve when all the presents were being passed out. After opening the package and barely glancing at the socks Racer, who had given me a more expensive present, threw them aside contemptuously exclaiming: "Agh, I got plenty o' socks! Them are no good anyway."

As a schoolboy he was famous all over the town for getting in and out of scrapes with a blithe, uncannily justified assurance of escaping any serious punishment. There was the time, for instance, when he marked the school principal for life by flicking a ruler at him over the edge of his desk and striking him right in the centre of the forehead. His story was that the boy behind him had thrown a book, the book had struck the projecting ruler, and thus the ruler had sailed by accident into the principal's face. When he came home from school that day, Racer told us the whole story again, with that evil, winning smile still denying his guilt, of course, and all but convincing Mom that he was telling the truth. "Racer, my love," she tried to scold him, "surely you wouldn't go and do the like o' that to your school principal?"

Inside our family itself, Racer was additionally notorious for the amount and kind of devilry he could get away with unknown to the Old Man. His imitations of him in a sour or violent mood were quite hilarious, as were also his take-offs on the language and idiom the Old Man used on the frequent occasions when savagery possessed his mind and ruled his body. Over all this Mom used to be in stitches of laughter, and the rest of us were never slow to follow her lead.

But it was on the question of money that Racer showed his real ability and daring. Being an enterprising lad, he had secured the paper route for Humber Heights – the Milltown *Messenger,* a weekly at two cents per copy – and as this whole area was too much for him to cover all by himself, he soon subcontracted the steepest and remotest hills out to Crawfie and myself at a fixed rate of ten cents per week, summer and winter. In this way he made a good profit without suffering any of the worst hardship in the actual selling of the papers. There was a settled rule in our house that part of whatever we earned had to be given to Mom "to put away," and Racer's method of paying her an absolute minimum was to cook up a list of poor people who regularly took the paper on tick, thereby cutting down his profits and each week preventing him from putting very much into the household kitty. Names on his list varied from week to week, but the number of creditors was always about the same. This list he would always present to Mom before settling down over our Saturday pea soup to count all the money he and Crawfie and I had brought in, and as far as we could tell, Mom believed him in spite of the loud, sarcastic doubts uttered by Crawfie and myself. After our dinner Racer usually brought out the large chocolate bar he had bought that morning, gobbled it all up in two or three bites, and then swiftly passed the wrapper under my nose and Crawfie's with a taunting laugh. "That's all ye two gets – a smell. That's all ye're wort'." Again Mom joined in his laughter, only half-heartedly reproving him for not sharing equally with his brothers. The only way Crawfie and I could get revenge and a chocolate bar of our own to eat when we went to the Saturday movie matinee on our weekly salary was to invent a short credit list of our own and keep it going from week to week until Christmas tips brought everything square and enabled us to start a new year with new hopes of justice from Racer.

Once Dad came home early with one of his stomach attacks and heard Mom reading out to us with great relish Racer's housewife credit list. Apparently there was an unlikely name on it, for when he checked later with the woman's husband he discovered that this family had never taken a paper or anything else on credit during all their time in Milltown, and were insulted at the idea of anyone even thinking they would do such a mean thing as taking a two-cent paper on tick.

"You're spilin' him!" Dad once more accused Mom when he came home on the day of his discovery about the credit. "Mark my words, you're spilin' him, and he's the one that'll have to suffer for it."

"Don't be bawlin'," came Mom's standard reply. "Spilin' him! What odds about a foolish little newspaper?"

"What odds! Puttin a man's name all over the town like he was a bloody bum or a common t'ief."

"We was only havin' a bit o' fun, sure."

"That's not what I calls it. Do the young fella pay you reglar every week?"

"Yes, yes. Don't be fussin'. He gives me whatever he can, accardin' to."

"He better. And don't let me hear no diff'rent, or else I'll haul it offa him meself."

"*I* handles all the money."

"And let him be more partikler whose name he mentions. There's fellas'd radder be shot than owe money. I would meself. 'Specially if it was only two cents over that bloody little t'ing they calls a newspaper."

On the whole Racer's career in school was no less lively and successful than his budding business career. Only once was he actually expelled – and on that occasion Mom got him reinstated by going to see the principal herself and making certain promises on Racer's behalf before the incident had any explosive repercussions at home. As for his academic standing, that would have been excellent if only he could have been persuaded or forced to apply himself. By achieving Grade VIII he had already reached a higher level of education than anyone else in the history of our family. Perhaps the trouble was that having once acquired some reputation as a young daredevil and town sport, Racer felt continuously obliged to live up to his name.

After an episode in which Mom had once again to intervene personally by going down over the hill and dragging him bodily out of the Humber Pool Room and Billiard Parlour, where he was playing Boston for money, smoking, and also using foul language, Racer restored his prestige among the local bucks by landing in gaol. On a dare one Sunday evening he threw a stone through the main window of the Salvation Army Citadel right in the middle of the Main Prayer. The police did not nab him directly, but someone squealed and the result was that Monday morning found our Racer shoved into a cell instead of his usual seat at school. Yet again Mom had to put on her Sunday best and go begging for mercy for her wayward boy. The Magistrate let him go on condition of paying for the window and also a fine for vandalism, to all of which Mom urgently agreed if only Racer could come home that morning, right away, and get himself cleaned up and have a proper meal. When he made his heroic return home, we boys could all see how ludicrously Mom was torn between joy at having him back and a sneaking realization that she should be chastising him instead of kissing and falling all over him in this tremulous, tearful way. The fact that the Old Man did not learn the full truth of this whole affair until it was too late for rage only postponed but did not cancel out the reckoning that we knew from experience must one day be settled between him and Racer.

As a work-dodger, Racer developed a skill that none of us other boys ever achieved or dared to attempt right under the Old Man's nose as Racer did night after night from Monday to Saturday and all the way through again. Perhaps his best idea came when he joined the Church Lads' Brigade, an organization whose half-military and half-religious character made it unimpeachable in our parents' eyes as a connection for a wild boy like Racer. It might even put a check on his wildness. The C.L.B. met only once a week, but Racer improved his opportunities of freedom from labour at home by becoming a drummer, which made two more nights a week that he had to go out — for practice. So it was a common occurrence to see Racer, looking spruce and handsome in his square-cut, belted uniform, stepping out of the house after tea for one hour of beating the kettle drum in the church basement and three hours or so on the town, while Ank and Crawfie and I toiled away at the Great Wall and other large jobs that came so readily to the Old Man's imagination.

When every other excuse failed, Racer took refuge from manual labour in illness. Despite his ruddy look, he was not especially robust, and he already knew and used the fact that back trouble is one of the hardest things to diagnose as well as the most disabling where hard labour is in question. As Dad did not fancy spending any money on doctors for Racer, we never could find out for sure whether he really did have anything wrong with his back. Neither back trouble nor anything else hampered his later and more interesting activities. The Old Man just cursed, we echoed him in agreement for once, and Ank swore he would take it out of Racer's hide, back or front or any place else.

Racer glided past puberty without much apparent trouble or awkwardness, nor any incipient neuroses, and of course it was not long after this change in his life that girls came to occupy his thoughts and hours much more than studies, the C.L.B., or the problem of how to get all the cash he needed for his various operations. In retrospect

I see what it was that attracted the girls to him so much: it was the beguiling, challenging look of combined innocence and virility on his face, plus the assured, compact maleness of his body. At any rate, his success as a lady-killer was undeniable, even if there were now and then slight *contretemps* that gave us a laugh in return for those frequent occasions when, supported behind the scenes (if not openly) by Mom, he got the better of us. One of those mishaps occurred when Racer, squiring not one but three girls along Broadway on the West Side, casually said: "Let's go in for a coke." They all went into a café and each of the girls ordered a banana split at fifteen cents apiece. With exactly fifty cents in his pocket, Racer ordered a five-cent coke for himself and had to sit there sipping it as slowly as he could while the three girls gluttonously enjoyed themselves. We all relished hearing about this from a friend of Racer's, especially about his mortification and loss of prestige at being unable to leave a tip, and for a time we dubbed him the five-cent gentleman.

Perhaps what we marvelled at most was the boldly casual way he ventured – socially – into the townsite, an area that we and all our neighbours on Humber Heights considered almost as enemy territory. Racer felt no reluctance or embarrassment in mixing with the biggies; on the contrary, he seemed to take it as quite natural that he should add this area to the general extent of his conquests, and the whole thing became almost official in a symbolic way when it began to be rumoured around the mill and the rest of the town that Racer Stone was the boy friend of our minister's daughter. None of us had ever dreamed of, much less achieved, a like social eminence.

On these evenings when the C.L.B. was having a route march, we would observe Racer dressing more meticulously than usual and carefully picking his way down over the hill to keep the mud off and the shine on Ank's best shoes; later word came back to us that when the band passed by the minister's house Racer's drumming took on point and vigour in so noticeable a way that he was suspected of having a secret code known only to the girl and himself, though he managed to keep time and be a pretty good drummer as well. In point of fact, Racer never became established or recognized as the minister's daughter's boy friend, but what a lot of credit he had added unto his name by the mere rumour! And even Mom thought that a girl out of the Rectory would have been good enough for her handsome laddy-o.

Somehow Racer kept on at school until he had struggled through Grade X, at which point he balked at further study and actually demanded to be put to work – at anything, he insisted, except a job in the mill. Dad raised no objection at all, hoping perhaps that earning money would teach Racer the value of it, while Mom only vaguely regretted that Racer did not go on and finish, now that he was so near Grade XI and graduation. Racer's eye was now entirely focused on money. He had to have cash of his own if he were not to go on living what he considered a dog's life and earn the dreaded reputation of being a piker and a cheapskate. His first job was that of butcher's boy in the Townsite Meat Market. Naturally we all assumed that Racer would not long remain in such a lowly post; the salary too was, as we put it, nothing extra. But Racer had a foot on the ladder of success and with his very first meagre fortnight's pay managed to create another sensation. He went off to a shop all on his own hook and ordered himself a tailor-made suit, the first in our family and an extravagance and waste that immediately brought a menacing nod from the Old Man plus a cold glint in his eye, giving us all to understand that another point had been added to the score he had to add up against Racer.

When Ank married, things became worse for the rest of us instead of better because Racer, assuming all the privileges but none of the responsibilities of eldest son, threw added work on Crawfie and me, and moreover kept the Old Man in a continual state of irritability and blasphemous rage that poisoned each day of existence in our storm-rent home. Soon Racer found a new job as clerk in a property office which put him in a position to pay full board to Mom and still have a good bit of pocket money left over; but we soon found out that Mom was giving him a kickback of one-quarter to one-half the amount he paid, depending on the exigencies of his social and personal life.

With Ank out on his own, Racer and Mom drew more intimately together than ever before, and Racer's whole manner took on a confidence that might have been called swagger in any young man less openly, genially, and charmingly pleased with himself. There came into his manner too a kind of self-sufficiency that set new devils dancing in the Old Man's eyes. Why, Racer argued, should he slave at night around the house when he was out working all day and paying his board? Ank had done it? To hell with Ank. That was his funeral. If he was fool enough to have done it, all well and good. But not Racer. No sirree. Piss on that. "And piss on you too," Racer generally added in reference to the Old Man when the latter had turned his back and walked away in total disgust and out of hearing range.

The showdown between them came quite unexpectedly over a comparative trifle, as one more puff of breath will cause a long-glowing ember to burst into sudden scorching flame. One evening when Racer was about seventeen, we were all getting ready for tea as usual – that is, brawling, shredding another towel, and grabbing food from the stove – while waiting for Dad to arrive home. Racer finished washing first and was over in a corner with Mom, amusing her by giving once again his impression of the Old Man's accent and whole manner. We all stopped to watch, even Flinksy, who was setting the table, and could not help applauding when the truly devastating, accurate, and deadly malicious performance by Racer was done. Mom's appreciation took the form of a mere token warning at first and then a complete and laughing surrender to Racer's mimetic ability; unable to resist him, she threw her arms around his neck and began stroking his lustrous hair and kissing him in an ecstasy of love and adoration.

At that moment in walked the Old Man, his towering frame and mistrustful eye seeming to oppress us all more heavily and bore into us more scathingly than ever before.

"Well, you been at it again," he grunted at Racer and then slowly transferred his accusing stare to Mom. We all thought he meant the present performance and braced ourselves for immediate fireworks, but when Racer tried to bluff it out there came another development.

"At what?" said Racer as blandly as he could while disentangling himself from Mom's embrace and squaring his shoulders with a manly thrust of defiance.

"You knows what. You and two udder fellas – ye had a girl over the hill last night and ye was . . . was takin' advantage of her, one right after d'yudder."

"Who said so?" demanded Racer.

"I hearrrd it from good aut'ority. From a man who seen ye, and he's no liar like some people I could mention."

"He is if he claims he saw me doing that."

"I should say he is!" Mom chimed in vigorously.

"That's right! That's right! Take up for him again, like you always does," Dad bawled at her.

"How crooked is you!" she countered, trying to divert him. The word "crooked" in our family meant cantankerous, not dishonest.

"Crooked or not, I'm sayin' the young scut ought to be ashamed of hisself."

"Ah, he's only mischeevious. He's not evil like some. Is you, Racer?" she invited him to deny the fact that he was a precocious young ram who took his tail wherever and however he could get it.

"No, I'm not, Mom," Racer gave her his captivating smile.

Somehow we assembled ourselves for the meal without any more than verbal violence and with only a little further growling from the Old Man about disgrace to his name again and the nauseating worthlessness of the younger race. As usual, we males were all served first, then Flinksy sat down with a heaped plateful, and finally Mom appeared ostentatiously bearing a small plate with one or two bits of turnip and potato and a rind or so of meat and took her place at the foot of the table. All this was merely a blind, for we knew she had been eating most of the time the meal was cooking; moreover, I often saw her, as economic conditions gradually improved in the family, take a whole cubic inch of butter on the end of a knife and swallow it straight down with a gulp and a little shudder of sensual delight. She ate and drank with no more thought of calories than a hungry child let loose on a barrel of ice cream. Her tentative pose at table came from a knowledge that before the meal was over she would be up from one to twenty times for the purpose of tending on Dad or one of the boys until all were satisfied.

On this particular evening some wicked spirit must have got into her or Racer or both of them; or perhaps the showdown came simply because Racer had been made more reckless than ever by his easy escape from the raping incident and felt in a gloating way that nothing could touch him now. As Mom handed him his second helping of vegetables, she also gave him a conspiratorial wink. Racer grinned, and from behind his hand he made another face imitating the Old Man in sour mood — mostly for the benefit of Flinksy, Crawfie, and myself. In spite of ourselves we began to giggle and smirk and snort, soon borne along by Racer's bravado to the point where we could not stop even if we had wanted to. A warning from the Old Man took no effect whatever, and he relieved himself for the moment, and had his revenge for being left out of our joke as usual, by reaching out suddenly and giving Crawfie, the least self-controlled of us all, a cuff on the ear with the back of his hand. It was an injustice that brought tears more of indignation than of pain to Crawfie's eyes. "See if that'll shut ye up," said the Old Man coldly.

"Hush up now, all o' ye, and finish yere tea," Mom urged us anxiously, no doubt recognizing danger signals in Dad's manner more readily than anyone else.

Far from recognizing or heeding any danger signals, Racer kept on tormenting us with surreptitious looks and gestures and, at last, in answer to an innocent question from Flinksy, who with a little of Mom's instinct was trying to head off a fuss, he put a match to the gunpowder he had so blithely scattered around himself and all the rest of us. All he said in answer to Flinksy was: "I *hearrrd* diff'rent," but that was more than enough. With a snarl of animal rage the Old Man sprang up, tipping the table and sending most of the food and dishes sliding down to Mom's end in a tinkling avalanche. He seized Racer by the hair with his left hand while with the right he began pounding him over the face and head, each blow a grunt of satisfaction and of vengeance achieved.

"Mock me, willya? Mock yer own fawder! And t'ink you can get away wit it, be the Lard Jesus! Shore signs, we'll see about that." He plucked Racer upright until their eyes were almost on a level.

"I . . . I wasn't mockin'," Racer gasped, cowed by the suddenness of the attack. "I wasn't makin' fun." And in truth we others were not at all sure he *had* meant to imitate the Old Man this time. Racer's academic progress to Grade X had softened and toned down the more grotesque of the errors and crudities of speech habitual with us, but by no means removed them entirely.

The Old Man chose to think he had been deliberately mimicked. "Liar!" he yelled. "Bloody liar along wit' all the rest of it." More blows fell now on Racer's head. "You does a t'ing, and then you're not even man enough to own up to it."

"Now that's enough, Dad, that's enough," Mom begged frantically.

"Enough my arse! I'll give him a damn good lickin' while I'm at it. Somet'ing he wunt forget in a hurry. He

been askin' for it for years, and now he's goin' to get it."
Seeing more punishment coming, Racer tried to pull out of the Old Man's grasp and even raised a clenched hand as though he might be intending to strike back. The mere gesture was taken as an attempt at retaliation.

"Oh, you would, would you? T'ink I'm still not able for you, hey?" The Old Man viciously jerked up his knee and sank it in Racer's belly, dangerously low down. Racer sucked in breath with a kind of rattling gasp and collapsed on the floor.

By now we were all on our feet crying out in protest and staring in horror. Flinksy screamed when Racer fainted, and I saw the blood draining from her face as though someone had stabbed her directly in the heart. When the Old Man raised his boot and made a motion to stamp on Racer, Mom tried to intervene physically but was sent reeling back over the table by a brutal shove. Somehow Flinksy now found the courage to speak out against such violence.

"You shut yer mout'!" the Old Man barked. "And ye too," he rounded on me and Crawfie. "Not a Jesus word, or ye'll get it worse than him. Yes, ye're all alike. Just 'cause ye got a bit o' education ye t'inks yere shit don't stink. But I knows diff'rent. I been out there in the t'ilet right after ye. So don't go givin' me no lip. I should'a did this years and years ago to the whole goddam lot o' ye. Then maybe I wouldn't find ye makin' fun o' yere own fawder right to his face."

During the brief silence that came while the Old Man was recovering his breath, Racer must have come to and perhaps had a brief respite from pain, for suddenly his voice came up from the floor as clear and deliberate as a judge's sentence, startling us all by the manner no less than by the matter of his words.

"You goddam dirty old bastard."

After the first shock of realization had passed, the Old Man leaped for his razor strap that always hung on the wall beside his shaving mirror. This time Mom tried to wrest the weapon from him, but he pulled away and gave her a cut across the front of her dress with the two-tailed heavy leather strap. I saw her already ashen face contract with the pain as she once more fell back from the centre of the struggle.

"If you so much as *touches* him once more," she managed to cry out, "I wunt stay in this house another day. I'll take the two youngsters that's not workin' and I'll clear out o' this cursed hole for good. I'll go back home to Ma in Haystack."

"I don't give a good goddam where you goes. Go to hell, and take yer saucy brats along wit' you. Put that in yer pipe and smoke it. I'm tired tellin' you about the way you goes on wit' 'em. Hulderin' 'em and takin' up for 'em when you should be givin' 'em some discipleen. They're saucy as blacks, every one; but *this* one is goin' to find out for once he haven't got *you* to deal wit' this time."

"Oh, I wish Ank was here!" cried Mom in helpless agony. "He'd do something." She looked across the kitchen at her two youngest sons, but it was clear that Crawfie had not the stomach to tackle the Old Man at this time, and as for myself, apart from being too young and delicate for anything to be expected of me in such a situation, I was utterly absorbed, horrified, and fascinated by the spectacle of this creature called my father in the startling transformation of his fury.

His pale eyes protruded from sockets like bags of blood and I noticed how the slack space that always showed between his trousers and his belly opened and closed spasmodically as he panted for breath. When he began to give Racer a thorough lacing with the strap, dancing up and down in the ecstasy of his rage, he seemed to me like some huge emaciated monkey sprung out of the jungle to prey on an innocent world.

Racer threw his arms over his head, drew up his knees, and jack-knifed his whole body into the embryo position to protect himself from the whistling cuts of the strap.

"Will you ever do it again?" the Old Man thundered vengefully. "Will you ever mock me again? Hey? Will you?"

"No, no."

"You better not. I'll have me rights in this house – yes, by the crucified Jesus, I'll have respect from ye, even if I got to *swing* for ye." He went on like this for quite a while, more or less in time to the strokes of the strap, until fatigue slowed him down, and at last there came a momentary lull in the horror. Racer must have thought this was the end of his torture. He cautiously drew down his arms for an instant, but in that very same instant down came the strap again cutting right across his exposed face. Racer howled, blood spurted, Flinksy screamed again, and the Old Man, stimulated rather than sobered by the sight, kept on lashing at Racer until blood was spattering over himself and the walls, and the kitchen looked more like a slaughterhouse than the centre of our domestic life.

At long last it really was over. Sucking air like a bellows, the Old Man passed the back of his hand across his forehead to wipe away the blinding sweat, bloodying his whole face with the motion, and then turned to stare at the rest of us as if to demand whether we would like some of the same medicine. We all turned away in disgust, and with a sneer he flung the strap down on top of Racer, muttering contemptuously: "Now get out o' here, the whole bunch o' ye. I'm *sick* o' the sight o' ye. Get out and leave me alone."

Flinksy managed to rouse Mom from her dazed and terrified state to lead her out of the kitchen while somehow Crawfie and I dragged and supported Racer into our bedroom to examine his wounds and see what could be done for him. The minute we had passed through the kitchen door the Old Man slammed and locked it and then we heard him fall on his couch half-moaning and half-cursing in a totally inarticulate way. His radio remained silent the whole night.

We had to take a jug and go out the front way to get some water for cleaning up Racer's injuries, which however were not nearly as bad as we had thought during the conflict. It was a split lip that had caused all the bleeding, and when we had closed it with plaster and otherwise restored Racer to something like his normally clean, morning-fresh appearance, we were able to hope with some reason that no serious damage had been done. As soon as Mom had quite recovered herself, we broached the question of getting the police after the Old Man; she hesitated, pondered, but after spending a few minutes alone with Racer she decided against it. Apparently Racer's wounds were in a bodily way only superficial, though in another way they would never entirely heal.

That night we had no family prayers nor did any of us boys individually commune with God to thank Him for His general protection in our lives and the particular blessings of this day, fearfully needed though such a communication was in all our minds. From that day came other changes too. Silence was now more noticeable in the kitchen, even if we knew the Old Man was safely down over the hill, and Racer was for many days and weeks less ebullient than we had ever known him. Nowadays he did not pass by the Old Man when they met, but darted around him with eyes averted and his body hunched in a wary manner against possible further punishment. The Old Man was likely to explode again at any moment and for no adequate or predictable cause.

They never spoke to each other. From time to time the Old Man audibly muttered his disgust at Racer being so pig-headed and case-hardened, but still Racer only hung his head and keeping his mouth tight-clamped merely nodded as if to show that now he knew what he knew and there was nothing more to be said. Privately Racer swore to us he was going to *get* the old bugger and when we told Ank about the racket, ways and means were discussed; however, I seemed to notice that since he had become a husband and father Ank was not so keen as formerly on condemning the Old Man out of hand, and this time he did not encourage

Racer to any positive action or promise any support in the event that Racer should attack on his own initiative.

Racer seeming to be more talk than deeds, the cold war in our home continued cold, but Racer did keep up his campaign of mute resistance and what amounted to silent contempt against paternal domination. Even when the Old Man gave him a direct order he would not acknowledge it by a single word; he would simply jerk his head again and set about his task in a mulish way. For months the whole atmosphere of the house was oppressive as a dentist's breath.

What had frightened us all as much as the Old Man's seizure was Mom's despairing threat to leave him and go back to her original home, a place that we knew of only by hearsay. She never did carry out this threat, although she certainly meant it in spirit at the time it was made. The practical difficulties were quite insuperable and, in addition, she had not a cent of her own money nor any relative or friend who would stake her to such an unheard of and sinful escapade as leaving her husband. Among people like us, the private law was to take whatever came with marriage and, if you couldn't smile, then at least keep the misery to yourself and make the best of it. Besides, we all realized on reflection that even if Mom did take Crawfie and me with her, she would never be able to go away and leave Racer. So we had the assurance at least of keeping her with us indefinitely.

Nevertheless, the whole episode of Racer's humiliation and bloody beating was epoch-making in more ways than one. Already in reckoning dates Crawfie and I spoke in terms of Before and After Racer Got His Lickin', and Flinksy's face took on an anxious look that was not to disappear or at least soften until marriage promised her escape from the house altogether. The episode produced an aftermath as well, an event almost more crucial and dismaying than if Mom *had* packed up and gone away.

One evening in late summer, we were all gathered in the kitchen as usual over various indoor occupations and relishing the fact that we could all do more or less as we pleased for one whole evening. We were free of the Old Man, who was certain to work late on repairs because there had been a breakdown on number one machine in the mill, and Flinksy had had to take his tea down to him between two heated plates wrapped in cloth. Our freedom was good until midnight at least.

Mom was also in a good mood at the thought of the extra money come pay-day and by Racer's decision to stay in for one evening instead of going out gallivanting around and getting into more trouble. There was, in any case, such a violent electrical storm that even he admitted the uselessness of getting all dressed up only to have his best clothes soaked and nothing to wear on Sunday. So we had domestic peace for a few hours, with all serious work put aside and each of us able to give a little time to his heart's desire: Flinksy reading *True Romance*; Racer, *Gone With the Wind*; Crawfie at the mirror bunching up his curls and gravely assessing his looks in general; and myself with a piece of trouting line suspended between two door knobs, fascinated by the changes in pitch when I plucked the string after tightening or loosening it by moving one of the doors.

Mom was sitting comfortably near the stove apparently sewing, but really occupied in pleasant contemplation of nearly all her family quietly and peacefully assembled together with a hot nourishing meal inside them and adequate shelter from the storm. I had just tired of my musical experiments and like the others started on some quieter pursuit when in the cozy silence we were all startled by a question from Racer, who must have been prompted to it by something in the novel he was reading.

"Mom," he asked in puzzled tone and with puckered forehead, "Mom, did you ever love d'Ole Man?" Mom stared at Racer for a full minute as intently as we were now all watching her. She seemed transfixed by memory. The bit of sewing fell unregarded onto her lap, and while she continued to gaze at Racer, I saw her tawny eyes suddenly go dark, as they always did in sorrow, and her whole face settle into a pale mask of regret. Then to my horror huge tears welled up in her eyes and flowed down along her cheeks in glistening procession for several minutes, without any change in her expression or a single word issuing from between her lips. Flinksy, now weeping herself, went over beside Mom's chair and touched her diffidently but tenderly on the shoulder.

"Never mind, Ma girl," she murmured, "never mind," – as though to assure our mother that at least she was not all alone in the knowledge of her grief and still had us to stick up for her. The quiet words and gesture from Flinksy seemed to tap an even deeper well of sorrow in Mom, for now her face collapsed like a tent from which the ridgepole has been plucked away, and she leaned forward and covered streaming eyes with her hands.

"Ye'll never know," she sobbed, her vast form heaving convulsively and seeming to multiply her emotion by its very extent and bulk. "Ye'll never know what I've a went through with him. Not if I sits here from this till Doomsday and keeps on talkin'. 'Tis not so bad now. When ye was all small – that was the worst of it. God above only knows what I suffered from his temper then. But what could I do? I couldn't just go away and leave ye. What'd become o' ye? Who'd tend on ye and get yere meals? So I stuck it out somehow, but like I said, neether tongue nor pen could tell what I'm after puttin' up with and goin' through in this house."

Amazed, and all but paralyzed mentally by this glimpse into a past that we remembered only dimly, and also by a momentary view of our mother as a lonely person and a weak, suffering individual woman rather than our familiarly ribald and always-in-demand Mom – amazed and horrified by these revelations, we all did our best to comfort her by promising that things neither could nor would ever be so bad for her again. For one thing, we were now big enough and would soon be independent enough to take her away ourselves if things at home became unbearable for her or for us. It seemed to me that no matter how much we reassured her, some doubt remained in her grief-shadowed eyes.

I could see too that Racer, like all the rest of us, had been deeply shocked by the vistas that Mom's outburst of confidence had opened up, but when she had become somewhat calm he did venture one more question, and a most pertinent question it was. "Mom, what *makes* him so contrairy?"

At this Mom once more embraced us all with her eyes, shaking her head in a baffled way to show that even a consideration of this question was almost too much for her.

"I'm blessed if I knows," she muttered helplessly, "I'm blessed if I knows. I done me best – got the meals, kept the house, sent ye all off to school. I managed the money the best I could and saved and scrubbed and spent the half o' me time at the washtub. I don't see how any mortal could'a worked any harder. Ye all knows I don't get down over the hill no more than three or four times a year. But it's all the same. All no good. It just seems like nutting can please him, nor ever could. I'm wore out tryin'. Sometimes I feels just like I don't care no more. I feels like sayin' to heck with it all. And then there's all those rackets. Racer, my darling, I want you to promise me that you won't do anything to start any more fuss. And the rest o' ye too – no matter what happens. I don't believe I could stand much more. I believes I'd go right offa me head, that's all. Now will ye *promise* me?"

Racer led us in promising the thing she desired, with reservations, however, about preserving his health and life should the Old Man launch any more attacks on him. Racer was putting on flesh and muscle almost daily, so that the time was approaching when it could no longer be assumed by anyone that in anything like a fair fight, with no cowardly advantage taken by the Old Man, Racer would again be thrashed and at least momentarily cowed. That was our habitual mode of thought at this time, in terms of calculated chances and possible victory if and when hostilities were to break out again.

From time to time the Old Man continued to threaten us all and Racer in particular, but we got through several weeks after the big showdown without a major outbreak. Little by little Racer lapsed again into his feckless and reckless ways. He was doing well in his new job, dressed more than ever like a village Clark Gable, and soon began bringing girls around the house as well as spending most of his evenings in what we regarded as high living. This was nothing but showing off on his part, all of it, for as Flinksy had come to realize only too well, anyone wanting to love it up a little or foster the spirit of romance would have chosen a damp church at four in the morning rather than our house at any time for the carrying out of such a purpose. No, Racer just wanted to prove to us what smart-looking girls he could fascinate and capture.

When Flinksy got married, Racer did not improve the family atmosphere by presuming on his new status as the eldest now at home, and again exasperating the Old Man to the verge of violence. He would still make his own decisions or even spend a considerable sum of money without any reference at all to Dad; or he would, through mere vanity and by way of codding him, tell the Old Man a whopping great lie just to see how long it would take the old tyrant to find out the difference. We others, who had been in on the whole thing from the start, always reckoned or hoped that if and when the Old Man did ferret out the truth too much time would have passed between Racer's lie and its discovery to precipitate another crisis in the kitchen.

For months we went on like this, daily expecting Racer to go too far and get himself either murdered or thrown out of the house and disowned forever by the Old Man. In the stress and the passionate tension of Racer's mounting defiance, promises to Mom were almost totally forgotten; now and then she still begged us not to start anything, but she might just as well have begged a poisonous plant not to grow while she was quite powerless to pluck it from its nurturing soil.

The whole situation was shaping up into a contest that centred around the question: would Racer provoke an ultimate and perhaps fatal crisis with the Old Man over his love affairs, or would one of these affairs lead him, as Ank had been led, along the path of an early marriage brought on by premature fatherhood? Neither catastrophe occurred, but from Mom's point of view something much, much worse.

One Sunday morning in 1939, when we were all lined up in our church pew according to custom, the minister climbed up to his pulpit in a more solemn mood than he had ever exhibited, and before going into his sermon made an announcement that was to affect our obscure, backwater lives as profoundly as it shook the lives of those remote and legendary figures at the very centre of the world's affairs.

War! That morning Britain had declared war on Germany, and of course it followed automatically and without question that, as Britain's oldest colony, Newfoundland was also now at war with Germany. In the atmosphere of wonder and awe that prevailed in the church as this news crystallized in the congregation's mind, very little was inwardly heard and still less understood of the sermon on *Dulce et decorum est pro patria mori*.

Over Milltown's Sunday dinner the eager buzz of talk in all families, as in ours, could be centred only in the sudden reality of war and its probable consequences for all our lives. For one thing we soon arrived at and accepted perforce the conclusion that every family in which there were grown sons would be expected, if not compelled, to send one of them overseas to fight for King and Country, and beyond that point it was a short and inevitable step to the realization that from our family Racer would have to be the one to go. Ank was married and had a child, Crawfie was hardly old enough, and I would not be of military age for about two years.

The moment during our dinner when this inescapable process of elimination became clear to Mom, she looked fearfully at Racer and then clung to him with her eyes, her whole face taut with yearning and with the dread that he would not be able to resist all the pressure to make him into a soldier. Dad looked grave, neutral, expressing no opinion in so many words. Racer himself took it all with his usual blitheness; not only did he accept his position as a logical fact, but the very next day on his way home to dinner he dropped into the Recruiting Office that had been set up overnight in the courthouse and offered himself for service in the Royal Artillery, Newfoundland Regiment.

With sinister speed there followed his x-ray and a medical examination during which nothing was found wrong with his back or any other part of his body, and then came his orders to be ready for departure to England via St. John's in two weeks. This period of waiting was, if possible, more painful and full of tension for all of us than the days following Racer's great beating at the hands of the Old Man.

Once we children overheard a long-drawn-out acidulous dogfight between Mom and Dad in which she hysterically accused him of being the one and only cause of Racer's enlistment. "You druv un to it! Yes, you druv un to it," she cried. "If it hadn't a been for all your fuss and fights and bein' so hard on him, he'd never a gone and jined up. That's one t'ing for sure, and I wunt forget it in a hurry — you can mark that down in your book, once and for all."

Of course she was all wrong here. Racer would have gone off to the war under any circumstances, but there was no convincing her of this fact. Every time anyone mentioned the war, and the knowledge came upon her like a midnight avalanche that she must soon lose her heart's darling, Mom sank down on the nearest chair and wept as helplessly and disconsolately as an abandoned child. If only she knew for *how long* he would be gone, that would be something. Every one of us was quite aware, but naturally none of us dared say or even hint, that Racer might never come back home at all. In Dad we noticed a slight relaxation of the hostile glare that was his usual rampart of defence around the house; once or twice, in speaking to Racer, he called him by name instead of beginning, as he generally did, with that arrogantly abrupt gesture of the out-thrust right arm and the words "Why, look'a here. . . ."

It was most certainly a relief when at last the day came for Racer to go away on his great adventure. Mom had got everything ready for him a couple of days previously, knowing that she would be quite incapable of remembering or seeing to anything on the ultimate day. It was again a Sunday, and soon after our chicken dinner, cooked special for the occasion by Flinksy, we all prepared to accompany Racer down to the little country-cottage style railway station where all the volunteers were to muster before taking the express to St. John's. Crawfie and I had agreed to carry his luggage between us, but a half-hour or so after dinner and before train time, Dad astonished us all by sending Crawfie into the townsite to order a taxi, in which Racer and Mom and Dad would ride down to the station, taking the luggage with them, while all the rest of the family came along on foot to the momentous parting.

On arriving at the station, we saw that the volunteers had already fallen in to be numbered off and checked and inspected. There was a motley double rank of fresh-faced boys, all about Racer's age, nineteen, and all visibly eager to have these enervating preliminaries done with and be on their honoured way. The entire scene was given a stamp of official urgency by the presence of a neatly moustached British Army officer in full uniform, medals, ribbons and all, whose commands our boys obeyed with a vigour that seemed to acknowledge, with every click, his right to command and their cheerful duty to obey.

All the parents and relatives and friends were massed at one end of the station gazing in sorrow and pathetic pride at the brave show their boys were making, and easing pent hearts by an exchange of their real anguish and fear. Not until we heard the train blow a mile out of Milltown was Racer, along with the other recruits, allowed to fall out for the purpose of saying his good-byes.

Showing only a slight pallor of the face and a tremor in his voice, Racer came over to us and began saying good-bye; he started by shaking my hand and saying a few gruff, patronizing words, worked his way up through Crawfie, Flinksy and Rome, Ank and Mavis and the baby, and then came to Mom. She clung to him convulsively, pouring out a stream of incoherent words and passionate endearments all jumbled together with admonitions and good advice, and made more painfully incoherent by the cascade of tears that she could no longer make any effort to control. It was not until the aristocratic bark of the British officer called Racer back to formation that she could be persuaded or forced to loose her hold of him.

Now it was time for Racer to face the Old Man, who stood rigidly waiting but austerely self-controlled, a little behind and to one side of Mom. He and Racer met almost eye to eye. As we all furtively watched with a kind of fascinated curiosity, we saw Racer sway toward him ever so faintly, and we also noticed Dad making an almost imperceptible forward motion of his body. For a second or two it looked as if they would embrace, but into their eyes came what seemed to be a last-minute questioning, a hesitation and an awkward self-consciousness; then before they could surmount this barrier, their moment for reconciliation had gone. The screech of the train's whistle cut into us all like a sentence of death.

Once more Racer was summoned by that commanding bark; he stuck out his hand and Dad took it, muttering two or three words that might have been, "Take care o' yourself," or "Take this" – I could not hear them distinctly

– but as Racer turned away I saw him open his hand and stare downward in wonder at a twenty-dollar bill that lay crumpled in his palm. Pausing for another second to call out, "Thanks, Dad!" he fought his way through the milling, murmuring throng, fell into line as before, and was instantly hustled aboard the train and whisked out of the station and out of our lives. It was all as swift and efficient and final as an execution.

That night as I was passing through the hall on my way to what we called the boys' bedroom, I saw Dad on his knees beside his and Mom's bed and heard him slowly and in a strangled voice muttering the familiar prayers, going as usual through the Lord's Prayer and the Creed, and finally arriving at the Blessing with which we all ended our nightly devotions. I could just hear his inarticulate appeal: "God bless Gert and Ank and Hilda and . . . and Raymond—"

Here his words cut off abruptly and gave place to violent racking sobs that made his body jerk as if somebody were pumping bullets into his back. Unable to watch for long, I moved on toward our room, but I did hear Mom call out, "Saul?" in a tone I had never heard her use before and soon after that came the sound of Dad getting up off his knees and into bed.

For a long time I heard the sound of Mom's crying and Dad's moaning; at long last a subdued talk in which the uttering of comfort-laden, conciliatory words from Mom was the predominating note. Though Crawfie and I had plenty of room in the big bed now, we drew closer together to discuss what I had seen, and the strange, grotesque sounds now coming from that forbidden parental bedroom. As a basis for explanation we agreed right away that, whatever else was happening, the Old Man must be having his bad stomach again.

CHAPTER

7

CRAWFIE

It was a favourite theory, many times and variously expressed, that with Crawfie there entered into our family a certain decadence. Quite often Ank would inform Crawfie and me that we were not worth the powder to blow us to hell, or when we failed to satisfy his standard of brute strength, he would growl savagely, "Get out o' me way, fer Christ-sake! The two o' ye put togedder are not wort' a pinch o' coonshit." Once he declared that Crawfie ought to be "took out some winter morning and shot wit' a ball of his own shit," and Racer used to go still further by saying that Crawfie's execution should be by shooting in both knee-caps, with dumdum bullets, after which he should have his nuts cut out. In a more general way, "soft as shit" was the family verdict that fell on and dogged Crawfie throughout his childhood and youth.

Yet in Crawfie's early years there was nothing in particular – no incident or habit or bodily mark – that would seem to justify the harshness of these comments on his ability and character. True, he was never far from the chamber pot while he was about the house, and at night he had to keep it beside the bed so that it would be easily got at in case of emergency. All this was no more than childish incontinence, however, and might have been regarded by us as more unfortunate or more humorous than ominous had not other bodily peculiarities been joined to it in the total picture of Crawfie's development. The truth was that in several ways other than the purely mental Crawfie was a backward child.

Often Mom used to remind us, and anyone else who happened to be present, that Crawfie had sucked the nipple until he was three years old and even at that time could never be quite satisfied. He was querulous as a sick old man. "I can't peacify un," was Mom's way of putting it. "No matter what I does, I can't peacify Crawfie."

Until the age of three he had likewise neither talked nor walked, nor shown any sense at all. What I remarked first about him in our baby intimacies was his strikingly large head and the unsteady, top-heavy, comical appearance he had when finally he did begin to stagger about with no support except his own rickety legs. Perhaps in all things Crawfie was unconsciously inhibited by another frequent comment of Mom's to the effect (this with a world of weariness and a suspicion of wishful thinking in her voice) that he had almost died when he was born and had hovered on the brink of extinction for several weeks afterwards.

Life became a little better for Crawfie when he started school and soon showed that inside his huge head there was something else besides sawdust and apprehension. We started together, he being only nine months older than I and having been held back by lingering physical weakness. At this time he could already print and often showed the pleasure he took in his rather unusual name by squeaking out CRAWFORD STONE on his slate and holding it up to me across the aisle of the kindergarten. Seeing his achievement, I challenged it by scratching down my own treasured identity and showing it to him; and thus on our first day in that primitive, chaotic little schoolroom up on the Humber Heights we began that academic rivalry which was to continue and drive us on until we had both scored the triumph of getting farther along in school than anyone else in our family.

As Crawfie could hardly hope to equal the personal and social success of the egregious Racer, he gradually came to take refuge in school-work as a means of fighting his way to a place of recognition, if not of respect, among our unimpressionable crowd, but here again he was subjected to mortification and frustration, whenever Mom announced to anyone who happened to drop in at the house of an evening while we were doing our homework at the kitchen table, that Crawfie did not "ketch on so quick" as I and would no doubt have a hard enough time of it in all the higher grades.

At this wanton injustice, tears would well up in Crawfie's eyes. With a show of temper, he would snatch up his books and mouthing an outlandish oath – "Criney Jesus" and "Allah's Curse" were our favourites – he would flounce off into our bedroom to sulk for a while and then continue his work kneeling on the floor with his workbook on the seat of a chair. Later he would reappear in the kitchen and angrily, self-pityingly storm at Mom: "What do you want to go sayin' that for all the time? Juju is nutting exter. I beats him every time in Hist'ry."

Mom was in the habit of laughing at these passionate protests. "Ha-ha!" she cried triumphantly, "look at un – he's jealous again." Crawfie's reaction to this certainly confirmed her taunt, and more than once another fuss would have started – a little sideshow, as it were, in the large gritty drama of our family life – if Dad had not impatiently and somewhat surprisingly intervened on Crawfie's behalf.

"Aw, leave the youngster alone, girl," he admonished Mom. "I don't know but what I agrees wit' him on this. You got no right to go runnin' him down and makin' him feel small in front o' udder people."

That was the way is often went until Crawfie and I had passed through the early classes. On reaching the eighth grade, we moved to the big school in the townsite, at which point Crawfie revealed other talents that helped to soothe him when his intellectual pride was hurt. For one thing, there was his undoubted ability in the acting line. On account of his already imposing bass voice, he was chosen to play the God of Thunder in one of our school pageants and was such a success not only vocally but in representation as well that he took to playing parts and acting out little scenes in private life just to see how many people he could fool and hoodwink. Once he even tried it on us.

There had been another murder in Crow Gulch, and the *Messenger* was putting out daily extras which Crawfie and I had to take all over Humber Heights outside school hours. It was shivering, sleety March weather. After four or five days of it we were both tired out, and on the climactic Friday of that murder week, a day on which there was such a hail storm on the hill that it seemed as if a million ice-tipped arrows had been released from across the bay at one-second intervals, Crawfie was unusually late getting home. We had all finished our tea and Mom had worriedly put Crawfie's in the oven while we began settling to our evening tasks, when his step was heard on the back porch, and then the kitchen door was shot open as though by a desperate fugitive.

Crawfie's form appeared in the doorway, but instead of walking in as we expected, he flumped through it and collapsed across the kitchen floor in a sopping, seemingly lifeless heap. We all gaped. A minute passed, perhaps two. At last: "Water. Water!" Crawfie croaked, his eyes sepulchrally shut and mouth gaping like that of a dead codfish.

Mom was just rushing into the pantry to fetch a glass, but Ank motioned to her to wait and dashed as quietly as he could into our bedroom, reappearing a moment later with Crawfie's chamber pot. He showed it to us – about half full – and then sluiced the contents straight down into Crawfie's face. We all burst into uproarious laughter; even the Old Man cackled appreciatively and tossed back his head as though to declare once again "them youngsters is hopeless."

The taste of his own water soon roused Crawfie from his swoon. He spouted like a small whale, sprang up with an oath, and seeing Ank holding the pot fisted into him just as if they were on quite equal terms physically. Ank thrust him aside with casual contempt, but Crawfie was so enraged over the ruin and above all the anticlimax to his performance that he kept coming back at Ank for more; finally the Old Man was once more obliged to intervene in order to prevent copious bloodshed. This was the occasion on which Crawfie threw the scissors at Ank and scarred him for life. It was a very long time before they were back on anything like brotherly terms again.

Since from an early age he was inclined to take himself seriously, Crawfie felt he had good reason to resent the fact that so many of his aims, inspirations, and actions were turned by us into farce and occasions for mocking laughter. It all started again shortly after Crawfie and I were confirmed, a ceremony which Crawfie took so literally and heavily that for weeks after the Bishop had cleansed us from all unrighteousness he wouldn't, in Ank's phrase, "say shit if he had a mout'ful." He never swore now, he never told any lies that we could detect, and he even did a stroke of real work around the house once in a while, whenever he felt that the Fifth Commandment demanded such an effort. He even began calling the Old Man "Father" and addressing him as such. Worst of all, his mind had been seized on by the words "at the Name of Jesus every head should bow," and at the most unexpected times would therefore give himself occasion to use the Name so that he could stand at attention, pause for a dramatic moment, and then bob his head in a most reverent manner and with a far-away look in his eye to suggest that he actually was in communion with a Holy Presence. It was like one of those old film sequences where the hero suddenly freezes, registers a key emotion, and the action then continues at normal speed.

We all protested that Crawfie was only using this holy fake to curse as much as ever he did before Confirmation, only now he was getting away with it entirely, escaping protest from Mom and cuffs over the ear from the Old Man. Why, we demanded, should he have these special privileges? After all, Ank and Flinksy and Racer and I had gone through Confirmation without any humbug or "putting on" like this and, besides, Crawfie's naturally long face had become so much longer in his piety, so much more solemn and gloomy, that it was beginning to get on all our nerves.

Ank and Racer resolved to break down his pose of holiness, their chance coming when a skin and beauty specialist arrived in town and put up at the Milltown Hotel for a limited time only. At this stage in his growth, Crawfie was going through his worst agonies of acne, a condition that irritated and humiliated him even more than Mom's comparisons of his learning power with mine or Ank's refusal to accept his moral transformation as genuine. In dead secrecy he made an appointment with the specialist to have his face treated, using for the purpose every cent of his earnings and a little money wheedled out of Mom on false pretences. Unfortunately for him, one of Flinksy's friends was taken on as local assistant by the specialist, so it followed that even before Crawfie's treatment took place we knew all about his plans. We determined, however, on a family compact. No one would mention a word about Crawfie's intentions to anyone at all until the deed was done.

On the Saturday evening of Crawfie's adventure into beauty, Ank, who at this period had just started working in the paper sheds, came into the kitchen a bit later than usual and innocently sat down at the table for his tea. We had all finished earlier, and Crawfie was also at the table doing some homework, head bent and one hand masking his face. We could see at a glance that Ank was primed with beer and ripe for mischief. Abruptly he reached across the table and plucked Crawfie's hand away from his face, revealing a truly ghastly sight. Crawfie's expansive face had a mottled, splotchy look, his pimples, blemishes, and inflamed lumps standing out more purulently than ever against a pale pinkish complexion.

"Who crapped on yer nose?" Ank demanded, and shoved his thumbnail into one of Crawfie's suppurating lumps. Crawfie pulled back his head and tried to brush Ank's hand away. His sudden blush made his skin look worse. "I hear you're after bein' *treated*," Ank went on. "Never done you a hell of a lot o' good. Haw!"

Racer led us in appreciation of Ank's verbal attack, and then Mom put in her two cents' worth. "Wastin' your money like that!" she frowned at Crawfie. "Better you'd a give it to me for your school fees. Tellin' lies over it too."

"What?" Ank shouted. "Tellin' lies? *That's* a sin, and no mistake. Now you're not Confirmed no more. You're not goin' straight up to heaven when you dies like Elijah, any more than the rest of us; no sirree. You'll have to scrap for it same as everybody else."

"I never told no lies," Crawfie protested.

"You said it was all for a good cause – the money I went and give you, foolish-like. You said true's-the-Bible." Mom was adamant in her accusing tone.

"So it *was* a good cause. To *me*, Mom."

"Pomps and vanities o' this wicked world," she quoted. "That's not good." As Crawfie would give no sign of admitting her argument to be true, she clinched it with: "I'd never a give you that cash if I'd a knowed what it was for."

"There you are!" Ank resumed. "That proves you're a liar, no matter how you tries to crawl out of it."

"I'm not a liar."

"Own up!"

"You ought to be ashamed o' yourself too," Mom added. "A big b'y like you goin' off to a beauty parlour. Whoever heard tell o' the like?"

"Yes, it was pomps and vanities, that's all it was," Ank would not let Crawfie escape. "And you're a liar in the bargain. So be a man for once, and own up."

"I wunt own up!" cried Crawfie obstinately, still pushing Ank's hand out of his face. Ank seized his wrist and burned it by twisting his hands around it very hard and in opposing directions.

"Own up, you bloody hypocrite," he bellowed.

"Let me go. Ow! Ooooow! Mom, make him let me go!"

"Yes, that's enough, Ank. Let un go, and I'll punish him myself for what he done." But Ank well knew the futility of her words and intentions in this regard, and by this time the Old Man was no longer present to put an end to the quarrel. Ank burned more fiercely. Now there were tears in Crawfie's eyes and we could see as well as Ank that his temper was rising by leaps and bounds. Ank added the last straw by spitting in his face, while Crawfie cast about with his eyes like a man seeking a weapon.

"Oh no, you're not gettin' any scidders this time, you cowardy bugger," Ank grated out the words and gave another twist with his vise-like hands.

"Let me go," Crawfie screamed. "You stop hurtin' me or by Jesus . . .!" That very instant Ank dropped Crawfie's arm and burst out in triumphant laughter.

"Haw-haw!" he cried, "you done it that time. And you never bowed your head needer. So don't go makin' out. Ye all heard him?" Ank demanded our support. Too late Crawfie had pulled himself up, clapped a hand over his mouth, and bobbed his head in his practised apologetic manner. No use at all. It was clear to each one of us that he had taken the Name in vain and under the worst possible circumstances too – in blind anger.

Crawfie withdrew in tears to pray, but after such an obvious fall from grace no amount of prayer or atonement on his part could restore his sanctity in our eyes. Ank had got him fair and square, as he expressed it, and he was ready to oppose with further violence the least presumption that Crawfie might show of being on better terms with the Almighty than anybody else.

In spite of all this opposition, Crawfie did make one more attempt to acquire spiritual merit. He could not be confirmed again, but one Sunday evening not long after Ank's attack on him he hurried up to the Salvation Army after our own church service and installed himself in a seat quite near the altar and under the direct influence of the colonel who was preaching that night. Racer and I followed him to the citadel, seating ourselves up in the gallery at the back of the congregation, where we would not be under close observation by the ushers and yet had a good view of whatever went on down in the main body of the hall.

We could hardly believe our eyes when, the sermon over and Saving Time come, we saw two Salvation brothers close in on Crawfie and obviously begin exhorting him to repentance. They were massaging his shoulders and fishing for his soul to the tune of "Will There Be Any Stars in My Crown?" We were even more astonished at seeing motions of Crawfie's body indicating response, and the climax of it all was the sight of him suddenly rearing up to his full height and, in a state bordering on frenzy, crashing his way straight up to the Mercy Seat at the foot of the altar. There he fell down in a passion of tears, blindly and remorsefully banging both fists on the solid planks.

Racer and I waited just long enough to see him rise from the Seat and give the usual testimony to prove he had sincerely repented his sins and now considered himself no longer a lost sheep, a man on the high road to hell; we galloped home with the great news. "Crawfie got saved! Crawfie got saved!" Then we stood by to witness the reaction our announcement would provoke. The Old Man just muttered something about our own religion not being good enough for us and gave a grimace of disgust. Mom laughed incredulously, exclaiming, "Go on, he didn't!" Ank swore it was all baloney again. Only Flinksy smiled with a certain amount of sympathy, though she too said she would like to have been there to see Crawfie flump down at the Mercy Seat and later testify to his own salvation. She would never have been able to make a show of herself like that.

On his arrival home, Crawfie was greeted by a chorus in which all of us children took a part:

Hallelujah, 'tis done!
I believes in the Son.
I am saved by the Blood
Of the Crucified One!

He smiled sheepishly and went straight to bed, later keeping up with some fortitude a pretence of sleep when Ank and Racer and I went to our bedroom and began questioning him about his Big Experience. This time Ank's boring into him was nothing like the severe punishment he had previously inflicted, because neither he nor any of the family could take a Salvation Army saving as seriously as we took the idea of Confirmation in our own church and by a Bishop from the Old Country too. We just took turns tormenting Crawfie in a mild way, needling him about his face being so long again, about his moony ways, and his infuriating habit of forgiving us all our trespasses on his private holy ground or in any other connection.

As we expected, his backsliding began sooner this time than after he had been absolved and made whole and pure by the Bishop and without any sharp provocation from anyone at all. We merely placed a little temptation in his way. On a berry-picking expedition over the hill, a few of us boys began as usual by gathering some crisp alder leaves and crunching them in our palms the way we had seen old-timers of Milltown shredding their cut-plug tobacco, and then rolling our dust in tissue paper to make cigarettes. For a while Crawfie kept aloof from us, although we could see that the harsh pungency of our smoke was tickling his nostrils and causing a struggle in his soul. Only a little urging sufficed to make Crawfie, with a foolish grin, scoop up the makings of our tobacco and roll himself a clumsy cigarette. After his first puff it was all over and Crawfie was welcomed back into our pagan gang on the same terms as anyone else, for of course smoking was considered by the Army as a definite sin, and therefore Crawfie could no longer pretend to any special virtue or lien on paradise from which we others were excluded. This marked the close of his early religious phase.

All through puberty Crawfie had to continue his fight for a place in the sun of our family life, though on the sexual side he showed a certain unexpected precocity that perhaps made this fight somewhat easier than his religious crises. One day he and I were out in the privy together, and having made water were tossing our tools as boys will when Crawfie's suddenly stood up at a sharp angle like the muzzle of a cannon. One or two extra flips from his hand were then enough to send him off.

"I got it, I got it!" he squealed in jubilation as a jet of semen splashed against the wall and another followed instantly. Crawfie danced and crowed in his ecstasy; the moment he had breath he challenged me to an equal performance.

I managed a little squirt to begin with, but was interrupted by Racer, who came banging on the door and calling out in pain, "Let me in, ye two! Open the door. I needs a piss so bad, I can taste it." Ignoring him, Crawfie and I continued our experiments. Racer pulled at the door so hard that the inside hook came off and he burst in angrily, dancing about in the urgency of his need. While relieving himself he noticed the sliding stains on the wall, which brought from him an accusing stare and a few words of warning from the height of his seniority to us and his reputation of knowing just about all there was to know about the subject of sex.

"Ye better quit doin' *that*," he warned us darkly, "or else ye know what'll happen to ye. Ye'll turn yella in the face, like them Chinks, and be weak as rats. Ye wunt have no stren't a-tall. And then, when the time comes, ye wunt be able to satisfy a woman, see?"

Crawfie nodded gravely and submissively, but I did not see at all, and knew almost enough at this time to ask why then the Chinks were able to produce so many children. On putting my point to him, I was rudely overborne by Racer and alarmed by his concluding threat: "If I ketches ye at it again, I'll have to tell d'Ole Man, and then ye knows what *he'll* do to the two o' ye." That was more than enough to give us pause, if not to inhibit us altogether from any further sexual motions.

Fortunately it was not so many years before Crawfie's energies were directed into the approved and proper channels. In the meantime, he had the satisfaction of growing quite rapidly out of early semi-invalidism and his childhood bodily miseries. Very proud he was of shooting up to be the tallest one in the whole family, topping Dad by half an inch, and prouder still of the luxuriant tangle of auburn curls that crowned his lofty form. His hair lacked the lustre of Racer's though, and his equally blue eyes were less clear and candid, or seemed so, because of a certain wavering that passed over them when you demanded his attention for any length of time. The glasses that Crawfie now wore were delicately cut and parsonically gold-rimmed instead of being the grotesquely iron-clad things that had been forced on him in childhood.

He had gold in his mouth too – a triangular filling in his right front tooth that gave his smile a certain distinction and contributed to his marked individuality. To achieve this distinction, Crawfie had fretted and stormed like a *prima donna* against having his decaying tooth yanked out, and finally he had won his point of getting some kind of a filling, a mad and wasteful novelty in all eyes, rather than a butchering by the town's cheapest dentist and a ridiculous appearance afterwards. The filling of gold was Crawfie's own idea, not mentioned until he returned home from the dentist and gave us his first opulent, triumphant smile. In this whole operation Crawfie showed a certain naive cunning, as he calculated that once the job was done the Old Man would sooner pay the bill than owe the money, or allow anyone belonging to him, and under age, to owe any man a red cent beyond the fortnightly time for settling bills.

Yes, Crawfie managed to achieve an impressive appearance from top to toe, from his massive head, shaped and more or less poised like an inverted pyramid, down to his number eleven shoes; but those who saw him pass by in the street as a stranger were much more impressed than we of the family who knew and assessed him from the inside.

The fact was that in spite of his towering form and considerable weight, the physical elements in Crawfie never quite "jelled" into a co-ordinated and manly whole. He had softly rounded wrists, for example, a plump arse which drew the grossest innuendoes from Ank and Racer, and he was all but useless with his hands. Furthermore, he was never able to ride a bike, nor skate properly (he yawed like a cranky dory when he tried to turn from left to right on his skates), nor master more than the slowest and most elementary steps in dancing. His timing seemed always off. When he walked down over the hill, you saw him go cautiously like an old man studying the ground in front of him and not ready to trust either it or himself to get him safely on his way.

With such handicaps Crawfie naturally had a difficult time at those endless practical jobs and improvements that Dad seemed to delight in undertaking, especially during our summer holidays. The friction between him and Crawfie originated and developed around these jobs, just as it did with Ank and Racer; even the most trifling things added fuel to the glowing fire of antagonism that stood always between us and our father.

Once Crawfie and I accidentally broke a saw blade while sawing up a load of paper cores from the mill—an almost capital offence unless we could persuade Mom not to tell the Old Man until we had had a chance to earn a bit of money and replace the blade. That Monday morning she was in a playful mood.

"What'll ye gimme if I don't tell?" she asked.

"We haven't got nutting to give."

"Lies. Yes, ye have. Crawfie have." And laughingly she flourished a few coins that Crawfie must have had hidden away in our room. Her bed-making was always treasure-hunting as well.

"Well, what do you want?" Crawfie demanded indignantly.

"Ye wunt run down over the hill to do a message for me without I gives ye five cents, so now I wants a . . . a box o' choclates, or else I tells Dad on ye when he comes home." Dad had been working overtime all Sunday night and was due home any minute.

"That's too much," Crawfie protested.

"Get 'em, or I'll blow the roast." Urged on by me, Crawfie refused, and this time Mom did tell. On arriving home, Dad was too tired to give us our licking then, but he did not put his head to the pillow without assuring us that our punishment was coming as soon as he woke up again. So Crawfie and I were left to speculate and quarrel over the question of how severe it would be.

All that day we lived in the anteroom of hell, and then the chastisement turned out to be relatively mild after all, or at least the dreaded moment was not dire enough when it came to leave any scars on us; but the strangest thing was that, although in this case Mom had been the direct cause of our pain and the Old Man only the instrument, it was against him alone that our resentment was cherished. Of course we cried at her with some justice and much heat that if it had been Racer who broke the blade she would never have told on him; in fact, she would, as we put it, have ponied up the cash for a whole new saw and hushed up the whole incident. No use to rail at her. She only laughed again at our protests, blandly hoping that the next time she fancied a few chocolates we would be a sight more nippy about going down over the hill to get them.

To one of Crawfie's rather vindictive nature, a genuine resentment such as he harboured against the Old Man, deepened by this and many other such incidents, was not to be as lightly forgotten as Mom's little squeeze-play against him over the chocolates. The summer Crawfie was fifteen and I was fourteen, the Old Man had the most fiendish idea of all concerning the improvement and modernization of our home. He decided to deepen the well under the house and put a concrete wall in it, as he claimed that the old wooden walls made the water taste fusty. This was as rough and mucky and brutal a job as any prison warden could have dreamed up, and for our sins Crawfie and I were ticked off to be the chief assistants on it. We had just got to the stage where all the mud had been hauled up in buckets from the bottom of the well, and we were passing down some two-by-six planks to the Old Man for use in the new form, when Crawfie, who detested soiling his hands in any way, partly released his grip on the slimy plank we were holding to scrape some of the pug off his right hand. It so happened that at this moment I was off in one of my daydreams and had only a slack hold on the plank myself. Down it went like a plummet straight into the centre of the Old Man's back. He let out a howl and began to hop up and down in the mud at the bottom of the well, clutching at his spine and cursing us in his pain. "Lard Jesus Christ! Ye're after breekin' me back. Goddam ye, I'm crippled fer life. What are ye two young bastards tryin' to do up there? Wait till I gets me hands on ye!"

Having watched the Old Man's agonized gyrations for about a minute, Crawfie and I looked at each other; his eye flickered, and then a corner of his mouth twitched; I responded, and in a trice we both found ourselves obliged to turn away from the edge of the well and clap a hand over mouth and nose in order to keep quiet.

Now the Old Man was scrabbling up the side of the well. His hold gave way and he slopped down into the filthy ooze again, half burying himself in the stony sludge that he also brought down with his fall. Crawfie and I took another brief, cautious glance into the well. The sight was too much for us. Like a couple of lizards we wriggled out of that confined space into the lower part of the basement and then jumped out into the lane where we could stand up and stretch and run. Once out of hearing distance from the house, we both collapsed on the ground and burst into peal after peal of wild, hysterical laughter. It was a long time before we could control ourselves, and a longer time again before any reference to this fiasco lost the power of raising a good laugh between us.

On that particular day only hunger could drive us back to the house, but finally we did go back, plotting our story with each step of the way and trying to settle what our course of action must be should the Old Man inflict on us, or try to inflict on us, a licking of the classical kind that Racer had recently suffered. My own suggestion was that with Crawfie's bulk and my determination we should be able to do more than just protect ourselves from injury. Crawfie frowned on this suggestion from the very first either because he had no stomach for a fight, which I suspected all along, or because he had lost confidence in my suggestions after the saw-blade affair, or perhaps because he had a better idea of how to avoid the threatened slaughter.

When we got home more or less braced for an appearance before the bar of judgment, our judge was stretched out on his couch with an extra cushion under his back, moans and groans issuing from his lips, and in his eye an expression of total disillusionment with all mankind. Crawfie took him and me completely by surprise by rushing up to him and crying out in a tone of the most extreme solicitude, "How is your back, Dad? Do it hurt very much?" The Old Man reared up as far as he could, gasped with the pain of sudden movement, and gave us his sourest look and surliest growl.

"Fat lot ye cares, if me back *is* broke. Goddam young savages. Sure signs, though, when I gets on me feet again I'll give ye droppin' planks! See if I don't, be Christ."

"We're sorry about the accident, Dad," Crawfie came back, his face lengthening under the stress of sincerity and an anxious, ingratiating look taking possession of it. He oozed repentance. "But sure, Dad, we never done it a-purpose."

"Never done it a-pur –!"

"No! No, sir. That plank slipped. I swear it. Didn't it, Juju?"

The Old Man looked hard at me after scrutinizing Crawfie's immobile face Not trusting myself to speak, I nodded as firmly as I could to support our defence. "It's true, Dad b'y," Crawfie pleaded urgently and respectfully. "We never *meant* to do it."

"Never meant to, hey?" the Old Man studied us with as much suspicion as ever. "Come over here, the two o' ye, where I can look ye in d'eye." Crawfie and I exchanged another look, made silent agreement to risk it, and cautiously moved within eyeing and striking distance of the Old Man. For the moment no blows flew at us. "Now then," he continued, "if ye didn't do it a-purpose, tell me this:

116

What did ye run away for?" Here I was quite nonplussed myself and marvelled at Crawfie's readiness with an answer of undeniable plausibility and force.

"We were afraid you *would* think we tried to do it and you'd give us a lickin' for it, right away." This the Old Man received with a grunt of scepticism perhaps mingled with some satisfaction over the indirect tribute to his power. He kept us standing there in front of him, and went on glaring at us balefully, each eye a cold, relentless probe. Had it not been for Crawfie's lead in this instance, I could never have maintained a straight face, but whether from the fear of pain or simply enjoyment of his own performance, Crawfie on this occasion surpassed himself in duplicity and pulling the wool over someone else's eyes.

Although he and I knew perfectly well that there had been more intent than accident in the dropping of that plank, his eye did not waver during the long inquisition, nor did he smile in a silly way as he often did when discovered in iniquity, nor in any way reveal his true feelings. Later in life, when we were all out on our own and more or less out of touch for long periods, I was not surprised to hear that Crawfie had earned the reputation in Milltown of being able to talk his way out of hell and get away with murder.

We escaped without punishment that time at least, and for a little while my respect for Crawfie was accordingly increased. When our trial was a thing of the past, we often discussed the technique he had used to achieve victory, and gradually Crawfie became so impressed with its merits that he wondered whether it might not get results not only in a crisis where punishment threatened but also in the everyday affairs of life where the chief object was to get ahead and beat the other fellow in whatever you undertook.

Our everyday affairs were mainly school work, but here too Crawfie showed some enterprise by nabbing the second seat from the front of the classroom, just behind me, on the pretext of his having weak eyes and therefore needing to be near the blackboard, whereas his real purpose was to copy work from my exercise books in English and French. His height enabled him to do this with very little risk of detection. In many other ways he showed a capacity for humbug and wangling during our career at the central school, notably in the fact that although sport was the surest way to popularity among our fellows, Crawfie achieved a certain amount of recognition without showing any more athletic prowess than I did myself.

Debating was one means of his doing so, as here a certain garrulous charm that he undoubtedly possessed, and perhaps too the come-hither quality of that gold-enriched smile, helped him to forge ahead toward distinction. If these assets failed him, he took unhesitatingly to underhand means, chiefly in the historic Spelling Bee of Grade X in which we were opposing captains and before which it was Crawfie who first suggested collusion. By virtue of this prior agreement, he was able to create a sensation when he survived the word "antidisestablishmentarianism," and nobody could prove a thing.

All in all, Crawfie's later school record was an official credit to him and some compensation for the continuing miseries of his life at home. The truth is, we ragged him mercilessly about his peculiarities, and no doubt he was to some extent a born victim in such an environment because of his proneness to fear and the want of iron in his whole constitution. In adolescence he still believed in Jackie-the-Lantern, a legendary light essentially evil that followed you on dark winter nights when you were alone, stopping whenever you did and starting again on cue, but still drawing gradually a little closer – until finally you turned once more to see if he had gone and then he pounced on you with a demonic screech, revealed himself fully as a raging devil and gobbled you up altogether.

It was no wonder that with his profound sense of sin Crawfie seldom strayed far from home by himself after dark. Sometimes, if he were a bit late, one of us would swipe one of Mom's white sheets and leap out on him in the guise of a ghost just when he was hurrying into the safety of home ground. All during this period he suffered from nervousness, not lessened by the cruelty of our domestic sports, and from headaches and sweating at night. We other boys daily witnessed his misery, but Ank especially had no mercy on him. One day as Ank was walking home in his dirty working clothes, and Crawfie was coming the same way all dressed up as usual in emulation of Racer, Crawfie deliberately and unmistakably hung back so that he would not have to walk along the road with Ank while he was in that shabby condition. How could Ank or any of us forgive him that?

During our last year in school, a day came when Crawfie had his revenge on the whole lot of us, not in the form of any hostile act but through a spectacular triumph that got his picture in the *Messenger* and his name and his own personal identity rather than "Racer Stone's brother" on every tongue in town. This personal triumph was winning The Trip, a Scholarship Cruise to England on one of the Company's paper boats given each year to two boys from the graduating class and lasting well over a month of the summer holidays. Even pocket money was supplied to the two winners. It was indeed a prize, this trip, and all the more treasured by Crawfie and honoured by Humber Heights when we remembered that nearly every time it was boys from the more well-to-do families in the townsite who achieved this signal honour.

Although the winners were informed of their success well beforehand, Crawfie showed a rare self-control in not breathing a word about it until the official announcement was made; then he flourished the newspaper in all our faces and with a radiant smile seemed to challenge us *now* to call him a big bluff, not as nice in disposition as Racer or quick to learn as Juju. For once we were all obliged to take him seriously and to congratulate him on a genuine, honest achievement.

During the time Crawfie was away, there was much optimistic speculation among us about his future, now that he had passed the milestone of Junior Matriculation and so added academic success to the social prestige of winning

The Trip. It was generally felt that with such a good education and all the rest of it he could go on from there and become almost anything. Crawfie himself had had early leanings toward the church, as everybody know, but more than one obstacle stood in the way of such a career. There was his regrettable lapse from sanctity shortly after his Confirmation, and also a more concrete and in a sense public difficulty that began at one of our church garden parties.

For some years our minister had had his eye on Crawfie, not altogether in a favourable way, and his hostility crystallized over the incident in which Crawfie was put in charge of the Bean Board, a game in which you threw small bags of beans at a board with numbered holes in it and tried to come as near as possible to a top score of one hundred. First prize for the nearest score was a cheap pocket watch, which Crawfie had coveted from the moment he saw it. Accordingly, he placed himself in the competition, and on the first day of the garden party there appeared on the scoreboard, with a few other names below it, the bold legend: CRAWFORD STONE – 98.

When the minister spotted this, his jaw fell and he took Crawfie aside to protest the impropriety of a member of the house, so to speak, entering into competition at his own game, but Crawfie in turn protested that there was no rule against it and then backed up his case by producing a sheet of paper on which two of his pals attested that he had made his fantastic score in the usual and proper way. Thereupon the reverend gentleman had all but lost his temper in public, giving Crawfie the choice of withdrawing his score or withdrawing from the management side of the garden party altogether. Crawfie took the watch, but he lost all hope of ever getting the local recommendation and blessing that were necessary before he could even hope to be accepted as a Divinity student at St. John's or to take advantage of the subsidy offered by the church to needy but promising students.

What about Crawfie being a lawyer, we all wondered? He should be good at anything where the gift of the gab was rated high. Crawfie thought so too; but again, who would supply the funds for five to seven years' study at college and then two years of clerkship followed by the expense of setting up a practice and waiting to build it up? Since, therefore, the Law was quite out of the question on practical grounds, and nobody came up with any better workable ideas, Crawfie returned home from England with the matter of his potentially brilliant future still unsettled.

The day he arrived back there was a little disturbance at home due to Crawfie's loud complaints about how he was neglected by the family the same as always, and how little honour was done him even at the climactic moment of his progress across the ocean to the Mother Country and all the way back again. It appeared that, when the ship docked at the Company wharf, relatives and friends of the other young man on The Trip had rushed up the gangway and with a cherishing pride of welcome had whisked him off in a taxi. Crawfie was left high and dry and dismal on the dock, obliged to pick up his own suitcase and walk through the mill grounds and up the several hills to our house without a soul to say "welcome home" or to help him carry the heavy case. He had spent every shilling of his pocket money and could not afford a taxi of his own. So keenly did Crawfie feel the humiliation of all this that during tea on the evening of his return he kept up a chant of self-pitying protest and finally succeeded in upsetting us all by making us feel somewhat guilty. The truth was that almost any one of us could have managed to take an hour off to meet the boat, and this was especially true of me, because we were in the summer holidays and I was completely at leisure.

Consequently it was with a malignant eye on me that the Old Man summed up the situation in his usual devastating way: "Ye t'inks no more about one anudder than ... than *dogs*." I was about to defend myself from the accusation when Mom, to avert another fuss, jumped up and scattered us all by clearing the table and bawling at Flinksy several times to come and help her. There were reasons why I had not turned up at the boat and treated Crawfie to a hero's return, reasons known only to myself but sticking in my mind like burrs. Nor was I made to feel any more cordial toward him when he now turned on me, after the Old Man's brief outburst, and gave that characteristic little sniff of self-justification and victory which I always found more maddening than a whole week of the verbal gloating to which he was also addicted.

Though tension between us continued for some time, Crawfie's feathers were eventually smoothed and his pride fully restored by the offer of a teaching post from the Department of Education in a rocky little hamlet away up on the north shore of Newfoundland grotesquely called Flowery Cove. He was to teach Grades I to VI at a salary of twenty-eight dollars a month. It wasn't much but Crawfie bravely took it on, young as he was, and thereby settled his immediate future and brought off another achievement that was not inconsiderable when we thought of earlier departures from our home – Ank's fight for self-determination, Flinksy's tormented courtship and desperate marriage, but above all the horrible tension in the house that had preceded Racer's going off to war.

Crawfie got away without suffering any racket or violence from the Old Man (although this most fateful year in Crawfie's life *was* to have repercussions under the paternal roof later on). His tearing up of the whole house and stowing into his luggage almost anything he could lay hands on around the place was more the result of nervousness in the face of his great adventure, and his natural greediness, than of any emotional crisis with the Old Man or anyone else in the family.

As far as I was concerned, Crawfie did not get away too soon, because after Racer had left and Crawfie in his turn began to feel his position and dignity as eldest remaining son, the fights between him and myself became more frequent and bitter, finally ending in a savage battle that after many years I still do not like to recall. At home there was a brief and most welcome lull when he had gone; we had a letter or two giving lurid accounts of the diet and cold and other hardships in Flowery Cove, always followed by the request for a little cash to supplement his salary and buy some extra food when the coastal boat came on its monthly visit with supplies.

And then the next thing we heard was that Crawfie was married. After Mom had read out this part of his letter, the Old Man made a loud and prolonged hawking noise in his throat as though to expel some poison from deep down in his system. "Jumpin' Jesus!" he muttered bitterly, "what next?"

"Yes, he's wonderful young to be takin' responsibility." Mom took up Dad's train of thought in a milder and more sympathetic tone. "Only eighteen, and haven't got the best o' sense eether, in some ways. I dreads to think what'll become of him if he goes and gets a fam'ly."

"More money t'rew away – that's all it is." Dad followed his own harsh reasoning. "Goddam it, you wears out yer guts and spends half a fartune tryin' to give 'em a good education so's they'll have it easier and maybe do a little bit better than you and me, Gert, and then the minute you lets 'em out o' yer sight they goes to work and does somet'ing so foolish a... a cat wouldn't be caught doin' the like. There's times I t'inks their education only makes bigger fools of 'em than they was in the first place."

"Wait and see, wait and see," Mom protested against his premature judgment. "Maybe she'll be all right and knock a bit o' sense into Crawfie and make him stand sound. That's just what he needs, for sure."

"You got more hopes than brains. You knows as well as I do what kind of a wife he's likely to find way down there in a place like Flowerdy Cove."

Here Mom sniffed in mock pride and gave her answer sharply. "I s'pose Flowerdy Cove now is no worse than Haystack when we was young, and I 'low you never done so bad marryin' a girl from there. And what's you talkin' about? *You* comes from Raggedy Cove."

"Diff'rent t'ing altogedder. Them times, you was a man or a woman be the time you was fourteen, let alone eighteen; but now," the Old Man waved his right arm scornfully as if he would sweep away the present and all its works, "now, fer God's sake, the young people expects somebody else, or the Government maybe, to feed 'em all their life. And anybody foolish enough to do it, what do they get fer t'anks? A good kick in d'arse."

"There's some not frightened of a day's work, and saves money too."

"Aw, they're all alike, I tell ya," the Old Man yelled. He was getting himself steamed up. "You does 'em a good turn, and then the minute yer back is turned all they does is give you a curse and a boot up the hole, if they t'inks they can get away with it."

"You always exaggerates." Mom wound up the conversation because like so many others in our family it was tending rapidly to argument and threatening to boil over into a quarrel. I was glad she did so, because my own belly nerves were beginning to quiver as the Old Man went on ranting and it would not have been long before he and I would have been into it over his blanket condemnation of the younger generation. Above all things I desired calm.

Nevertheless when Crawfie came home with his bride for Christmas, we all had to admit before many days had passed that on some points at least the Old Man had been right. Her name was Eunice, which all of us pronounced Eye-neece, and the poor girl had not been in our house an hour without arousing against herself a storm of criticism that she must have heard, or at least been aware of, even though at first we did not say anything to her face. From her first moment in the house, she took on a bewildered expression and never lost it. Crawfie's letter having informed us that she was not a fisherman's daughter but the heiress of the local merchant, we had been expecting somebody perhaps a little better-looking and more refined – more "grand" as Mom put it – than this plain, rather dowdy young woman who now sat among us painfully trying to be one of the family. "She looks right *common*," was Mom's additional complaint that first day of Eunice's life in the house.

"What in the hell is the matter wit' her, anyway?" the

Old Man grumbled. "Haven't she got a tongue? You looks at her, and you speaks to her, and all you gets out of her is a kind of a half-smile, like she didn't have a word in her jaw about *anyt*'ing. She can't carry on a conversation."

"She do seem kind o' *strange*," Mom had to admit.

"Brings my words true! Brings my words true!" the Old Man crowed. "I told you what kind of a woman the young scut was likely to bring away from a place the like o' Flowerdy Cove."

In her dismay, Mom called Flinksy over to the house for the purpose of meeting – inspecting and pronouncing upon – our new sister-in-law, but her opinion too was flatly unfavourable. In brief, the family all decided separately but irrevocably that in his marriage Crawfie had gone and "made a proper fool of it" and now he must take the consequences.

"I half believes she's expectin' too," Mom said dolefully the next day, when Eunice had been more closely and furtively examined. "I don't know what Crawfie wanted to go and get tangled up with the likes o' her for. Curses, I daresay if he'd a went over to Crow Gulch and closed his eyes and said eeny-meeny-miney-mow, he might a come up with just as good a chice as *that*." So with Mom dead against her too, Eunice had as little chance in our home as Crawfie had had in Flowery Cove. There had been no element of choice in his courtship and marriage, once he took the first fatal step of paying any marked attention to a girl within the narrow and barbarous confines of such a place.

During an hour when we had the kitchen all to ourselves shortly after his return, Crawfie told me all about it. "You got no idea what it's like down there, Juju b'y!" he began, his eye big with memory. "If you so much as looks at a girl sideways, people think you got to marry her. I was only after takin' the wife out twice, and then one night when I took her home again and we went into the front room for a little bit o' sport before I said goodnight, the trouble started. Well, I wasn't really *gettin'* it, you know – I was just feelin' her up, see, when in comes her Old Man with his two hands behind his back, and a look on his mug that'd sink a battleship.

"I jumped up offa the chesterfield and told him I was just leaving. He looks at Eunice with her blouse all undone and her skirt up around her hips, and then he looks at me. He takes his hands away from behind his back and I saw he had a rifle in them. A bloody great blunderbuss it was, the gun he used for shootin' seals, about this long." Carried away by his narrative, Crawfie rose up from his chair, extended his arms to show the length of the gun, and then proceeded to act out vigorously the rest of his tale. "This long, and with the muzzle starin' me right in the face, like the Black Hole o' Calcutta.

"First I thought he was goin' to shoot me right offa the bat, but he only waved the gun at me like a club. Even so I felt a breeze o' wind whistlin' across my face and I thought me time was come. Anyway, her Old Man said, 'When are ye two plannin' on gettin' hitched?' with the gun pointed right at me again. Well, what could I do, Juju? What could I do?" Crawfie insisted pitifully. "You don't realize, my son. Down there in Flowery Cove they're not even civilized. They'd just as soon shoot you as look at you. Sooner."

To myself I said that here was one situation Crawfie had not been able to talk his way out of. "What *did* you do?" I asked aloud.

"I told her Old Man we were planning to get married real soon. And after that, by the Criney Jesus, he never let me or that gun out of his sight, hardly, till we set the date and actually got married. Well, what do you think of her, now Juju — on a fair shake?"

"Eye-neece?"

"Yes."

"I don't know, b'y. I suppose she's all right. Give her a chance and we'll soon find out, hey?"

The fact was, we did not give her a chance — especially after we began to suspect that Crawfie's tale to me about the shotgun tactics and all that was a lot of his blarney. We soon heard that early in the school year the principal at

Flowery Cove had got married, and it was our secret but firm opinion that Crawfie had also got married just to follow his superior's example and be in the style. Eunice had been simply the only eligible girl around, and on her not-too-powerful mind Crawfie must have exercised his notable powers of persuasion.

Now he found himself landed with a dawny young woman of weak understanding and doubtful durability. Even if we had been the most sympathetic in-laws in Milltown, it is very doubtful whether anything we could have done would have lightened the burden that Crawfie had taken on himself by this hasty marriage. We summed the situation up in another way by saying that Eunice's father had gone and pawned off his half-cracked daughter on Crawfie because she was getting on (she was several years older than Crawfie) and nobody else would have her.

As for Eunice, she certainly did nothing to raise herself in our estimation. From the very first morning of her stay in the house she began to get on Mom's nerves, especially in the pantry and kitchen, "arsing everything up" and doing absurd things like bringing out a small cup of sugar from the pantry when asked to fill up the bowl for the family breakfast. That alone might have been enough to raise Mom's domestic doubts about her, but it was nothing compared with the incident a few days later in which, on setting about to wash up the dinner dishes, she asked Mom if there were any rubber gloves in the house that she could use to protect herself against dishpan hands.

We all laughed on listening to Mom make her characteristic puffing noise with her lips and reply that as far as she knew rubber gloves were only for nurses and people like that. Later on she said to us in private and rather grimly: "I expect she'll have more than *dishpan hands* before she's finished with Crawfie, or he's finished with her."

Crawfie did no more than Eunice to help things along; he was feeling his new dignity as a teacher and even went so far as to complain, after an occasion on which we had had some rare visitors in the house, that Mom should refer to him now as "Mr. Stone," and not Crawfie or even Crawford, when speaking to anyone outside the family. This was greeted by a derisive howl from all of us who were present and another explosion of *pff*! from Mom.

Utterly frustrated along this line, Crawfie took refuge in his self-importance as a husband and expectant father, but here again he was (in our eyes) so far short of having achieved anything praiseworthy that all his straining toward responsible and dignified behaviour came out as mere pomposity. Then too he kept fussing and nagging at Eunice, exhorting her to please Mom by helping around the house and at the same time expecting from her a standard of conduct and refinement a cut above what we at home were all used to. Apparently he felt that a teacher's wife should in some respects serve as an example to the common working people.

Between Crawfie and Mom, poor Eunice was like a ship tacking against two winds. She could make no headway whatever, and by bowing to one of them could only expect to be buffeted by the other. Apart from her frequent sighs and puffs of martyred patience, Mom bore the strain of Eunice's visit very well, though she confided to us that she would be glad when the Christmas holidays were over and Crawfie took himself and his bride off to Flowery Cove again.

"I'm after doin' me best bringin' 'em up," she declared, "and now Crawfie is married he got to do the best *he* can too. Him and Eye-neece got to make a go of it by theirselves now – that's all."

Beyond his critical outburst after Eunice's first evening with us, the Old Man said little during the painful days that followed, until the news came out that Crawfie was not returning to Flowery Cove at all, a revelation that set the devil right back in the Old Man and caused him to back Crawfie into a corner and bellow at him in the same old style he had used when Crawfie was a relatively carefree bachelor.

"I sees what you're up to! Don't t'ink I don't. You figures

you can come home here any time you likes and plank yourself and that t'ing you calls a wife down on me, and expect me to start supportin' ye again? Well you got anudder t'ink comin'. Put that down in yer account book and pay heed to it. What's the reason you're not goin' back to Flowerdy Cove, anyway?"

"I . . . I resigned," Crawfie replied lamely. Of course we all understood him to mean what he could not say right out – that he was afraid to go back there and face such a hostile, murderous father-in-law.

"You *resigned*," the Old Man mocked him heavily. "And what in the hell's flames are you goin' to do now? And her wit' a youngster comin' too."

"I guess I'll find another teaching position."

"That you will damn quick, or else a job o' some kind, 'cause what I'm just after tellin' you, I'm only tellin' you once. When I sez a t'ing, I means it. So govern yourself accardingly."

For some days after this warning, Crawfie had a more than usually sober look, though as one day followed another and Christmas drew near he still failed to bring us any news of another appointment. With each day the smouldering heat of the Old Man's resentment was threatening to burst out into a flaming crisis; it kept intensifying until the atmosphere of the entire house was almost as jumpy and electric as in Racer's wildest days at home.

Again Mom did not help things. Once she made the mistake of getting Eunice to mix the family bread, and either from ignorance or nervousness the poor girl forgot to put any salt in the dough, with the result that the whole batch of bread came out as flat-tasting as wet paper. To throw it away was out of the question, a sinful waste, and so every time the Old Man, who could not be persuaded to sprinkle a little salt on it, took a slice of that bread, he munched it slowly, sourly, all the time giving Crawfie and Eunice such a scowl that you would have thought they had just been discovered in a plot to poison him.

The final racket started on Christmas Eve. In the afternoon Crawfie had been over on the West Side shopping, and arriving back home just before tea, had poked his head in through the kitchen doorway to ask, "The Old Man is not home yet, is he?" In reply, Dad swung around from behind the door and stuck his nose into Crawfie's face.

"Yes, d'*Ole Man* is home," he mimicked. "What about it?"

Crawfie's long face paled all over and his jaw dropped in dismay just the way they used to do when he was an errant schoolboy and Dad a more dreaded judge of his misdeeds than even the school principal. He had forgotten that on Christmas Eve all the millworkers except a skeleton crew were let off early to bring home their gift turkeys to the wife for pre-cooking. Mom and I could not help smiling at his discomfiture.

"Oh, nothing special," Crawfie's mouth stretched in a weak, fatuous facsimile of a smile. "Just something about a Christmas present I was looking for."

"Better you'd be out lookin' for a job. That's something you needs a bloody sight worse than any Christmas presents. And remember this: When Christmas is over, your holidays is over; far's I'm concerned."

That was the start of our celebrations – a little warm-up for the domestic fireworks that were to come on the holy day itself. Going to church at midnight did not really draw the few remaining members of our household together, as Crawfie was by that time three-parts gone (but carrying his liquor surprisingly well), and I was half-heartedly tipsy myself, at the same time hovering between elation and nausea after two or three drinks of whiskey and a couple of bottles of beer.

Early on Christmas morning, Mom, the first one up as always, heard Crawfie calling out to her, and in response to his tone of misery went into the bedroom where he and Eunice were sleeping, returning almost at once to the kitchen to make a cup of tea. The Old Man too must have heard Crawfie call out; he himself always had his breakfast in bed on days off, but so far he had had nothing at all, and now out of childish jealousy or mere cussedness he hauled himself out of bed and met Mom in the hall just as she was going into Crawfie's room with cup and saucer and some toast on a small tray. I saw and heard this whole scene through the half-open door of Flinksy's little cube of a room where I had been sleeping since Crawfie and Eunice came.

"What's that you got there?" the Old Man demanded of Mom.

"What do it look like, a bunch o' roses?" Rapidly assessing the crookedness of his mood, Mom first tried to jolly and then to pacify him by making light of her kind-hearted indulgence toward the young people. "Sure it's only a cup o' tea. Now you go on back to bed and I'll bring you in yours in a minute. I got the kettle all bilin' and a lovely bit o' salt fish for your breakfast. Right tick and tender too."

The Old Man lingered surlily. "I know you wants bringin' *him* tea this hour o' the morning, and you yourself without a bite in your mout' yet, prob'ly."

"How foolish is you! I can have something whenever I wants it. Get out o' me way, or the tea'll be cold."

"Too bad if he got to drink cold tea."

"Oh, it's not for him, anyway. It's for Eye-neece."

"What! For her!" If Mom had searched her mind she could not have made a more unfortunate statement. The Old Man's eye blazed up at once in indignation and his whole body began to tremble. His tone rose two or three notes. "I'd like me job! You tendin' on the likes o' *that*. Take it back to the kitchen. Go on."

"What odds, sure? Only this once. Besides, 'tis Christmas. And she might not be feelin' too well this time o' the morning. You knows how it is in her condition."

"I knows how it is, all right. And I knows something else. We don't have no goddam *ladies*...."

"Ssshh! Keep yer vice down." Mom tried to pass by him quietly.

"Hell wit' me vice. I'm sayin', and I don't give a damn who hears me – we don't have no ladies in this house. Anybody wants their morning tea can bloody well get up out o' bed and get it."

Suddenly his hand came up under the tray and before Mom could realize what he was doing, or draw back, cup and saucer and plate and tray and all were dashed out of her grasp, making a horrible splash and mess on the wall and over a good part of the floor.

"What in the world is wrong wit' you this morning!" Mom cried out in protest, anxiety now uppermost in her voice. Before the Old Man could reply or offer further violence, Crawfie's deep and ponderous bass made itself heard in an effort at what he probably considered conciliation.

"Never mind the tea, Mom, if it's going to cause any fuss. We'd just as soon do without it."

Like a wild animal distracted by a fresh scent, the Old Man now turned away from Mom and, in his flapping long underwear and nothing else, barged into Crawfie's room, while Mom distressfully set about gathering up the broken china and dabbing at the stain on the wall.

"You're cursed well right you'll do without it, and *her* too, long as I got anyt'ing to say around this place. Who the hell do she t'ink she is, anyhow – the Queen o' Sheba? Dragged up down there in a hole like Flowerdy Cove; never saw nutting, and be the looks o' t'ings, haven't even got sense enough to wipe her own arse. And then she comes up here and lays around in bed half o' the day and expects y'mudder to tend on her. Well, she can expect away."

Next I heard Crawfie reply with a rather tremulous, self-defensive pride, and at the same time I could easily picture Eunice cowering back against the wall driven half looney by all this premature Christmas spirit.

"I'd like you to know," said Crawfie, "that's my wife you're referring to."

"*Wife*. Christ, like y'mudder said, I could do better over in Crow Gulch."

"Are you calling my wife a prostitute now?"

"Call her what you likes. I'm proper fed up wit' the whole scroungin' lot o' ye."

"I think you ought to apologize – sir." I fancied now that

I heard an unaccustomed note of danger in these few words by Crawfie.

"T'ink away," the Old Man spat out. "A slut is a slut whatever you tries to make out of her." He moved slowly out into the hall again with this parting shot: "And you're a proper fool to go gettin' tangled up wit' her."

To my surprise I deduced from the next bit of commotion in Crawfie's room that he was jumping out of bed and following the Old Man out into the hall. I too leaped up and stood in my doorway to watch the fun. "Just a minute," Crawfie called out peremptorily at the Old Man's back. "I'm not finished what I got to say." The Old Man turned abruptly, bringing himself face-to-face with Crawfie, and there they stood toe-to-toe, audibly shivering through their winter combinations but for once ignoring the cold in their passionate hostility. "I still think you ought to apologize for what you're just after saying," Crawfie insisted.

"You go to hell, and all belongs to you."

"You won't apologize?" This was an ultimatum delivered by Crawfie, crescendo.

"I wunt."

"All right then, by Christ – put 'em up!" Crawfie doubled up his futile fists and took a fighting stance, as if he really meant it.

I burst out laughing, and yet at that moment I did feel more respect for him than I ever had before. Then as a minute passed in silence and then another, while Crawfie stood there on the icy linoleum, trembling all over but not backing up an inch, I finally understood that he *did* mean it. The Old Man finally understood too; he gave Crawfie a look of mingled contempt and astonishment, but he made no move to attack him.

"Well, come on!" Crawfie jerked out, "it's up to you. You're the one started all this." There was now a long pause. On my part an agony of expectation. At last: "I wouldn't sile me hands," the Old Man brought out coldly, turning away toward his own room; but that was not good enough for Crawfie, who went so far as to reach out and try to slew the Old Man around by one shoulder. Even then the Old Man did not strike. He only shrugged off the detaining hand morosely and went on to the door of his bedroom. By his final look at Crawfie and the manner of his turning away, I was suddenly reminded of his wordless good-bye to Racer.

"A-ha!" Crawfie called out after the Old Man's retreating figure, and I could detect in his tone, in addition to self-justifying triumph, a secret gladness at gaining his point and saving his face without having to fight for it. "I see there's some people pretty quick and nasty with their tongue, and then when they're in the wrong they haven't got the manners to admit it, or the guts to stand up to what they said in the first place. Some people got more bark than bite, when it comes down to brass tacks."

The only reply made by the Old Man was a violent slamming of his door and a turning of the key. For me this action confirmed his cowardice, though as a matter of fact I did not need much confirmation, as I had for a long time suspected the truth of what Crawfie implied in his remark about barking and biting. One thing at least was certain. No sentimentality about the Christmas season had stayed his hand against Crawfie. We all knew he had no soft scruples of that kind.

On hearing the Old Man turn his key, I went up to Crawfie, thumped him in a brotherly way on the biceps, and in effect congratulated him on his clear-cut victory. Crawfie shook himself like a boxer clearing his head after a gruelling round and contined in his former style, not troubling to keep his carrying voice below normal pitch, "Old bugger! He's lucky I don't burst that friggin' door down and go in there and give him what he got comin'. If it wasn't for Mom's sake and all the fuss, I believe I would."

"Now you looka here," the Old Man retorted unexpectedly. "You shut yer gob and pack yer duds, and get the hell out o' here. And take *her* wit' you. I'm goin' back to bed for a while, and if I finds ye here when I wakes up, I'll call the pleece, so help me Jesus, and arder 'em to t'row ye out on the street. You wants to be saucy and independent.

All right then," the old familiar stridency returned to his voice as he worked himself up to another bout of rage. "You goes and gets married on the sly without lettin' on a word to your own people, and now you can keep on on yer own, fer good. Don't you ever come sniffin' around here expectin' me to keep ye. Just get out o' me sight from this on, and stay out."

"Don't worry," Crawfie assailed him with equal bitterness, "I wouldn't stay here now, not if the rest o' the world burned down."

Coming back on the scene at this moment, Mom intervened as expected and begged the opponents to wait until Christmas Day was over at least. What would everyone on the hill say if they saw Crawfie and his wife leaving at such a time? Being quite as determined on immediate flight as the Old Man would have him be, Crawfie stormed into his bedroom and commanded Eunice to pack all their portable luggage and get dressed for a prompt departure.

"But where'll ye go to?" asked Mom, her face a little more taut than ever with anxiety and pain.

"That's all right, Mom. Don't worry," Crawfie reassured her. "We'll find a boarding-house and stay there until I get another teaching post."

And so a few minutes later there was Crawfie making his formal exit from our home, indignantly bumping out through the front door with a large suitcase in his hand, and Eunice streeling dejectedly along behind him with various flung-together bags and parcels dangling from her arms and shoulders.

"Shockin'," Mom cried softly as she watched them go. "I feels awful bad about this, and it Christmas time too."

We were a small crowd for our Christmas dinner that day, and apart from the trouble with Crawfie, Mom had already been in tears off and on for weeks over the thought of what Racer might or might not be having for *his* Christmas Dinner away over there in North Africa.

CHAPTER

8

JUJU

For some reason which I never thoroughly understood, I was nicknamed "Jewish" by the family in early childhood. According to our quaint reasoning, Jews had tempers that blew hot and cold at a moment's notice or over the least trifle. At the time I used to have little fits when my cold, underground resentment of some injury suddenly broke out into a passionate rage. Therefore I was at such times said to be "getting Jewish," and the word clung to me in one form or another throughout my life at home. Somewhere along the line it was softened to Juju, becoming further modified by Flinksy as I grew up, into "pore Juju" – perhaps on account of the girlish, brahminical slenderness of my bones.

My first memory is of shovelling a path through deep snow from our gate to the back steps, proudly awaiting Dad's homecoming from work, so that I could show him the result of my lengthy labours, and then being told by him on his arrival that I should have cleared a path to the front steps and shovelled them off, because there was a man coming to the house that evening on business and we didn't want him falling down before he got to the front door and breaking his back.

With Mom too I had some difficulty in establishing early rapport, since in my first years of life I developed a secret conviction that she never gave me quite enough to eat. I was one of those thin-as-a-rake youngsters who have three platefuls of dinner every day yet never put an ounce of extra flesh on their bones. When they watched me eating, all hands used to say, "He must have a worm."

On one particular occasion, being determined to have enough of something I liked for once in my life, I laid a plot and very nearly had my way in the matter of food. Mom had sent me out to buy half-a-pound of cooked meat (one thin slice each, with fried potatoes and bread) for our Saturday tea; but having enough money I asked the clerk for a pound, and when I brought it home told Mom the store had made the mistake, at the same time refusing to take the extra meat back on the implied grounds of shyness. Though she railed at me for not having a grain of sense, Mom kept the meat, but still only laid out one slice each for our tea; the rest she put away in a little cubbyhole under the pantry floor where it would keep cool and fresh. Having watched her every move, I took the extra half-pound of meat when she was not looking and hid it temporarily under the kitchen table, for future reference, and then after tea, when for a moment I had the kitchen to myself, I dived under the table intending to put my hoard in a safer place, but as I was lifting it out from under the linoleum the paper came off it and the fragrant meat fell on the floor. The piercing aroma was too much for me. I sat on the floor under the table and began to gobble up the whole half-pound.

Before I had quite finished bad luck brought into the kitchen the envious Crawfie who immediately began to bawl out: "Mom, Juju is at the meat! Juju is at the meat!" Of course the elephantine charge made by Mom into the kitchen soon brought all the others as well, so there I was helplessly caught in the act by the whole family. My first reaction was to stuff the remainder of the meat into my mouth and swallow it, after which I sat back and stared up at them all and waited unrepentently for my punishment. When Dad reached in and dragged me out, I shuddered as always at his raspy touch and the musty reek of his clothes and body, but even as I dangled in his grip and cowered as best I could in that position, the expected blow did not fall.

Perhaps I was saved by Mom; she suddenly began to

laugh over the whole episode, since the meat was irrevocably gone, and to marvel once again at the peculiarities of her youngest child. "How cute is he a-tall!" she cried. "And how *evil*. The young schemer. I do believe he done it all a-purpose, right from the first goin' off. You got to watch 'em every blesséd minute like a hawk, or else before you knows where you're to they'll have you in the porehouse." She laughed good-humouredly again at the devilry of one so young, and her good humour must have brought the others, even Dad, around to a lenient view of my greediness. I was let out of his grasp with a warning that if I was hungry I should say so and not sneak around robbing food that must be shared out among us all. I could always have another slice of bread and lassie. From this adventure there were no further repercussions, although it may have been from about this time that I began to acquire the reputation of being the odd one in the family.

In those very earliest years of my recollection, something was always happening to throw me into confusion and stir up to exasperation point my amazement and wonder at the human powers by which I was surrounded and on whom I depended to make the world not only a safe place but also a place that made sense. There was one puzzling afternoon when Crawfie and I were left in the care of a neighbour while Mom went in town for a couple of hours. On our return home Mom was there as usual, but she was a changed, hardly recognizable Mom as compared with the person I had got used to: Her mouth had suddenly fallen in on itself like that of an old woman, and as she went about her work, paler than usual but fussily busy as ever, she kept spitting blood into an old bucket and munching up her lips like a thirsty old grandma. It was some time before my imagination could take in the grisly fact that on that afternoon Mom had had all her teeth out at the dentist.

Another time, as I was coming home from school, I saw Dad throwing stones at a car, which seemed to me a very strange thing for a grown-up to be doing, and I continued puzzled even when I learned that he was throwing stones because the car had splashed him with mud in passing by him and he had sworn with a vicious oath that he would break a window of the car to have his revenge.

Again there was a certain evening on which we had company in the house, and before they all settled down to the game of cards somebody turned on the radio and got some barn-dance music. I saw Dad begin to hop about in a grotesque way and with no reference at all to the tempo of the music; after watching him for a while and listening to the salty comments of Mom and the others, I suddenly realized that he was dancing. I just could not take it in – the association of Dad with a joyous activity like dancing. How strange the idea seemed!

There was also the time Dad was brought home from the mill in a taxi at half-past three in the afternoon and hauled into the house, his feet dragging loosely and crazily on the gravel of our lane and his mouth blubbering agonized oaths, by two men who worked with him in the forge. Once in the kitchen, he was stretched out on his couch and then gave himself over to retching and drooling sea-green bile and vomit into an old pan that Mom had hastily slid under his mouth. This alarming occurrence was accounted for, though not explained, by a brief conversation which I overheard that night between Ank and Racer when they thought I was asleep.

"What happened?" said Racer with cynical casualness. "The Old Man get loaded for once?"

"Naw b'y. You knows he don't drink like that, and cert'n'y not in the daytime on the job. Might be a good idea if he did take a good belt or two before he comes home, though. Then maybe he wouldn't be so goddam cranky all the time."

"Did he have a accident?"

"No, it wasn't no accident eether. A fella down in the mill hit him in the gut with a maul."

"A what, Ank?"

"You knows, a sledge hammer. The big fourteen-pounder it was, too."

"What the hell for?"

"They got into a argument."

"Over what?"

"Religion. You knows half o' them fellas down around the forge is dirty Micks. Well, the Old Man was givin' them a few tips about what he t'ought o' the Pope and the Virgin Mary and all their ole rigmarole, so one o' them up with the maul and let him have it – right fair in the gut."

Personally I was glad when I reached the age of six and was sent off with my hand in Crawfie's to the first great adventure of school, for here I began to feel that I had at least some small measure of control over the things that happened to me, in a violent and bewildering world. By close attention and diligence I could influence and therefore predict my rulers' behaviour toward me – a refreshing contrast to the arbitrary government and frequently shattering chaos of our home life, and one that gradually gave me a sense of power and even security within myself.

I scarcely had to be taught, since nearly all that was told me came to my mind as recognized knowledge rather than strange facts and figures to be conquered and possessed; and I rushed ahead of each daily lesson to feed my hungry mind on things already half-guessed at from the suggestive power of earlier acquisition. It was not until we reached the second grade that Crawfie and I began to get proper school reports, and then my very first triumph over him was marred by what I felt to be a lack of enthusiastic appreciation at home.

Having lingered at school to compare marks and share in the general post-mortem over the exams, I arrived home clutching my precious report just as Dad was sitting down to take off his boots for tea, but when I proudly handed him the proof of my good behaviour and better marks, he only gaped indifferently at my sheet and with a strange smile half-shy and half-guilty said: "You done good, hey?"

"Yes, I done good. Excellent. Look!"

"Show y'mudder." In hope of getting more reaction from him than this, I thrust my pencil into his hand telling him the teacher said he had to sign my report on the bottom line. Again he drew back awkwardly and indicated with a jerk of his head that I should take it all over to Mom for her to deal with. For a long moment I stared at him, puzzled and hurt, while at the same time a momentous suspicion was dawning on my mind. It seemed to me possible, from the uncomprehending way he had eyed my report and the unbusiness-like limpness of his grip on the pencil, that Dad himself might not be able to read or write at all! When later this suspicion became a confirmed fact, I needed a good deal of time and pondering to get used to the idea that in one way at least *I* had power over *him*, or a skill and a means of dealing with the world in which my father not only did not surpass me but in which he had no share at all.

It was as if the whole universe in its motion had changed gears. Though my physical fear of him remained, I already felt somewhat liberated from my childish helplessness and the over-all atmosphere of constraint and subjection in our home. Shortly after this revelation of his ignorance, Crawfie and I began, like all the others, to refer to Dad as the Old Man. Was there any truth in his frequent accusation, in later years, that we all "t'ought nutting about him" and looked down on him because he had no education? My private experience seems to have borne him out.

The rest of my elementary schooling was smooth and gratifying, and when I graduated with Crawfie to the townsite school, I even began to extend my knowledge beyond the merely academic toward wider fields of appreciation.

There had scarcely ever been a time when I had not suffered from the barren ugliness of our home both outside and within. There was our room, for instance – the boys' bedroom, with absolutely nothing in it but two beds, a chair, and a dresser in mass and design like some half-hewn boulder. There was the hideous flowered paper on the walls made more hideous by the roughly parallel lines of the partition boards showing through, and the whole gaunt box of a room biliously lit up and exposed at night by a single fly-specked, unshaded bulb hanging straight down from the ceiling. I was pained by all this horror, and must in my child's inarticulate, yearning way have pined for some touch of art or beauty as an antidote to the poison of clashing colour and grating disproportion all around me.

Not that we children were utterly without some touch of art in our lives. There was the poetry in our literature courses, for one thing, and even an occasional vivid piece in our other school books – the only volumes in our home apart from the Bible and hymn books. One little stanza I recall from our Hygiene textbook on the theory of germs and the perils of uncleanliness in the home:

> *The fly comes gaily unto us*
> *His feet all gummed with poison pus,*
> *And singing clear his song so sweet,*
> *Alights and cleans them on the meat.*

It went on to give a macabre picture of what would happen to us if we dared to taste that meat before it had been thoroughly cleaned. But even this direct style and all the heroic ballads we read in school did not satisfy my longing, and since there were no paintings in our home and no such thing as sculpture or architecture in Milltown, my vague desires soon found their focus in music.

There was no music in our home either, but there was the radio to which in solitary hours I eagerly turned for the beguiling sounds I could draw from strange, far-off places just by turning a knob and giving the set an occasional bang with my fist. When this began to pall, I bought a cheap violin through Eaton's catalogue from my share of the prize money Crawfie and I had won in a newspaper slogan contest; and as I had no more aptitude for music than all the rest of us, it could only have been a deep need for something that might counteract the violent disharmony all around me, and lodged within myself as well, that induced me to spend several dollars on such a fantastic purchase.

In the way that Crawfie seemed to hunger for divinity, so I craved for melody, regardless of the pain I inflicted on those who could not always escape from my attempts to draw a tune out of my violin. The end of my active musical studies came when the Old Man smashed up the instrument – not because of such pain but in a fit of rage and frustration at the mere sight of the thing and the thought of all the money I had secretly gone and wasted on it that could have been used for a sensible purpose.

It was generally like that. Anything at all could touch off his temper, and apparently he did not always need direct provocation to destruction. On an average of once a month he would seize the heavy iron poker that always hung on a nail behind the kitchen stove and vengefully bring it down on our huge family teapot standing nearby on the back of the stove. While pieces of crockery were still flying about the kitchen and we were all ducking to avoid scars, he would stalk out with a grunt of satisfaction and relief.

Once he took me fishing on his day off, but when we had reached the edge of his favourite pond, a slight breeze came up and on the very first cast my line got tangled with his and he had to spend about an hour cutting and pulling the lines apart while all the time fat trout were saucily jumping and showing their numbers not more than ten yards out from where we were standing. Never at any time, not even during my later naval career, was I ever cursed so continuously and so contemptuously in a single hour. I never cared much for fishing in any case.

The Old Man and I tacitly broke off all relations after I sawed up four of the two-by-six, twelve foot planks he was using on the well and some long pieces of pipe laid aside for the same job. Tired of Flinksy's "pore Juju" and of giving her the "cold shivers" by my thinness, I decided to expand and solidify my frame by doing a Charles Atlas course all on my own, and for this purpose needed first of all a set of parallel bars.

Those planks and pipes were just right when cut into six-foot lengths for the frame; but I never finished my project because the Old Man's first sight of the havoc when he came home that day very nearly gave him an apoplectic fit. He roared for a reason, and when none was forthcoming (I was too shy to tell him the truth) he seized me by the ear and dragged me into the kitchen to stand once again before the bar of judgment. It must have been that same delicacy which by my offence I had been planning to remedy that saved me from heavy corporal punishment, for to my surprise he limited himself to one crack over the head and another good "tongue bangin'" and a warning that next time anything like this happened I would not get off so easy – I could bet my boots on that.

I refused to acknowledge his threats or his power in any way, merely hanging my head in silence. "How case-hardened are they a-tall!" he squealed. "How pig-headed! Even this young tallywack. I might just as well be talkin' to the stove." In a frenzy of exasperation and with an expression of concentrated loathing, he then jumped up and hustled me into the hall out of his sight. Shortly after this, to further ease himself, he started on Mom. "I blames *you* mostly. Couldn't you see what the youngster was at?"

"Oh yes, 'tis always me," she echoed him bitterly. "Blame me! Hell's bells, I can't be watchin' 'em every minute of the day, can I? I got me own work to do home here."

"Well, you knows I'm down in the mill all day, and *somebody* got to check up on 'em."

"Then hire a constable to do it. That's all I knows. It's no good you shoutin' and screamin' at me all the time when the youngsters starts actin' up and doin' away wit' t'ings. I told you: They're gone right cracked, wild as loos; and that young mite of a Juju is gettin' just as bad as all the rest."

"But goddam it, Gert, I can't make no headway like this, the way they goes on. Next t'ing I knows they'll be choppin' the place down over me head."

"I don't care what you does. Now! It might get me out o' this hole for once, if somebody did chop it down. Now eat your stew before it gets cold. Juju! Come in and have your tea. Come on, this minute." It was only my everlasting hunger that drove me back to the kitchen and to the ordeal of avoiding that poisonous scowl of the Old Man's during yet another of our tense, belly-griping family meals.

As Crawfie and I together climbed the short, steep hill of puberty there was no relaxation of the tension in which I lived from one day to the next. About sex we were told absolutely nothing by anyone in authority, and my first clear idea of the mechanics of sexual intercourse had to come from a poem that Racer recited to me and Crawfie as summing up the whole subject in four lines and giving us all the actual facts that were required:

The girls got a cushion,
The b'ys got a pin;
The girls lays down
And the b'ys sticks it in.

After that it became imperative on my part to stick it in, or try to stick it in, somewhere, but when Crawfie and I together had a nervous little go with an old bag over the hill named Jinny, whom Racer and his cronies were suspected of having raped, and when Mom heard about our escapade, she gave us her most frowning look and scolding tone.

"Ye bad b'ys" was all she said; "ye *bad* b'ys," her manner suggesting, however, that this particular badness of ours was more heinous by worlds than anything we had ever perpetrated in our lives before.

So horrible was it that she was afraid to tell Dad on us this time. Crawfie did not seem to mind her upbraiding, as he claimed to have enjoyed total success with Jinny ("Me gun went off the very same minute she started squealin'," he boasted), but I was in a different and less happy situation. For me the whole experience had been a fumbling fiasco, and so I felt especially bitter at having been hanged, so to speak, for not having had a real taste of either mutton or lamb.

When I complained to Crawfie, he immediately consulted with Racer, after which the two of them came down on me together with the news that there must be something wrong with me if I couldn't "get it" even off a practised and willing performer like Jinny. After that I tended to keep my own counsel on the subject of sex, though I did now and then fish for more information in a roundabout way.

Once, at the tea table, I remarked on how strange it was that all those movie stars had babies but still they never seemed to get big and fat as all the women on the hill seemed to do after they had had two or three children. But this sally of mine brought no information or enlightenment – merely a guffaw from all the men and an exchange of deeply secret smiles between Mom and Flinsky. Thus I soon learned to despair of them and to beware of Crawfie. On being told by Racer about the diseases and agonies and disgrace that could follow from too much association with old bags, especially anyone from over around Crow Gulch, I pretty well made up my mind that sex was not for me. Taking all I was told as the literal truth, I considered even at this early age that the game was not worth the candle.

My turning away from sensuality was encouraged and not reversed at the critical time when I fell in love with Flora, a slender little beauty from our own class of people and having much the same educational and moral background as myself; in fact, she was originally a young baywop whose family had recently moved to Milltown and settled there. Her stranger-in-town shyness gave me the courage, during our precious moments alone, to tell her how I really felt about things like poetry and religion – and sex. Her mother complained that Flora and I spent far too much time away from the other young people and all by ourselves, but whenever I cut Flora out from the herd of all the other girls she went around with and made off with her privately, it was not for any sinister purpose of seduction or even just feeling her up, as Crawfie and all the other boys swore they started doing the minute they got a girl alone.

We two would sit on the grass at the ocean's edge and with mere words and half-spoken longings work ourselves up into a purely uncarnal ecstasy complete with religious texts, quotations from Wordsworth, and perhaps a remark or two on the evil that we suspected lay all around us and had even corrupted already some people in our own grade at school. We thought it was all too shocking to say very much about. Alone, or together, we lived for a year or so in a hot haze of idealism which in my case shrank morbidly away from any cold fact that might condense it into reality. Flora seemed to glory in all this as much as I did, her only untoward remark being that at times I *did* seem a little unsociable.

My love affair had a good effect on me too in that it inspired me, for Flora's sake, to step up my efforts in school work and raise my performance in exams and other activities from good to outstanding, so that as Crawfie and I moved into our Matriculation year, and the question arose as to who would win the coveted Trip, there was general agreement around the school and also at home that I had a pretty fair chance.

Secretly I thought so myself, though I tried to maintain a cautious modesty about my hopes, and I was encouraged in these hopes by Crawfie; right up to the hour of the school voting he was rubbing me on the shoulder and forever saying, "You got the best chance, Juju b'y, you got the best chance." At the moment of seeing Crawfie's name in print as the winner, I thought it was a mistake, but at last, and after checking with the school, I realized the full, ghastly truth, and once again my inner world collapsed in ruinous confusion. I taxed Crawfie with his treachery. In front of our whole family crowd he gave me a wide stretch of his golden smile and said gleefully, "Well, you *almost* got it. You got the most marks for Study and all that, but where you fell down was in the voting for Popularity. There you got Zero." At my expense there followed a general horse-laugh, which I cut into by passionately accusing Crawfie of being a liar as well as a deceiver, since I had good reason to know that Flora for one had voted for me in the personal category. I determined on revenge.

Before I tasted the full sweetness of getting my own back on Crawfie, there was a painful episode between us that constituted a triumph for me but to my surprise brought very little satisfaction. It started with an overnight quarrel as to which one of us was to have the best and softest spot in our bed, right in the middle, Crawfie maintaining that being the older he should have first choice, while I argued that it was not a question of age but of democracy – fifty-fifty, or nothing but war between us. We kept on shoving and shouting that night until the Old Man had to come in with his strap and try to settle us for the night by a few cuts that even through the bedclothes were sharp enough to make us yell and then quiet down for a little while.

Of course Crawfie swore *I* had started the dispute, thereby earning me an extra swipe or two and causing the Old Man to decide that Crawfie should have the soft hollow for the first half of the night and I for the second, regardless of anything else. "And don't let me hear so much as anudder peep out o' ye," the Old Man concluded, "or else I'll haul them clo'es offa ye and reelly redden yer arse. Mind now!" With a self-satisfied chuckle Crawfie stretched out in the favoured spot; and when I woke up next morning he was still there. I glanced at the clock – time for the Old Man to have left for work but not late enough for us to get up and get ready for school. My movements roused Crawfie, who spread himself luxuriously down the middle of the bed and treated me to a glaucous laugh.

"You forgot to claim your half of the night," he said, and when he added that little sniff of superiority something clicked behind my eyes, sending me momentarily blind. I was on top of him in a flash; I battered him with fists and elbows and knees and demanded "surrender" in both word and act before I would leave off. His greater bulk was useless against the surprise and ferocity of my attack; once we had rolled off the bed and I had him on the hard floor, I fought even more fiercely, like a starving tiger, and never gave him a chance to recover or retaliate in any effective way. No doubt his ineffectuality was caused partly by the fact that he could not believe my stringy muscles capable of such force or tenacity, or my quiet nature of such implacable violence.

After I had banged his head on the floor for about five minutes without pause, there finally came a sound – a sob – from Crawfie's throat. I searched his eyes, probing for the flicker, and then the word of capitulation. At last it came. With a growl of victory I sprang up, squared my shoulders, and marched out to my breakfast. But my elation did not last long; all that day, after an hour or so of savouring conquest, I was troubled and half-sickened by the memory of that appealing, supplicating look in my brother's eyes just before he muttered the word "surrender," and later in the same day I was glad when he was the first to break the silence between us by speaking in a conciliating way and so easing the painful tension. What had troubled me most was the obscure but overriding thought that in such a victory I had lost more than I had gained.

My real revenge came in the form of a success so unforeseen, so pure and sweet that in the warm glow it gave me I was able to forgive Crawfie for anything he had ever said or done against me. Only a few days after he had returned from The Trip, there came to the house a telegram, addressed to me, announcing that I had been awarded a two-year scholarship to Memorial College in St. John's on the strength of the marks I had scored in Junior Matriculation.

From that moment I was plucked out of the mist of all our family dissension and pain into a sun-shot, glorious vision of my future. When Ank came unexpectedly into our room, and finding me rolling back and forth on the bed, asked me what that future was to be, I found myself pondering for a moment, but then I gaily dismissed the question as one that did not have to be answered for two whole years. All I knew was that I would study Arts and that anything in the way of professional or technical studies seemed faintly absurd.

Meanwhile I too had asserted myself inside the family group, with my own name in the paper, needing no association with Racer, and I was particularly gratified by Flinksy taking the time and trouble to run over and give me a kiss of congratulation and to predict a creditable not to say brilliant future for me. Even the Old Man gave me a nod and almost a smile when he came home that evening. He had already heard the big news about me in the mill, but he gave no further sign of pleasure in my success, nor was any word of congratulation or acknowledgment actually spoken between us.

One small moment of dismay did come to me when Mom, though she rejoiced with me as much as anyone else, told me once more the tale of what she had said to the nurse on the day I was born. "I said to her, 'I didn't want no more youngsters. I got enough.' 'But never you mind,' said the nurse, 'you might be proud o' this one one day. You never knows. He might turn out to be the best one o' the whole crowd.'" Sweetest of all and unalloyed by any reservations was Flora's kiss as soon as we found ourselves alone that night.

All in all, it was a genuine triumph and one that caused local people to take notice of me as an individual, with the result that I began to take a sharper and more appraising notice of myself. Though still as lean as a cross, I had grown to medium height or a little over – about the same height as Racer – and my "Spanish" eyes and luxuriant raven hair might have lent some plausibility to Flinksy's description of me as dark and handsome in the rather smooth style of Robert Taylor.

My interest in girls and sex took on a sudden intensity, and I even began to wonder (although I did nothing positive about it) whether Flora and I were not missing something in our devotion to each other's purity. Once or twice after I had sailed into the limelight I had what seemed an opportunity to get a deeper and certainly a more immediate satisfaction from girls on the Heights, but in fact I did nothing crucial about that either. I did swell with secret pride at having had the chance.

Even when a bit later some of my friends began to get married and to come back with lubriciously epic tales of life in bed, I remained an active, earthy, and conquering lover only at the movies and in my imagination. As time went on, I also spent a good deal of time wondering how all those nice-looking girls who were getting married could have done so without having first been considered and rejected by myself.

Perhaps to my inner self the greatest boon of the scholarship was that it would take me away from Milltown and the hill for at least two years. I could not remember a time when my foremost and altogether obsessive desire was anything but escape from the place, from the sleet and mud in spring, from the greyish clogged heaps of slop and garbage that stood and stank in the ditches outside our homes all summer, and above all from the paralyzing cold of the long winter. My hands were always cold from October to May, and on my paper route on Saturday morning I used to leave my shoes off and put on three pairs of heavy woollen socks with my rubbers tied on over them, which was the only way I could find to keep my feet warm during the three hours of outside work.

There must have been something rather strange and disturbing to others besides myself in my sufferings because Flinksy often remarked that, no matter how long I stayed out in the frosty air at work or at play, my olive-tinted face would never turn red while I was out nor glow freshly and healthily like all the others when I came into the warm kitchen.

For me the departure from Milltown essentially began with the poignancy of saying good-bye to Flora. I spent a whole day and evening over the delicious exercise, at the end of which, with a perversity stopping somewhere short of perversion, I informed her, without any preamble and without giving any specific reason, that I was not going to write to her while I was away. My idea must have been that we should not by wordy anticipation dull the drama or blunt the point of our reunion in the spring after a separation of eight or nine months. And so I went off to college in St. John's with the drums of destiny beating in my heart.

My career in the capital city turned out to be something of a fiasco. In the first place, there were six movie houses there as compared with one in Milltown, so that every evening, after the prose of the day had been got through at college, I rushed off by myself to feed my gluttonous imagination on the poetry of MGM or Warner Brothers, and thus slide out, for another hour or two, from under the burden of reality. I was captivated most deeply by pictures starring Claudette Colbert, because she looked so demurely and breath-takingly like my own Flora.

In the second place, my career was a fiasco in that the daily prose itself was mostly quite intolerable, including as it did a large number of dry technical pages which were compulsorily a part of my five-subject course but which I found about as palatable as broken glass. It was chiefly the French prose that I liked, nearly all of it poetry to me at this time, and what reasonable person could be expected to have any interest in a thing like organic chemistry when he had the opportunity and the skill to read Balzac in the original?

Finally, I had some difficulties of personal adjustment on moving from the forthright atmosphere of our home and Milltown to the more sophisticated world of university life in what was to me a big city. There was, for instance, my unfortunate habit of referring to the material of my professors' lectures (in personal interview with them) as "stuff," of snatching rather than accepting anything that was offered me, and of publicly classifying any fellow student whose appearance or manner displeased me as a toad. Somehow I got through the two years without being expelled or beaten up, but I never did recover from the disorientation and the morbid shyness as well that seized on me when I first left home; and the upshot of my college career was that in the final exams I won the French Medal but did not even bother to write the papers in any of the other subjects except English.

My return home was all irritation for me since I was perplexed by the family's attitude of disappointment and even hostility toward my venture into higher education. After all, I reasoned, Memorial had given me what I wanted and needed (an open gateway into the world's literature), and the money spent had been mostly my own. If Mom and Dad had not been prepared to spend a few hundred dollars extra on me, then they should never have let me go to college at all; or, to take it deeper than that, they should never have begotten me in the first place if such a fuss was to result every time I went my own way on a path toward which they themselves had proudly steered me.

My arguments made no impression whatever on the Old Man. The day I returned to Milltown I could tell by the look on his face, when he came home from work, that the news of my *débâcle* had already reached him in the mill. When he opened the kitchen door that evening and saw me stretched out on his couch by the window calmly reading, he gave me the blackest scowl I ever saw on human face, and in the bitterest tone I ever heard accused me of making a fool of him.

Now began a period in my life that was at once the most painful and the most delicious of all the feverish years of my youth. I was deeply cast down by the fact that Flora had taken up with someone else in my absence, and as she avoided me I could purge myself of festering pride only by writing her letters – somewhat in the style of Lord Chesterfield – accusing her of riding high on the crest of the romantic wave that had apparently swept over Milltown since my departure two years before. To my intense irritation she never replied to these letters, and so never gave me a chance to put my case and my indictment against her with all the decisive and argumentative force of which I believed my pen to be capable.

Then there was at home the chronic nuisance of having Mom and Dad nagging at me about getting out to look for a job. To me the very word seemed a tiresome thing, such was the intensity of my private intellectual life ever since I had been let loose in the Memorial library, and such the importance I attached to the slow ripening of my thought.

Quite hopeless, I soon learned, was the effort to make anyone in the family understand this point of view or any point of view that did not embrace a plan for me to pay my own way in life now that my education was finished.

The delicious side of my life at this time was chiefly the leisure I had for reading. Now that Crawfie was away teaching, I had Mom all to myself during the daytime, and usually I could persuade or bully her into letting me alone for a good many hours out of those precious eight. I would get up as soon as I heard the Old Man go off to work, have a large leisurely breakfast, and while Mom served me my second cup of tea, settle down on the couch to my favourite of all luxuries, a book in my hand and quietness all around me in the morning-fresh hours.

In that way the mornings passed until our dinner time, after which I took a little exercise, perhaps even did a tap of work around the house or outside; then a clean-up and another cup of tea and a sweet biscuit as I once more established myself on the couch to pass the hours until our evening meal in passionate reading. Those late-afternoon hours were never as pleasant as those in the morning time. There was always in my mind the mounting apprehension of the Old Man's arrival home and Mom's reiterated fretting over what he would say or do if once more he came and found me acting, it not looking, like a young gentleman. "You knows, Juju, when he sees you stuck down *there* again, how dirty he gets." Dirty was one of our extra words for angry.

"What's the difference, Mom?" I countered. "If I wasn't here, I'd only be on my bed reading."

"Yes, but it's just him layin' eyes on you there the minute he pokes his nose in the door. It's the idea o' the t'ing, see?"

"*Let* him lay eyes on me. Hell with the old bugger."

"Here! Mind y'self, now, Juju. Mind. If he ever heard a echo o' you sayin' that, why he'd . . . he'd *kill* you."

"I'd like to see him try."

But even Mom was not altogether sympathetic to my

attitude here, nor to all the reading and philosophical speculation – which I sometimes tried out on her.

"Better you *would* be goin' out to look for work," was her frequent reply. "All that stuff you're reading and all this fancy talk you goes on with – all that is nutting only the height o' bullshit."

Though I kept on at her for many months I could never make her see that some things which did not bring cash or another immediate benefit into the house were not necessarily all bullshit. Perhaps she was just worn out with all the fuss and worry she had had with the other children and so lacked the patience to indulge me in my theories.

Meanwhile the war of nerves between the Old Man and me went on toward its inevitable climax with occasional flare-ups to mark its progress. There was the affair of my boat, to begin with. It was my custom in fine weather to vary my sedentary routine by an overnight camping-out expedition across the bay, for which purpose I bought a small punt for seven dollars and fifty cents out of some money I had saved from the last payment on my scholarship before I left St. John's. Knowing that he would object to anything I might plan on my own hook, as we used to say, I resorted to Crawfie's technique of presenting the Old Man with a *fait accompli* and then simply waiting to see what he would do about it.

I went ahead and bought the punt without saying a previous word to him or anybody else. Of course the day he found out he came home frothing with rage and swore he would smash my punt to smithereens if I didn't return it the very next day and get my money back. All his raging I met with a stubborn, haughty silence, and with no more intention of returning the boat than of swimming across the bay on my camping trips. I was also curious to see whether he really would destroy my property as he threatened, and as the days went by I felt my position solidifying when the time stretched to a week and my boat remained afloat and intact. To top off the whole affair, he one day brought home from the mill a huge chain and padlock for mooring the boat properly at the wharf and keeping it safe from thieves.

Yet this silent gesture of capitulation, or goodwill, or good sense, did nothing to improve relations between us, for the reason that as long as I had the punt there arose further trouble over my going away on Saturday evening without asking his permission or at least letting him know beforehand; and in addition there were continual rows between him and Mom over the danger of my rowing across the harbour all alone, no matter how high the wind was blowing or in what direction. My argument was that I was now eighteen, and why couldn't they trust me, without all this fuss, as they would any other man? Even if I did weigh only one hundred and twenty-eight-and-a-half pounds, I was resolved to go my own way across the bay, or anywhere else, and in spite of the Old Man, in spite of the devil himself — only I no longer believed in that kind of superstition.

Despite this growing enmity between the Old Man and myself, an enmity that had gone on growing ever since the first time in boyhood I had asked him for five cents and watched him draw it slowly out of his pocket, and then throw it on the floor for me to pick up — despite this incident and its many varied sequels, I found now that it was chiefly on Mom's behalf that I resented and condemned his general behaviour. She seemed to be always in a state of tension bordering on terror, and I noticed that the most trifling things were enough to shatter her composure entirely if they threatened to ignite the Old Man's temper and thereby precipitate another fuss. A pair of socks mislaid when he was getting ready to go to Lodge, a moment's delay in finding a match to light the fire, or any little annoyance like that was enough to start him tut-tutting with impatience and then cursing with rage if his wishes were not instantly gratified.

Day after day I observed Mom tending on and chasing after him, never able to keep up with his whims and never once earning a word of recognition for her efforts to keep him pacified. At this time in my intellectual life I was reading John Stuart Mill, and to me the entire home situation smacked of one thing: tyranny. It was monstrous the way the Old Man harried and bullied her, and although I said nothing to him, as we were no longer on speaking terms and did not even say good night or good morning, I did try by working on Mom to make her see the gross injustice of his attitude in the house and her folly in yielding to it without a fight.

A test case unexpectedly presented itself one afternoon when we had a little trouble with our electricity. It was a very bad day to tackle Mom on a matter of principle, since earlier in the afternoon we had had our annual visit from the minister, on seeing whom Mom flew into a panic because she had not yet tidied herself, and on top of that she was afraid the parson came to tell her Racer had been killed in the war. She lived in mortal dread of a call from the minister or a policeman. The casualty danger past, I was hustled out through the back door, while the minister sat in the front room, to run down over the hill and buy half a pound of fancy biscuits so that she would have something nice for parson's tea.

When all this was accomplished and we were alone once more, we found out that none of the lights in the house would come on. It was quarter past five. Instantaneous fret and dithering from Mom, exasperation and protest from me. "Now, Mom, what are you getting all flustered about?" I demanded, trying to calm her by using a deliberately even tone.

"But what's we gonna do? Dad'll be home directly." She started running to and fro like a decapitated hen.

"You don't need the electric power to get tea."

"No, but you knows he's goin' firkin' around down in the basement again right after. He got the extension cord all laid out and everything, and if there's no juice he'll be ragin' mad, ragin'."

"Look, Mom," I said, doing my best to remain cool and patient; I forced her down into a chair. "Will you promise to sit still for five minutes while I say something?" Anxiety shadowed her eyes and puckered her whole face as she looked up at me, but she did promise. "Now then – will the world come to an end if there's no juice right after tea?"

"No, I s'pose not."

"Well, what are you getting excited about?"

"We got to do *some*thing."

"Why?"

"Oh, you knows what he's like."

"Yes, I do. He's damned unreasonable. He can fix the wiring himself. So why don't you just relax for five minutes, like I said? Then you'll be nice and calmed down for tea."

She stood it for about five seconds more, jumped up in greater anxiety than before, and even dragged a chair under the fuse box in the hall, getting up on it and poking her fingers into it regardless of possible shock to herself or danger of fire to the house. "Mom," I groaned, "you know perfectly well you don't know any more about the wiring than I do, so why in the name o' God don't you leave it alone?"

"Maybe 'tis only a fuse blowed. Come and see, Juju. Come on now – just to please me. Will you? I feels awful tormented."

But I remained seated as before and felt only irritated at the way she teetered with her tremendous bulk on the soft bottom of the chair.

"It's not that I wouldn't do it to please you, Mom. It's the idea of the whole thing. Something has happened that we can't help and didn't cause, and I don't see why the whole house should get in an uproar just because you're scared of what the Old Man will say about it. It doesn't make sense."

"I hates tellin' him about anything gone wrong. I dreads it."

As she continued to dab and poke at the fuse box in the intervals of fretting over the pots and pans on the stove during the few minutes before tea time, I saw it was quite useless to attempt any reasoning with her or any stiffening of her resistance to the Old Man's rancorous will.

I confronted the Old Man as soon as he entered the house and said in a somewhat implacable recitative manner, "Something has gone wrong with the wiring, and there's no power. It was nobody's fault. Nobody *did* anything to it; it just happened. So it's no good bawling at Mom about it. Now, do you want me to help you fix it, whatever the trouble is, before tea, or after?"

To my great surprise and relief he did not fly off the handle, but merely gave me a strange, almost embarrassed look, shoved me to one side, and marched into the hall to have a look at the fuse box. I followed him closely to make sure he did not start taking his spite out on Mom. As it happened, there was nothing wrong except a frayed, loose wire behind the box which he was able to repair at once with electric tape; nevertheless, I felt that my bold approach to him had prevented another racket and for once had protected Mom from its harrowing consequences. I began to wonder whether it might not be a good idea for me to deal with the Old Man directly in cases of threatening storm among the three of us.

This idea, or my solitary success, must have gone to my head, for I kept on silently, and often openly, taunting him, until Job himself might have lost patience with me. The simple truth was that in mind and spirit I was rapidly outgrowing and soaring beyond Milltown, which at this point in our relationship I definitively christened the Hell-Hole, while my body remained there in a restless and dependent condition that continually exacerbated the nerves of both my parents and myself.

I seemed to provoke one minor crisis after another, and one day when Flinksy was in for lunch and some previous little incident with Mom had roused my impatience, Mom suddenly cried: "Ha-ha. Look at un! Look – just like the Old Man! Ent he, Flinks? Just like un for the world." This remark brought me up sharp, if only by the intensity with which I repudiated it. Perhaps I was acting up all the time in a half-hope of stirring myself out of my physical lethargy or even of being kicked out, though I knew too that Mom lived in constant fear of my running away, in that event, and enlisting in the Forces.

In any case, the ultimate crisis between the Old Man and myself had to come soon, and come it did over a little matter of finance. Having decided that in the intervals of reading I would teach myself to type, I ordered a portable from St. John's and received it on the strength of the down payment I sent along with my order; then I set happily to work for a month or so, at the end of which time, the first payment coming due, I realized that I had not enough money left to cover it. My solution was simply to ignore the demand with a feeling of some annoyance at being troubled about such mundane trifles, and also a cloudy idea that if I paid no attention to the typewriter company, they might not pay any more attention to me.

Next month came a letter from them addressed not to me but to Dad, which Mom opened and read as she did all the private and business correspondence the two of them had; and this letter we decided to hush up, Mom begging me to send back the machine and so cut our losses and end the whole tormenting matter. That was exactly what I could not bring myself to do. What action could they take, I argued, with me in possession of the typewriter and more than four hundred miles away from them? The following month I found out: The amount of two whole instalments was deducted from the Old Man's cheque at the mill and the cashier had explained the whole matter to him in detail.

That evening he came up the hill with longer strides than usual, and he burst into the kitchen with much more than the customary fire in his eye. As usual I was reclining on the couch with a book hiding my face. "Christ Jesus!" he spluttered for the tenth time while washing himself before tea. "Christ Jesus, haven't ye got a grain o' sense a-a'tall? Not one? You'd t'ink ye'd be ashamed. Curse it, ye goes ahead and does what ye likes and then expects me to pay for yer foolishness. And *you*," he switched his bilious glare onto Mom, "you knew all about this. Same time you never said a goddam word. You're *worse* than the youngster." So they began to bicker over the money and the deceit, and went on until we had sat down to our tea, each reviling word that passed between them like a sword that had to pierce my brain before it reached its mark in the other's consciousness. About ten minutes of it was all I could bear. With the blood pounding behind my eyes again, and my whole body trembling in passionate protest against their hateful disunion, I once more intervened directly to save Mom from any more of his abuse.

"Look!" I shouted, to command their silence for a moment as I turned full on the Old Man, "Mom is not responsible in any way for me buying the typewriter. It was all my doing, and I'm the one to blame – if anybody."

"You little shit," he answered. "You got no business orderin' t'ings without you tells me. You're under age, and they comes back on *me*. I'm the one got to pay up."

"Maybe so," I held to my main point, "but what I'm saying is, whatever I do is done entirely on my own, and I am the one to be held responsible for it. I and nobody else."

Without giving me a chance to continue, the Old Man blew out his lips in a farting sound, his rank breath whistling right under my nose. "You're some independent all of a sudden. And not a red cent to back you up. You couldn't pay fer a one-cent candy, let alone a typewriter. Haw!"

"Yes, I *am* independent," my voice vibrated with defiance. "You needn't keep on about the few measly dollars. I'll pay that back. I am independent, I say. I consider that I have full and complete liberty to act by myself. Is that clear? Is that finally and utterly *clear*, once and for all? Well, is it?"

There was a long, tense moment during which I felt sure he was going to strike; but no – something, perhaps a silent supplication from Mom or even a potential danger to himself in my fierce passion, held in check his violence. My eye did not flinch from his nor my body recoil an inch from the anticipation of its pain. A moment more, and then the decisive thing happened: Our eyes locked, and it seemed that neither of us could pull away, that each of us was turning up the other's soul by the naked thrust of his stare.

I *could* not yield, especially now that the time for physical combat had passed. This was my ultimate declaration of independence, to renege on which would plunge me back into the moral and spiritual morass of uncertainty that I had lived in for many months now. I saw the blood drain slowly from the Old Man's face, his lips turn a dirty violet colour.

"Don't you turn pale at *me*," he croaked, and I realized that my own face must be as bloodless and bitter as his. Yet there came no wavering in my gaze. The crisis went on for another whole, intolerable minute, even Mom's vocal distress over our battle making not a shred of difference, until I felt myself going dizzy with the strain. Just as I was beginning to feel that the Old Man's intense, ineluctable hostility would crack my inner control, I thought I saw a slight flicker at the back of his eyes and a flutter of his lashes – yes, yes, he was mentally retreating, on the verge of giving in! Or at least of withdrawal. A moment more and his pupils had shifted, then turned completely away in a weak, embarrassed pretence of observing something through the kitchen window.

"Ha-ha!" I cried, and I sprang up from the table with this shout of triumph ringing through the whole room. I left my meal half finished and strode into my own room like a boxer retiring after his arm has been raised. This mood lasted for a whole day, perhaps two; but soon there came a reaction in my mind and every time I recalled the look in his eyes at the crucial moment of our struggle I realized with sick certainty that I had gained nothing but another Pyrrhic victory.

After this painful experience with the Old Man, it was only a question of time before I made a decisive change of direction in my life. Within a few days I had found myself a clerical job and, after beating Mom down to ten dollars a month for my food, I bought a lock-up cash box out of my first fortnightly pay and began to save my dollars with as single-minded a concentration as I had formerly applied to my reading.

Everything of my own that was not absolutely essential to my new plan I secretly sold at the second-hand store; even my books would have gone too if they had had the least market value in Milltown. In Mom's mind and Flinksy's, there was now some idea that being employed and saving money I would soon find another girl friend to succeed the faithless Flora and go the way of Ank and Flinksy herself and Crawfie into an early marriage; but such a possibility never once entered my mind, nor did I ever think of staying home and contributing something over my board to the family expenses.

To get away – that was my one idea, my one ambition and hope of salvation. Apart from the home situation, I had by this time brought myself through reading and solitary cogitation to such a degree of intellectual ferment that my existence in Milltown was no more than that of a live body going through its daily motions and routines as a temporary but also necessary evil. The Old Man I now ignored completely as one who no longer had the power to hurt me or interfere with my plans. Between Mom and myself there was still communication on a human basis, though I felt that she was over-critical of me (beyond her usual scolding attitude toward anyone who was saving money only to waste it) and of my inevitable emigration.

My financial campaign received a boost when Racer's civilian clothes came back from the Army. They were only a little too big for me; by always wearing a sweater under the jacket of his good suit and braces on the trousers, I could make use of them and so spare myself the expense of buying any new clothes for going away. I was a little hurt by Mom's lack of enthusiasm at the proud moment of my first appearance in Racer's garments and my asking her eagerly how they looked. It seemed to me that she was positively cranky these days – not herself at all. She was always brooding, and out of character in her frequent silences.

"Juju," she pleaded with me one day when I had got her to talk a little, "is you goin' to jine up too when you goes away? *Is* you? Tell me the truth now."

I could not answer that question with a definite no; all I could do was not promise *not* to enlist, and so be sure of not deceiving her or raising any false hopes. But after I had told her this as gently as I knew how, and she with a shuddering sigh of weariness finally accepted the verdict in its worst light, there yet remained a trouble in her eyes that I could not entirely fathom.

Six months after starting my job and with two hundred and seventy-five dollars saved up after I had made the final payment on the typewriter, I quit and bought a train ticket for Montreal. My departure from Milltown and Newfoundland took place with some apprehension on my part but with little sentiment and no regret. Montreal had been chosen as my destination almost at random. I liked the sound of the word and so was curious and eager to see the place. Also it was in Canada, a foreign country and one that appealed to my imagination, and it was a hundred times as big as Milltown.

On the day of my leaving home all went well, and I managed to remain calm during the whole painful operation, very glad that the Old Man was at work and not hanging about the train to see me off. We had silently shaken hands the night before. I did have one shock that day. I found out from Flinksy what was wrong with Mom and why there had been so much edginess in her behaviour over the past two or three months. It was not on account of me or my unshakable resolve to leave home at all. No. At the age of forty-four, and with all her labour, as she had thought, blessedly behind her, Mom was now going to have another baby.

CHAPTER

9

FUDGE

He was christened Frederick Yeovil Stone, but before he was old enough to say all that himself, his name and whole identity in the family were reduced to the one syllable – Fudge. I never saw him until he was over eight years old, when I made a flying visit home to Milltown during a summer vacation.

Eight years. Eight rather eventful years for me. And yet, as the train whistled its way around the rocky curve of Crow Gulch and I inhaled again the pungency of salt water and fish and low tide – that great seminal smell of the ocean and all islands – I felt as if I had been away for no more than a few days; and as we chugged past the mill and the nauseous reek of sulphur dioxide was thrust into my nostrils by the north-west breeze, I certainly did not need the sign "MILLTOWN" at the station to assure me that I was home again. Instantly I was plunged back into the atmosphere of the Hell-Hole as deeply as if I had never been away at all.

Being familiar with Fudge's general appearance from letters and snapshots, I spotted him as soon as the train came into the station, but as a matter of fact I would not have needed any previous knowledge of him in order to recognize him instantly as my brother and one of our family. He had the very same, almost-perpendicular forehead that we had all inherited from Mom, although there was not much of it, and in his young eyes there was already that yearning look – a look as of one staring into eternity and not seeing much of anything there, certainly nothing of a heartening nature.

It was the mark that sooner or later came to brand us all like a crowd of Ishmaels. When I spotted him he was looking up at the train with his mouth wide open ("ketchin' flies"), his brow puckered against the sun, and his entire form looking wretched in dirty jeans and a cheap striped jersey that hung down over one shoulder in a limp, neglected way. Though apparently a chubby little fellow, he had none of the cheerful aspect that goes with physical robustness, I thought; for as soon as I had taken him in all over, I was irresistibly reminded of that boy-man in *Jude the Obscure*.

Fudge recognized me too as soon as I had stepped off the train and caught his eye, but he did not come forward as I expected and eagerly pick up my smaller suitcase. Instead, once he was certain it was Juju, he seemed to panic, and before I could call out or do anything to stop him, he had turned and run away out of sight behind the station. Puzzled and rather dismayed, as there was nobody else but Fudge there to meet me, I spent a few minutes hunting around for him, all to no avail.

He seemed to have disappeared completely, so that I was obliged to pick up both my bags myself and somewhat dejectedly start on the long uphill climb to our house. On the way I noticed signs of prosperity and material progress that had come about, I assumed, in the galvanization of Milltown's economy during the Second World War and in the years of continuing upswing since 1945.

There were a good many cars about, even up on Humber Heights. There was paint on more of the houses than formerly, though dull and sombre colours were still very much in favour; and some of the bigger places even had asphalt shingles on their roofs instead of the cheap tar paper that had once been in general use. I fancied too that many of the people were better dressed and able to pay more attention to personal appearances now that the fundamentals of food and shelter were assured them by full-time production in the mill.

Many of the people I met on the trek from station to home either did not recognize me at all or only guessed at my identity and were perhaps too shy to speak to one who might be a total stranger. As a result I had this good opportunity to observe undistracted the changes in people and things around my part of the old hometown. In return, passers-by stared at me, at my clothes, my luggage, my walk and my whole bearing as though questioning and inwardly disputing my right to come among them at all. On the strength of my eight years abroad, I felt how primitive it all used to be and in many ways still was. Not until I reached the foot of our hill and was once again called Juju Stone did I feel the old atmosphere of our family life close down over me completely as in childhood days.

When I had reached the house and given Mom a good hug and a kiss, and restored myself with a cup of strong tea, I saw with pleasure that she at least had not changed very much. She was still fat as ever and glorying in her fat as some women glory in a mink coat. Her ribald humour was ready as ever, no matter how much lip-service she might pay to the fact of my maturity and my superior education. I had not been in the house five minutes nor spoken a dozen words before she was at me, more or less in the old style, about my peculiarities.

"Ha-ha," she laughed, "I see *you* got 'em too."

"Got what, Mom?"

"Them glasses."

I adjusted my new horn-rims a little self-consciously. "And that *foreign* way," she added with some disapproval.

"How do you mean?"

"Well, that *ass*-ent, for one thing."

"Don't be so foolish! I haven't got any accent."

"Yes you have! You got that real Canadian twang. Some words you says I can't hardly understand you a-tall. I s'pose

Newfoundland talk is not good enough for you now, after bein' away so long."

Since it was obviously useless to argue her out of this, I decided to change the subject.

"What's the matter with young Fudge?" I asked her point-blank.

Her habitual expression of anxiety deepened (almost a double-take) to one of terror.

"Why? Do you think there's anything the matter with him? I sent him down to meet you. Didn't he go?"

"Oh yes. I saw him – for a minute. But he ran away from me."

"Ran away, did he? The little cod. You don't want to mind him. He's wonderful shy and . . . and odd on times. He don't know what to make o' you, see Juju? When he comes home, just let on you never noticed un."

In some bewilderment I agreed, and when Fudge finally did come home, driven by hunger, I found that my first impressions at the station were more or less confirmed. He was an odd-looking, sad-looking little boy, another painful touch being added to his appearance by the fact that he was already getting his second teeth in front, and they were already beginning to rot. As to his personality, that was extremely hard to gauge because at first he kept his distance from me in a nervous, mistrustful way, his head forever turned aside as though in shame and his light-brown eyes fastening on me in perpetual query only when he thought I was not observing him. Had I been a genuine man from Mars he could not have gaped at me more curiously.

I was prevented from coming to any conclusion about Fudge that evening by the Old Man's arrival home from work and then our being mutually saddled with the task of trying to forget some of the past and making a go of things for the immediate present. He shook my hand in a non-committal manner, or rather he allowed his hand to be shaken, but did not go as far as to say, "Welcome home," or even to call me by name or nickname then or at any time throughout my entire visit.

The truth was that from Mom's letters I had not been led to expect any geniality from him or any great improvement in the family atmosphere; he was increasingly unwell, she had written, and tormented by pain continually in one part of his body or another, so that if he managed to keep his tantrums under some measure of control, that was about as much as we could expect. I knew too that, like all hands at home without exception, he was disappointed at my not having become rich during all the time I had spent up in Canada. For my part, I was determined, and I had promised Mom, to keep the peace between him and myself as long as I remained at home.

Covertly studying him, I could see that what Mom had said about his health was true, though it was also a family joke that if he got a little pain in the head he was immediately terrified of a brain tumour, or if he had cramps in the stomach it was cancer of the bowel, and so on to the point of absolute hypochondria. He was now fifty-six years old, and the deathly physical drain of his thirty-odd years, those twelve thousand days he had spent toiling in the mill and then climbing the hills to more work at home, was certainly beginning to show. From scalp to ankles he looked like a man into whom somebody had stuck a tube and then pumped out all the juice. Nor was his expression such as to give me any hope of an improvement in his disposition, for he still looked out at me and all the world from those chill cavernous eyes with all the mistrustfulness and the flickering malignancy of some wild beast at bay.

But it was not in relation to myself that I now studied the Old Man's reactions; it was his relationship to Fudge and the child's predicament as inheritor of all the strife of earlier years that now chiefly interested me. What I saw that first evening was very much in the old style of our family life. I noticed right away that Fudge never passed by the Old Man; he always circled around him more or less out of arm's reach, and once when he was caught up in the Old Man's grasp for some trifling cause I saw Fudge's little body quiver all through and his eyes blur in sightless panic like the eyes of a snared rabbit.

Of course his refuge and consolation after such an ordeal was to fly toward Mom and hide his head in the folds of her skirt just as if he were still a mere toddler instead of an eight-year-old boy. If Mom was not around the place, I gradually observed, he was the loneliest child in existence. "I haven't got nobody to play wit'!" he frequently wailed in long-drawn-out *patois*, his head thrown back mournfully and copious tears flowing down his face and into his mouth. From such indications I gathered that Mom and Fudge were already very close. Apparently she had got over the revulsion which we all knew she had felt while carrying Fudge and now, perhaps in a reaction of guilt and remorse, she clung to him and treasured him as deeply and violently as ever she had cherished the youthful Racer.

Before I had been home a week I could see that the same old familiar pattern was repeating itself in the house; that is, an alliance of mother and child against a common enemy and aggressor called the Old Man, who was barely tolerated as being a necessary evil – breadwinner, and supplier of extra cash on demand. The very least thing was enough to show up this division in the household. For instance, if Fudge wanted ten cents to go to the show on Saturday afternoon, Mom's first impulse was just to hand it to him and let him go on and the Old Man would break out cantankerously: "That's right! Go on. Go ahead and spile *him* too. Just like you done all d'yudders. Give the youngster whatever in the hell he wants, and then see what t'anks you gets."

"What odds about ten cents, for mercy-sake!"

"How many times am I after tellin' you? 'Tis not the money. It's the principle o' the t'ing. If he wants ten cents, let him go out and earn it. Then he'll value it, see?"

"He's too young for that, sure."

"Too young – my arse!" The Old Man shook his head in exasperation, just as though someone persisted in telling him that black was white. "The rest of 'em was out sellin' papers be the time they was his age. Let him do likewise."

At this I pricked up my ears, never having dreamed that our boyhood labours would one day be recognized by the Old Man and certainly never expecting him to hold up me or Crawfie or Racer as a good example for anyone to follow.

No matter how much the Old Man raved and ranted, however, Fudge never sold a single copy of the *Messenger* and Mom nearly always gave him whatever money he wanted for shows, candy, and other childish expenses. Privately I now agreed with the Old Man that Fudge would be none the worse for a bit of honest, gainful employment, but Mom had her own way as usual in spite of domestic upheaval, and I had a very strong feeling that Fudge was getting too much of his own way with her.

Several times I made an effort to wean him from Mom, the more so as I quickly became aware that he was a very nervous child, more riddled with fears and fantastic inhibitions than a honeycomb is with holes. Once when by accident I closed our bedroom door and left him alone in the dark, he burst out in a sudden howl of terror; another time I saw him run away from a fair fight into Mom's arms, and at all times he showed a morbid fear of going anywhere near the townsite, especially by himself.

If he and I happened to go in there together and we met anyone like the minister or one of Fudge's teachers or any young girl, no matter whom, Fudge would dodge around behind me or to the far side of me and squirm along making himself as invisible as he could, never uttering a word to me or the people we met until we had walked past and were in the clear again. Only on the hill was he quite himself, in so far as he had any self to be at this time, and only at home during the day was he at all relaxed or recognizable as an individual human being.

I noticed as of old that the minute Dad entered the house shadows fell, and as the bickering rose higher and higher to its normal pitch of recrimination between him and Mom, so Fudge became correspondingly more silent and withdrawn into himself. One of the worst times of all was when Mom went over to the West Side and bought Fudge a new suit to wear to church on Sundays. Fudge was proudly trying it on that day at the very moment the Old Man arrived home, and of course it did not please the Old Man either because it had been bought at a Jew's, or the material was not strong enough, or the price was too high. Any nail would do on which to hang the string of his complaints. He insisted on her returning it the next day. "I'll do no such of a t'ing!" Mom declared bravely. "It's a nice suit, ent it, Fudgie my love?"

"I likes it all right," Fudge replied tremulously, looking away from Dad.

"There!" Mom's glance returned complacently to his face.

"What do he know about it, fer Christ-sake?"

"Well, he's the one got to wear it."

"But *look*," the Old Men seized hold of Fudge's coat sleeve and tugged at it impatiently, "that material wunt stand him a week; it's t'in as paper." Mom plucked at the other sleeve and obviously tried to persuade herself as well as the Old Man.

"Oh, it'll do him the summer, anyhow."

"I tell you, woman, you might as well go heave the money out in the harbour as keep the like o' that." He gave another contemptuous jerk at Fudge, Mom gave a further, self-justifying demonstration on her side, and so they went on again.

"You got to take it back."

"Buggered if I will."

"Then me next cheque goes all in me own pocket. Ye wunt get a smell of it, so help me Jesus."

"Yes, yes! And what'll I run the house on? What'll we eat?"

"I'll eat dandelines and grass before I pays fer the like o' that trash."

This went on, back and forth, until Fudge began to

bawl in his distress and, fighting clear of the two of them and the coat as well, ran into the bedroom in what must have been a totally schizophrenic condition. Going after him, I heard Mom finally agree to the return of the suit, but I had my doubts as to whether she really meant it.

She certainly did not; and to achieve her ends or impose her will in this particular contest, she used once again her delaying tactics. There wasn't time next day for her to go down over the hill, much less away over to the West Side; the weather was too bad when she did have a chance to go; the stores were closed for a half holiday when another opportunity arose. In finding excuses she was as prodigal as a codfish laying eggs. Finally, it was too late to get her money back from the store, so that the Old Man had to content himself with a few anti-climactic, face-saving growls and one more spasm of rage the first time Fudge wore his new suit to church on Sunday.

I had to laugh at Mom's bare-faced, hypocritical way of lying to the Old Man; she was so earnest and convincing that while listening to her I might almost have thought, but for the pitch of voice, that it was Crawfie making one of his corrupt special pleadings in order to pull off another swindle. There was no point in my trying to reason with her about all this humbug she went on with. I did not try very hard, but I might just as well not have bothered at all.

"I cods him along, Juju," she answered me with her broad smile, half pride in her own power and half contempt for the Old Man's helplessness in some things. "I cods him along. I *got* to."

"Why not come right out and tell him you had no intention of returning the suit?"

"Oh no. That would only start a worse racket."

"But it's . . . it's ridiculous to go on like that year after year about everything that crops up in the family."

"It's the only way," she replied rather wearily. "If I didn't make out I was givin' in to un over that suit, why, he'd tear the place down – while we was having the fuss, I mean. No. I just got to string him along. He's as bad by that as he is over the grub. Claims he can't eat lamb 'cause it's too fat and greasy and hurts his stomach, so I gives him a big plate o' lamb but I calls it veal, and he eats it all up as calm as a clock, and it don't trouble his stomach no more than a glass o' water."

"I still think an honest show-down, and a final one, would be a lot better."

"Ah, you don't know un like I do."

"He's no better than he used to be then?"

"Better! My son, he's ten times worse. I couldn't even start in to tell you what I've a went through since Fudge was born."

"That's what I was coming to, Mom. These everlasting rackets – don't you think they're having a bad effect on the young fella?"

"What can I do? I don't want murder in the house. But I do worry meself on times over Fudge. It must be awful lonesome for a little b'y here in the house with just the two of us, and we not gettin' any younger. You'll be comp'ny for him now. He do be *strange* sometimes. Will you talk to him, Juju, and try to find out what in the world he's thinkin' on all the time? You're older now, and you got th' education, see? You're able to onderstand."

At least I did understand what it must be like for a small child to serve as a buffer between two parents advancing in years and still unable to agree on what day of the week it was; but any attempt at approaching Fudge I found as difficult as picking up a hedgehog. If I promised him candy he seemed to doubt my word, and if I took him to the movies it was not until the picture was all over and we were coming out that he seemed to be sure the promised treat had come to pass. Lack of confidence in others as well as himself – that was clearly one of his problems, combined with a peculiar passivity, as it seemed to me, of both body and mind. The boy often gave me the feeling that he was not quite sure whether he really wanted to go on living or not.

And yet in some ways he was also an endearing little fellow. He had a lisp that was worse than Crawfie's had been in childhood, and yet he was extremely comic at times. In his whole nature there was a certain clinging softness that was not altogether unattractive in a child of eight. If only I could bring him to regard me not as a stranger from a strange land but at least as one who sympathized with him and wished him well! (I had no hope of getting him to treat me as a brother unless I remained home indefinitely and really worked at it; then perhaps I could do something to take away that disturbingly lost look in his eyes.)

After trying various dodges I stumbled almost by accident on a gateway to his confidence. I came across my old copy of *Grimm's Fairy Tales* and was sitting over it one day in a half-sentimental mood when Fudge wandered into the kitchen, visibly bored by the length of his summer holidays and seeking some kind of distraction.

"What's you doin'?" he asked in his childish *patois* that now struck oddly on my ear. I then read him a bit of the tale I was looking into, and I was surprised to see a look of attention come into his eyes. As I went on, not watching him but very much aware of the effect, a gleam of interest followed, and finally I was rewarded for my efforts by a little gulp of pure pleasure that was as gratifying to me as the story itself apparently was to him. He was especially amused and charmed by the one about the "flounder, flounder in the sea" with whom the fisherman had such realistic, person-to-person conversations. Perhaps, after all, Fudge's saving grace would turn out to be a spark of imagination.

After that first day, once I had assured him that there were millions more stories like those I had read to him, it was difficult to escape his importunities and what came out as his sudden dependence on me. He was not yet able to read a book for himself, and so all day he followed me around and pestered me with some book in his hand; as evening came on there came also from Fudge the anxious, inevitable question: "Thuthu, is you goin' out tonight?"

The implication was that if I were staying in I might spend the time in reading him more stories—almost any kind of story would do him now, so hungry was he for mental food and so delighted to escape in fancy from the tensions and terrors of his ordinary home life. Once or twice I did stay in just to please him, evenings that were marred only at the very end when all the reading was over and it was time for him to go to bed.

Perched on my shoulders and steering me by the chin, Fudge would start his slow progress toward the bedroom, submitting to Mom's kiss on the way; but after that came an awkwardness and hesitation because he would *not* say good night to Dad or make any acknowledgment of their temporary parting. It always fell to me to bridge the gap between them by saying Fudge's good night for him as the only way to spare abraded feelings and avoid the risk of yet another fuss. I noticed many times that Mom was grateful to me for this mercy.

Through literature and private conversation I soon won Fudge's confidence to the point where he revealed to me his private fortune of seventeen cents in a mangy little purse hidden under the mattress. He also showed me another of his secrets. This was a baby picture of himself with butter-coloured ringlets for hair, dangling down almost to his shoulders, and a general look of fruity girlish sweetness over his whole face. Having stolen this rather nauseating photo from Mom's bureau drawer, Fudge wanted to destroy it not only because its very existence embarrassed him but also because it was somehow associated in his mind with Susie Moore, a tow-headed, tubercular, and quite grotesque little girl who lived farther up the hill and who was said by Mom to be Fudgie's sweetheart.

Whenever she wanted to torment him after he had been "bad" or would not obey her, all she had to do was declare her intention of telling Susie on him, and then it was truly comical to see the writhings of shame and rage he went into at the mere mention of this child's name. Mom's hearty laughter only made him worse, and although I sympathized with him in a way, I could hardly keep a straight face myself when I saw him squirming on the couch in agony, begging Mom to shut up about Susie, passionately promising to be good if only she would leave off and let him alone. Not long after one of these crises Fudge came to me holding up the tattered, hated photo and seeking support for his wish to destroy the pestilent thing.

"Does Mom know you've got it?" I asked.

"No, I don't t'ink she do. You're not gonna tell her, is you?"

"No, no. Here," I put him out of this particular misery by taking the snap and tearing it into four pieces. "Now get rid of them where they'll never be seen again." Laughing at the ease and simplicity of it once a decision had been taken, Fudge stuffed the scraps into an already bulging pants pocket and nodded his head gleefully.

One of the pieces must have fallen out – enough to tell what the picture had been – and Mom must have found it, for some hours later I was taken aback by the strong look of bewilderment and dismay she fixed on me when she learned for sure how I had been a party to the destruction of her favourite baby picture of her darling Fudgie. "He was so sweet-lookin' when he was a baby!" she said in a tone of sharp nostalgia, bereavement, and accusation against me.

In spite of this one alienating episode, Mom encouraged the idea of my staying home for a while, seemingly on the grounds that in general I would be a good influence on Fudge, as long as she gathered together all her private treasures and kept them under lock and key. Certainly Fudge needed guidance as well as company, since there was no one to tell on him if he misbehaved in school or mooched from Sunday School. There was no effective check on him at all unless the principal or superintendent sent home a special complaint, which as likely as not would never get beyond Mom, or achieve anything more than one of her futile resolves to chastise Fudge with her own hand and for his own good.

It was over the matter of Sunday School that the big fuss started while I was at home. Mom and Dad rarely went to church now, because on Sundays when not on repairs in the mill Dad was always too tired to go anywhere, and Mom said she felt out of place if she went alone. Nevertheless they insisted on sending Fudge to both church services and Sunday School, there to be exquisitely bored in direct proportion to the utter incomprehensibility of the things that were told him.

It came out one day, through a chance meeting of Dad's with the superintendent, that Fudge had not been to Sunday School in over two months, even though Fudge had himself been reprimanded by the authorities already and a note had been sent home calling attention to his delinquency.

"Why haven't that youngster been goin' to Sunday School?" the Old Man demanded without delay the moment he arrived home that evening. As soon as he heard the words "Sunday School," Fudge lit out for the front door, but the Old Man was too quick for him this time and seized him by one ear, holding him firmly while waiting for Mom's answer to the question. Fudge began to whimper and wail, his eyes fixed on Mom imploring an excuse or at least an explanation that would set him free for the moment.

"I didn't really know he was moochin'," said Mom without much conviction.

"No, 'tis lies you didn't! You was sent a note. So don't you go tryin' to pull the wool over *my* eyes."

"I only got the note a day or two ago."

"Two weeks. Two weeks. Jesus, can't you tell the troot for once in yer life?"

"Well, you knows Fudge is too young yet to onderstand. He don't know the difference. So let un go now – do."

Irritated by this characteristic change of direction but far from diverted by it, the Old Man grimaced and shook his head from side to side in rising rage against the two of them. "He's plenty big enough to know when he's after doin' wrong. Ent you? Hey?" He waggled Fudge by the ear and made him howl. "Goddam it, Gert, the rest of 'em was goin' reg'lar when they was the age o' him. You knows that as well as I do."

"Yes, but they all had somebody else to take them and

look out to them and . . . and explain it all, see? Fudge is all by hisself, he's kind of afraid and all that."

"What's you afraid of?" Another waggle and louder howling, which deepened to screams as if the child were being tortured.

"Let un go!" cried Mom with sudden fierceness. "Can't you see you're hurtin' the youngster?"

"Aw, shit on ye!" the Old Man gave Fudge two or three back-handed clouts and flung him out of sight into the hall with a command to get to bed without any tea, threatening him also with real punishment if ever he skipped Sunday School again. "There's no sense wit none o' ye. I'm fair pisoned wit' ye all," he summed up his disgust before sitting down at the table.

Then over our tea the fuss continued with every inch of the present ground for dissension between Mom and Dad gone over and over in exasperating detail and reiteration. After that they gradually worked back into the past, seeming to quarrel over almost everything that had happened not only since Fudge's birth but further back to that remote, and to me unimaginable, time when they had been a young married couple and Ank was only a baby. All of it, or as much as I stayed at the table to hear, stank in my nostrils like a vast field of stale manure.

After about an hour of it I felt my nerves jumping so painfully that I excused myself on the plea of wanting to catch an early movie and bolted out of the house feeling just as disgusted as the Old Man had looked on arriving home that evening. As for Fudge, there was not much need to worry about him at the moment, since I felt quite sure that later on after the Old Man had gone out to do his puttering around the house and in the basement Mom would sneak Fudge's tea in to him, probably with an apple and a couple of sweet biscuits as well by way of compensation for what he had just gone through.

A major fuss of this kind once in a while might not have been so bad, but they were always at it. We had almost the same scene and a similar boring rehash of the past when the

Old Man found out and complained to Mom that Fudge had stolen a nickel from a drawer in their bedroom.

"Curses," he snarled in rounding off this new uproar, "yer own flesh and blood. You can't even trust them no more. Why, if I'd a done the like o' dat when I was a b'y, me mudder would a kilt me on the spot. Yes, she *would*. The udder youngsters wasn't t'ieves, anyway. Was they?" I smiled at all this, remembering my own boyish burglaries of Mom's purse and bedroom drawers when I desperately needed an extra five cents. I suspected that the Old Man himself had not been much different as a child – only he could no longer remember. "Nowadays, be Jesus," he concluded, "you got to lock up everyt'ing, even against yer own. They'd whip d'eye from yer head, if you give 'em a chance. Yes, if you wasn't watchin', they steal the milk out o' yer tea."

Even if I had been intending to please Mom by staying in Milltown for a while, this unchanged and unchanging home atmosphere would soon have driven me away. For the rest of my short visit I took refuge mostly in the bathtub while I was in the house. The installation of a bath seemed to me the only really sensible improvement made out of all the work that had been done around the place. By means of an electric pump and a large tank attached to the kitchen stove we got a good supply of hot water, and in this I wallowed for hours on end with a book propped up in front of my eyes and the knots in my nerves gradually untying themselves in the delicious warmth and silence of that tiny bathroom.

Of course even this harmless luxury of mine could not be indulged in without a certain amount of protest from the Old Man; he swore that I was wearing out the pump, and both he and Mom darkly warned me that too many hot baths were *weakening*, whereas I contended that surely the only point of having a tub, after years and years of birdbaths, was to make good use of it. And as to my being in some way weakened, I could not see any logical connection between cleanliness and sexual potency, nor was I backward in telling everybody so.

To me it was quite clear that the longer I stayed at home the more friction there would still be between the Old Man and myself; there was simply no reconciling the semi-hysterical prejudices and sombre superstitions of a man like him with the calm reasonableness and the enlightened world-view toward which I felt myself to be continually striving in my intellectual life. My concern for Fudge was entirely genuine, but he would have to grow up and protect himself as best he could in the terrible isolation and tension that were his fate. We continued as pals right up to my last day; then there came, not any difference between us, but on Fudge's part a sudden and unforeseeable reversion to his earlier eccentricity.

The minute he clearly understood that I was going away and not coming back, that mournfulness seemed to flow back into his eyes; and on the day of my departure he ran away from the house and hid himself just as he had done at the station when I arrived. Since he did not show up before train time, I had no opportunity of saying good-bye to him or leaving in his mind any thought that might be a help or comfort to him in the future.

The other members of the family I had hardly seen at all, so brief was my stay and so taken up had I become in those few days with the problem of young Fudge. Beyond noticing that Ank now looked out on all the world, including me, with a glowering hostility and even malevolence; that Flinksy was flourishing in body and purse; that Racer too was gaining flesh but beginning to look fed-up and browned-off with everything; and that Crawfie's wife had a black eye – beyond these observed facts I had had almost no contact with the rest of my brothers and my sister or their families at all.

HOUSE OF HATE

PART TWO

CHAPTER

1

FAMILY REUNION

On my next return to Milltown some thirteen years later, I was met at the station by Mom and Dad in their car. This in itself was a sufficient indication of the changes that had come over Milltown and its people. Apart from cars, almost everyone up on Humber Heights had TV now and many of the viewers had also a chesterfield to sit on while viewing, though Mom declared there were not so many who had it all paid for.

This transformation had come about as the result of a breakdown in our historic isolation as Newfoundlanders, for we were no longer an obscure, neglected, and bankrupt island-colony of Britain but a Province of the Dominion of Canada. Since the Act of Confederation in 1949, a steady, fertilizing flow of money from Ottawa, in the form of pensions, allowances, baby bonuses, unemployment insurance, and a dozen other handouts from the semi-welfare state had brought a measure of plenty or a means of subsistence to most of the island. Even the people in God-forsaken, workless places like Raggedy Cove were no longer half starving.

In Milltown the Act had brought much additional money to the working man through the powerful international unions which had soon moved in and taken control of the mill's wage rates, working hours, and all aspects of labour and the worker's company life. Added to the prosperity that Milltown had always enjoyed, as compared with the rest of Newfoundland, all these regulated and cumulative benefits should have made the place a little paradise for people who had lived on the edge of want for much of their lives.

All over the town I saw and heard evidence of the forward steps that had been taken since my last visit home. Some of the streets in the townsite and the main road leading from there to the mill now had asphalt paving and concrete instead of the old wobbling plank sidewalks of my earlier days. Telephones were everywhere and radio and TV stations banging away sixteen hours a day seven days a week. There was even a traffic light where the mill road joined the main traffic artery running from the townsite to the West Side. To crown it all, we now had a mayor and a town council and amalgamation of the heights and the West Side with the townsite – all the ceremony and apparatus of a miniature metropolis. There was no longer any Shacktown, which had been taken into the embrace of the west side district and made official and respectable. Only Crow Gulch remained beyond the pale, although no amount of technology or civic improvement could change Milltown from what it essentially was: an industrialized village mushrooming into a small town and masquerading as a city.

On the first day of my return, having survived the perils of the Old Man's driving from the station to our house, I was amused and astonished to see that our hill now had a name. It was called Ocean View Road. Not much else about it had changed, however, as I could tell from the hollow scratch and the frequent spinning and bumping of the tires on the loose gravel of the road which tended, as always, to be forever sliding downhill toward the salt water, leaving great jagged outcroppings of rock along the difficult climb to our house.

In spite of superficial marks of material progress, the crazy line of the houses, after my long absence from home and my dwelling in many strange lands where town planning was taken for granted, jarred more than ever on my eye. The houses had the same old tentative, temporary look against their background of mighty mountains, just as if neither human life (nor any of its manifestations) had ever taken root or stabilized itself on this sharp incline of rock and gravel.

Our old place was much as it had always been, except that over the rocketing years Mom had added many family photographs in the front room and even in the kitchen — her pathetic attempt to fill up the emptiness of the house after we had all gone off and left her stranded in that big barn with Fudge and the Old Man.

She herself was not looking well. The first ravages of age and acute diabetes showed in her yellow-leathery skin and whitening hair, and (most startling to me) nobody could call her Big Gert any more, for the necessary check that had been put on her appetite by disease had drastically cut down her weight and sent her into mourning for the loss of all that rosy flesh she had once so comfortably owned.

"Look at me, Juju," she cried pitiably, pulling the folds of her dress away from her once-mighty bosom and letting them fall back loosely, "I'm gone away to nutting. Me cloes is fallin' offa me."

She dreaded the thought of getting on the scales at any time for fear that she might have gone below the mark of one hundred and sixty pounds. I noticed too that her powerful jaw seemed to have moved forward over the years, giving her face now an underslung, almost prognathous look which I found disconcerting in its suggestion of desperate and baffled determination. Her entire head was carried with a marked forward thrust as though she were perpetually and anxiously waiting for some terrible news or a final blow that should end her misery once and for all.

There was only a very slight flicker of her old good-humoured railing at me that first day of my return. I had grown a moustache in the interval of my two visits home, and neither the style nor the density of it seemed to please Mom.

"Get in the bat'room and shave it off!" she scolded me about ten minutes after I had got my nose in through the kitchen door. "What in the world do you want a musstache for? It makes you look like I don't know what – like a . . . like a eye-Talian gangster. It's only a smudge o' dirt, anyway. I tell you fair and square, Juju my son, it looks as foolish as a odd sock."

I went into the bathroom to have another look at the moustache but I did not shave it off, as I had always considered Mom so strong already in her salty, passive way that too much exercise of the will would not be good for her.

Dad seemed to have put some flesh on his bones since he had been retired from the mill three or four years previously. One might have thought he was adding weight and gaining health in proportion as Mom lost them; yet his face gave the lie to such a thought. It was gaunt and terrifying as ever, with hollows above the upper maxillary bone so marked that you could lodge an egg in them. His bitter mouth was now permanently fixed in a grimace of pain and immemorial grief. Those translucent blue eyes were rheumy and dim, but if anything more frightening than they had ever been in the days of his vigour because they had taken on that ghastly, inhuman stare of extreme (and in this case premature) old age. His chief physical complaint was pain in the chest and inability to stoop without great discomfort – palpitations, I thought, until Mom showed me a paper the doctor had given her after carrying out a thorough examination of Dad. I read with a shock the sinister words "*angina pectoris.*"

In terms of daily life there was not a great deal of change in the atmosphere of the old homestead, no late softening of the asperity and intolerance that had been our continual burden while we were all growing up. Mom could not even fart without bringing on a burst of impatience and complaints from the Old Man.

She had always been a free-and-easy, a prodigious farter,

specializing in everything from what we called her baby putt-putt to the champion rip-snorter like a cross-cut saw going through knots, but now that her stomach had gone back on her she was always letting them go, in all degrees, and every time she did so the Old Man threw back his head with a glare of indignation, calling out in the tone of a prosecutor: "What in the world is wrong wit' *you*? You're *always* at it now."

"Oh, mind y'own business! Can I help it if I got wind in me stomach?"

"Wind! You got a gale up there, woman. And it never stops blowin'."

"You got no room to talk – stuck there day and night, morning and evening, on that couch, hawkin' and spittin', coughin', gruntin', moanin' and groanin' till I got to run out o' me own kitchen to give me ears a rest. You gets right on me nerves. I wish you was back workin' again."

"Yes, well I can't help what n'ise I makes, see, with the trouble I got."

"Well, no more can I! How foolish you talks."

"Go on! You does it a-purpose. For God's sake, get somet'ing for that stummick o' yours next time you goes down to the doctor."

This latter was another sore point between them because, although she often complained of feeling ready to give up, Mom was very reluctant to visit any of the doctors in town on the grounds that they were all too nosey.

Listening to this sample of what I knew must be their daily exchanges, I immediately had doubts about the wisdom of coming back after so long a time and also about the possibility of any reconciliation (if that was the right word) to my family and Milltown and of my remaining there indefinitely. Though I still had no ties elsewhere, everything that happened during those first few days at home once again filled my mind with dismay and a drastic feeling of homelessness in the midst of my nearest kin and all the sounds and sights and prejudices into which I had been born. Mom did her best to dispel these apprehensions of mine, even though she did not fully understand them, while Dad kept himself carefully neutral on the subject of my plans for the future.

"He's welcome to stay if he wants to," he said to Mom without looking at me when she urged the folly of my going away again, and he said it with the air of somebody making a general statement for the benefit of anyone at all who might be within hearing distance. That too seemed to rasp on Mom's nerves, so much so that she determined right away on some kind of gesture that would give me a more direct and heartfelt sense of where and to whom I really belonged. The best thing she could think of was a little family party in celebration of my return, and no sooner had she thought of this than she was on the phone urgently inviting all hands for Saturday night. Throughout her many conversations the Old Man sat near her tut-tutting disgustedly (he refused to use the phone himself and hated to hear Mom on it, just as he could not bear to see her reading a newspaper) and swearing all the time that no matter who came – the family or the whole of Milltown or Jesus Christ himself – not a drop of beer or booze would he allow her to buy or pay for on his money. Mom just hushed him up as usual and went on making her plans.

Accordingly it was with some anticipation that I waited for all the family to show up on Saturday evening for my little party. Fudge and I had already seen each other again, of course, as he was still living at home, and my astonishment at his appearance could hardly have been greater if he had turned into a perfect Beau Brummel. He was now as tall as Crawfie, or just about, and weighed two hundred and forty-seven pounds, making me feel like a futile runt and of no physical consequence whatever when I found myself standing beside him.

The others when they arrived at the house also showed this startling accumulation of flesh. Ank with his blocky frame distended and sagging most painfully all over;

Flinksy oozing rich fare and prosperity and with much of it bursting out along the zipper of her dress; Racer arriving belly-foremost with self-important aldermanic tread; and last of all Crawfie coming on the home scene with the doleful majesty of some great actor whose youth has fled and who has let himself go to obesity and to seed.

And what a shock their faces gave me! Each one of them except Fudge seemed to have donned a mask to hide the features of youth by which I had known them and kept them in my memory; but I realized with a jolt that it was only middle age they had put on, and as I again scanned their rueful faces it came home to me that they must all be making the same reflection on me that I was making on them. I too must be showing on my face, though my body was still slim, that shadow or mask which proclaimed like a tolling bell that youth was gone. It was a thought I could hardly accept, for in spite of my eyebrows beginning to sprout and go haywire and the appearance of tiny hammocks tinged with purple under my eyes, I flattered myself that my face still had a reasonably fresh and gleaming look. Surely it couldn't be as faded and fallen as the faces of my brothers and sister?

It was in Flinksy's compassionate but also candid eyes that I read the death of my illusions, and then in the silence that followed all our greetings and meagre compliments I lapsed into a morbid reverie on all that I had failed to accomplish since my first departure from home more than twenty years before. I reflected too, as we all gathered around the table for a game of cards, on how much we Stone children resembled one another in spite of marked differences in individual feature: We were all very much alike in the way that portraits are alike when set into identical frames.

It was a relief to me when the card game started and we grouped ourselves into two tables of six (Ank having brought along his eldest son Jim as well as his wife Mavis to make up an even twelve) and in the course of the game began to move around and change places and partners according to victory or defeat at the end of each game. But I found too that more discomfort and even pain must mingle with my pleasure and my gratified curiosity throughout what was to me a memorable evening.

It could only be painful to feel my blood relations covertly staring at me and studying me as though I were not only a suspicious but also a foreign character, and one who might be secretly inclined to look down on them. I could hear the thought turning behind their eyes: "Juju is after gettin' high notions," and I could almost feel the word "traitor" pushing at their lips, demanding utterance. I felt as alien as a Hottentot at the North Pole. It made no difference that I had this time arrived home from a place that had become a sister province of Newfoundland, no longer a foreign country but the mainland of Canada – no difference at all. Acts of Parliament bear no reference to insularity and the village virus.

Ank was the worst one of all in his attitude toward me, and in the unfriendliness he showed in direct proportion to any little incident or contretemps that tended to illustrate how far, for better or worse, I had travelled from the speech and manners and mores of twenty years ago on the hill.

"*Pawss*," he kept saying, imitating the way I pronounced the word "pass," with a sarcastic grin and mocking inflection about as subtle as a fist in the face. The others all laughed with various degrees of sympathy (on Ank's side). I made no protest to him, not wanting to cause any friction in the clan so soon after my return; in any case, there was soon friction enough in that crowded, steaming kitchen as the cards and insults began to fly and the heat of battle to come to its full, old-time intensity.

Mom and Dad were soonest at it; he jeered at her savagely whenever she went down on a bid and she retaliated fiercely over and over again: "I wish you'd *shut up*. You keeps on at anyone till you makes 'em feel right small, just like two cents. I *hates* that." In fact, the Old Man himself was no longer any great shakes at the cards, as I saw when he once or twice bid twenty on the jack of diamonds thinking it was the jack of hearts and made a horrible mess of his entire hand. On our gleefully pointing out his mistake and the trouncing he was in for, he would give a start and then hold his jack of diamonds at a distance of about two feet from his eyes and stare at it indignantly for being diamonds instead of hearts. We would not allow him to change or take back his bid, and we kept to the ancient practice of showing no mercy at all in a game of cards. I reflected, while taking in the whole rowdy scene, how nothing else, quite apart from the long-sightedness he now suffered from, could have shown his decline into old age so clearly as did this failure of his powers at the cards. Each time he went in the hole he howled and swore, blamed it on his partners or his position at one of the tables, and eventually he tried to take his revenge on all of us by starting a fuss with the mild-mannered, easy-going Rome when Rome rather foolishly bid thirty for sixty over Dad's twenty-five when they were partners, only to be absolutely slaughtered by the other side.

I saw Flinksy turn pale and begin to tremble as the Old Man lit into Rome regardless of their temporary partnership, yelling at him that he had no business going over his own partner, especially when he did not have the cards for thirty, and that he could only have done it for spite because no other reason could be found for such a foolish bid.

"No sir," Rome kept repeating quietly but stubbornly, "no sir, there's no spite in it. I 'ad the cards, and I went. That's all there is to it."

His very mildness seemed to ignite the Old Man's temper, which was like dry straw to a flame whenever he was losing, and soon I observed Flinsky digging her elbow into Rome's side, saying more plainly than any words: "That's enough, b'y. For God's sake, agree with him and keep the peace. Never mind who's in the right of it."

But obviously nettled by the Old Man's calling him

down in front of everybody, Rome seemed not at all inclined to give way, with the result that our game might have broken up then and there had not Mom, emboldened perhaps or made reckless by the years and the Old Man's obvious decay, vigorously entered into the argument on Rome's behalf and so diverted the Old Man from his main quarrel.

"How childish is you gettin' a-tall!" she scolded him. "For glory-sake, let Rome alone and give your tongue a rest. You'd t'ink a million dollars was staked on the hand, the way you goes on. You never stops once the cards is on the go, and yet you knows as well as me and all the rest that Rome had enough to try t'irty on. To *try*," she smiled charmingly at Rome, having been the chief cause of his downfall in this case, and went on more gently. "So hush up now, the both o' ye, and have a drop o' beer. That'll cool ye down, I hope; and we'll take a little spell while I sees to me pots and pans." She acknowledged with another broad smile the laugh that greeted this sally, for it was another family joke how she managed to produce a drink for any of our gatherings at home despite all the Old Man's prior warnings and without anyone knowing when or how she smuggled it into the house.

The refrigerated beer, and the break, and another change of partners, did cool us a little and helped to keep our voices down to a raucous shout whenever another little disagreement threatened to arise. Each man grabbed a bottle and, tipping it greedily to his lips, drank off most of it in two or three long sensual gulps; and so as not to feel entirely out of the mood, I went into the pantry during the break and made myself a cup of Nescafé; but it turned out that I was not entirely alone among the men after all, because Jim also preferred coffee to beer and, as I learned not long afterwards, had some very good reasons for doing so. "Juju don't touch a drop, not even beer," said Mom with a mixture of pride and wonder in her tone when I returned to the table with my cup and saucer.

"That so?" Ank regarded me without much enthusiasm.

"That's where he got sense," Mavis put in unexpectedly. "Some people ought to folley his example."

Ank merely glowered at her for a moment, then removed the bottle from his foamy lips. "And *some* people," he grunted heavily, "ought to mind their own goddam business."

All through the evening I had sensed that Ank and his wife were not exactly on the best of terms and as the card game warmed up again while Ank put away more beer and Mavis gritted her teeth in growing exasperation, my guess became an undoubted and embarrassing fact. Not unless they were opposing each other at the card table could they take any real pleasure or satisfaction in the game; then each time Ank beat her and she cursed him for a scheming cheater or a gloating fool, he would stick his nose into her face and say, "You kiss my *arse*." He would intone this with the deliberation and emphasis of twenty years' repeated use.

"Paugh, you stinks!" was the standard reply that Mavis gave, turning her face aside and pushing Ank's away with the heel of her hand. To all of us these well-known antics were cause for laughter – to all, that is, except young Jim, who smiled with us but blushed also and squirmed on his chair as the slanging match went on. The real antagonism between his mother and father showed more clearly in its ugly truth with the steady flow of beer and the renewed fraying of nerves during the rest of the card game. Once, when the young fellow's temper flared up over a grossly unjust and profane criticism of his card sense from Ank, I was carried back with a shudder to that seeming yesterday when Ank had cried out in exactly such a tone against the furious criticisms of the Old Man.

Somehow we got through my homecoming party without anything more than verbal attacks being launched by one generation of Stones against another. At twenty-past-twelve, we stopped playing cards in honour of the Sabbath (we just had to finish that last hand), and all the males were driven with their beer and tobacco and arguments into the front room, leaving a clear field in the kitchen for the women to set about clearing the tables and getting a cup of tea.

When we came back to the kitchen half an hour later, a huge platter of salt pork and cabbage stood in the centre of each table, with places laid all round for everyone and bottles of sour pickles on the side. At sight of it all I felt my stomach quail. To touch food like that after midnight would be for me like committing suicide, or at least running the risk of screaming nightmares and a week or so of total collapse. My old enemy-in-residence, dyspepsia, forbade me any but the mildest food outside of regular meal hours. Mom too was forbidden this diet that was salty as the ocean; her eyes filled with tears of longing as she gazed at those great steaming slabs of brick-red meat and the blistered layers of fat lying between them.

A real Newfoundlander she was in her love of a good feed of pork and boiled cabbage after a riotous card game; but now she had to deny herself and suffer the double misery of being unable to enjoy a meal that she herself had taken a great deal of trouble to cook. Her only compensation seemed to lie in the vicarious pleasure she took in watching Fudge devour two platefuls of the steaming mess, but toward the end of the scoff we all smiled tolerantly to see her at her ancient habit of picking a rind or two of meat from Dad's plate, plus a small stump of cabbage, and gobble them down as if the speed and unofficial manner of her eating might cause her stomach to overlook this imprudence for once.

The Old Man dug into the feed as heartily as all the rest, although Mom and Fudge and I knew he would be groaning all through the rest of the night and complaining for days after this about his constipation and the cramps in his stomach. It was no use at all reminding or trying to restrain him in any way. When I saw him greedily relishing that huge meal, the two sharp parallel cords in his throat leaping outward each time he chewed, I was struck again by the way he seemed to have lapsed into old age since my last visit home, and I realized with a terrible weariness how futile it would be to try and reason with his frozen mind about food or anything else, much more futile than in the days of his strength and implemented temper.

The cup of tea finished, the men had one more smoke, and then prepared for the short but in one or two cases unsteady and perilous return to their own homes. They all invited me to come and visit them, and naturally I accepted, with a new stirring of curiosity to see what they had all become and made of their lives out on their own. Yet ready as I was to accept, it appeared that I was not quick enough to please Ank in his present mood; or perhaps the load of beer he had taken on had just brought him to that cantankerous stage where he was disposed to quarrel with anyone about no matter what. "Christ!" he exploded, "you're not the Bishop, are you? You don't have to wait for a written invitation." Hastily I assured him and Mavis that I would be over to visit them very soon. Anything less than that, and the faithful carrying out of my promise, would have landed me in the danger of being considered and condemned on all sides as Stuck Up.

CHAPTER

2

ANK

Two evenings later I made my way over to Ank's house just across a field and on the hill parallel to Ocean View Road. I was reflecting all the time on the way in which Ank and all the others, despite the harsh manner of their several departures from our original home, had clustered around the Old Man – satellites around a darkening sun – in setting up house on their own. Racer was just next door to Mom and Dad, Flinksy had her business and home a little way down the hill on the other side, and Crawfie lived in over the brow of the hill only a few minutes' walk from the rest of the families.

Ank himself had got along in his married life in a respectable and independent way, or so at least I understood from the regular letters I received from Mom and the occasional gossipy-epic ones from Flinksy during the past thirteen years of my absence from Milltown. He stayed on as a labourer in the company paper sheds, sweated it out for ten years, and at the end of that time was promoted to the job of checker out on the wharves where the paper and wood boats were forever loading and unloading in the traffic of large-scale commerce.

In the beginning his house was built mainly from packing cases pilfered from the mill, but gradually the improved conditions of labour in the whole town and the rising wages enabled Ank to dress up and extend his place until it began to take on a startling resemblance to our old home, except that Ank had not the ambition to make as many or as fantastic improvements as the Old Man had made in our never-quite-finished house. Ank's home was just a family shelter, no uglier than most of the other houses all around that looked as if they had been blown there by a gale of wind and never properly settled to their foundations.

His family of four had come at decent intervals after the unexpected arrival of the eldest boy Jim, but the strain and expense of raising and educating this family in a criminally expensive town turned Ank, who was always older than his years, into a middle-aged man long before he reached that stage of life by the calendar. It also obliged him to supplement his income in various ways if he were not to fall shamefully, perhaps hopelessly, into debt. One of his money-making and saving dodges was to keep a few hens and pigs, which were still a family joke and about which I had often heard in the letters I received from home.

Such was his life: a long, day-by-day struggle to keep his head above water and maintain some sort of decent social position on Humber Heights according to the primitive standards that had guided Newfoundland families like ours over four centuries and more. As in our own family history, births were the major events in Ank's married life, and these were by no means regarded as unmixed blessings. The old pattern was repeated in almost every other detail, with no appreciable change in morals, manners, or even in speech on Ank and Mavis' part, though later on I noticed that Ank's better-educated children were veering away from the traditional *patois* of our class.

All during the early years of his married life, Ank had apparently no relief from the harsh monotony of his routine, no amusement or recreation at all except the radio and an occasional day's fishing. Only as he approached middle age could he afford to spend any money on trouting equipment and the more expensive refinements of salmon fishing, and even then it was understood by the rest of our family that Mavis complained in her most cutting style if he stayed away from home for more than a few hours at a time.

The more I turned all this over in my mind, the more I pitied Ank and congratulated myself on an early flight from Milltown and what I had gradually and, since my return, shudderingly come to think of as the local *marriage-à-la-mode*. I saw no sign of Ank himself as I came up to the front door of his house, although I had been invited for tea and it was just on that hour, but I did hear voices from the back yard and paused a moment before ringing the doorbell.

"We got to wait for d'Ole Man, b'y." I recognized Jim's voice.

"What for?" – obviously the second boy, Dick.

"He'll give us hell and put 'er up if we goes off troutin' on our own hook."

"Hell wit' him. We'll shove off right after tea."

"Yes. Piss on d'Ole Man," the youngest added. "Let's frig off anyway."

How strangely those words "the Old Man" fell on my ear in reference to anyone except Dad! With a rueful adjustment of my time sense I realized that Ank had now entered on that lonely and bitter estate and was no longer to be thought of as essentially a big brother to all of us in the original Stone family.

That scrap of defiant talk from the boys having made me more than ever doubtful about the possibility of domestic bliss among a hard crowd like ours, or of anything like a pleasant evening at Ank's, I nevertheless rang the bell again and was let in by a tight-lipped, obviously tense Mavis and planted uneasily on the sofa in the front room. Just for the sake of conversation we chatted about this and that, but it was clear that even if Mavis had not been jumping up every two minutes or so to check the meal cooking on the kitchen stove she would still have been unable to fix her mind on any subject or line of thought whatever. After about ten minutes of such nervousness she called in the children, including their little girl of twelve, and decided that we should go ahead and have our tea, as it was now well after six and we were all getting hungry.

"Where's Ank?" I asked innocently.

"God only knows, b'y." Mavis replied.

"And he won't tell," Dick shot in saucily. Mavis paid no attention to Dick. "I can imagine easy enough where he is." The children looked at one another furtively and giggled, almost sneered, as at a long-standing and not extra-funny joke.

Toward me their attitude seemed peculiar, being made up of shyness and curiosity in about equal parts; they could hardly be got to say a word to me without prompting from their mother, but I could sense their wonder and their secret amusement at my style of speech, my mainland clothes, and my air of genteel prosperity as against the general family knowledge that I had no money to speak of. Throughout the entire meal I was reminded of Fudge's first reaction to my presence on my last return home.

We had almost finished our tea when there came an irregular stomping noise from the direction of the verandah, as though some blind or crippled monster were trying to climb up the steps and enter the house. Taking a deep breath and grimacing in the manner of one praying for patience, Mavis got up from the table and went out to the front door. Even as she stood there opening it we could all hear her voice raised in savage scorn.

"Goddam you, look at you! Where the hell were you to? Don't tell me! I knows. Didn't I tell you a dozen times Juju was comin' for tea tonight?"

Ank came into the kitchen, mumbling obscenely at his wife and showing no concern at having missed an hour or so of my society. He was an appalling sight: boots unlaced, the grey woollen socks he always wore hanging down over his boots in rolls; the fly of his pants was all open to the breeze, mouth drooling at the corners, and to complete the picture he had not shaved for three or four days. Sopping drunk—that was the only way to describe him; utterly soused, and this was not even Saturday night or payday. Mavis must have been shamed by the look of wonder on my face, for she gave Ank a stare of contempt even more open than any I had seen her fix on him while we were playing cards, and then spoke to me again in a tone of hopelessness. "He's always like that, Juju b'y. Whenever he got the cash, that's it! Saturday and Sunday is all alike to him. I haves to fight with him just to get enough money to run the house."

This I could hardly believe. What could have happened to Ank? As a young man he used to take the odd bottle of beer, a drink of rum or whiskey, but nothing out of the way, to use our phrase for moderation; that is, nothing that ever made him stinko in his youth or indicated for him an alcoholic future. Surely what Mavis had said must be a bitter exaggeration, and yet as I looked at the tight faces of Ank's children and almost smelt the excretion of fear from their young bodies, I began to wonder if she had not spoken the literal truth. The expressions and attitudes of those kids had something horribly habitual about them.

Ank himself was still in the more or less genial stage of drunkenness, though whenever he looked at Mavis his bloodshot eyes narrowed instantaneously and became as ugly and malevolent as a wild boar's. I thought in those moments how much he looked like a man who has a grudge not only against his mate but against the whole world, against life. After he had been in the room for about ten minutes he seemed to recognize me and even to remember in an elementary way his duties as a host, and master of the house. Sticking out a calloused, dirt-encrusted hand, which I took with more embarrassment than reluctance, he welcomed me to his home and offered hospitality. "Have a little snort," he urged, pulling a bottle of Pale Ale from a side pocket and grinning at me slyly. "Go on, b'y. Do you good." I was just about to refuse as inoffensively as I knew how when Mavis snatched the bottle from his hand.

"Oh no you don't!" she cried, and smashed the bottle into a garbage can. "You knows bloody well Juju don't drink, and God knows *you're* after havin' enough for one night." Ank swore at her but offered no violence. Then without having washed or combed his hair or made apology of any kind to me or the others he sat down at the head of the table and demanded food.

"Gimme me tea," he shouted as Mavis dallied and thereby partly punished him for present and past sins. "I wants me tea!" Ank went on, "and you better be quick about it, or else, by Jesus," and here Ank's voice lowered to a menacing growl, "I'll put this place, this whole shebang, sky-high, and you along wit' it." After a while Mavis slapped a plate down in front of him. "Here. Eat that, and shut up. You got the kids half-frightened to death already."

"Kids!" Ank retorted. "Christ, they're old enough to go out to work, two o' them, and at least one o' them t'inks he's big enough to go courtin', if you please." Here his voice became heavier with the weight of sarcasm it carried, and his baleful eye rested for a long moment on seventeen-year-old Dick, who straightened up defiantly in his chair and muttered a curse as he looked sheepishly all around the room – anywhere but into his father's eyes. I sensed another family drama here, and one that was not altogether a comedy.

Now Ank's mood, changing as abruptly and capriciously as that of a child, became genial again and he began to chuckle to himself. "That Morton," he giggled, apparently recalling some character or incident on the job or perhaps in their favourite beer parlour. "That bastard, he tells more lies than the Divil."

"Mind your dirty mouth!" Mavis warned him while she glanced at me and continued apologetically. "Don't pay no heed, Juju."

"That fucker," Ank went on with his private train of thought.

"Shut up! Animal!" Mavis attacked him again before

she turned back to me. "See what we got to listen to. F, that's his favourite word when he got the liquor in him. It's no good me talkin' to him, not a bit."

"Fucker," Ank repeated. "You know what he went and told me, Juju? Well, he claimed he couldn't get alongside o' the wife, see – not for love nor money, and no matter how much he coaxed or wheedled her. She was like a block o' ice. So he goes to one o' the fellas offa the boats and gets some o' that stuff they calls the Spanish Fly, and that same night when he puts it to her —"

He got no further. Mavis gritted her teeth and, giving the little girl Jenny her dessert of blueberry pie and ice cream, sent her into the front room and shut the connecting door. "Now you hold your filthy tongue!" she snarled, and with the words Ank got an equally sharp cut across the head from the side of his wife's hand. "I won't have that kind o' talk in the house and in front of the children. And you can do what you damn well likes about it."

Ank rose unsteadily from his chair, looking for a moment or two as if he would do battle. The three boys formed up resolutely on their mother's side. Ank raised his hand to strike Mavis, but even as he did so I saw his face turn pale. He gave a ghastly *gawp* from the depths of his stomach, and we all knew what was coming next. Though Ank did veer toward the kitchen sink, he did not reach it in time, and vomited all over the kitchen floor. While Mavis was clearing up the nauseating mess, we all moved into the front room where Ank collapsed on the sofa now that his retching was all over and apparently sank into a kind of post-orgy coma.

Mavis came in again after she and Jenny had finished the dishes, and she and all the rest of the family talked quite freely, I noticed, just as if Ank were completely unconscious or even as if he did not exist at all. Watching Mavis and listening to the torrent of her words, I was once more struck by the fantastic changes that the years had wrought. Where in this hard-eyed, taut-lipped woman of forty could I find any trace of the blushing, self-consciously pregnant and crazy-for-Ank young girl who used to come to our house so often and so eagerly in those long-distant years just before they were married? Mavis was now visibly implacable in her hostility toward him, so much so that even to me, as unknown a quantity to her now as she appeared to me, she poured out a tale of married misery that in many of its features was already to my mind crushingly familiar.

Caught up in the stream of private confidences that women had often and unaccountably made to me, Mavis even told me the story of Dick after that young fellow had excused himself and gone off on what was obviously a heavy date. Boiled down from the seething mass of her resentments and irrelevances, it all came to the fact that Dick was a randy young buck, a roving billygoat, and at the age of sixteen had already got a neighbour's daughter in trouble and was bent on quitting school in order to get married. To this plan, although Dick's girl was no better or worse than most of the kids on their hill, Ank had been instantly and violently opposed.

So deep was his hatred of the whole idea that he and Dick had soon declared war on each other and split the home into two camps with Ank on one side and all the rest of their family on the other. This war had gone on in much the same fashion as other domestic wars I had known, but it was some of the details that caught my ear and added new features to the pattern with which I was already familiar. There were frequent brawls, of course, with Dick finally resorting to a switch-blade and threatening Ank with it in case of further brutal aggression.

Then there was the common occurrence of Dick coming home at three in the morning and finding that both front and back doors were not only locked but nailed up on the inside. Dick's ultimate action was breaking down the basement door and crawling up into the house through a hatch in the kitchen floor. Ank came down to prevent him from doing even that. Mavis entered into the fight, and at last the whole family came down and ganging up on Ank until he was actually forced to let Dick stay in the house where he belonged.

This had now been going on for some months, and I gathered from Mavis that what irritated and enraged her most was that Ank could never be brought to express in so many words the reason for this hysterical hostility to Dick's romance and impending marriage. The boy's youth was simply not enough to cover the whole story. When the possibility of Dick's getting married was finally broached to Ank, he simply told everybody concerned that they could go square to hell and do as they goddam-well liked, because he wanted nothing to do with the whole affair in any shape or form.

That was the current situation as Mavis related it to me in her own tumbling and bitter words. How much of her story Ank had heard or even been conscious of during her recital, or throughout the TV session that followed, I could not be sure, for he still lay there on the chesterfield with his mouth hanging loosely open in a repulsive yet pitiable way, the densely matted grey stubble of his hair and beard framing his face like thorns. From time to time he groaned, rolled over, and resumed the mutterings and murmurings that had been coming from him ever since he had passed out. At first I thought he was only protesting against the bias of Mavis' outlook and her frankly high-voiced condemnation of him and all his acts, but as I listened more closely, bored by the raucous TV noise and the stultifying commercials, my ear was caught and held by some of the words and phrases coming out of Ank's stupor that, because of their repetition and intensity, seemed uppermost or at any rate most irritant in his mind. "Old Man . . . old bastard . . . right after all . . . maybe . . . right after all . . . goddam women . . . never let you alone . . . cunts . . . never . . . work yer guts out . . . no t'anks . . . expect no t'anks . . . kick in d'arse . . . that's all . . . Lard Jesus . . . kids . . . cost a bloody fortune . . . fortune . . . goddam slave . . . that's it . . . slave . . . bringin' in money . . . t'rew away . . . finished wit' dat . . . fuck it! . . . nutting but work . . . all work and no pay

". . . ha-ha . . . no more . . . by Jesus . . . never done nutting but work . . . all work . . . since when I still t'ought I only had it to piss through . . . so they looks down on me . . . young farts . . . down on me . . . me own flesh and blood . . . I won't stand it! . . . they got no right . . . saucy young buggers . . . her too . . . worst one o' the lot . . . Jenny, my duck . . . sweetheart! . . . what did *I* ever get out out of it? . . . fosh in d'arse . . . nutting else . . . that's about the size of it . . . and them lookin' down their nose . . . curse 'em . . . curse 'em all! . . . sufferin' Christ . . . I'll kill 'em . . . if they keeps on . . . kill 'em . . . kill . . . kill . . . *kill*. . . ."

Tears now began to stream down Ank's face making dark stains on the light-coloured material of the sofa, and Mavis, giving an exclamation of disgust, ran out to the kitchen for a rag, then came back and slopped it over his face just as if he were a fractious, messy child. "Aw, *dry up*," she barked, not with any humour (she meant only "shut up") and paying no more than the bit of physical attention to his tears. I realized with an inward start that she perceived no meaning in his mutterings and ravings, that Mavis saw Ank only in the light of what she had learnt about him since their marriage, whereas I knew him and judged his words from memory of an earlier time when he was still an integral part of our own family; therefore I heard with more sympathy and perhaps understanding too these things that seemed to burden his mind like chains.

While I was reflecting on this, Ank suddenly reared up on the sofa and seeming to recognize me again, cried out to me in a tone of passionate woe: "Goddam it, Juju, I been workin' like a dog for twenty years, and how much money have I got in the bank?" He sobbed convulsively and soberly. "Not a cent. Not a *measly* red cent. Now is that justice? Hey? You tell *me*."

In the lurid flash and glimmer of the TV, Ank looked for a moment like some ancient prophet demanding of Jehovah the reasons for all his suffering and long-continued woe. I would hardly have known how to answer Ank, but in any case Mavis was determined to save me the trouble.

"And whose fault is it?" she demanded. "D'you expect to have money in the bank when you goes out every blessed night and spends it in them beer dives, and then comes home and pisses it all down the t'ilet or vomits it all over the floor? What can you expect, for God's sake?"

"Who ast *your* opinion?" said Ank nastily, and they probably would have launched out on another slanging duel had not a diversion come from a not unexpected quarter.

"Aw, can't we have a bit o' peace?" Jim cut into their argument with more impatience than respect. "I can't hear the program." Ank shot an evil glance at him and tried to brace himself belligerently, but I saw that now the film was coming back over his eyes and in a moment he left us again, subsiding on the sofa with a moan of agony and end-of-the-world weariness.

He slept or dozed for an hour or two, at the end of which time he appeared to wake up in earnest. At least he struggled to a sitting position, and after a long visit to the bathroom came back to the sofa, now demanding more food and a cup of tea. As the minutes passed and Mavis made no move to tend on him, he became plaintive, and when he spoke again there was a crack of self-pity in his voice.

"Come on, girl. Get us a cup o' tea. Hurry up, will you, Mave? I'm thirsty as the divil. Hungry too."

Mavis went out to the kitchen and Ank fell once more into what looked like miserable meditation, ignoring me completely. While I observed the painful spectacle he made and wondered how he had come to this more-or-less permanent state of beery despair, I searched back into my own experience for some basis on which I might come to understand, and perhaps even to sympathize with his present misery. Ank was not so much older than I that his life-experience might not be regarded, at this date, as providing some basis for comparison with my own. We were only five years apart in age.

I recalled my own introduction to the booze, which had taken place shortly after I joined the Canadian Navy in 1942, which in turn had come about in Montreal some months after I had left home with my stake of two hundred and seventy-five dollars in my pocket. On going broke I had taken refuge from poverty and loneliness in wartime service rather than return to the Hell-Hole or saddle myself with a permanent job in trade. On receiving my first Navy pay, I felt obliged to rush out like all my mates who yearned for saltiness and spend the money in guzzling beer or hard liquor before starting out on a wolf-hunt I never made much of a hit as a wolf, and as for the drinking, I started out like Ank with beer as my staple drink. At first I experienced some pleasure and even rose to *bonhomie* on occasion, surrounded by acquaintances with whom I came closer and closer to terms of friendship the nearer I got to my limit of twelve glasses.

But a few months of these piss-ups, as they were termed in the Navy, and I began to suspect and tire of the spurious palsy-walsy warmth they generated no less than I tired of the beer itself. My heart was never in it. Reason moved in and took control, stressing the awful pointlessness and the circular futility of these minor orgies and bringing the waste of it all so sharply to my consciousness that I began to discuss my state of mind with my drinking companions themselves. They did not care for introspection. I became a loner again and I suffered from my solitude, but still I knew with a hard comfortless certainty that no strong drink of any kind held the power to ease my pain. That was how I felt at the time.

Later in my life, when the pressure of circumstances came down on my mind with greater urgency, I would have been grateful to seek refuge in even a momentary forgetfulness of myself and life's problems through any drink, but by that time my stomach was in no condition to deal with anything stronger than Nescafé.

What had been the pressure of circumstances on Ank from the day of his marriage to this present moment in which I viewed him with mingled disgust and pity? Heavy enough, no doubt, yet not so much heavier than what other men like him endured, that it would explain or condone his gradual descent into alcoholism. I was convinced that the root of evil went further down in his mind than the time of his marriage: It went down to the arid and rocky soil of his childhood and youth, to the emotional starvation that our family life had clamped on him like a harness for so many crucial years.

What consolations Ank had missed in life during childhood he had again failed to find in marriage and fatherhood, and perhaps the disillusion of this continuing void was too much for him to accept or overcome. How could Mavis or any of Ank's children, unless gifted with a delicate and also a penetrating imagination, see him as the victim and not the villain of a family situation? How could they see him as anything but an alcoholic, would-be tyrant, when factors that bore so heavily on Ank's development and formed part of my own recollections were to them a completely unknown quantity?

Lost in these musings, I was hardly aware of her when Mavis returned to the front room bearing a large enamel pan full of a sickly-smelling mash, steaming hot. "Where's me tea?" Ank said impatiently but got from Mavis only a hard-faced stare.

"The pigs is not fed yet," she warned him. "After that you can have your tea."

"Can't you do it for once?"

"No, I can't. Nor the kids neether. It's your job. We agreed on that and now you got to stick to it."

Every moment I spent in Ank's house showed me how completely he had lost whatever dominion he may once have had over his household.

"Well, gimme me tea first, and a bite to eat."

"That I won't. You'll fill your gut and then you'll fall asleep again. No sirree."

"Aw, shit on you, then," Ank belched morosely; but he pushed himself up from the sofa, shook his head to clear it, and took a bearing for the kitchen. Though staggering dangerously, he managed to take the pan from Mavis and pass through the kitchen out through the porch as well, and to start down the back steps. Suddenly we heard a series of terrific thumps, a clatter, and a wild howl as if Ank had been teetering on the rim of hell and had just fallen in. Mavis and Jim and the other boy rushed out to see what had happened to the pig feed while I watched the whole scene through the kitchen window.

Ank's renewed motion or the stimulus of his re-awakened anger must have sent the beer-laden blood to his head again; he now lay prone at the bottom of the steps, out cold by the look of him, with the horrible *purée* of the mash spattered all over his face and clothes. I heard Mavis swear at him viciously, then call out to Jim to take Ank's head as she and the youngest boy seized hold of a leg apiece in a practised way that suggested frequent occurrence. Naturally I supposed they were going to help Ank into the house and see whether he was injured, and I was just stepping out to ask if I could lend a hand when to my surprise I saw them heading down the garden path dragging Ank along between them.

Jenny rushed ahead of the grotesque procession holding one of her father's boots that had come off, and opened a gate in a low fence down at the bottom of the garden. Finally they arrived at the gate with their burden. I could hardly believe my eyes as I saw them shove Ank into the enclosure – right in among the pigs – and shut the gate with the obvious intention of leaving him there until he was able to get out under his own steam. As if to emphasize this, Mavis took the boot from Jenny and threw it in on top of Ank before turning back with the three children toward the house.

I left them shortly after that, in a disturbed and pensive mood, pondering Ank's immediate future as well as what appeared to be the awful abyss of his past twenty years. After all, it was no joke to spend several hours or a whole night on the slushy clay floor of a pigsty during the cool of the dark hours in a Newfoundland September.

CHAPTER

3

RACER

Racer came out of his six years in the Artillery and campaigns in as many foreign countries with no wounds at all and no disability except a little trouble in his ears from the booming of the guns. On his return to Milltown as a sergeant, he shared fully in the glory of all the original volunteers and at home received what amounted to a hero's reception, with a great WELCOME HOME banner slung right across the front of our house, Union Jacks protruding from every window, and a mass gathering of relatives and friends and neighbours to cheer him as he was driven up the hill and proudly deposited at the gateway to our festive home.

In the time immediately following his return, good fortune seemed again to walk by his side and protect him from many of the pitfalls that we others stumbled into so readily and had so much trouble climbing out of over the years. There was the obvious blessing that his war service had saved him from the kind of premature marriage which became such a crippling drawback to Ank and others in our family.

When Racer did marry some two years after demobilization, he chose a young woman, well-educated according to Milltown standards, nice-looking in a pinkish, fluffy-brown way, and in addition partly trained as a nurse. In our circles this amouted to distinction, even though Rhoda had not finished her training by the time she and Racer were married and she never afterwards used her knowledge and skill in any practical way except around the home. From all I heard of their wedding, it was a brilliant, even memorable affair in the town, Racer wearing his full-dress uniform with medals for the ceremony, and Rhoda rising from prettiness to fairy-tale beauty in the halo of her bridal veil. Everyone bent on them looks of admiration and envy while predicting a rosy future for bride and groom and any little ones who might come to complete their happiness.

Indeed Racer had wasted very little time after his return in taking his future by the throat and making it promise an abundance of success. After a short period in the real-estate office which he had left to join up, he launched out in business on his own, at first conducting it from a desk in the corner of our front room, then from shared office space lower down on Humber Heights, and finally achieving an office of his own with a secretary next door in one of the main office buildings of the original townsite.

His rise in the local shark-fight of business was undeniable, meteoric. As he gradually came to get on first-name terms with the big-dealing men who secretly ruled the town through the mill and an elementary knowledge of what the law would let them get away with, his position became that of a solidly entrenched member of the inside group, the boys in the back room of municipal government, who could even challenge the law and the government if it came to a show-down between them and the constituted authorities. Racer took on flesh and assurance at an equal rate, it seemed, and moved not too ungracefully toward middle age in a cushioned world of small-town success and honoured if not altogether honourable reputation.

Socially too he climbed with vigorous rapidity whatever ladders there were to be climbed in Milltown, attended cocktail parties at which he shook the manager of the mill by the hand, used the Milltown Haven (slick successor to the old slapdash Company Inn) as a second home, and ultimately achieved the laurels and perquisites of being elected to the local branch of Rotary. Nearer home, one of his best real-estate deals was to buy up their shack from the old couple who lived just below us on the hill, burn it down for the insurance, and on the proceeds start building a home of his own, which soon became almost a social centre (though not for people on the hill) in the town. Primarily, it was business people from the townsite whose cars blocked Racer's driveway several nights a week, and whose revelling voices late on Saturday night or early in the Sabbath often scandalized the more sober-minded and joyless among our neighbours. Racer Stone was getting a bit above himself, they murmured more and more frequently, as the years passed and the howling parties continued in his home.

One cloud on Racer's horizon and his wife's for a good many years after their marriage was Rhoda's failure to produce a surviving child and the consequent grief she suffered over her own failure and Racer's obvious disappointment. After three miscarriages and a warning from the doctor, Rhoda desperately broached the subject of adoption, the end result of which was that she and Racer decided to take as their own, legally and for good, one of Crawfie's legitimate children who apparently were regarded by Crawfie at this time as eminently expendable. It was soon done, and the new parents reaped a harvest of praise for their generosity.

Then, within the next five years, Rhoda produced four healthy, handsomely blue-eyed boys of her own and Racer was all the more solidly established on the local scene in his character as father of a thriving family. Moreover, Mom's smile now shone on him with a greater radiance than ever before, or so at least I heard from Flinksy. Certainly Mom regarded Racer and the four grandsons he had given her with more favour and fondness than she bestowed on any of her other children or grandchildren.

The decade of his thirties saw Racer scale the peak of his many-faceted success in Milltown and reach the acme of his personal triumph over our common past. It was during this period that Confederation took place, nor was Racer by any means the last to take advantage of the forward jolt in Newfoundland's economy brought on by this epochal event.

All at once people had more money to spend, or to make payments with. What better way to help them dispose of their cash than to buy up rows of shacks all over amalagamated Milltown, even in Crow Gulch, and sell or rent them to local families or outport people who flocked into the town from their isolated villages now that the federal government had given them enough money to stir at last out of their boredom and misery?

The whole situation being a natural for any enterprising moneymaker with a bit of capital, Racer threw himself into it with zest and ferocity, and he came out of this boomtown scramble not exactly a rich man but one whose business and credit position all over the island were so solid that it would have taken almost a revolution to dislodge his foundations. Personal fame was added to his achievements by means of the very frequent occasions on which his picture and business advertisement appeared in the *Messenger* and was copied by all the other important papers from the capital city to Port-aux-Basques.

So it did seem that Racer at forty was sitting on top of the world, and from what I had heard in letters I was inclined to believe it; but I had heard the good about him in all its fullness through the reflected pride of a family success story, while only a hint or suggestion of the bad ever reached me in the distant parts I visited for many years. That was why it was such a shock to me when Racer walked into the kitchen that evening of my homecoming party and I saw a wheezy, belly-distended, semi-apoplectic man of a grossness of appearance that was distressing to contemplate, even if one had not known him in earlier days. The shine had gone out of his eyes too; they were now perpetually bilious, looking very much like a couple of blueberries stuck into a custard veined with strawberry flavouring.

My first thought on seeing him again after so many years was that I had never met a man who looked so utterly fed up, browned-off, and disgusted with the whole world — except of course the Old Man himself. The out-flowing, conquering geniality of Racer's youth had been replaced by a surly, suspicious manner that was compounded of the apparent need, amounting to a compulsion, to praise himself and at the same time habitually run down other members of the family.

What had happened to Racer, then? What was the worm in the bud that had eaten all the joy out of his success? Nobody knew for sure, not even Mom; but if nobody could tell me the cause of his private discontent, everybody could agree on the effects of this secret canker in Racer's life. In brief, he too had taken to the booze. At some point along the glory road, all the public and private successes of his career began to go sour, or at least failed to provide him with any satisfaction adequate to his efforts, unless he could regard them through the warm haze and in the heightened glow of alcoholic stimulation.

It had all started in the usual way, I was told, with an occasional social drink, business lunches where liquor was served, dinners at the Haven that went on until after midnight and became so boisterous that the Mounties had to come and cool the fuddled diners down and then drive most of them home or see that they got home in safety. The next step was the appearance of beer and hard liquor in Racer's home.

These unfortunate developments had come about since his marriage and his dramatic rise in Milltown's business and social life. From what I heard I gathered that his drinking had become much worse after he had been elected president of the Canadian Legion and got into a habit of spending all his evenings and most of Sundays at the Legion Hut, the most notorious booze-hole in a hard-drinking town. What horrified me personally was the news that Racer went so far as to drink three bottles of cold beer every morning for breakfast. Of course various members of the family had remonstrated with him in a friendly way, notably Mom and Flinksy, and even Ank, who was not quite as heavy a drinker as Racer, if only because he could not get his hands on the necessary money.

"You're spilin' your looks, Racer b'y," Flinsky had appealed to him more than once, gazing at his congested eyes and bloated body; and from time to time Mom had tried to reason with him in hopes of at least moderating his suicidal habit. But by the time such appeals had become necessary, Racer was already too far gone, it seemed, for anyone to reach or influence him on a personal basis. Certainly if Mom could not induce him to put a check on his drinking, nobody else in the family had much chance of doing so.

With tears in her eyes she told me, shortly after I came home, how one night he had come in, when she was alone in the house, already tight, but with a fresh bottle of Johnny Walker carefully cradled in his arm, his face and whole person darkened by the mournful remoteness they had taken on in recent years. That night he confessed to Mom in a maudlin way that he no longer had the will-power to resist the lure of the bottle.

"But why don't you try, my son?" she begged him. "You knows we'd all help you any way we could."

"I can't, Mom. I *can't*."

Although they had been alone with each other for more than two hours, they never really came any closer than that to their old trust and confidence, Racer finally taking refuge in his extra bottle and keeping on at it until Mom had to drive him home before Rhoda began to think she was encouraging him in his wicked and unmanly ways. The Old Man said nothing at all to Racer and not much to anyone else; he just took in the whole unfortunate situation as the years went by, grimly nodded his head, and waited for time to give Racer the chastisement that his whole way of life now deserved.

This then was the cruel, cardinal fact about Racer in

his middle age: He was a drunkard. When he arrived at my party I had suspected no such drastic thing, as his manner had been fairly quiet and he spoke to me in a pleasant, almost refined way. In general he appeared to have turned out more or less as I would have expected—save for the deplorable and incredible increase in his physical bulk. Only as the evening wore on and Mom's supply of beer ran out, sending Racer down to his own house for some real liquor, did I begin to have an inkling of the true situation with regard to him. The amount he drank and above all the gurgling, yearning way in which he sluiced the whiskey down his throat, immediately reaching for another once he had burped and felt the previous drink settle in his stomach, soon gave me an idea that booze was more to him now than money or sex or power, or anything else in the way of gratification that Milltown had to offer. Also, the fact that no one in all the family, not even Rhoda, tried to check him or reason with him suggested that his alcoholism had long since been accepted by them all as an incurable evil.

Still more painful than Racer's private fall and consequent physical grossness was the manner in which the coarseness of physical fibre seemed to have passed into his moral nature, his character, as well. I had always known that in his mind there were large areas of insensitivity that to anyone who suffered from them seemed very much like mental cruelty, but I was not prepared for the nastiness that came out of him once or twice during our family reunion.

When he won at cards he was pleasant enough, emitting a wheezy asthmatic laugh that sounded and smelt as if a few gallons of all the liquor he had recently drunk were permanently lodged in his lungs and gullet. When he lost, and Racer was a man who took losing at anything so hard you would have thought someone had rasped his skin to the bone, it was a different story. The first time this happened he glared contemptuously at Fudge, who by crossplaying had been the cause of Racer going in the hole, and grated out, "Dat t'ing! He's the one done it. Mom, go out and get a ole dog and put it there in his place, for Christ-sake."

I was amused at the way his careful realtor's English was totally forgotten and our childhood *patois* rushed back into his mind when he was heated with whiskey and anger, but Fudge seemed unaware of this side of the present situation; he shoved his head down into his hands, scratched his scalp, and sighed like a man fighting for time and self-control. In a little while he came up for air, with his face brick-red, little globules of sweat at his hair-line, and his large chin trembling like that a of a stricken child.

"When you speaks to me," he warned Racer with a certain dignity despite his careful and rather pompous language, "kindly speak in terms of *men*, not t'ings – or dogs eeder. I would appreciate it if you didn't forget that."

Though Racer laughed self-consciously and pooh-poohed Fudge for being so touchy, I could see that Fudge's protest had taken some effect and was likely to restrain Racer somewhat in his drunken attacks on our youngest brother's card sense, human qualities, and want of emotional maturity. Perhaps Fudge's height and weight had something to do with it too. It was clear also that Fudge did not really enjoy the card game after this incident, for he soon became rather listless and seemed to be just going along with the game and all its ups and downs for the sake of putting in the time.

Later that same evening there was an incident with Crawfie that to my mind again showed Racer in a poor light. The contributing circumstances were much the same as in Fudge's case, with Racer again going in the hole and this time blaming Crawfie for his ignominious defeat. Crawfie defended himself with all the force of his agile tongue. Racer again lost his temper, and as usual the quarrel rapidly turned into a contest of personal abuse instead of remaining a debate on the playing of a particular hand.

"Go waaaay, b'y," Racer denounced Crawfie with a final

devastating remark, "*you're* not wort' talkin' to a-tall. Even a bitch wouldn't leave her own pups."

This reference to Crawfie's shortcomings as a father had some power of truth behind it, but we all felt that Racer was guilty of very bad taste in throwing it up in Crawfie's face at this time in front of the whole family, in-laws and all. Crawfie himself was jarred by Racer's bitterly scathing remark, and I saw by his wobbly, vindictive smile and the whole set of his hollow, treacherous countenance – symptoms, one might say, so familiar to me from our childhood days – that if ever Racer's back were turned and Crawfie happened to have a knife in his hand, some throwing might very well be done. For the present there was no sequel to Racer's attack.

Even I, the long-departed and in a sense the prodigal son, was not to escape censure and abuse from Racer at my own party and likewise in the presence of three generations. When the game was over and we had settled in to our cup of tea, the conversation moved from the cards onto more general topics, so it was only natural that the limelight should fall on me for a moment as I gave a sketch of my doings over the past few years. From all sides came sympathetic enquiries and friendly or at least not hostile reactions as I skimmed uneasily over the years and tried to get out of the spotlight as soon as I could.

The truth was that I had not much to show, or to tell, that would impress my present audience, which gave Racer a pivot on which to turn his attack on me. What seemed to trouble him chiefly was my failure to make money, my approach to the age of forty without any cash in the bank or real property to give me substance and status in some community.

"My Christ, b'y!" Racer came down on me in an elder-brother tone that I found both embarrassing and infuriating, "my Christ! A fella with all your education, and *still* only a bum."

"Here!" Mom struck in reprovingly. "Don't you call your

brother names like that. You leave Juju alone. Leave un *alone*, I said," as Racer drew breath for a fresh onslaught.

"Yes," Flinksy added. "Juju got his own ideas, and he's entitled to them, I s'pose, same as you and me. Besides, he don't owe you any money, do he?"

Not troubling to answer Flinksy at all, or Mom, Racer laughed in an ugly choking way suggesting his private opinion not only of educated bums but of any man who lets himself be defended by women. He concluded his remarks to me in this fashion: "You ought to be ashamed o' yourself – that's all I got to say. And I says it right to your face, what everyone else is only thinkin'. Jesus, man, if I'd a had your education I'd a owned the half o' this island now, and not just a good slice o' Milltown. What in the hell's flames are you waitin' for? You're not a b'y, not young any more, you know."

Stung by his stupidity, I began to answer that if I was waiting for anything, it was for something worth doing and not just a blind accumulation of money and clutching at power; that I preferred poverty in freedom to wealth in business, leisure to luxury. But as I went on talking I was gradually discouraged by the dull stare of incomprehension or incredulity in Racer's eyes. Clearly it would be useless trying to explain my position to such an unreceptive, beer-sodden, Milltown-shackled mind; anything that rose above or moved out from under the local criterion of achievement and success would be Greek to him.

Racer just gave me up with a farting sound from his loose lips. "Agh!" he added finally. "Don't gimme that kind o' fancy bullshit. I haven't got no college education, but I graduated from that crap twenty years ago."

My fury at Racer's present attitude toward me was only temporary, as it was swallowed up in my passionate curiosity to find out what had happened to him. I could hardly begin to imagine or to fathom what events or experiences or recurrent obsessive thoughts had transformed the shining youth into this caricature of a successful but discontented and obviously disillusioned bourgeois of forty-three. Even the most casual observer could have seen from the ill-timed and quite gratuitous nature of his insults that these were merely a projection of some deep-seated anger he harboured against himself.

In the days that followed my party, I often spoke to Mom about Racer, trying to get some clue to his unfortunate development and what seemed to me the tragedy of his life. I thought that if Racer had confided in anybody it would be Mom, however secret she might keep the confidence, but in her now habitually grief-stricken way she assured me that Racer hardly ever came into the house any more, drunk or sober, and that she could tell me little more about his inner life than I already knew from letters and my own current observation. The only new fact she gave me was that his drinking had increased in direct proportion to his prosperity, had finally outstripped even that, and had lost all reference to it by becoming an end and an obsession in itself.

Was it the double strain and responsibility of business and family life that had driven Racer to the point where he could hardly take a single step in his daily life without the crutch of alcohol to support him? Somehow I doubted it. True, he had worked like a slave in the early years of building up RAYMOND STONE REAL ESTATE, and his five boys took some looking after and controlling, but other men in Milltown with fewer advantages than Racer had survived and were surviving much greater strain without taking refuge in the booze.

Besides, he did not work so very hard any more, often not getting to his office at all until Tuesday at noon, and leaving for the Hut every evening about six and after lunch on Friday. Apparently he had brought his business to such a degree of solidarity and smoothness that it could almost run itself and still bring in an abundant income with the aid of good salesmen and a reliable secretary. All hands in the family swore it could not go on for long, and some waited impatiently for the whole far-flung edifice of his business to crash in on Racer's head; none the less, it had gone on for several years now and the money was still coming to him in a steady stream.

Could it be that Racer's marriage had turned out badly, at least the side of it that the world never saw, and that brooding on this had sent him into the lonely world of the alcoholic? He had made a love-match under the most favourable circumstances, as everyone agreed, finding a life partner who could hardly fail to be a comfort and a credit to him in all the ways that a man could desire. Was he then suffering from the disillusionment that follows nearly all love-matches, or had he gone sour simply through the gradual erosive process of disenchantment which dogs all men into middle age and was bound to come down most heavily on a youth such as Racer had been?

In my eagerness to solve the mystery of his decline I thought of having a friendly confidential talk with Rhoda, but when I mentioned this idea to Mom she immediately tried to steer me away from it. Why, I asked, was she so insistent that I should not stick my nose in? Well, Rhoda might take it the wrong way; or Racer might hear of it, get dirty, and start a fuss with me; or other members of the family might be brought in and a big racket started all round. I could see right away that these generalities and excuses were only stalling on Mom's part. I pressed her and kept at her for the truth, which at last she gave me with (I thought) a little relish along with her reluctance.

"She's just as bad as him, sure." Mom came out plainly with it, though at first I was not sure of her meaning.

"What! Rhoda?"

"Drinks like a fish, my son." My mind now shot back once more to Racer's wedding and all the generous tributes that had been paid to the bride's looks and fair promise for the future. So this was how it was all ending. Rhoda a boozehound too. From what I gathered, once Mom's tongue was loosened, this made another heinous tale and was a separate tragedy in itself. The definite estrangement between Racer and Rhoda had begun of course with his heavy drinking and had proceeded with all the traditional stages that divide a man and his wife: a thousand meals cooked and thrown out by Rhoda because Racer never came home to eat them; the entire burden of raising the children shoved off on her; her rebellion as a woman; Racer's buying a share in a whore subsidized by three or four of the leading businessmen in the town; his consequent spending of a good many nights down in Crow Gulch; and his ultimate arrival at the point where he and Rhoda hardly ever spoke to each other at all except in irritation and mutual contempt.

At last, in desperation, or perhaps in a blind panic over the thought of losing her husband altogether, Rhoda had thrown in her hand and begun to drink too. At first it was just a temporary escape from her heart-crushing misery and the monotony of her neglected existence, but these intervals of relief were so sweet after her long struggle with Racer, and worry, that soon she was longing to extend them into a lasting forgetfulness. Perhaps she thought that in the warmth and sentimental glow of their intoxication she might begin to draw close to him again.

Rhoda concentrated on gin, and soon the word went around the family and the hill of how the liquor controller's truck drew up outside her back door once a week and delivered her gin not by the bottle any more but by the case. Her pathetic and desperate idea did not bear fruit, however, so far as Racer was concerned; he railed at her all the more for being so unfeminine as to get soused, even in the privacy of home and in front of the children. Instead of bringing man and wife together, her drinking only alienated Racer to the further point where he bought another TV and often sulked with it and his bottle down in the children's basement playroom several nights a week and well into the early morning, while Rhoda sat upstairs with her gin and watched the same programs on the house TV until she passed out from exhaustion or plain drunkenness.

That was what their marriage and home life had come to, and the tale was written as clearly on Rhoda's face and body, though in a different way, as on Racer's. In the Old Man's phrase, she now looked like "a gutted fish"; her once plump figure seemed to have fallen in on itself, her eyes were haggard as hell, and about her entire person there clung an aura of long-endured misery and settled wretchedness that would have better suited a gaunt widow of sixty than a well-to-do matron with a good home and five robust children to her credit.

In her daily routine Rhoda had gone completely slack. There were no regular family meals at all now, the children living out of the fridge mostly, and there was no discipline in the home whatever, which again left the kids on their own, thinking who-knows-what thoughts about their parents' boozing and cat-and-dog manners toward each other.

It turned out that I did eventually have a brief talk with Rhoda, or rather she with me, that gave me some further knowledge of her true state of mind. One day I dropped idly into her kitchen and sat down to pass an hour or so over a cup of coffee. It so happened that on this morning Racer had hauled himself out of bed and gone off to the court house to pay a fine for reckless driving, and Rhoda's comment when she had finished telling me all this about Racer was somewhat revealing.

"That's just like him, Juju. I just don't know what to do with him. Everybody calls him a successful man, but you know the truth is he has no sense of responsibility at all – not in his private life. I'm frightened to death all the time that his private life is going to catch up with him in business and we'll all be on the rocks. He's forty-three now, and he still thinks he got to be a young sport and run around with the b'ys every night of the week just like when he was twenty. Well, if he don't care, why in the hell should I? You want to know how I really feel, Juju? I'll tell you: I just don't give a *god*-damn, and that's the truth." Her tone implied the words "about anything," and for so young a woman they held an unforgettably disgusted quality – an end-of-the-tether bitterness.

But all this took me little further in my attempt to understand Racer, since I held the view that he as father and titular head of the home was mainly responsible for this domestic havoc instead of having been driven into it by his present wretchedness. There could be no doubt that Racer too felt wretched. A mere glance at his face in all its gloomy wrath was enough to prove that. Each time I took that glance my mind again went back to Racer as he was on that day he left home to go off to war. I knew pretty well what he had been, up to that time; then what else had happened after that to turn him into what he now seemed to be? I thought of my own wartime service in the Navy and the education in human bestiality provided by life in the lower ranks; and I had been only a dry-land sailor, a Sick Berth Attendant, a chancre bo'sun, as it was called, whereas Racer had been a fighting soldier dragged or driven through six whole years of the war in Europe, Africa and Italy.

Had it all been such a shock to him at the time that it preyed on his mind ever afterwards, leaving him with little or no faith in man's decency and no hope at all for a good life as one of such a sordid mass, however much he might achieve in a private and personal way? It was a possible though partial answer, and yet one that I did not find convincing as a reason for his later taking to the booze. There were too many men of our generation, even right here in Milltown, who had managed to withstand the reverberations of wartime horror in their minds while yet remaining sober; and Racer could not be considered one of those delicate, sensitive spirits who became pathological cases because they could not forget the horror and the blood.

I felt that I must again come nearer home if ever I were to find a satisfactory answer to the riddle of his inward collapse. Could it be simply boredom, a sort of Alexander-the-Great feeling that he had achieved all there was to achieve in Milltown, which now to his grief and chagrin offered him no more worlds to conquer? And had the conquests to date been really worth-while to him? If all this were so, why then did he not move to the mainland where there were new and limitless fields to conquer in the world of real estate? Racer did not even show any sign of moving down off the hill and into the townsite, but wherever he chose to live there could be no question of his success in the terms that Milltown whole-heartedly accepted and approved. And still disillusionment was written in every listless fold of his face. When he was not on his guard and holding up his body and chins, he looked as sad as Lucifer.

I had another glimpse into his real state of mind one day when he picked me up in his car as I was walking back home from the library and we had a brief sober conversation on the subject of life. "You know, it's time you started facing facts, Juju b'y," he began more or less amiably, while yet glancing critically over my somewhat shabby clothes and silently disapproving my whole casual manner in the face of his brotherly advice. "You're not young any more, you know."

"What facts?" I said, determined to ignore the tiresomeness of his second remark.

"What facts? Christ, man, you're not *gettin'* anywhere."

"I'm not acquiring things?" I replied with a touch of the stubborn idealism that nobody at home could understand and everybody smiled at behind my back. "Like a wife and kids, a house and money in the bank? I have my mind on other things, some of them not available here in Milltown."

"That's all there is, b'y. Can't you see that? That's all there *is*." But Racer said this fretfully, just as though he were saying it with only one part of his mind, the other part demanding a refutation of his words. I was reminded too of Ank's well-known views on this general subject and his emphatic way of expressing them: "You *lives*, you *dies*, and that's all of it."

"What other things?" Racer demanded petulantly. "What else is there?"

"I don't know."

"Well there! Like I said, you're only goin' on with your bullshit again. Fancy words. What do you keep on like that for when you nor nobody else really knows if there *is* anything else?" He was getting angry now. "What's the difference between you and me, when you come right down to it?"

"Well, I'm willing to spend my life trying to find out what else. That's the difference."

"Agh!" Racer treated me again to his elder-brother growl of impatience and took no pains now to hide his opinion of me as a fool. We were both relieved when we reached his place and immediately went our own ways again, he to his liquor and I to my books. It was hard for me to judge how much boredom had entered into and caused Racer's misery because I had never suffered from that awful disease, not for long.

My time in the Navy was followed by five years at the University of Toronto at the expense of the government, a change that I came to regard as my ascension from hell into heaven; never again in the future was I to experience the priceless boon of leisure sweetened by relief from money cares and absolute freedom of thought. College life gave me new ideas or "high notions," as Milltown viewed them, and it gave me also expensive tastes while at the same time rendering me unfit to earn the money that would gratify them; but those five blissful years provided me above all with a fund of intellectual sustenance – a built-in supply store, as it were – from which I could draw and comfort myself no matter how intense my solitude later became or how meagre and uncertain my physical diet.

Perhaps, after all, the grinding materialistic horror that was our hometown had much to do with Racer's plight and the terrible prospect of his future as an alcoholic invalid. Would he have been different, and in better case now, had he cleared out of the Hell-Hole and both deepened his mind and broadened his vision at an earlier age? That was doubtful. He had made a good many business trips to the mainland, as far afield as Banff, and had had abundant opportunities of glimpsing greener pastures and appreciating a more variously human way of life than Milltown could show; yet it all seemed to have made no difference. As far as I could see, Racer at his present age was as deeply and viciously impregnated with the village virus as he had been before he ever set foot outside of Milltown for the first time in his life.

Hours and hours I spent as the days passed and the total picture of Racer's development was revealed to my mind, contemplating its strangeness and seeking the reasons for his failure as a man. One might have thought from the boastful pride he took in his monthly income that it was simply money that had corrupted him. Not so. It was quite clear, if we could judge by the way he and Rhoda wasted it, that Racer also held his money in contempt and took no real satisfaction in it at all. That seemed to be the way with everything in his life: fatherhood, social position, pull with the police, his family cottage up on the Humber River, and his whore down in Crow Gulch – none could be enjoyed without the preliminary of a bottle, and all were maintained with a coarse pride that reeked of immodesty. And all partook of this dual valuation with which Racer seemed to look on everything in his life. The self-esteem he derived from them was balanced and cancelled out by an equal disgust, and poor Racer was left wandering in a no-man's-land of nothingness where the sting of liquor was the only immediate consolation he could find and its promise of oblivion his only hope.

I had one genuine clue as to the cause of his state on an unfortunate occasion when most of us once again assembled at our house to mark a family milestone. This took place some time after I had returned home, and so I was able to consider Racer's outrageous behaviour in the light of all I had heard and the personal knowledge I had gained about him in the meantime.

The occasion was Dad's seventieth birthday, for which none of us felt any great reason to rejoice but which at Mom's instigation we decided to recognize with a little family party as usual. As Mom reminded us, the Old Man was getting so childish that if we did not mark the occasion with some kind of good-will gesture, in addition to the few presents some of us gave him, she would be blamed by him for our neglect and would never hear the last of it.

Racer did not show up for the party until our game of cards was over and we men were sitting around in the front room waiting for our cup of tea. When he did make his appearance, he bore no gift and neither spoke any good wishes nor shook Dad's hand. Racer came in supporting himself against doorpost and wall, and it was plain to us all right away that he was stewed to the gills. I saw Rhoda give him a glare of revulsion mixed with a hint of fear, and turn away. She had not brought any of her gin to the party.

Ignoring her, Racer let his eye roam over the rest of us as he slouched in an aggressive yet mournful pose against the mantelpiece. Meanness was in that bloodshot eye, and an extreme nervous irritability amounting to perversity. We could see that he was bent on being unpleasant, but I think none of us was quite prepared for the volley of nastiness that came out of him. As always, Crawfie, Fudge, and myself seemed to be the prime objects of his loathing. "Bunch o' lazy, ungrateful, scrounging bastards," he muttered thickly at us, his words barely articulate but his meaning and intention only too clear. Crawfie and Fudge were feeling high themselves by this time, and so may not have taken in the insult. As for myself, I was cold sober, and after the strain of a full family gathering with four hours of card-playing just behind us, I was not in a mood to misunderstand or bypass any reflection on myself from one whom I had come to view as a pop-eyed, tub-of-guts, oafish nincompoop. I opened my mouth to tell Racer so, but the Old Man forestalled me.

"Here! You got no right to be takin' it out on them, just

'cause you're after gettin' loaded again." He was already boiling over with indignation because Racer had either ignored or forgotten the celebration of his birthday. "At least they come here a decent hour and acted half civilized. That's more than you done, wit' all yer money. So don't go comin' in here and layin' into them. You got no right, I say."

"No right, haven't I?" Racer drooled a little but pushed his body upright and became dead serious. "That's what you t'inks. Well, I got a diff'rent idea. I got a position to keep up in this town, a reputation; and *them* three, by Jesus, they're enough to drag down a saint. And that's a fact. No respect for nobody. I'll tell you anudder fact: they're a disgrace to the name I got built up in this town."

The Old Man was disposed to go on with the argument, but suddenly, when it dawned on me with absolute clarity that Racer regarded Crawfie and Fudge and myself as an embarrassment to his dignity and status in Milltown, that he believed us capable of saying or doing anything likely to bring more shame on the Stone family than he had already brought on it himself – when I realized all this my anger suddenly dissolved and I rushed into the bathroom to give vent to my laughter. The Old Man did not see it my way at all, as I knew the minute I returned to the front room and was plunged back, if only as an amused spectator now, into their quarrel.

"Better you'd do somet'ing about yerself, 'stead o' criticizin' udder people," the Old Man was saying. "And regard o' respect, I'm after livin' seventy years in this world now, and I can swear I never saw any man that calls hisself a man behave wit' less respect to his own fawder – than you. Lower than the beast. That's what you are. You got a holt o' the bottle, and you lowered yourself lower than the beast."

At this challenge Racer advanced with a ponderous, jolting attempt at dignity, stood over the Old Man and let his malice pour down on him unrestrainedly. "Seventy years, hey? By Christ, that's long enough for any man to live, specially an old bugger like you." All of us were shocked by the suddenness of the onslaught.

The Old Man gasped and started to struggle out of his chair, but even as he thrust himself upward a muddy pallor overspread his face like dirty water rising up from his heart instead of blood; he gave another gasp and fell back clutching at his chest in agony. Racer did not seem to take any notice, or else he saw the effect of his attack but chose even now not to check this outpouring of long-suppressed hate. His eyes were glistening from the overflow of the liquor in him, or perhaps it was with tears, as he bent over the Old Man and eased himself of his feelings in a brief passionate flood.

"You *pounded* us, by the sufferin' Jesus. You pounded us, when we were small, just like we were made out o' wood or iron instead o' flesh and blood. You went into your rages and your tantrums, and you put the fear o' God into us day and night, Sunday and Monday – it made no goddam diff'rence to you. And now you're an old man and can't get away with it, you expects us to come crawlin' up to you and *congratulatin'* you because you're just as crooked as ever you were but haven't got the stren't' to pound us any more. Well, all I can say is – you got some hopes, far's *I'm* concerned. Some *goddam* hopes, that's all." And with that, Racer stumbled out through our front room heading blindly for whatever refuge or security he could find in his own home next door.

CHAPTER

4

CRAWFIE

As for Crawfie, there seemed no end to the saga of his troubles nor to the expedients and crimes by means of which he struggled to escape from the net of his own weaving. It was a dark enough day on that Christmas morning so long ago when Crawfie bundled himself and his bride out of our house in a storm of self-justification and defiance of the Old Man, but many years were to pass before anything like a brighter day was to ease his path in life.

Having quit his teaching post in Flowery Cove and severed all relations with the Old Man, Crawfie eventually got another school, in Milltown itself, and seemed in a fair way to prove that he could get along without depending on or being beholden to anyone in the world. It was multiplying worries and responsibilities that held him back – the birth of his first son less than a year after marriage, then another child each year for the next five years regardless of his static salary and his wife Eunice's uncertain health.

Money troubles were probably the original cause of his own poor health and chronic migraine headaches. He began to slide into debt, and in those days still retained enough sense of responsibility to worry over it; also, Eunice soon began to show the mental as well as the physical strain of caring for five babies and a rowdy older boy on the fantastically inadequate income of a poorly qualified teacher. Crawfie never had a home of his own, being obliged to drag his wife and large family from one rented place to another

233

year after year as he changed schools, though he always managed to find a position somewhere in the Bay of Islands. All in all, his professional and domestic life must have been a series of nightmares during those early years of his married life. In the Second World War he saw a hope of escape from all his bondage by enlistment, and the story as we heard it was that Crawfie had in fact offered himself for ground crew in the Air Force and later for the Army and Navy, but in each case had been turned down on account of his weak eyes.

So there he was, trapped in a dirty hovel with six hungry, screeching children and nothing in his future, so it appeared to him, but a great deal more of the same misery. Whenever he contemplated his plight, Crawfie very nearly gave way to despair. Somehow he managed to carry on through the first few years, but it was known that he was paying the price in a sinister slackening of his moral fibre. Debts came to be ignored, money borrowed (until people learned to beware of him), and it was not long before Crawfie developed a habit of gypping anybody he could out of any sum he thought he could get away with short of going to gaol. As Hilda put it in one of her letters to me, his name was soon "all over Milltown," but this fame was more a sordid notoriety than any sort of credit to him.

He too tried booze as a relief from his misery, from the hideous impasse that his position in life had become in so short a time. In spite of his wobbly constitution and the pangs of migraine, Crawfie unexpectedly had a head of iron where the liquor was concerned. He could down a pint of rum or a large case of beer within two hours or so and show no ill effects beyond a more noticeable vagueness in his eyes behind their distorting lenses, or a solemnity more pronounced than usual in his whole manner. He could never achieve even a temporary forgetfulness on the quantity of liquor he managed to bum or buy or borrow.

If Crawfie himself was not able to break out of his prison, his temper was under no such restraint; it showed more clearly, and more dreadfully, as his position gradually worsened than it had ever done in his childhood and passionate youth. For the most part he managed to keep his fists off his infants, but the same could never be said for his unlucky wife, who was frequently seen on the hill and around Humber Heights with a messy black eye or even worse injuries.

She had neither the physical strength to defend herself nor the good sense to make some formal complaint against Crawfie with a view to having him restrained and bound over to keep the peace in his home. And so she went on suffering and becoming a litttle more self-enclosed and neurotic as the years of their married life dragged on. Since Crawfie lacked the insight to see, or was prevented by his ferocious vanity from seeing, that it was his own folly which had brought about the marriage in the first place, all his wrath over its sequel came down on the head of his wife. Utterly failing in the searing test of character that every marriage becomes, Crawfie let loose on her all the violence of his nature, "calling her down to the dirt," threatening to drive her back to Flowery Cove, and ultimately clubbing her into total submission to his will.

In the year 1949, when Eunice told him she was going to have another baby, Crawfie's fury reached such a crisis that he very nearly murdered her on the spot. On that occasion the police did come, called by neighbours who heard Eunice and the children screaming, and Crawfie was forcibly saved from criminal proceedings. Later on he did in fact make an effort to burn down their rented house while the kids were all away from it and Eunice was sleeping inside.

She survived; but the shock of what Crawfie had done and the fact that she had barely escaped seemed at last to be too much for her. Her mind began to give way; she was eventually reduced to a chronically blubbering mass of self-pity and fear, quite unfit to manage the house or handle the kids or even look after herself in her advancing pregnancy. Crawfie acted with furious energy. He seized the chance to have her removed to an institution on the grounds that in her incompetent state she was a menace to the other children. That was what he plausibly wrote down on his application for Eunice's committal, and the medical and welfare authorities who examined and interviewed Eunice in her home could hardly deny the truth of it. Not long after this, Eunice was taken away as a provisional and temporary patient to the Mental Hospital in St. John's, known and dreaded all over the island simply as the "Mental." There her child was born dead, and there she herself remained permanently as one of those border-line cases who were not at all insane or even suffering from any distinct malady but yet were obviously incapable of coping with life outside the walls.

Crawfie lifted his head and squared his shoulders like a man relieved of an intolerable burden, and to those of our family with whom he was still on speaking terms, he announced that as far as he was concerned Eunice was now dead. Everybody frowned at this, but at least it was expected that from now on Crawfie would do the sensible thing by hiring a housekeeper, giving his children some kind of a steady home, and in general trying to get back on his feet again in every way. Not a bit of it. Having disposed of his wife, Crawfie now set about disposing of his children. His first try was a total success when he legally gave his eldest boy to Racer and Rhoda — who were still childless at this time and could certainly give the boy a better home than he would ever know with Crawfie — but the moment Crawfie began trying to place the second child with Hilda and Rome, also still childless, and the family realized what he was up to they all drew back and closed in to form a circle of resistance to his scheme.

Hilda and Rome refused point-blank, and the Old Man had his revenge for Crawfie's declaration of independence on that memorable Christmas Day; he did not, however, instantly say no to Crawfie's request that Mom and Dad should take one of the kids; he kept Crawfie dangling and sucking up to him with the adoption papers in his hand and hemmed and hawed for months like an irresolute judge, while having no more intention of letting Mom sign the papers on his behalf than he had of giving Crawfie a straight answer himself.

At last Crawfie flew into a rage one night when the whole plan was being chewed over once again at home, and as a climax to his frustration he vigorously invited the Old Man to go fuck himself, if he was going frig around like that, because Crawfie couldn't stand it a day longer. This time the Old Man made no verbal or violent reply at all, merely sitting back with arms folded and a cold half-smile on his lips to watch Crawfie gathering up his tattered papers and storming out of the house again with a final farewell curse in his mouth.

This defeat drove Crawfie to a scheme for the wholesale disposal of his other children. Somehow he learned that the Church of England Orphanage in St. John's took in children of their faith if one of the parents was dead or quite incapacitated as a parent, and he made so good a case out of Eunice's mental illness and committal that in no time at all the five young children were shoved aboard the eastbound express with cards in their lapels directing them to their new home in St. John's. They all remained in the Orphanage until they were old enough to go out to work on their own, receiving no help or support and hardly any communication at all from Crawfie other than a card at Christmas for each of them and a present of one dollar bill apiece.

Thus Crawfie was at last free again, though there were rumours and signs that he was not leading the sober and continent life that our family and public opinion expected of him after the series of disasters he had been through and the questionable recoveries he had made. His teaching career continued, though he was now a marked man, doomed never to pluck one of the administrative plums in the Department of Education at St. John's. Nor was his character raised in official Milltown eyes after rumours began that he was carrying on with another woman and even spending nights and whole weekends with her at a cheap hotel on the West Side.

The result was that he was not invited back to the school on Humber Heights for the next academic year, after which his only recourse was to look for another school in some out-of-the-way place, similar to Flowery Cove but not quite so barbarous, where his reputation was not known, or perhaps would not matter in a place that had difficulty hiring any teacher at all. It was relatively easy for him to find such a post in Isle-au-Mort, a few frame houses huddled together on kelpy boulders near the town of Port-aux-Basques; and once he had gone there family feeling was that in his career Crawfie was no further ahead than when he had started out teaching some years previously. The chief difference was that this time he committed the incredible folly of taking his west-side woman along with him to Isle-au-Mort and passing her off as his wife.

It was not long before the inevitable happened: a travelling salesman from Milltown who knew Crawfie and all his history penetrated to Isle-au-Mort and, taking in the situation at a glance, reported to the parish clergyman in Port-aux-Basques that one of his teachers was living common-law. The clergyman got in touch with his bishop, who got in touch with the Department in St. John's – and in a matter of days Crawfie was dismissed from his position without warning and with no right of appeal. Later he was struck off the Anglican Teaching List for the entire Province of Newfoundland.

His means of livelihood gone, and his old yearning for the church now quite dead, Crawfie came back to Milltown with hardly a dollar in his pocket and no prospects in life whatsoever. His first act was to set up house with his mistress, on credit, and start living openly with her no matter what the family or anyone else might say. It was this act more than anything else that alienated the family from him, and when they all heard that Crawfie was once more to become a father bitterness broke out with all the intensity of which our crowd was capable.

Whenever the Old Man referred to "dat ole bag" now (meaning Crawfie's woman), he pronounced her name, which was Moira, in a long-drawn-out, savage way, exaggeratedly Irish and horribly expressive of his hate. Irish was in all our eyes equivalent to Roman Catholic, of course, and this was Crawfie's real offence – that he had taken up with such a one and was beginning to breed on her in his former prolific way. The mere thought that any grandchild of his, even a bastard, should be born of a Roman Catholic mother was in itself enough to send the Old Man into one of his epic obscene rages. When the child was born and immediately disposed of to the local Roman Catholic Orphanage, he declared Crawfie to be no longer a son of his.

"Shore!" he cried out at Mom, who was also scandalized by the whole affair but not so bitter about it. "Let the priests grab it. The more they gets their hands on, the better they likes it. One more Catleek and one less Protestant. But it better not have my name. No sir! It never will. If ever I hears the little bugger is called Stone I'll go to court, so help me Christ! I'll have it changed over to somet'ing else if it's the last t'ing I ever does in this world, and drains me dry. If it takes every cent I got in the world, I'll do it."

When Crawfie and Moira produced another son the following year, likewise "snapped up" by the priests, even the Old Man gave up his cursing and yelling and more-or-less settled down like all the rest of the family to regarding Crawfie as a hopeless case.

Crawfie himself realized at last that something must be done, if only because of his desperate financial state, and in his need he resorted to contraceptives that could be medically relied on. Later when I heard the whole story I wondered how he had been able to persuade Moira to consent to any such thing in spite of their domestic circumstances; but of course she had already violated religious as well as social law by going to live with Crawfie in the first place, and in any case Crawfie literally forced contraception on her, threatening to sling her out altogether and send her back to her implacably hostile family if ever she dared to become pregnant again.

That was the situation with regard to Crawfie when I returned home after my thirteen years' absence. He and Moira were still living together all by themselves in what was little more than a shack located just in over the brow of the hill. In his present social relationship to the family and his status in Milltown, Crawfie could now be accurately described as *déclassé*. The area where he lived had not the sinister reputation of Crow Gulch, but it was definitely not nice and certainly not respectable. His nearest neighbours were a released murderer, a crazy old woman who told fortunes by the cards, and two or three odd bachelor bums who had long since given up all hope of belonging to any Milltown social group whatever.

To avoid being sued for his debts and paying taxes, Crawfie had evolved a way of life whereby he worked only in the mornings, at a routine clerical job, while Moira had a similar job for the afternoons; and thus from one gliding year to the next they managed to live together without seeing much of each other except in bed or across the barrier of the TV. We all wondered how a sociable and talkative person like Crawfie could endure such an existence, but the fact was that his continual worries and agonies during his life with Eunice and the children had given him such a distaste for anything like racket or strife that all he desired now, it seemed, was to be left alone as much as possible. His chief and only real pleasure, apart from sex, was to settle down in his tiny front room after lunch with his case of beer close by (he could not afford hard liquor), put his feet up, and consume his quota of drink each afternoon while watching "Movie Matinee" on the TV.

With his recent history, and these details about his present mode of life in the front of my mind, I was especially curious to see Crawfie arrive at that party of mine. He came alone, as Mom had ruled that no matter what he did short of murdering his children Crawfie would always be welcome at home, but when it came to Moira – no. Mom wouldn't have her in the house, and that was all of it; and so I had an opportunity of observing Crawfie without being distracted by my equal curiosity about Moira.

He did not look happy; in fact, the mournful hollowness in his cheeks that had been so noticeable even in youth had now settled into a kind of morbidly hopeless look as of a man who had seen everything, experienced everything, and henceforth expected nothing. His distended beer-belly, a thing which I had come to think of as inseparable from middle age not only in our family but throughout Milltown, gave him no appearance of health or jollity, and I had an idea that this pervading air of bodily *malaise* extended again to the moral nature as well.

After settling in with Moira he had made one or two attempts to retrieve his fortunes and set himself up as a respectable if not universally respected citizen, but it was all no use. His name was mud, and when he learned that all his creditors would expect him to pay one hundred cents in the dollar plus accumulated interest over the years, he ceased all communication with them and fortified himself against legal attack by seeing to it that he had no assets in his own name that were attachable or of any great value. Crawfie just dug himself in with his woman and silently, lugubriously defied the sharks and hypocrites of Milltown and Newfoundland to do their worst.

Perhaps what finally broke his spirit was the upshot of his great scheme, only a year or two after the fiasco in Isle-au-Mort and the return home in disgrace, to clear off all his debts from St. John's to Port-aux-Basques in one master stroke and in addition leave Crawfie several thousand dollars to the good. This scheme was related to me with considerable relish by Mom, and amounted chiefly to the fact that one day Crawfie had found a French safe (used) in a pound of hamburger he bought at the Milltown Supermarket, and in his indignation and disgust had started out at once to return to the Supermarket and give the manager a piece of his mind. But along the way there flashed on him the thought that here was a possible source of quick and large-scale revenue. He would sue the supermarket (there must be something in the Food and Drug Act to clinch his case) and recover damages in proportion to the implied menace to his health, not to mention the outrage on his sensibilities.

Ten thousand dollars was the sum that instantly lodged itself in Crawfie's mind, a pleasant round figure that remained with him as his lodestar throughout all the journeys he made in and out of lawyers' offices as he eagerly pursued his case. The trouble was that none of the local men would touch a case against the supermarket, which was a company project, for fear of offending the mill manager and other high-ups in the town on whom their advancement in social prestige, and consequently in their careers, would ultimately depend. They put Crawfie off with abrupt legal jargon and succinct advice to drop the whole thing for his own good and that of everyone concerned.

Crawfie turned stubborn. As a last resort he took his evidence and his case to the local magistrates with the intention of launching a private prosecution with legal aid from the Crown, but when he realized that the magistrate too was going to reject his idea out of hand, he stormed out of the court house in a temper, declaring to anyone who would listen to him that in the Province of Newfoundland the law too, like the church and the teaching profession, was nothing but a goddam big bluff and a monstrous fraud.

By the time I met him again at my party, this painful experience and all such efforts to get his hands on some easy money were far behind him and he had lapsed into the rather remote and cloudy existence he and Moira led in their shack at some distance from all the rest of the family.

As in the case of Racer, I wondered why Crawfie had not pulled up stakes and hightailed it out of Milltown, especially after Confederation and the beginning of that great exodus to the mainland and flight from the nineteenth century which so many Newfoundlanders plunged into, following our leap into the Dominion of Canada.

Perhaps he was already a little too old in spirit to face the task of establishing himself in a new way of life. Whatever the reason, he clung now to the shabby security of his irregular *ménage* and seemed to take a sombre satisfaction in it at the same time that he was half-ashamed of it; at least his own place gave him a refuge from his conviction that we others were inclined to look down on him as a failure and a coward in the face of responsibility.

This I partly realized when like all the rest he invited me to come and visit him and Moira some evening for tea, because he put the invitation in a tentative, almost apologetic way as if he were half-afraid that I might instantly refuse or even be offended by his boldness. Of course I had no such idea in my mind and accepted at once. I noticed too that Crawfie made no reply beyond a sickly smile when Racer made that nasty remark about his treatment of his kids. In the old days there would have been bloodshed over a thing like that.

As for Crawfie's invitation, I myself was not so well-off in any way as to be justified in taking up a critical attitude toward his present home or his lack of status in Milltown. On arriving at his place one afternoon about four o'clock, I was greeted with a surface cordiality, found him installed as I had been led to expect with his case of beer, "Movie Matinee" finished but one or two bottles left, and sat chatting with him while he finished his case. I noticed when he sat down after receiving me that he clutched at his sacroiliac and lowered himself cautiously into the chair. "Me back is broke, Juju," he groaned by way of explanation.

"What's the matter?"

"I can't satisfy her."

"Moira?"

"Yes. Every night she wants it, and sometimes a nooner too. I don't believe *any* man could satisfy her."

"You did a pretty good job on Eunice," I said without any idea of being unpleasant; in any case Crawfie let it go without comment and rambled on about Moira's sexual appetite while I observed the room and was struck by the terrible barrenness of it – a puzzling inhumanity which I could not put my finger on until I realized that its chief cause was a complete absence of those family photographs and other mementoes or objects of sentiment that the living-room of almost any home in the world contains. A dreadful impersonality was the note of Crawfie's surroundings, in spite of some half-hearted, obviously feminine efforts that had been made to give them an air of comfort and domesticity.

In such an atmosphere Crawfie seemed no more wretched than Ank and Racer in their homes. He did not seem actively unhappy at all, as a matter of fact, but more like a man who has reached the ultimate harbour of disillusionment and there gathered about him whatever scraps of shelter and self-protection that he was able to filch from a treacherous universe. This came out clearly in a few remarks he made about his present set-up and "the wife." I listened to him with growing wonder and amazement.

"Here's how it is, see Juju? She can't get pregnant any more. I got that fixed. And we can't get married, of course, because Eunice is still alive. And I can't get a divorce either. I went to see the bishop about that once. Did you know?"

"No, I didn't."

"Oh yes. When Eunice went into the Mental. And do you know what he said to me, the soapy old bugger? 'Go back, my son,' he said; 'go back to your wife and try to love her.' *Try*! Allah's curse, Juju, how could anyone love a lunatic like her, and me after goin' through hell with her like I did? Flesh and blood could never stand it. Anyway –

no divorce. So like I said, Moira got no hold over me at all by law. I can fly off free as a bird any time I feel like it."

"Why don't you?"

"Oh, I didn't say I wanted to. It's just the idea of the thing, see?" As Crawfie ran on with all the loquacity of a lonely man and an outcast, my mind began to stray somewhat and even to find his conversation, which some people said was beguiling, more irritating than anything else. It seemed to me he had over the years developed a habit of pointless lying, and I found this even more exasperating than I used to find his abrupt little sniff of triumph when he had gained some point in the long game of our childhood rivalry. His tall tales lost some of their bite and force if you knew the true facts in his personal life on which they were based. I wondered how Moira could put up with them year after year; in truth, I wondered how she or any woman could have taken up with him at all with any knowledge of his record and then continued to live with him on Moira's present footing.

Part of the answer to this puzzle came unbidden when Moira arrived home from work and Crawfie introduced us. Observing her face, I could hardly restrain myself from exclaiming out loud. Crawfie had done it again! I saw at once that his concubine bore on her features and in her whole expression the very same dawny and stunned look that had become so familiar to us all in Eunice. Moira's eye had the very same wandering way which gave you the feeling that she was not wholly present in your company, and might be contemplating anything from instant flight to your assassination.

When Crawfie sent her off to her lean-to kitchen and she stayed there preparing a meal, I felt an urgent need to express my thoughts about her, but of course I could hardly do so to Crawfie himself, and with Moira only a few feet away; and so all through the meal I was only half-listening to Crawfie's monologues, preoccupied as I was with the mystery of their union and above all by its duration. I could not help feeling that only a part of the explanation was to be found in Moira's apparent limitations of intelligence and personality. Yet she proved each day that she was quite capable of earning a living on her own. What else was it then that kept her faithful to him on these unsavoury and quite disadvantageous terms of union?

Was it possible that she *loved* him? Moira had once been authentically quoted as saying that she would "follow Crawfie to the gates of hell," but that quotation came from the early days of their association. Somehow I felt certain that a discount would have to be made from it now. Was her remaining with Crawfie no more than the result of fear – a terror of the absolute loneliness she would have to suffer if she left him, and the disgrace she would have to bear in Milltown or anywhere else in Newfoundland once her story was known? That seemed to me a strong reason for their continuing together, but still not the strongest.

I decided after long pondering that it must be a sexual bond that was the real cement of their shacking-up and rather sordid union: It must be a simple case of their not being able to do without each other or at least without the regular satisfaction that each was able to give the other in bed, despite Crawfie's complaints about Moira being insatiable, and no matter how grotesque were their relations in other departments of daily life.

It was commonly remarked in the family that I was not only like the Old Man but also a little bit like Crawfie in some of his ways, but what a contrast I now found between us if I compared our sexual and personal histories! First there was the motive for marriage. God alone knew for sure why Crawfie had married Eunice down there in the arctic hell of Flowery Cove, whereas I was in no doubt at all as to the chief reason for my own marriage, which took place some time after I had finished college and when I was twenty-eight years old. I got married to still my sexual cravings and so be free to continue my intellectual life undisturbed. I assumed that Crawfie's reason could not have been the same.

Remembering the lubricous ease with which he had produced one child after another, I dwelt particularly on the pain and difficulties I had experienced in that very sphere in which Crawfie had proved himself so active and so very much at home. There was with me always, from the first night of the honeymoon onward, that cramping reluctance just at the moment of crisis. Always in my efforts at copulation there was the sickness before, and the sadness after; and eventually there came disgust, breeding a suspicion in my wife's mind that I did not really want any children at all. I myself did not understand my strange fear of launching life into this world, but nothing my agonizing wife found to say or do could take the fear away. As for the actual pleasures of sex, she was totally inhibited by my demand that she use a contraceptive at all times (I was one marriage ahead of Crawfie here) and by my finally informing her outright that I was simply not interested in increasing the population of Canada then or at any time in the future.

What could have been more different than Crawfie's experience and mine in these vital relationships? And in our subsequent actions too? Crawfie told me that when Eunice was taken away and he became in effect a bachelor, he had gone without a woman for almost two years, and yet I knew for a fact that during this period in his life, before he took up with Moira, he was to be found two or three nights a week making his way along the railroad track toward Crow Gulch, a bottle of Screech in one pocket and two or three French safes in the other.

This was a good instance of the pointless lying which Crawfie now indulged in and which irritated me so much, most especially as my confidence to him regarding my complete sexual abstinence, after my wife and I had separated, was the literal truth. I found it was almost impossible to have any real or satisfying conversation with a man like

Crawfie who habitually told you only as much as he wanted you to know.

So for the rest of that evening I listened to him more vaguely than before Moira had come, more and more lost in wonder at his complacent account of himself and his life during all the years since we had last met. My whole conception of the thing called conscience was revolutionized if not altogether destroyed by Crawfie in a few hours. Would a psychiatrist be able to explain him, I wondered, or to help him in any way? Somehow I doubted it.

I recalled how I myself had spent some time and money trying to dredge up my woes on a couch just after the breakup of my marriage (which Crawfie characteristically and infuriatingly assumed had come about through infidelity on my wife's part), and how after many sessions my psychiatrist had come up with the discovery that what I lacked was spontaneity. Before breaking off treatment I told him that I could have given him this information myself without ever lying down. Besides, it certainly did not apply to Crawfie, I reflected; it was not by any means the exact word to sum him up, as until quite recently all his actions had had about them a good deal of abrupt ruthlessness in their implementation. For all I knew his domestic life might still feature these elements. It was certainly clear that Moira was a submissive woman and easily bullied.

While walking back home that night I was still fiercely mulling over the puzzle of Crawfie's character and life story. More puzzling than even Racer's decline from glory was the reason for Crawfie's turpitude and also the question of how he had been able to get away with so much wickedness for so long a time without any of his misdeeds catching up with him or effectively checking his free passage through life. Was he simply a moral monster, some kind of a freak? That was the verdict of some people in Milltown and within our own family, but again this explanation did not satisfy me, perhaps because I knew at first hand the story of his early years and the struggle he had been obliged to carry on in such a family as ours. I knew too from personal experience what the atmosphere, the emotional temperature of our house divided had been, and so I scouted the conclusion that Crawfie was not to be held entirely responsible for all his misdeeds.

In my endless pondering over the collapse of my own personal life, I had evolved a phrase that seemed in some measure to account for my desolation: "chilled in childhood." Now I thought that in this general way perhaps Crawfie and I *were* alike. I wondered if he too had never entirely recovered from the arctic exhalations of the Old Man when we were quite young, never got far enough away from the chill to thaw out and become a whole-hearted man capable of a normal man's warmth and affections in the various relationships of his life. I also rejected the common idea that Crawfie gloried in his evil ways and felt no remorse at all for what he had done in the past. His deliberate movements and that faraway mournful look that never left his eyes, even while he was half tight, suggested to my mind his inner sorrow, and were an expression of this naturally gregarious man's longing to return from his isolation and exile to mingle with his family and the world again.

But I doubted if that would ever happen now. Habit and the relentless avalanche of the years had swept him into his present way of life, and there I saw him tragically doomed to remain until old age overtook him and from the dim past his own children rose up in their turn to curse him for the warmth and affection he had denied them in the helpless days of their childhood.

CHAPTER

5

HILDA

To pass from association with Ank, Racer, and Crawfie into the home and company of our sister Hilda was like sliding into a warm bath after long wandering through a cold, muddy swamp. By this time I had come to think of each of my family visits as a kind of quest, a search for the child I had known in my brothers and sister, and up to now I had had little success, beyond my own private speculations, in surmounting the barriers of time and change that separated me from all my elder brothers.

With Hilda it was happily different, though I was obliged to adjust my mind to the changes that the years had wrought in her too. But on the whole they seemed to be changes for the better – which was the more surprising in view of what we had all considered her undistinguished departure from home by her marriage to Rome Robinson. On that bleak day of her pathetic little wedding none of us dreamed that in middle age Hilda would have risen above all obstacles and above her own and her husband's limitations to a success in life far more genuine and impressive than anything we boys had achieved.

Where Hilda was concerned, the first thing I noticed among the family group was that she was the only one of us who had lived down her nickname. Nobody ever called her Flinksy any more, and I felt that this was an unconscious tribute to her character as well as an indication of the way in which each of us had followed his own path as the years passed and evolved a separate life that touched the others but rarely, and then with none of the rough and ribald intimacy we had known in childhood. To all of us she was Hilda now, and to the hill and Humber Heights and a good part of Milltown she was well known as Mrs. Robinson, a solid citizen in every sense of the word.

She and Rome had started out in life twenty years previously with nothing. He was a common labourer and she a store clerk of the lowest grade, and the two of them had hardly a word of learning to bless themselves with. As Ank was fond of putting it, they "didn't have a pot to piss in"; but each of them must have been desperately determined that such a scorned condition should not last very long. This may perhaps have formed the chief bond between them once the honeymoon mists had cleared away and they stood facing each other in the clear light of reality. I could well imagine them forming a joint passionate resolve to get ahead and redeem themselves from the low estimation they felt themselves to be suffering from inside their own families and in the eyes of the world.

Their first step was the decision that Hilda should keep on working after their marriage, a revolutionary and almost a disgraceful thing in the Milltown of that era, but despite all criticism they stuck to their plan and by means of fierce economies had soon saved enough money to buy the shabby little house they had rented at the time of their marriage.

Next came the conversion of their front room, facing the hill, into a candy, coke, and cigarette store which they ran by themselves on weekends, holidays, and in the evening. It was all done slowly, diffidently, no step being taken without cash in hand to cover it and a margin in the bank as well. But in a year or two the store was two rooms and required to be run on a full-time basis if they were to service all their customers with daily groceries on top of all the incidentals they were now handling.

The result was that Hilda could quit her job and work

only for herself and Rome, and the books soon showed that her profit far exceeded what her salary as a hired clerk had been. Though aching over all these years for a child, she forced herself to wait, devoting all her energy to the building up of the business, using every trick she had learned at the old company store and also rapidly acquiring a name as one who knew how to meet the public and satisfy all their needs and whims. Certainly she was most apt and in her element behind the counter where gossip and goods were retailed and so a double profit made, for it was just as important to find out who was good for credit as to keep the goods moving in and out of the store.

Several years passed in this way, with Hilda and Rome steadily driving on toward their desired haven of security-plus in the business world of Milltown. For them as for almost everyone else, the Second World War meant the shift into high gear for their business, following a sudden rise in both population through an influx of extra mill workers and prices through the over-all wartime boom. She and Rome plunged with all their young strength and deep resources into the local fight for quick and large profits, and they were not defeated.

Rome too left his job and attended to all the outside work of the business while Hilda remained behind her counter shovelling out the goods and raking in the cash in ever-increasing quantities. It was not long before the store took up all the house. Rome put in a basement apartment for their living quarters; they bought a truck for deliveries; taxes were evaded or minimized by means of an accountant and by sinking profits back into the business.

Before they quite realized it themselves, Hilda and Rome were running the biggest general store on the Heights. Real prosperity had come at last, and they revelled in it with a deep secret joy all through the week but especially after closing on Saturday night when they both settled down to the delicious task of totting up the week's profits and dreamed together of even greater wealth to come.

The end of the war brought some slackening in the pressure of business, though nothing that could be a source of worry to them or a threat to their established position with regular cash customers. They continued to make a fat living from the store and to swell the amount of those bank savings that were now a cause of much speculation throughout our family. Mom claimed to know for a fact that Hilda and Rome had fifty thousand dollars in the bank, an estimate always denied by Hilda in some irritation – with a coy smile that as good as said Mom might not be too far out in her busybody calculations of what sum exactly had been salted away.

Of course such a success could not have been won without the payment of a corresponding price in human terms. Hilda herself told me that formerly she and Rome used to be so harried and tormented by the strain and responsibility of it all that they sometimes began to growl and snap at each other like dogs. I learnt from her too how some nights on coming down from the store she was so tired she simply collapsed on the bed, clothes and all, and did not care much if she ever got up again. To my mind the heaviest price they had paid and the most fearful thing they had achieved was remaining in Milltown for twenty years without any real break or change of scene or long holiday of any kind.

Not so Hilda, whose profoundest fear had been that after some years of a childless marriage she might have to continue in that state while all around her the other family members produced their children, legitimate or otherwise, in easy abundance. All her money became trash and the sweet taste of security a sour abomination whenever such fears assailed her. Eight years in all she had to wait for a child, but finally she did come through with two boys who flourished from the day of their birth and gratefully filled out their mother's heart like water flowing into a potentially fertile but arid valley.

After the first birth, Hilda gladly made some changes in the pattern of her life. She hired a girl to tend the store and spent most of her own time downstairs, though after three or four days of maternal bliss she did sometimes find herself itching to re-enter the store just to check up on the stock, catch up with the gossip, and keep an eye on the new girl. Her days took on, however, a less hectic tempo, gradually piling up into years of quiet substantial living as her boys grew to school age and left her an odd hour or so when she could sit back and catch her breath after so many years of anxious and strenuous activity.

This was the comparatively placid way of life in which I found Hilda on my return home in 1961. When she came into the house on that night of my party, I unintentionally raised a laugh at her expense by remarking on how well she looked. As a matter of measurement, she was now a rival to Mom in her best days, admitting to one hundred and ninety-five pounds but probably sinking the scales at two hundred and twenty or more and providing the family, by her girth and her futile attempts at dieting, with another of its standing jokes.

It was no joke to Hilda – being incapable of gracing any clothes now that she could at last afford to buy whatever she fancied. The edge was thereby taken off her triumph over a miserable girlhood. That first evening on making my unfortunate remark I was also amused to observe that in spite of time and all changes in her circumstances Hilda blushed as readily as ever. It was delightful to be assured in this involuntary way that she had changed so little fundamentally.

One or two other things I noticed as well which struck me as more odd than amusing in a grown woman who had now been established in her own home and in complete independence for many years. I knew she smoked, but when I offered her a cigarette she shook her head with a puzzling admonitory grimace, at the same time sliding her eyes in an almost furtive way toward the head of the table where the Old Man was sitting. For me it was quite a shock to realize that she was even now afraid of smoking in front of him.

Then again while we all were saying goodnight I had an impulse, though none of us was by any means a demonstrative person, to give Hilda a parting kiss, and I was taken aback when she drew away from me rather nervously and self-consciously. I was somewhat hurt, until on turning around I saw the Old Man standing directly behind us, watching, and I knew without a word from Hilda that his presence was the cause of her untypical behaviour. "Never mind, Juju my dear," she half whispered to cover her own embarrassment and to soothe my feelings, "you'll run over and see me soon, won't you?"

For my first of many pleasant visits with Hilda, I chose Wednesday afternoon, a time when the store was closed, the boys at school, and Rome off on a fishing trip, so that she and I could have the house all to ourselves and feel quite free to talk about anything we liked. This weekly visit of mine soon became the foundation and centre of our pleasant adult relationship, and it was only natural that our long intimate talks should take the form of retrospective gossip concerning our old home or the present state of affairs among all the other Stone families.

The very first thing Hilda said to me, on my mentioning that things at home were not really much different from what they used to be, was: "I'll tell you now, Juju b'y, without a word of a lie – the day I got out of that hole, for good, that was the *happiest* day of my life." With a deep sigh as she said this, Hilda sank down on the sofa opposite my armchair and visibly relaxed like a person still savouring the joy and relief of a lucky escape from bondage. My mind was carried back to the struggle and the undoubted trials of her start in marriage, and I had perhaps a little more insight into the extent and depth of what must have been her misery at home.

"As bad as that, Hilda?"

"Oh worse, my son – worse!"

"You know, I always had an idea it was, in your case. But I was never sure about all the reasons."

"There was always that *dread* hangin' over me, Juju. Half o' the time I was frightened to move a step or open my mouth in the house. 'fraid *he* might take it the wrong way and fly into one of his tantrums."

"Dad?"

"Yes. You knows what he used to be like."

"My dear, he's no better, only he can't get away with so much now, on account of his heart."

"Shockin'," Hilda said, with deep sympathy for all who still had to live with the Old Man. "Me and Rome, we're after havin' our hard times. It wasn't always like this, you know," she ran on with a complacent glance around her well-appointed front room; "but there was never a time when I wanted to poke my nose into that old place again, not to live – no sirree!"

"Well, you haven't done so badly on your own."

"We got a few dollars, Juju." Hilda gave me her secretive smile again. "Not dependin' on nobody, anyhow."

"And are you satisfied, Hilda?" I quietly asked, remembering what I had already seen of Ank, Racer, and Crawfie in their own homes. Hilda smiled reminiscently and gave me a sincere answer.

"I wasn't, for years. Not really. It's the children. I was never contented till I had one. After that I settled down to marriage, I guess you could say."

Hilda rose from the sofa, or rather she ponderously rolled over to one side and eased herself up with a thrust of her left arm. But instead of being inwardly critical of her distressing bulk, I found myself smiling at it, whereas I found the fleshy masses of my brothers' bodies a little repulsive. Why the difference, then? Suddenly I realized it was because there appeared no bitterness in her face.

As she bustled about getting things ready for tea, and I helped her, I had for the first time a good opportunity of studying her face at close quarters, which previously my short sight had prevented me from doing. Hilda had still that defensive set to her mouth which I remembered so well and which had been stamped on it during her solitary, despised girlhood. Later the fight for success had etched a kind of calm sternness into all her features, but her eyes were kind and mild and above all she had none of that nervous edginess that was so marked in all the rest of us. Under her benign influence my own body relaxed a little, my mind unbent, and I felt that our conversation could flow on spontaneously for hours.

"You seem to have made a better job of marriage than the others, not omitting myself. Look at Ank and Mavis, for instance," I said.

"Ah, I pities them. It's something awful, the rackets they haves up there. I can't understand what happened to Ank. And poor Racer too. What in the world do they see in the booze, I wonder? I can't go near it myself. If I takes just one little drink o' whiskey my knees starts to wobble and I goes trembl'y all over. Right weak. I don't see how they can take it. But it's Rhoda I *really* pities. She drinks herself now, of course, but I can imagine what she's after goin' through with Racer. I dreads the sight of Rome takin' a drink, you know."

"Why, does he take many?"

"Nothing out o' the way. Only on special occasions. But then sometimes he gets wonderful crooked and I can't get no sense out of him. I hates all that for the children's sake, see?"

"Rome hasn't got the head for liquor that Crawfie has, then."

"Oh, Crawfie! I can't understand him a-*tall*. Not only his drinkin'. But to go and give away those poor little children like that! Every single one of them. It don't seem possible. On a fair shake now, Juju — do you think there's something *wrong* with Crawfie? He's our own brother, but you can tell *me* what you really thinks."

"Not much more than is wrong with the rest of us."

"Yes, I know what you mean. We're all kind o' warped.

Even me. Rome says so too, and gets real dirty with me sometimes, but I can't help it."

"Rome?"

"Oh yes. And that's another reason why I dreads him takin' too much to drink, 'cause then it all comes up – whatever is down there in the bottom of his mind."

"I would have said you're the only one of us that is not warped. But what comes up from the bottom of Rome's mind?"

"Oh, a lot of old foolishness and sometimes remarks about our crowd. True, most of it; but it's not his place to keep on about it. I'm not too keen about some of his foolery, either. He starts talkin' about gettin' a divorce if I don't get slim, and all that kind of stuff."

From the hardening of Hilda's tone despite the humorous side to what she was saying, I had a brief insight into her continuing dire need for reassurance and kindness, especially where anyone close to her was in question.

"Juju," she put me on the spot with her pathetic appeal, "do you think I'm much fatter than when you were home before?"

To avoid giving her a direct answer, I countered with what I hoped would be another reassuring question. "What difference, as long as you feel well and all that?"

"'Tis difference to me. I feels self-conscious – you know. Half the time I'm ashamed to walk in town 'fraid people are gawkin' at me. And I can't get near a pair o' slacks, though I know they're all the style now. Rome says if he ever ketches me in a pair he won't recognize me and won't come home any more at all. I gets right depressed over it sometimes."

That was the way Hilda would chatter on through one weekly visit of mine after another, all of them merging into one long conversation punctuated by meals and ended usually by the arrival of Rome with his trout and a roaring appetite some time after dark. Often if I closed my eyes while listening to Hilda, I could almost hear Mom talking;

that is, Mom as she had been in the days of her vigour and hope, and the resemblance again came to my mind whenever Hilda and I sat down to a meal.

Usually she began in a virtuous mood with a few slices of tomato, lettuce leaves, and a boiled egg, leaving the chicken and roast potatoes to me, but as the savour of the crinkled chicken skin and buttered potatoes gradually got past her guard, she would first pick off a tiny piece of white meat, then snatch guiltily one small potato, a spoonful of creamed corn, and finally she would shove aside her small plate and slew around the big platter of chicken directly in front of her, diving into it hands first with an abandon that was both awe-inspiring and revealing to watch. Always she came up from the attack looking at once ashamed and gratified, and at such times I had no trouble believing from her smile that the jollity of her nature was a genuine thing not dependent on booze to bring it out or to keep it alive. As a wind-up to the meal, she often sent me upstairs to the store for a chocolate cake and a brick of ice cream, which she again enjoyed without restraint.

Observing her and sympathizing with her, I could not doubt that this capacious lust for food was little short of gluttony. I realized that years before she must have lost all self-control in this line, once she had got her hands on enough money to satisfy this long-frustrated appetite. No power within or outside herself had been able to put a brake on her indulgence. The reason for her two hundred and twenty pounds and the misery she correspondingly suffered for every ounce over one hundred and sixty was abundantly clear now. Perhaps it was this she had meant, in part, by admitting that she too was warped in some ways.

I found myself on the lookout for other extremes of behaviour in Hilda, but in the course of our marathon talks not very much that seemed significant came to light. On the whole she impressed me as no less stable in character than solid in her citizenship, and only odd fragments of her confidence suggested hidden worries of which I now and then had an inkling.

"I frets about the b'ys on times, you know," she once told me.

"But why? They look well enough."

"Oh yes. Thank God for that. But I mean, where Rome is concerned. I gets afraid he's too stern with them. I'm too soft, I knows that; but I don't like the thought that they'll grow up afraid of him. You know what I mean."

"Indeed I do, Hilda. Still, between ourselves – Rome is not dangerous, is he?"

"Not really, I s'pose. It's just that when he got to check up on them I'm always scared he might go too far, and there'll be a big fuss and they'll start in fightin'. Gilbert is a big b'y now, and I dreads the thought of him and Rome gettin' into it."

"But *surely* Rome is not violent like the Old Man used to be?"

"He's not soft! Make no mistake on that, Juju. But not crazy either. And he never raised his fist to me, not since the very first day we were married. Good job he didn't, too, or else I'd a put a darn good bump on his nut with me rollin' pin. No mistake there either."

I smiled, but it was clear from the flush on Hilda's cheek and the tremor in her voice that this subject was not primarily a joke to her. "Seems to me," I put in soothingly, "Rome has come along in life pretty well, all things considered." Hilda did not take this as a patronizing remark but smiled at me again and answered with all the confidence of prosperity.

"Nobody laughs at him any more – tall or short, rich or poor."

To this I quickly agreed, fancying I could detect not only a hint of self-satisfaction in her tone but some touch of vindication or even revenge as well.

However deep the pride she took in her money and in her rise from exploited clerk to capitalist and employer of labour herself, she nevertheless managed to advance through life on a pretty even keel and to avoid those more destructive vices that had fastened on all the rest of us Stone children. It was quite true that at one time she and Rome had been in deep danger of avarice, of a total and obsessive preoccupation with the getting of money for its own sake. But as Hilda herself had suggested, the blessing of her children had diverted her main energies into less profitable yet more rewarding channels, leaving her more or less content with the capital they had amassed and a continuing livelihood from the store. To my mind the best proof of Hilda's stability lay in the fact that she was satisfied with the state of marriage. Again, how different from all the rest of us! "I tell you, Juju, and I means it: if Rome died tomorrow, I expect I'd be married again inside of a year." These were the surprising and quite sincere words in which she more than once assured me of her marital contentment.

I myself could hardly imagine happiness for anyone who had lived her narrow and strenuous life and seemed incapable of imagining, much less appreciating, a wider and more varied and spiritually richer view of things. Reconstructing in my imagination the calm and steady procession of her days since she had been a mother, I felt what a contrast they made to my own way of life over the past ten years following my divorce from a childless wife and my being let loose upon the world with no money but with an unquenchable thirst for new scenes and foreign faces.

Having shaken myself free of the galling yoke of marriage and a partner who must be attended if not catered to, I had thrown myself into an odyssey which took me from the essential primitivism of Mexico City to the tatters and remnants of civilization in the king of cities – London. From the deathly gloom of post-*débâcle* Paris to the retrogressive priestarchy of Dublin; then to the stench of tyranny in Madrid, the clanging grossness of West Berlin, and the ultimate nightmare of New York. Back and forth I stumbled from one capital city of the world to another in an ecstasy of mere motion, returning at intervals to my base in Toronto for the purpose of earning enough money to start me off once again on the open road.

All that I craved was six months of absolute freedom out of the twelve for travelling, and for leisure to read in the world's libraries when I became so weary from foot-slogging over asphalt or so hungry from an austere diet that I could do little except exercise my mind while the aching body found rest. After living this nomadic life for several years, I found that it had swept me along to the point where I suddenly abandoned whatever slender moorings of personal acquaintance I still had in Toronto, sold all the gear I owned that would not go into one portable bag and, in effect, cut myself loose from humanity altogether. The exhilaration of this state far outweighed my occasional spasms of terror and fits of depression.

I became a mobile speck on the vast globe of this world, having no more intimate connection with my fellow inhabitants than a star; often I asked myself what it was I sought in all these frantic wanderings, but no answer came clearly, not until world-weariness and an abrupt descent into middle age had at last driven me back home again and I came to realize that in these exotic places I had been seeking to prove to myself my passionate childhood conviction that all the world was not like Milltown.

Now, at forty, I wondered whether my early dreams had deceived me. Certainly I had found more culture than there was in my hometown, more breadth of mind, and less beery sottishness and general filth, but still there were times even now when the dark thought assailed me that this whole world was essentially a Milltown in which I should find no home nor any place of refuge this side of the grave. At such times I felt the hard, clear crystal of my sanity sinking and dissolving into chaos.

In contrast to my homelessness, I found Hilda as integral a part of Milltown life as a brick is part of a building.

Though she was interested in hearing of my travels, she showed no wish to imitate them in any way. I marvelled again at her escape not only from my pathological restlessness of body and mind but also from the other extremes of conduct that were making havoc of my brothers' lives. Hilda was the only one of us who had tempered her success with a measure of wisdom by putting what amounted to a moral rein on her behaviour as a private individual.

How had she escaped the havoc? Sometimes I thought that this was simply another of the mysteries of sex. At other times I fancied that the infusion of alien blood and alien seed into her body had made the difference by diluting the bad blood and the dark essence of Stone that was in her, and so she had been saved from the worst excesses of all the rest of our family. I noted with satisfaction that in both her boys there was much more of Robinson than of Stone. Mom used to say with a triumphant laugh that the way Hilda turned out showed that she had done a good job of raising her one girl, whereas the Old Man must have made a proper shag of handling all the boys; but of course that was all nonsense. As far as the rearing of our family went – that is, the actual day-by-day contacts and all the decisions of our growing up – Mom had had everything to do with each one of us, and in fact we all knew perfectly well how in years gone by she had never paid much attention to Hilda beyond scolding her for vanity and seizing a good part of her pay every Saturday night after Hilda had started working. It was only indirectly and on a much deeper level of consciousness that Dad had been the formative influence in our lives.

Perhaps what I found most refreshing about Hilda in middle age was her ever-welling and utterly feminine humour. She shook with incredulous laughter when I told her the chief reason for my divorce. "Well, Hilda my dear," I explained, "after about one year of marriage I simply reached a point where a decision had to be made: freedom or slavery. Every time we turn around in this life we're faced with a choice. I chose freedom. I had no money, as you know, and I just didn't want to be another economic slave. What are you laughing at?"

She studied my face as if I were joking, or as if that could not possibly be all there was to it; but I did not mind her scepticism, and in this case felt it would be quite useless to elaborate my point of view. It did not matter, the whole thing being now so far behind me. What did matter to me, in a more general way, was to find Hilda (though she was touchy as an inflamed tooth) entirely untroubled by the flow of black bile that was so strong an element in the circulation of all males in our family.

Nor did Hilda bear any grudge or savage resentment against the Old Man. When I tactlessly suggested that there might be a touch of hypocrisy in the way she catered to his prejudices, gave him presents on occasion, and in general jollied him along, she shook her head and answered me with conviction.

"No, no, Juju. I knows what he's like, and I don't forget what he done in times gone by. But I pities him too, you know. He's gettin' old, and sometimes I can't hardly stand it to look at his face. So *down*. I hope Rome and me . . . and *I* . . . won't be like him and Mom when we gets old."

"Somebody ought to shoot you first!"

"Sssshhh! Don't say that." Hilda admonished me for my harshness and at the same time laughed at my vehemence. "We never knows what we'll come to, Juju b'y. It don't pay to be too hard on people, specially your own."

In principle I agreed with that, but except for Mom and Hilda herself I was not able to achieve much sympathy in dealing with other members of the family. Maybe, I thought, it was the free flowing of love between Hilda and her children that had made all the difference in her life, or maybe it was that mysterious thing called, simply, force of character. Not without reason did everyone who knew them say that Hilda was the dynamo behind her and Rome's success; and yet I did not need Hilda's own reminder to convince me that her childhood had been the most crippling of all in our family. I knew it in my blood and bones and nerves.

And so her triumph over life was a pleasure to contemplate, not only because she offered to share a little of her home and her means with me, should my solitary wandering ever become too much for my health or human nature to endure, but also because inside her walls I lost for a time the feeling of coldness that I suffered from in all the other family houses up on Humber Heights.

Each Wednesday night when I left Hilda I felt a pleasant calm in my mind and found myself in a mood to feel and appreciate the beauty of Milltown at night as I, standing on its rim, looked down into the gigantic bowl of mystery that was the harbour, and saw reflected in its blue serge depths the lighted windows of the paper sheds, like bars of gold strung on invisible wire. Often, as I crossed the hill, there would be a solitary rower making late way across the water, fire dripping from his oars, and a steady light shining from the other side of the bay to guide him safely home. For a little while peace entered my heart as I took in this magical scene whose hushed beauty was almost enough to reconcile me for the moment to the human darkness and chaos that Milltown really was.

CHAPTER

6

FUDGE

Apart from their intrinsic pleasantness, these weekly visits of mine to Hilda became more and more a necessity the longer I remained at home caught in the suffocating triangle formed by Mom and Fudge and the Old Man. Fudge was now twenty-one years of age, and thus in a physical sense enjoying the full flush of young manhood. But his use of this exhilarating and potentially dangerous gift left very much to be desired.

Having last seen him as a lonely, peevish little boy of eight, I had some difficulty in getting used to his great bulk on seeing him again, despite the fact that I had had some reports of his sudden growth from Mom and Hilda. His history since childhood was much as I had predicted to myself it would be, except for several incidents that were all but incredible, and the one great weakness that soon came to dominate his life. School for Fudge was a spotty struggle from kindergarten to Grade VIII, after which it became for his teachers a nightmare of trying to cope with and overcome the insensate loutishness of an overgrown and totally uninterested boy.

Most years he was promoted because of his size, but he took no trouble to pass any exams, as far as I could learn, and seemed to exist in a kind of trance from which only food or violent excitement, such as Mickey Spillane movies, could effectively rouse him. The most frequent remark on his report cards was: "Could do better, if he applied himself."

Applying himself was a thing Fudge did not understand or did not intend to do, whether he ever came to understand it or not. I heard too that in Grade IX Fudge and one of his cronies at the back of the class, now big enough not to fear physical punishment from any quarter, had set out to drive their teacher nuts and had in fact reduced her to hysteria followed by a nervous breakdown which incapacitated her for an entire school year. This achievement Fudge followed up in Grade X with outright hooliganism, so that he was eventually dismissed from school having got no diploma at all and no distinction whatever to keep up the name that Crawfie and I had made for academic success.

Apparently his life at home had been no smoother or more fruitful than his school career, since I had heard a year or two after leaving home in 1948 that Fudge (being then considered old and strong enough to help Dad in his endless household repairs) had either proved so clumsy that he was no use at all, or within a year or two more had braved the Old Man and his wrath by open rebellion against hard labour at home.

According to all I had been told, the fuss and racket and violence with Fudge had for some years been just as bad as I remembered it with the rest of us, until Fudge suddenly grew to such a size that it was dangerous for anyone at all to cross him. The last fight between him and the Old Man took place the night Fudge got soused and set the house on fire by falling asleep with a cigarette in his mouth. The house was saved and the Old Man went nearly mad, but this time Fudge subdued him without ceremony.

In Mom's words, he "hove un down over the back steps like a sack o' potatoes," and left him yelling curses of disownment while Fudge himself flumped back on his sodden mattress and slept off his anger and his booze. After that he sponged more mercilessly than ever on the Old Man, treated him with silent contempt, and at the least sign of protest merely shouldered him to one side with casual rudeness, paying him no more attention that he would give to a yelping puppy.

For two years after his expulsion from school, Fudge did absolutely nothing but eat, sleep, and hang around. As long as Mom would provide him with cigarettes and food and a bed at home, he felt himself under no obligation to look for a job or contribute in any way to the family expenses, no matter how sourly the Old Man might rage and bluster – not at Fudge any more but at Mom when Fudge was well away from the house. At one point the situation reached a stage where the Old Man swore he was going to get the police up and have Fudge forcibly and permanently put out of his house and right off his property altogether, but then Mom swore in turn that if Fudge went she went and the Old Man could stew in his own juice or starve on the spot as far as she was concerned; he was bringing it on himself and nobody would pity him, whatever happened.

It was a deadlock. Of course the Old Man may have had a shrewd idea that when it came down to brass tacks she would not really go and leave him, yet age and trouble had by this time worn him down to a condition in which he no longer had the nerve to risk it. Mom held firm in principle, and the result of the whole uproar was precisely nothing. Fudge continued his rapid development into the typical village lout and loafer, despite an outcry of criticism from all the family and the pretended – or perhaps in some ways genuine – concern of Mom as well.

I heard also that the social shyness and regressive tendencies which had struck me as so comical and painful a part of his character in boyhood were becoming even worse as he grew up, gradually merging into a morbid self-consciousness which inhibited him from all society except the family and one or two neighbourhood adolescents just about as bad as himself. Girls were anathema to him, a source of pain and fear which he made sure he would not suffer any more than the raw demands of his nature required.

What eventually drove him to take a job as freight clerk with the Canadian National Railway I never really understood until I had been home again for some time; I was at first so taken aback by his appearance, finding it bizarre to say the least, that it was a considerable time before I could set about assessing his character or calculating the motives for any step he might have taken. Massive bulk and a touch of the grotesque were apparent not only in his torso: Fudge had an extremely large head too, rather flat on top like Crawfie's but showing only about one inch of forehead as against three inches or so of chin, and surmounted by a dense mass of straw-coloured hair worn in the brush-cut style which in Fudge's frequently expressed opinion was the only way for a man to wear his hair. I never did find out what had turned his nose awry, but in fact it was slewed to one side toward the base, while at the other end it was overshadowed by two fearsome eyebrows pointing upwards at each other in an expression of permanent perplexity. As for his lisp, that I was assured was not as bad as it had been in childhood, but this was hard to judge because just before I returned home Fudge had had all his teeth out.

His daily routine began with Mom in the hall outside his bedroom calling out in strident repetition: "Fudge, Fudge! Fudgieeeee! Get up now, my son, and don't have me callin' out to you half the morning – like a good b'y."

That went on for about twenty minutes, during which time the Old Man from his bed grumbled at all the noise, and I said nothing but for once agreed with him in principle. "Now, Fudgie – get up," Mom continued coaxingly without paying the least attention to anyone but him. "Get up, my dear, or else you'll be late for work. 'Tis almost nine o'clock."

After another ten minutes or so of this, Mom always had to go into the bedroom and haul the clothes off Fudge before he would stir at all; finally she managed to drag him out to the bathroom, shove his head under the cold tap, and then after stuffing a huge breakfast into him get him on the way to work no more than fifteen or twenty minutes behind what would have been a proper schedule. Once he was gone, peace came down over the house for a few minutes until the Old Man hauled himself out to his breakfast of salt fish and bread and tea, and after that snarling interlude another brief calm before I, calculating that the Old Man must have finished by now, put down my book and moved languidly from bed to kitchen table in want of my own breakfast.

Midday dinner was a meal that Fudge always took by himself, as he had arranged his time so that he did not arrive home until one-thirty when we had all finished and the table was cleared and more or less laid again for his return. Most days I noticed Mom keeping an eye out for him through the kitchen window, and I soon became aware that Fudge after a few hours on his own was a sight to see. He would come rolling up the hill with his coat flying wide open, even though it was now winter, his shirt billowing out from his pants and leaving bare a great swath of salmon-coloured belly just above the indentation of his belt. Nothing could persuade him to wear a tie in the daytime or button up his collar, since he thought such refinements on a weekday affected and even effeminate. From all of this I gathered that one reason for his taking this railway job was that it required no dressing up at all.

Once he had entered the house and flung off his coat, he and Mom settled down at the kitchen table for their meal, he making away with two huge platters of bologna and potatoes and gravy, she feeding avidly on every little detail that Fudge would give her about the events of his morning – the people he worked with, whom he had seen, and what they had said, and so on – to the point of acute irritation for Fudge and speedy boredom for me. They were like conspirators, those two, in the way they sat close together at the table, with Fudge bent low over his plate piling one mess of food after another against his huge forefinger that lay along the edge of his plate, and then shovelling each pile into his mouth, while all the time Mom leaned toward him and poured out her questions and comments in a low-voiced, never-ending stream.

She stopped only to bring in his dessert, usually a large pudding boiled in a bag and leaden with starch and carbohydrates which Fudge ate up as quickly and greedily as he had put away the main dish. Once or twice I remained at table after Mom and Dad and I had finished dinner, with the idea of having a little general conversation with Fudge and perhaps getting to know him again. But whenever I took the initiative from her in talk, Mom suffered me impatiently, and before I could develop any thought to my satisfaction or Fudge's enlightenment she always broke in resentfully and bore the conversation back to her own enquiries and Fudge's weary replies.

Our tea followed much the same pattern except that Fudge was generally a bit more gay and lively than at dinner because he was looking forward to another evening out with the "b'ys" and usually had a little money in his pocket or knew he could wheedle some out of Mom, if it were near payday and he was quite broke. The amount he ate for tea was no less, nor was it any more balanced, than his dinner. Whatever was put in front of him he thoughtlessly shoved down into the capacious furnace of his stomach, so that from thinking of him as a sport of nature I soon came to regard him as a sport of Mom's, in every sense of the term.

But if I protested to her (Fudge's weight having shot up past the two hundred and fifty mark), she merely laughed in a way that showed how completely she held his bulk to be a tribute to her cooking and motherly care. When I hinted at the advisability of medical or even legal interference for the sake of Fudge's health, she was at first puzzled, then angry enough to growl at me that I should eat like a man myself and so put some flesh on my scrawny little bones. She went on stoking Fudge up four or five times a day as if he were an empty boiler and was determined to keep on doing so, even if it killed him.

After tea there was nearly always a duel between Mom and Fudge over his plans for the evening. No sooner had Fudge finished his cigarette than he began to fidget and squirm under the barrage of Mom's trivial questions about what had happened during the afternoon, while she, baffled in her quest for information, soon attacked him directly on this matter that was now foremost in both their minds.

"You're not goin' out tonight surely, is you? Where to? What do you want to go out every blessed night for? I'd like to know what in the world you finds to do or how you puts in your time. Stay in tonight, Fudgie? Will you? Look, it's startin' in to snow. Stay in, and we'll have a little game o' cards and then I'll make you some cabbage rolls. Hey? You likes them."

Giving no reply in words, Fudge would move restlessly from the kitchen to the front room and glance at the *Messenger*, but it was clear that this was only a stall.

"Where's you off to, then?" Mom chased him wherever he went. "*Tell* me. Tell me what plans you got made, and then I won't be so oneasy." She kept at him with unflagging tongue.

"I haven't got no *plans*, Mom," Fudge muttered with a tormented twisting of his whole enormous face and body.

"Then stay in. What do you want to go traipsin' all over the Heights for on a cold night like this? Into God knows what ole dives, and knockin' around with that gang o' hard tickets you're after gettin' in with. Oh, I knows, I knows! And I can't see what *you* sees in it all, not for the life of me I can't."

A few minutes more of this and Fudge suddenly pushed himself up from his chair and fled into the bathroom, where he splashed his face around in a basin of cold water, blew like a spouting whale, and then dragged on his coat and made for the door. Mom dogged him as far as the gate, clawing at him until at the last moment he literally had to tear himself away from her, and she had to accept another temporary defeat by coming back into the kitchen and standing at the window to watch him go down over the hill. Fudge tumbled down past Racer's house like a newly released prisoner, hatless as always, his coat and shirt-tails again flying in the breeze, and in his whole attitude a hungry anticipation of joy that, so far as I could judge, never came to his heart.

The minute he passed out of sight, Mom turned on the Old Man with a look of irritation and disgust. "You gets right on my nerves, so you do. T'ink you might say something to Fudge to try and keep him in offa the streets once in a while. But no! You just sits there, glum as a owl, and you don't open your gob from one mont's end to the next."

"I'm tired talkin' to the likes o' him – *finished*," was the Old Man's standard reply. "I give that up years ago. And you knows just as well as I do that all *your* naggin' and fussin' don't do a damn bit o' good, anyhow. So don't you go keepin' on to me about him. I had enough." Even before he had finished this well-worn speech Mom had rounded on me, half in fretfulness and half in supplication.

"Juju, why don't you talk to un? Fudge might listen to you."

"What can I do, Mom? Fudge is of age, and in any case I have no authority over him. Besides, what are you worrying so much about? He's only gone out for the evening."

Privately I was always glad when Fudge went out because it relieved me of the nightmare of having to play one wild game of cards after another the whole evening. The game seemed to have become some kind of obsession with Mom and more than ever a means of pouring out her antagonism to the Old Man.

Nowadays I tended to find the cards tiresome and irritating, although there *were* times when I did wish that Fudge had stayed home permanently. The minute he was away from her supervision Mom started her evening's chant: "I wonder where he's gone to now? I hope he's not in any trouble with that *gang* again. If he is, I'll haul the scruff off of un. Sometimes I gets so dirty wit' un, I could flounder un. Not gone down to Crow Gulch, I s'pose, is he? Hey, Dad? Oh, *you* don't care if he's dead." She bore into the Old Man once more.

"Ah, give y'tongue a rest, fer the love o' Jesus!" The Old Man groaned and turned away his head in agony.

"Yes, yes! Give me tongue a rest. That's all you ever says. Sure signs, it'll be a diff'rent story if something *do* happen to Fudge one o' these nights. And you, Juju. You don't never offer to go out wit' un, nor nutting. You don't seem to treat Fudge like a brother a-tall."

"Mom, for heaven's sake, Fudge is twenty years younger than I am, and has his own set of pals. His own ideas about things too. He doesn't want to be bothered with me."

"He's still your brother, and you ought to try and do something about un."

The way she kept going all evening, until the Old Man switched on the radio in self-defence and I took refuge in a book, sometimes caused me to wish I had never had a brother or a mother or any relation at all. She never stopped for more than five minutes at a time, and as the long evening wore on she kept going over to the kitchen window to see if Fudge was coming up the hill, finally perching there in the attitude of one keeping a vigil. Ten o'clock came and I escaped to bed; eleven o'clock, and the Old Man called out for his cup of tea; that accomplished and midnight sounding, he too went off to bed; then after Mom's bout of complaining because nobody would wait up with her for Fudge there came a long interval of silence during which I usually fell asleep.

But I was wakened long before morning. The noise broke into my sleep like a herd of elephants stumbling up a huge stairway. This was Fudge arriving home, often about two, and his arrival was something like a circus act gone wrong. The first time this scene was enacted I got up and went out to the kitchen, thinking there must be some kind of trouble, but it was only the gigantic figure of Fudge standing full in the doorway with a monstrous great hotdog sticking out of his mouth and dripping ketchup all over his clothes, his eyes inflamed with the chronic conjunctivitis he suffered from and a look of unutterable woe clinging about his whole fantastic person.

He just stood there letting in the frosty air and seeming quite incapable of any further effort now that he had struggled in to home port. As I squeezed around him to close the door and got a whiff of his breath, I realized with a shock that he was loaded drunk. Then Mom got busy. She gave him a tug that brought him across the kitchen floor and up to the couch, on which he suddenly collapsed in a sodden jointless heap. One look at him lying there, and I knew for certain that he was prey to a wretchedness far, far deeper than anything we other boys had known at his age.

Mom bent over him anxiously. "Here, gimme that ole hotdog," she said with a grimace, hauling the huge cylinder out of his mouth and throwing it into the stove. "Got that t'ing down at the Chink's, I s'pose. Ugh! God only knows what they puts into 'em." Fudge's mouth now gaped like a huge fresh pothole. Suddenly he began to shiver and tremble as if he had been plunged into an icehouse.

"Where's y'overcoat?" asked Mom abruptly, and I noticed for the first time that Fudge was wearing only a shirt and jacket. He moaned in a helpless way, obviously only half aware of what Mom was saying. "He goes and loses five or six overcoats in the run of a winter, you know," she said wearily to me, poking up the fire in the stove and immediately concentrating on Fudge again. "Got any of your money left? Have you?" When Fudge failed to make any reply, she bent over him and went through every one of his pockets. "It's them young toughs from Crow Gulch. They folleys poor Fudge around and when they sees he's too far gone to help hisself they gangs up on him and robs all his money and the half of his clothes in the bargain. Oh, if

I only had a holt on them!" She quivered with rage and mortification.

After a while Fudge's eyes half-opened and he tried to sit up.

"Where *was* you?" Mom dug into him at the first sign of his coming back to consciousness. With a blubbering groan Fudge fell back on the couch clearly unable to answer any questions or hold any communication at all. His limp fingers began to grope in his pockets for a cigarette while he went on murmuring to himself in an incoherent, self-pitying way; at last he found a cigarette and, shoving about half of it into his mouth, demanded a light. "You don't want to go smokin' now, Fudgie?" Mom asked rather than told him.

"Light," Fudge muttered with childish obstinacy, and Mom took a match from the windowsill and lit his cigarette. After two or three draws Fudge passed right out again, the cigarette falling on his chest and beginning to burn a hole in his shirt. Mom snatched it away and otherwise tried to clean him up a little; she also hauled off his rubbers and shoes and did what else she could to make him comfortable there on the couch.

Fudge's next peevish order when he came to was, "Gimme sometin' d'eat, Mom," which puzzled me slightly until I saw Mom put the frying pan on the stove and shake up the big teapot. In a little while there was Fudge half-sitting up at the table gulping down a large meal of fried potatoes, ham and eggs, and seeming thereby to get enough strength to stagger off to bed and leave us all in peace for a few hours. It appeared to be only a very few hours indeed before Mom's anxious voice was again heard calling out, "Fudge. Fudge! Come on now, Fudgie. Get up, or you'll be late for work again."

That was the pattern on most nights, a horribly recurrent pattern which soon forced me to the realization that Fudge had taken to the booze at a much earlier age than all the others. It seemed in fact that he had begun his serious drinking immediately on leaving school and continued steadily and progressively until now he could not do without the liquor any more than I could get along without the consolation and drug of the printed word. I also felt sure that his main reason for submitting himself to a regular job was that it would permit him to indulge at will his craving for beer and hard liquor.

I never assisted at any more of Fudge's early morning homecomings but often I heard him and Mom, when he was half tight but not as far gone as on that night of my first witnessing his misery, talking in a repetitive, intimate way that was more than a little disturbing. "Fudgie, what in the world do you drink so much for? *Tell* me."

"Might as well, sure, Mom. Nutting else to do. No social life. You knows I'm queer-lookin'. Can't get no girls." The word queer had for us no reference to homosexuality: it simply meant, in this context, peculiar.

"You're not queer-lookin'! Besides, what do you want a girl for? You're too young. And they only costs money. You're better off like you are now."

"All the b'ys got a girl. I feels out o' place, see?"

"That don't say you got to go drinkin' all the time."

"If I don't, I got no chance a-tall, Mom."

"Why not?"

" 'Cause if I'm cold sober I got no nerve, and I always t'inks they're laughin' at me. The girls, I mean."

"Foolishness!"

"Anyway, I might as well inj'y meself while I got the chance. I believes I haven't got long to go in this world, Mom."

"Now Fudgie!" Mom pleaded, "don't you go talkin' like that again. You knows it gives me the cold shivers all over."

"Might as well tell you the troot' about how I feels."

"Yes, but..."

"Well, I'm not long for this world. That's it."

"Why not? You're healty as a horse. Look at the size o' you."

"A big built is not everyt'ing, Mom."

277

"What's goin' to take you, then?"

"Oh, I don't know. Soocide, I guess."

"I told you not to be sayin' wicked t'ings like that! They frightens me to deat', see?"

"I don't want to live to be over t'irty. Naw. I don't believe I could stand it any longer than that."

"T'irty! That's only a b'y. Besides, you're a long ways from that. Now, hush up, and act your age. Want another piece o' pie? Cup o' tea? Bad b'y! You're wicked on times. Yes, you *is*. Real wicked."

Listening to them going on like that hour after hour, night after night, I almost began to imagine – not without a vague sensation of horror – that there was some kind of abnormal relationship between Mom and Fudge. I noticed too how on Monday morning Mom always inhaled the odour of his semen-soaked underwear before throwing it into the wash; and when on Saturday nights she revealed a habit of going into the bathroom while he was having his bath, for the purpose of washing his hair, I even began to feel a little alarmed.

Fudge himself was also in the habit of doing things that struck me as odd and seemed to alienate me from this lumbering young man who had grown as far away as possible from the child of eight whom I had first come to know on my visit home in 1948. Quite by accident I discovered that he was ashamed to be seen walking down over the hill with me if I were carrying a book. He did not want to be known as the brother of anyone who did sissy things like that; and as for the slight spark of imagination I thought he had shown as a child when I read him *Grimm's Fairy Tales*, that seemed to have died a total death somewhere along the line of his peculiar development.

Another thing that acutely embarrassed him and which he kept a morbid secret from the "b'ys" was his middle name of Yeovil, which he regarded as almost a heavier burden to bear than his twisted nose or backwardness with the girls. Fudge's whole existence was limited to the physical aspect of things. He closely identified himself either with American baseball heroes, most of whom topped over six feet and weighed about two hundred pounds, or with National Hockey League players of similar size. So far as I could learn, the only non-athletic people who had any standing at all in his eyes were certain singing groups, again American, and one or two teenage pop-song idols of his own generation like Paul Anka and Andy Williams. When he was alone or thought himself alone, Fudge often indulged himself in imitations of these glamorously successful personalities and their songs, one of his great favourites from the pop charts being a revived oldie called "Prisoner of Love."

This one Fudge rendered with great feeling if not an equal musicianship, his massive head thrown back in ecstasy and his Gibraltar of a chin trembling, vibrating with emotion as he poured out in a startling tenor voice this mawkish chant of sentimental subjection:

She's in my dreams awake or sleeping,
My very life is in her keeping;
Upon my knees to her I'm creeping,
I'm just a prisoner of love.

I could readily imagine the Gargantuan fantasies which in Fudge's mind accompanied his solitary dwelling on such themes.

But no sublimation in music could ease for long the discomfort he suffered at home from the Old Man's scornful alienation and Mom's everlasting fussing and nagging at him. One day in desperation over the endless commotion he caused in the house, I suggested to him that he should pack up and go; I urged it also for the sake of his own body and soul, yet he only gazed at me with that active distress in his eyes reminding me again of Crawfie, but more alive with misery than Crawfie's settled sadness in middle age. "Where to, Juju?" said Fudge with his mouth hanging open blankly. "Where would I go to?"

"Hell, anywhere! St. John's, the mainland. You're not a cripple or anything. You could always get work of some kind."

"I don't know, b'y. I don't know." He said this in a tone of doubt and almost of fear which in so young a man seemed to me deplorable. He made no plans to go. Hilda had told me that more than once Fudge had fled from the house and arrived over at her place sobbing like a child, begging her to let him stay there for a day or two as a respite from Mom's tongue and the Old Man's unnerving silences.

These flights always ended in Mom barging into Hilda's house and either coaxing or bribing Fudge to come back home, at the same time promising on oath that she would leave him more to himself in the future. Then the first night he went out, there she was back at her old stand by the kitchen window; and when Fudge came home well after midnight, the whole fantastic routine of feeding him, questioning him, and getting him to bed started all over again. Not a half-hour's peace could there be in the house unless everyone was asleep; it was like living in a perpetual nightmare, and as the long winter of my return home wore on, it became so bad that I felt obliged to remonstrate with Mom for Fudge's sake no less than for my own.

"Mind y'own business!" she shot back at me when I first spoke to her on this subject.

"You're smothering him, Mom. Can't you see that?"

"Yes – smuddering him, yes! How foolish you talks! Go on back to your books. Four-eyed little monkey!"

"Leave him alone just once. Just *once* when he comes in the door, don't say a word."

"I got to say somet'ing. I got to check up on un," she laughed unexpectedly. From her whole manner during this talk we had, I realized with some dismay that in spite of all her protests and railings and complaints she did in fact enjoy all this futile racket, and that was why she kept it up so assiduously.

After that I made up my mind it was not much use

talking to her on the subject of Fudge or the way she coddled and tortured him. Fudge himself was my only chance. Though he shattered in a way that was grotesque and unpardonable my ideal of a quiet studious life, I did feel a genuine sympathy and even pity for him. I saw him not only as a youthful monster but also as the tragic inheritor of all the pain and torment and disunity that we others had suffered from in our childhood. I saw him too as the last in that long line of Newfoundlanders who stood rooted in time, storing up through the centuries, dumbly waiting for their Van Gogh to come and set down the pity and the terror of their lives.

As the last pawn in the half-century of war between our wildly incompatible parents, he was a figure to be pitied. Whichever way he turned he found Mom choking him with a hysterically prehensile possessiveness, while he and the Old Man lived in the tension of having no truck with each other at all. Yet in revenge for Fudge's crude arrogance in holding him of no account, the Old Man went on silently storing up his malice like a bee stock-piling some poisonous honey.

The whole atmosphere of the house was so charged with discomfort that I privately kept on at Fudge about a move on his part, a drastic move ending in escape, but I seemed to be making little impression on his mind – until one day on coming home from the library just before tea I found Mom in a ghastly state, thumping about the house like some frustrated idiot and ceaselessly pouring out a stream of lamentations. Before I was half-way through the door, she rushed up to me and cried out frantically: "Did you see un, Juju? Did he say anything to you?"

"Who, Mom? For heaven's sake, calm *down*, and tell me what all the fuss is about now."

"Fudge – he's gone!" Her tone was both an accusation and a knell.

"Gone where?"

"I don't know. A fella saw him gettin' on the train for

Port-aux-Basques and told Dad. Where in the world is he gone to, I wonder? I was never so tarmented in me whole life. Did he say anything to you? Hey?"

"*No*, Mom."

"It's so queer, him just leavin' his job like that and goin' off without sayin' a word to no one. Not even me."

I did not find that queer at all. From what I remembered and had recently seen of Fudge, I calculated that this was just the way he would do it if once he summoned up the nerve and the energy to leave home at all. He had always shown a morbid fear of anything like deep feeling or the recognition of a momentous event by the display of any emotion whatever.

"Don't worry, Mom," I said comfortably. "He's probably just gone up to the mainland to look for a better job. You'll hear from him soon."

"But he got no money, only what he had in his pocket, and I s'pose he spent the most of that for his ticket. I 'lows he'll be half-starved. And no clean clothes either. Oh, my!" she sighed so heavily, all of the world's woe might have come down on her overnight.

"Don't talk nonsense, Mom," I replied a little sharply. "Fudge is a young man in good health most of the time, and he'll no doubt be in some place where work is as plentiful as peanuts." Before I had finished speaking she directed on me as unfriendly a look as ever she could have given to one of her children.

"Didn't he tell you *anyt'ing*? You sure?"

"So help me, I don't know if Fudge is in Port-aux-Basques or Timbuctoo." Mom continued to study me suspiciously for a while but, getting no more information, rounded once more on the Old Man right in the middle of his listening to the six o'clock news on the radio. "Didn't the fella say if Fudge said anyt'ing at all about where he was goin' to?" she insisted.

"No, no, no. Just saw him gettin' aboard. That's all."

"I half blames you for the whole t'ing. You wouldn't never say a word to un or act like he was alive a-tall."

"Ye can do as ye likes," the Old Man muttered. "Him, or any o' the rest o' ye."

"Yes, yes. That's some way to talk, and him gone off to a strange country with hardly a cent in his pocket, and nobody to look out to un. Oh my, I feels half cracked! Are you sure you don't know where he's gone to? Hey?"

"Jesus – *no!*" was the snarling reply, and the sudden rise in the Old Man's voice sounded dangerous. "Nor that's not half the story. I don't give a good goddam where he's gone to. Now shut up and let me listen to the news, will you?"

"I never said nutting to hurt his feelings," Mom turned again to me and continued thoughtfully. "P'raps 'twas 'cause Dad wouldn't let un have the car. He was always after me about that."

"Let un have the car!" the Old Man cried at her again. "Talk sense. You knows bloody well he was forever drunk. If I gave him the car, any night a-tall he might a drove down over the hill and slaughtered half a dozen youngsters. You makes me sick the way you goes on!" Crimson with rage and bristling all over with frustration and disgust, the Old Man turned away altogether from Mom and her importunities.

During the next two or three days Mom drove us nearly mad with her ceaseless and repetitious demands that we do something about finding out what had happened to Fudge. In self-defence I reminded her that a bit of roughing it on his own would be good experience for him, but this again did not go down very well with Mom and every time I insisted on it I noticed that my next meal was not as abundant as my meals usually were.

Mom received no more comfort when all the rest of the family was summoned for the purpose of saying what they thought of the whole affair. "Proper t'ing! Proper t'ing!" Ank stuttered. "Let him fist around for himself a while. Knock the shit out of him."

Racer's verdict was similar. "About time he got up off of his big fat arse and started actin' like a man for a change."

"Well, Mother," said Crawfie ponderously, "he got a life

of his own, you know, and got to live it whatever way he thinks best."

Hilda was the gentlest in trying to say the same thing, softened by an assurance that Mom would soon hear from Fudge and see that he was all right. My own admiration of Fudge's abrupt stiffening into a vertebrate was gradually rising, and Mom was on the point of calling in the Mounties to start a nation-wide search, when out of the blue there came a telegram sent from Halifax, addressed to Mom:

NEED FIFTY URGENT LOVE
FREDERICK

Mom burst into a passion of tears and relief and laughter, and ran for her purse. The fifty dollars was soon sent, along with a telegram urging Fudge to write and to come on back home. There was another long silence after that, broken only by a few lines from Fudge to say he had received the money and was moving inland. It seemed likely that the Old Man and I would have to endure more days and nights of Mom's frantic fussing and grieving. Each time the postman passed our house without leaving anything, she broke out into the very same lamentations and wailings that had dinned in our ears for weeks. If we ventured to protest that Fudge should be left alone to carry through his little adventure to a finish, she turned on us angrily. "Ye don't care! Ye don't care if he was starvin'. Him all alone in some strange place wit' not a soul to talk to, and ye t'inks no more about it than if he was sitting right there at the table alongside o' ye. Oh, ye makes me dirty!"

We were all put out of our misery, in a sense, by the next scrap of news that came from Fudge. Having penetrated as far as Toronto, he found a job as assistant to a piano mover, which lasted one and a half days before he quit; and then, faced by destitution, he went and joined the army. This military phase of his career lasted only three days, and even in that time he had got into two fights, both of them caused by remarks from the other soldiers about Newfies.

After losing the second fight, and also perhaps because he could not endure the harsh loneliness of boot camp any longer, Fudge deserted.

On his escape from camp he turned blindly east again, still in his civilian clothes, and managed to beat his way down to North Sydney on foot, by hitch-hiking and by any other free means available. From there we received another begging telegram, and the money having been sent off once more by Mom without any delay, Fudge arrived home a day or so later in a state of near-collapse.

It had been no use at all telling Mom that she should send the money if she believed Fudge was in real want but should at the same time advise Fudge to return to his regiment and so avoid greater trouble in the future. We might just as well have told her to fly. All she could think of was that Fudgie was coming back to her, and when he did arrive she fell on him and all over him with a greedy glee that was almost frightening. He stank too, all his clothes looking as if they had just been hauled out of a damp old rag pile.

Mom washed him and fed him and cuddled up to him until you would have thought he was Lazarus. She was quite oblivious of everything and everyone else but Fudge and Fudge's restoration in body, mind, and spirit – a fact I came to realize with a shock on his first evening back home when she forgot to put up any tea for me at all.

Her bliss was rudely shattered by the arrival of a letter about a week after Fudge's return, from his Commanding Officer ordering him to report to Army Headquarters in St. John's for the regulation disciplinary measures. Apparently his enlistment had been genuine and formally completed (oath, signature, and all) so that if he did not voluntarily proceed to St. John's forthwith, Military Police ... etc., etc.

Fudge was hooked. "I'm never goin' back in d'army!" he cried with glistening eyes and a shudder of recollection. "No sir. That's what I'm not. They can shoot me first."

"Hush up!" cried Mom in terror. "And that's a fact, you're not goin' back in d'army. What do they want *you* for, anyway? No, my son, they won't get you, and that's all of it."

Nevertheless even Mom had to understand that there was not much she or Fudge or anyone else could do if the army authorities chose to press the charges of desertion. As an ex-soldier, Racer was called in to give his opinion on the whole mess, but in all honesty and drunk or sober he could not offer Mom any real comfort.

"Good job it's not war time," he said darkly, "or else the army wouldn't be writing him any letters, I can tell you."

"But will they really come with guns and take Fudge away if he don't go out to St. John's of his own accord?" Mom asked, her face a study in pain.

"Yes. You got to face it, Mom. Fudge will have to go, and it'll be so much the better if he goes now before his time is up. Otherwise they might be even harder on him, see?"

"What'll they do to un out there in St. John's?"

"Well, I can't say that for sure. Depends how his trial goes," Racer said not unkindly, "and what he got to say for himself. But they may not be too hard on him, in peace time."

Still vowing that he would rather die than go back into the army, Fudge grimly took the next train for St. John's; but again his departure brought us anything but peace in the home. As the days dragged on one after another with no news from Fudge to break her tension, Mom became pathological in her behaviour. Ceaselessly and tirelessly she fretted and fumed and speculated on what *they* were doing to Fudge, and nothing else could engage her attention or distract her mind.

Even to sit in the same room with her was to feel the vibration of her nerves and to be hopelessly discomfited by it. I was on the point of leaving in despair when Mom astonished us all by one day getting on the eastbound express and going off to St. John's herself to plead with the

Commanding Officer there for mercy on Fudge, and for his ultimate release.

Her return a few days later was dramatic in the news it brought. "They're goin' to let un go!" she cried jubilantly the moment we met her at the station. "I saw his Colonel and the Medical Officer and the whole bloomin' lot of 'em," she related her adventures many times that day, "and the army don't really want Fudge a-tall. Ha-ha!"

"Medical Officer?" I put in at one point. "Why, Fudge is not sick, is he?"

"No, no. But they *t'inks* he is, see? They t'inks he's mental. Fudge, he fooled 'em, see? He was only lettin' on."

"But what did the Medical Officer say was wrong with him?" I persisted.

"Oh, I don't know. Some big Latin word I can't remember."

"Try, Mom. I'd like to know."

"Oh, something like fousa . . . fussa . . . fussafubbia. Ah, I can't get me tongue around it!" After some thought I decided that she must mean claustrophobia, and the more I reflected on that the more I saw how it might be a good general diagnosis of Fudge's case.

"But are they going to let him off scot-free?"

"No. The Colonel said Fudge got to serve twenty-one days in gaol – detention, I think they calls it – and then he can get his discharge. He was started on his sentence before I left. Poor Fudge! I walked alongside o' Buckmaster's Field one day and saw un in there with a wheelbarrow wheelin' a big pile o' rocks from one corner of a field to the other. How foolish is that! I would a called out to Fudge only there was a big lump of a sergeant standin' right over him with a gun. I t'ought to meself – if I had that sergeant by the scruff o' the neck, I'd give un guns! But I s'pose they won't be *too* hard on Fudgie now he's leavin' d'army anyhow. Oh, I can't wait till I knows he's out of it all for good!"

Fudge duly arrived back home clutching an official paper which said that he was "unlikely to be of further use to the service" and was therefore discharged from Her Majesty's Forces. He spent a few days cursing the army, especially all N.C.O.s, and then gradually slid back into his old disgusting way of life.

The ribbing he had to take from us was not too violent or persistent: Racer dubbed him Major Stone, and I added a D.S.O. (with bar), and for a time we could easily get his goat by airing these terms in front of his cronies. But little by little the tale of his army career, his services to the Crown, and their inglorious end, became just one more item of family folklore that all of us carried in the back of our minds, though we seldom referred to it unless Fudge showed signs of getting up on a high horse or in some way attacking one of us in the matter of reputation or personal credit within the family circle.

Although he had come out of his detention looking more like a man and less like a refugee Fat Man from the circus, Mom declared he looked miserable all over, and she soon began to blow him up again with starch and sweets and all kinds of clogging messes four or five times a day seven days a week. Fudge himself made no bones about resuming his drinking and thus completing his own inflation on the same scale as before his military service.

Here he was, then, back in the same rut without a job and seemingly with no more aim in life than a jellyfish slithering about on a beach. The grand climax to this period of his existence came when he was found one frosty morning at five o'clock lying in a ditch on the West Side with nothing on but his underwear and in a drunken coma.

Mom was again forever needling him for information about his doings (it was the price he had to pay for her indulgence), and quite often I saw Fudge squirming at the table as Mom stood over him or sat close up to him pouring out her questions. He looked at such times like a man intolerably badgered and bedevilled but unable to escape from his tormentor. Once or twice I saw him break out into a sobbing appeal to be left alone at least until he had a chance to finish his dinner. I was beginning to think that

Fudge would crack up or I myself would start screaming if something did not happen to break this horrible pattern of our daily life, when Fudge himself (no worse in health for his adventure in the icy ditch) took a step forward, as I considered it, by suddenly acquiring a girl friend.

Nobody ever found out how he managed this, my theory being that it must have happened while he was only about one-quarter loaded, on the upswing of the manic-depressive cycle that his behaviour had fallen into, and so overflowing with that elephantine good-humour which was the most attractive feature of his personality. All we knew for certain was that the romantic lightning struck him at a dance and apparently struck this girl at the same time, for they soon became very thick and established themselves in the local mind as a courting couple. Perhaps the spectacle of Fudge engaged in dancing a jig all by himself in the centre of the floor (when he had become a little more than one-quarter tight) had roused all the maternal pity, which is so large a part of woman's love, in his sweetheart's breast.

Her name was Jean and she was an outport girl from a place very much like Flowery Cove, but unlike the ill-starred Eunice she seemed quite stable in personality; as a matter of fact, Jean showed clear signs of a well-formed character even at her present age of nineteen and we all agreed that she might be just the kind of girl who would be a good influence on Fudge by not coddling him too much and by making him "stand sound." Evidence of this was soon forthcoming in the way Fudge began to shed his morbid, oafish self-consciousness and mix in the society of his class and generation instead of always just hanging about with the "b'ys." Better still, he got his former job back and even made a start on cutting down his drinking.

Of course the great question in all minds was: How would Mom take this startling development of a romance in Fudge's life and, above all, how would she take to Jean? After one or two meetings she professed to like her all right, though finding her a bit hard and "too stern" for a woman. But Mom also said, when the possibility of an engagement soon came to be discussed, that it might be all for the best. "I wish he *would* get engaged, or do something, to get him offa *my* hands. I'm fair wore out with worry over him." None of us was quite convinced by this, and being on the spot I knew perfectly well that despite all the anxiety and fatigue that Fudge's wild escapades and late hours caused her, she would rather have him at home than win a million dollars tax free.

"Go on, you humbug," I said to her, "you know you don't want to let Fudge an inch out of your clutches."

Mom slewed around and faced me threateningly. "You dry up!" she growled. "If you gets your tongue goin' about Jean or anything I said – look out!" I laughed at her giving herself away so easily, and I promised to say nothing to anybody about Fudge or Jean.

The first idiotic mistake Fudge made after he had got his teeth and got married, was to yield to Mom's insisting that he and Jean should come to live in our house until they "got on their feet" and could afford to rent a place of their own.

Trouble started right after the honeymoon, its first specific cause being the question of who was going to cook Fudge's dinner and serve it up to him when he came home from work at one o'clock. Mom saw no reason why Jean should bother when *she* was already cooking for the family; and in addition, while Fudge was in the house for that hour, she not only served his meal but drew up to him at the table in her same old style of intimacy and tried to draw all his secrets and confidences out of him just as if he had never got married at all. She rode over Jean like a bulldozer in other ways too, and it was not long before I observed a glint in the girl's eye as the truth dawned on her about what kind of family and situation she had got herself into.

The climax of the dinner-time trouble came one day when Jean in a fit of exasperation threw out the meal Mom had cooked for Fudge and served up a cold one she had secretly prepared all on her own in the pantry. Fudge did not like cold food. He ate it, but after this incident an element of active dislike crept into the rivalry between Mom and Jean; furthermore, Jean got into the bad books of the Old Man as well by protesting against Mom's habit of filling up Fudge with scraps left on the Old Man's plate when he was still hungry after eating his own two platefuls and there was no more food in the pot. The Old Man only cursed Jean privately; it was Mom who stirred up all the trouble. Quite useless was my pointing out to her that she was behaving like the worst of all interfering mothers-in-law and at times like an absolute monster. She just warned me again about being saucy and sticking my nose in, and vowed she would never understand why I and apparently all her other children, except Fudge, were so much against her. That was partly why she now clung to Fudge all the more possessively, regardless of Jean's claims on him as his young bride.

After a month or two in the house, Jean started to take out her resentment on the only person available to her wrath—on Fudge, whose predicament was three times as pitiable as it had been in his bachelor days. He had Jean on him as well as Mom, and he had lost all his personal freedom. Now after enduring Mom's mosquito-like buzz-and-sting and blood-sucking at the table, he had to march into his own room and face Jean's wailing about how he neglected her and thought nothing about her, because if he did he wouldn't give in to Mom the way he did. More than once we heard the sound of Jean giving it to Fudge across the chops with a towel or scarf or anything that was within her reaching distance.

Naturally Fudge soon went back in full spate to the booze and the "b'ys," needing them now more than ever, and he again started wasting every cent he could lay his hands on, showing no more shame or sense of responsibility than a greedy spoilt child. On his beginning to slip into debt, Jean took matters into her own hands by going out to work herself, but soon after that she found out that she was pregnant and so resigned herself to the situation at home for a few more months.

The first day she was on her feet again after the birth

she took her baby son and went back to her home, leaving Fudge an ultimatum by which he had to decide whether he wanted to be with Mom in the future or with his own family. Mom did her feeble best to hide her satisfaction, though she did come right out and say that Jean was much too hard on Fudge (she had even tried to put him on a diet), and so perhaps in the long run he would be better off without her.

It looked as if their same old dependent relationship were to be resumed, but now during their huddles at the dinner table I noticed in Fudge's eye a new look of sadness – the consciousness and perhaps also the pride of fatherhood, along with the unease which this new status might have brought into his neglectful way of life. At any rate, I was aware of a new factor in his thinking. Mom too showed a fresh and growing anxiety, obviously brought on by the fear that she might no longer be able to rule and smother Fudge in the way she had been doing for so many years.

Watching them together, I gradually came to feel that they were a tragic as well as a comic pair, and their tortured interdependence no longer appeared in a light that was chiefly grotesque. Mom especially came forward in my imagination as possibly Fudge's only anchor in an ocean of loneliness and bewilderment and frequent self-pitying despair.

Nevertheless, she could not hold him or content him now, a fact that became a little clearer each time Fudge had a letter from Jean. Either he flew to the booze at once, and so tried to dull the piercing pain in his mind, or else he developed alarming physical and nervous symptoms which made us all realize that if he went on in this way of life indefinitely he might very well become a genuine mental case.

Sometimes, when we were playing cards of an evening, he would suddenly stop dead, begin to tremble all over his vast body, break out into an instantaneous mottled rash and glistening globules of sweat, and then give out one long asthmatic sigh after another as if his next breath might be his last. At other times he would give off a violent acrid stench like an over-galloped horse, and for these and other similar attacks there was no treatment that did him any good except to go out on the back steps all by himself and suck in the cold night air in slow, deep inhalations for about an hour at a time. That, and splashing his congested head around in a basin of cold water, was the only thing that could even temporarily relieve his distress and anxiety. When he came back from these solitary struggles for breath and self-control, he always had that gazing-into-eternity look in his shallow brown eyes again.

Whatever the inmost cause of his symptoms, it became clear that if something were not done soon Fudge would just rot away like an old potato left in the wet ground of autumn; and so between Hilda and myself we slowly persuaded Mom that Fudge and his family must be reunited no matter what her personal opinion of Jean was or how stiff the girl might be in dealing with Fudge.

Grudgingly Mom consented to use her influence in that direction, but then there came up the same old difficulty from Jean's categorically refusing to rejoin Fudge as long as he remained under the Old Man's roof. On the other hand, Fudge could certainly not afford to get a place of his own nor could he raise a sufficient sum to make any kind of a down payment. Neither Racer nor Hilda, both of whom had the means, had enough confidence in Fudge to make him a large loan. It looked like a dead end, a situation from which on the human and financial side there was no satisfactory escape.

It was at this point that Mom came up with her ultimate brilliant idea. They would build an apartment onto the back of our house for Fudge and Jean and the baby to live in all by themselves. Dad would go bond for a loan from the bank and Fudge would pay half-rent until in the course of several years the whole thing was paid off and everyone would be satisfied. Of this nobody except Mom felt very sure; in fact, a howl of warning went up from the family on Fudge's behalf, yet in his position there was not much he could do but weakly give in to Mom's persistent urging.

She had already nagged and ragged the Old Man into paying for her folly. As it was, Fudge still had a hard enough time persuading Jean, who would not hear of the apartment at all unless there was a vestibule (neutral ground) between the old place and the new, and unless she had her own key to the connecting door on her side.

After some pooh-poohing from Mom about vestibules and fancy baywop notions ("Who the hell do she t'ink she is – the Princess Marg'ret?"), Jean's conditions were accepted and soon the apartment was far enough along for her to come back and move in there with the baby and Fudge, on the understanding that their life was to be wholly separate and apart from anything that took place in the main household.

What some of the family did not appreciate was that in forwarding this plan Mom herself had made some personal sacrifice beyond the giving up of her cherished baby. Our pantry window was blocked off entirely by the addition to the house, as also the side window of the kitchen, so that with Racer's large house rising up directly below us, and partly blocking our main kitchen window, the kitchen needed artificial light at all times, and on a dull day was like a glimmering tomb. Here Mom spent the largest part of her time and did all her work, yet about this aspect of the new arrangements she never made a single complaint nor any demand for sympathy.

She stuck to the agreement about entirely separate quarters too – for a time. Gradually, however, as the dimness and solitude of the kitchen, reinforced by the Old Man's gloomy silences of marathon length and my own deep absorption in myself, began to get on her nerves and get her down, she would take refuge in the little vestibule and stand at Jean's door listening to what she was saying to Fudge and trying to make out how she was treating him.

Her fixation on Fudge was ten times stronger than any promise. Next she got into the habit of asking Fudge to take her into town to the big stores or just out for a little run in the car on Saturday afternoon whenever Fudge was not busy and the Old Man was in one of his surly moods. As to actual visits to the apartment, Mom at first confined these to times when Jean was away, giving her a clear field with Fudge and no repercussions; then as winter approached again, and the long nights left her forlorn and fidgety, her restraint broke down like a dam slowly overborne by accumulating pressure behind it, and she began to barge into Jean's privacy at any time of the day or night when Fudge might be at home and ready to talk to her. No longer did she pay any heed to past agreements or the danger of present strife.

A real crisis came the day Jean found out that Mom had had an extra key made for Jean's connecting door when the apartment was being built and had kept it all to herself. Within six months of Jean's return, all was as before, the ancient women's battle for possession of son and husband was out in the open again, and Fudge's life in particular was no better than that of a Labrador dog.

Once more his drinking rose to new heights – or depths – and Jean had to go down each payday to the railway office, collect Fudge and his pay, and escort him straight home if she were to salvage from his criminal wastefulness enough money to pay the rent and feed the three of them for another month without missing too many payments on their furniture or becoming saddled with a fresh load of debts.

Life for all of us around the place was just one crisis after another, with now and then a real explosion to mark the end of an old era or the beginning of a new. One day Jean quite unwittingly set the Old Man's temper ablaze in a trivial incident that anyone but the Old Man might have ignored. She had, during a brief interval of truce between the two houses, brought the baby in for a visit and a meal, and when it was over the boy was still crying for more food, keeping it up so long that at last the Old Man took some remains from his own plate, according to our old custom, and handed them to the child to chew on. But before he could even start on his new meal, Jean snatched it away from him in a way that did suggest her dislike of this casual unsanitary way of doing things. That was the end of any truce.

The Old Man saw red; he sprang up from the table, glaring straight down on Jean like an insulted old Mohawk warrior. "Now you get t'Jesus out o' here!" he screeched. "Take yer goddam brat and get out o' my house. Get offa my property altogedder. See how dat suits you."

"I didn't *mean* nothing," cried Jean in a voice tremulous with fear, and she stared up at the Old Man like one staring at a lunatic, observing him for the first time.

"I knows bloody well what you meant. T'ink I'm not good enough for him to eat after, hey? All right. Then I'm not good enough to give ye shelter eeder. So pack yere duds, and fly. Get the hell out o' this house by tomorrow morning or else I'll have ye hove out on the street like the crowd o' goddam bums ye are."

Clutching her child and visibly terrified by this uncalled-for violence on the Old Man's part, Jean rushed out to the apartment and began shoving things into a couple of suitcases with the intention of leaving right away. Something might have been done if Fudge and Mom had combined to resist the eviction, but Fudge was plastered when he came home that night and Mom could never have been more than half-hearted in any effort she might make on Jean's behalf. Apart from all that, Jean herself was determined to go for good.

That night she and the baby stayed with a friend, and the next day she once more set out with the child for her parents' home, leaving Fudge to do whatever he thought best or, as Jean put it in her parting words, whatever he was man enough to do in defence of his wife and son. Fudge did not attack the Old Man for frightening Jean; he just moped and boozed around for a few days, and I sensed that Mom was beginning to feel that if she bided her time she would soon be in full charge of Fudge again.

All her schemes and calculations were shattered to pieces when Fudge took the startling and unpredictable step of drawing five hundred dollars from the apartment account at the bank and running away again – not to his own family but to St. John's, where he went on a wild and lengthy spree that left him physically helpless and financially ruined inside of two weeks. After that he refused to come back home but instead managed to get himself transferred by the railway to St. John's, and there he stayed indefinitely, worrying the life out of Mom but somehow dragging out an existence on his own. The Old Man not only had to put back the money Fudge had taken on false pretences but he also had to look sharp about getting another tenant for the apartment if he were to avoid serious financial trouble.

Mom had a slight stroke the day after Fudge absconded; not enough to incapacitate her yet too much to allow her any clear thinking or power of concentration on any subject in which her emotions were at all involved. We all realized this change in her when, shortly after Fudge's flight, she began to insist that the rent from the apartment should be sent to him, since the place had been built for him and in his name. It was no use my explaining to her that Fudge had no claim to anything whatever, that if he had his rights he would be prosecuted and sent to gaol instead of receiving any benefit from property owned and rented by Dad from the very first. She refused to look at any papers or listen to reason and every now and then would launch out at me or Dad with her nonsensical arguments about Fudge's claim, becoming almost hysterical if her case was ridiculed by us. Any clear-minded person must have seen right away that *nobody* could appropriate the rent from the apartment until the bank loan was paid off and the title to the place clear.

I soon gave up trying to make Mom understand even this elementary fact, and still she would not let me alone on this or any other subject as long as my body was within her reach and no matter where my mind should chance to be. It seemed that to fill up the void in her life caused by Fudge's absence she was now going to clutch at me as a last resort and pour out on my cool and self-reliant head all the frustrated love and longing of her undisciplined nature. I did not want all this devouring attention from her, nor did my temperament take over-kindly to being an obvious substitute in her affections for my younger brother.

Time after time when tea was ready Mom would call out to me, "Now then – come on, Fudgie. Come on. Tea is on the table." She would even stand out in the hall at eight in the morning and again call me repeatedly in his name, so that eventually I got tired of reminding her that my name was Juju. The depth of her grief over Fudge's betrayal by leaving her thus alone was almost equalled by a morbid dread that I too would suddenly go away again and leave her altogether desolate.

This was strongly borne in on me one day when Mom and I had another of our conversations on the subject of my plans for the future. The truth was that on returning home this time I *had* had some thoughts of staying for a while, of easing my world-weariness by coming to terms with Milltown and all that to my mind it represented. But the more I saw of the unchanging situation in our old home and the ghastly conditions in all the other families except Hilda's, the less was I inclined toward reconciliation with my birthplace and toward a permanent residence there. Besides, my position in the house was becoming rather uncomfortable, as I had now been home for more than a year and I sometimes had the unpleasant feeling that if I stayed much longer I might be expected to start thinking about finding some kind of job and paying my board. I never knew at what moment the Old Man might "get dirty" and throw my whole dependent situation up in my face. All the family was in agreement on this kind of thing being his particular specialty. Look, we argued, how he had treated Jean. "Aw, piss on *him*," Mom said once in answer to my doubts about staying. "Don't mind him a-tall. That's only the way he gets on when he's in one of his tantrums."

"But I'll have to make a move sometime, Mom. You know that."

"I knows nutting o' the kind. What do you want to go

away to them foreign countries again for? I know you don't like Milltown, but I daresay there's worse places, and here at home you got most everyt'ing you wants and no worries that I can see."

"Well, I'll tell you, Mom," I replied judiciously, "if somebody offered me a thousand dollars a week, clear money, and no strings attached, then I might consider staying in Milltown. I *might*."

"Pooh! Too bad about you. You must think you're some big." She said this irritably but also with a wounded spirit, as I could tell from her expression. I was beginning to repent of my harshness when her whole look and manner changed abruptly to supplication. "Don't go, Juju, my son. Please. *Promise* me you won't go away and leave me. You're all I got left now."

"I can't promise you that, Mom. I might not be able to live up to my promise."

"Try, for my sake."

"You know how I feel."

"Yes, Juju, my love. But *you* don't know how *I* feels." Something in her voice, a strange undertone or a tremor deeper than usual, caused me to face her directly, and as she held my gaze I saw her eyes darken and glisten in the familiar way they had when sorrow overrode all her other emotions. I tried to soften my refusal a little more.

"It's not as if you'd be completely alone if I went. You've always got Dad here."

"So I have, so I have." This she said in an indescribable tone of disillusionment, while at the same time I noted the corners of her mouth turning down and remaining taut in an expression of what could only be called disgust. "So I have," she repeated again with bitter deliberation. During these painful private moments with her I had some further inkling of what her whole life with the Old Man must have been. I saw clearly and with a sobering thrill of horror that she too had felt and borne against him for many years the same emotions of repulsion and fear that we children had so intensely experienced, only her suffering stretched back so much further than ours. It went back to a time we could only guess at and perhaps contained the most intimate relationship that man and woman can know, agonies and fears that we had never even begun to fathom.

I seemed to understand a little better why she had been willing and eager to make Fudge an emotional cripple and almost to commit murder on him, in a moral sense, and why she was now unashamedly *begging* me not to go away from her. She was utterly dominated by fear of being left all alone with the Old Man. So many of her monstrous acts were explained for me by this dawning revelation. Both her mind and body were saturated by this dread of being left a solitary prisoner in his evil old house.

Yet I could not bring myself to give her a promise that I would remain with her indefinitely, and it was just as well I did not, for shortly after this talk between Mom and myself the Old Man ran true to form by speeding up my plans for departure with another bit of his well-known nastiness.

It was again at tea one evening that he started droning along on his favourite theme of the worthless young, using his own family as prime examples of degeneration. After some few minutes of putting up with his tirade, I broke in with a fresh and contrary example in hopes of getting him to discuss this quite interesting problem calmly, though I might have known better than to try and reason with an embittered, impassioned old man like him.

"But take Rome, for instance," I said, choosing Rome because he was generally recognized within the family as a pretty good man in any sense of the word. "Take Rome. Now, is he any worse a man than his father was, do you think? If so, tell me how." But the Old Man was not telling me anything except what was pressing on his mind, and it was clear that my reference to Rome served only to inflame his indignation against his own offspring.

"There's needer one o' ye acted right!" he howled, ignoring Rome altogether. "Needer one o' ye. Crooks and cheaters and drunkards, the whole goddam bunch, and God knows what else besides. Ye ought to be ashamed to look me in the face. If I'd a done to me own fawder the half – no, the quarter – o' what ye're after doin' to me, I'd never a lived to tell the tale. I'd a been crucified. Yes, *crucified*. I goes to work and drags me guts out fer ye a whole lifetime, and I don't get no more t'anks for it. No sir. A kick in d'arse, and a foul word behind me back. Oh, don't t'ink I don't know! I've a hearrrd yer whisperin' and back-bitin'. Sure signs, ye'll get nutting more out o' me."

His passionately self-justifying words seemed to be tumbling out endlessly while I listened and felt every nerve in my body quivering like a plucked string. I was just clear-headed enough, after about ten minutes of his railing directly at me, to know that I must hold myself in from smashing up the face and beating up the body of an old man who was also legally my father. The next thing I knew, my plate was flying in pieces all over the table, blood was flowing from my hands, and Mom was crying out: "Juju! Look what you're after doin'. You went and smashed up your plate with your two fists." Her shocked words brought me back to full awareness. I turned on the Old Man, who looked pale, deathly pale, and I realized more than ever that he really was a sick man.

"Bullshit," I said to him quietly. "You're talking bullshit."

"I *kept* you all this past year, bullshit or no," he gasped, seeking and stressing the one word that would sting me most deeply. To avoid attacking him I rushed into the bathroom, bathed my blood-smeared hands in cold water, bandaged them with Mom's help, and then began to pack. That very night I tore myself out of Mom's imploring clutches and caught the train to Port-aux-Basques as the first step in my return to Toronto.

But less than a year after my arrival there I received a telegram from Mom saying that Dad was dying and I should come home immediately.

CHAPTER

7

SAUL AND GERTRUDE

The telegram was a lie, or at best a bit of wishful thinking on Mom's part. I saw that the moment I had got back and seen the Old Man. What had happened was that while shovelling snow in the drive he had fallen down and blacked out for about half an hour, and when the doctor came and gave Mom warning that it could be fatal she panicked and began phoning all members of the family in Milltown and sending telegrams to those who were elsewhere.

Fudge had not come or even answered the telegram in any way. That grieved Mom too – more than any threat to the Old Man's health or life, I suspected; but as a matter of fact, there was no actual threat to his life, and after three or four days in bed he was back on his couch again looking little worse than when I had last seen him. There was no perceptible loss of the bit of flesh he had put on since retiring from the mill, nor any obvious sign that he was a doomed man whose days were numbered. The only real change I noticed was a deepening of his pallor and a slight trembling all over his body that was immediately noticeable when you passed close by him or observed him carefully at a little distance.

It was Mom's appearance that now shocked me and gave me pangs of conscience whenever the thought came to me that my absence over the past year might be partly responsible for this further and most deplorable change in her whole appearance and her outlook on life. From Hilda I had heard that Mom too had had a mild stroke some months after I left, but nothing in Hilda's letter or those I had had from Mom herself prepared me for the sight of an old woman who was partly paralyzed on her right side, and had in this brief period of time lost all confidence in herself as wife, mother, cook, housekeeper, confidante, and all the other parts she had played in our lives.

In a few months old age had seized on her prematurely in its worst manifestations: raddled, dew-lapped flesh, innumerable puckering lines like purse strings around her mouth, and a mat and muddy complexion that showed no variation at all except for patches and streaks of the olive-tinted skin common to many diabetics. She could not bear any of us to look at her for long, or closely. How deeply my scrutinizing though sympathetic glances disturbed her was startlingly proved when on the day of my return she came to the tea table wearing lipstick. Our mother wearing make-up! It was incredible, and this was the first time in her life she had ever done so.

"What's ye *gawkin'* at?" she demanded irritably of me and Dad before we had been two minutes at the table.

"For God's sake, girl, what've you got on?" the Old Man made no bones about his disapproval. "What's that — ras'berry jam you got smeared all over your face?" It was a fact that in her usual nervous bustle, increased no doubt by the momentousness of the occasion for her, Mom had overdone her lips and had a good deal of trouble keeping her hand steady for the unaccustomed operation. Anyway, that violent scarlet smear all over her mouth and a little way down her chin did show up in a frightening way against her awfully pale skin. If she was determined on make-up, she should have had Hilda over to assist her the first time.

"Have you been attending the beauty parlours like Crawfie, Mom?" I asked in a light tone intended to divert her mind from the present moment and relieve her embarrassment a little.

"None o' your business! No, I haven't. But I s'pose I can put on a bit o' lipstick if I wants to, same as any other woman, without the world comin' to an end. No crime, is it? But I didn't go and waste any money on it – no. Hilda give it to me out o' the store, if ye wants to know. And God knows I needs it! I looks just like somet'ing was dug up, so I do."

She was pitiable also in her efforts to do the bit of work that was still to be done from day to day around the house. In truth, she was quite unable to keep up with it, or to make any effecive pretence of looking after the place at all. I saw this at once when she started to clear away after tea. She took three or four dishes in one hand and, steadying herself against table or chair or wall with the other, made for the pantry holding the dishes out from her body in painful concentration like somebody entrusted with a precious salver; but at every alternate step her right leg would give way under the weight and she would lurch heavily to one side in a way that was perilous not only to the dishes but also to herself.

Quite often she nearly fell to her knees, but most of the time she made a brave staggering recovery and bore on grimly toward her goal. Whenever a dish or two did shatter on the floor, the Old Man burst out in his familiar tut-tutting and called out to know whether she was going to leave "air dish a-tall" for his breakfast. The whole scene got on my nerves so much that after this first evening at home I volunteered to wash up all the dishes as long as I was there, and so removed at least one cause of their endless profitless bickering.

The house itself now looked and smelt like a tenantless junkshop, with odd piles of dust-furred articles sticking out of every corner, smeary translucent windows, and over the whole place the air of seediness and neglect that time unopposed will soon shed heavily on any dwelling. The big old house had got on top of Mom on the inside, and as far as the outside was concerned, the Old Man just let it slide with a mumbled curse or a bitter word about all the backbreaking labour he had put into the place, and nobody to give him a hand now that he could no longer keep it up himself.

When the inside of the house became so bad that the woman who now rented the apartment used to stick to our kitchen floor when she came in to see Mom, the kind-hearted woman offered to come in and do a little cleaning, but after one or two visits the Old Man had had a fuss with her over something she said about his couch and the state it was in, and thus Mom was left all on her own again with the accumulating housework.

I could not help feeling that with a little more concerted effort he and Mom could have done better by the place, but anything like concerted effort was just what they were not prepared to make. Their verbal duelling began each morning about half an hour before they got up, when it was time for Mom's insulin injection, which she had to have before her breakfast and which the Old Man had learnt to administer, because at the time Mom started on them there was nobody else to give her the injections.

After that came always a slight fuss at breakfast – the only meal for which Mom had any appetite at all nowadays – because the Old Man had got into the habit of asking her if she was going to eat the house down, or what, her reaction being to throw down the piece of dry toast she was cracking into bits and exclaim, "My glory, it seems like you begrudges me the bit I eats! I got to take *somet*'ing, haven't I? That's all I lives for now, sure." Thus they went on all through breakfast and during the time I was clearing away until the meal was behind us and both of them settled down to the serious business of their present-day lives.

This was a perpetual spying on Racer and his family next door. Apart from all other distressing happenings, the Old Man had been carrying on a feud with Racer ever since he, in order to accommodate his increasing family, had put a second storey on his house and so blocked the fine view of the harbour that we used to have from our kitchen window. "He done it a-purpose! He done it a-purpose!" the Old Man shouted at me in the high whine of impotence that his former tone of growling complaint had now become. "He could a built across, instead o' goin' straight up in d'air. But no. Jest fer spite he goes to work and blocks me off till I can't hardly see a foot outside o' me own window."

That was all nonsense, of course. If Racer had built on to his place horizontally, he would have had something like a sprawling barracks on his land and been crowding his fences front and back with no room for the kids to play around the house. However, I was immediately convinced that it would be foolish to try and reason with the Old Man on any subject touching Racer's doings or intentions with regard to the Old Man himself. In revenge for what he called Racer's contrariness, the Old Man sat every morning at the kitchen window, with Mom just opposite him, taking in every least move that was made next door and passing appropriate remarks on it.

There the two of them sat all afternoon engaged in the same pastime too; they seemed to be eternally perched at that window, and nobody next door could so much as go to the toilet without the fact being noted and discussed and criticized in our house. Chief among the Old Man's amusements in this line was to count the deliveries of beer, whiskey, rum, and gin that were made at Racer's back door, but he also took delight in assessing the groceries and other supplies that came.

"Oh, she's gettin' dinner ready!" he used to cackle when he saw a carton of canned goods being handed to Rhoda from the delivery truck. He included Racer's wife in all his ill-will and sarcasm just because she was Racer's wife. His greatest pleasure of all was to rise rather early on a winter morning after an overnight snowfall and gleefully watch Racer (never one for strenuous work) struggle to clear enough snow away from his car and driveway to let him back out onto the hill and get a run down over it. I could always tell by the Old Man's satisfied grunts if Racer were getting stuck in the snow and ice of his drive.

Mom was almost as bad as he, though not malicious in her spying, and as I watched them day after day I was troubled by the way in which the less admirable qualities of each seemed to have permeated the mind of the other. For instance, Mom's well-known, nosey-parker tendencies had by this time become a fixed quality in the Old Man, while his vindictiveness seemed to have tainted somewhat her liberal and easy-going nature. It was uncanny how in one year they had had more influence on each other's character – a sharper process of mutual attrition had taken place – than in all the previous part of their life together. But again what disturbed me was that this influence apparently extended only to their darker habits and harsher qualities rather than to any of the softer elements in their natures. Mom now exhibited too a good deal of the Old Man's touchiness and excitability; he had suddenly lapsed into her notoriously sloppy ways, and there they were, railing at each other all day long about trifles or actively quarrelling about some domestic incident that anyone else would have passed over in silence. Peace was as much a stranger to our house as it had ever been.

My own mind was continually palpitating with the horror of it all, and I found that I had to revise all my ideas about the calm of old age, the quiet evening of life, and other such naive notions. The entire place was electric with discontent and ill-feeling and suppressed hatred. None of the other families ever came into the house now, except for Hilda on her weekly duty visit to Mom, and this neglect shown through the absence of all the boys was characteristically put down by the Old Man to the fact that since his retirement he had had no more money to give them and no favours or benefits of any kind to pass around.

Again I found it futile to try and remind him that all, bar myself, were quite independent of him in a financial sense and were doing fairly well on their own. So I simply held my peace. Mom was deeply puzzled and hurt by the dismal solitude in which she had been left, before I came back, from one week's end to the next. How could I explain to her that anyone who came near the place and stayed for any length of time was apt to feel the foundations of his mental balance being undermined by the cross-currents of hostility flowing between her and the Old Man?

All of us in the family felt these cross-currents most acutely and were repelled by the atmosphere of our old home, by the painful spectacle of our father and mother not only failing to show any sign of reconciliation in old age but actually behaving worse in some ways than in the time of their youth and vigour when they could implement their opposition to each other. Living there with them I had daily proof of their failure, and it filled me with bafflement and despair and sometimes with horror. Each noon when Mom called out to the Old Man to come and peel the vegetables for dinner, he made a fuss over it, giving as his reason that this was not his job, even though Mom was quite incapable of handling knife and potato together adequately since her last stroke.

Perhaps the worst proof of their profound division came one morning after the Old Man had complained of a little puddle of water on the kitchen floor and Mom took a rag and bent down to mop it up. Suddenly she keeled over completely and came down on the floor with a tremendous thump; and all the time I was struggling to raise her unmanageable dead weight and get her to a chair, the Old Man just sat on his couch with his mouth open cackling with impatience about her clumsiness.

Mom was laid up for several days after that, a result which forcefully brought home to my mind the possibility that she and not the Old Man would be the first of them to go. Somehow all of us in the family had come to take it for granted that the Old Man would die first and so leave her victor in the ultimate duel of their half-century of running combat. The rivalry between them for mere survival was out in the open now. It came out most unpleasantly in Mom's case through the bitter and disgusted way she was always going on about how the Old Man would soon be married again if anything happened to her and thus waste his bit of money on some old bag when he should be spending it on his wife here and now.

Very strange indeed I found this forward-reaching kind of jealousy, but when in a quiet moment I tried to reason with Mom about it (what possible difference could it make to her what the Old Man did after she was gone?), she only brushed me aside with an even greater impatience than she used to let loose on the Old Man whenever this subject came up. No matter how she went on, I found that a radical readjustment of my thinking was needed in order to conceive the mere possibility of her dying first. Perhaps I too was guilty of some wishful thinking, which received fresh stimulus from time to time at this period by continued attacks on me from the Old Man.

There was one crucial episode just after tea one evening through our somehow getting onto the dangerous subject of the duty of children toward their parents. I had still not thoroughly learnt the lesson that it was out of the question to have an impersonal theoretic discussion with the Old Man on any subject, much less on one like this. The Old Man took violent refuge as usual in reiterated statements about all that his children owed to him.

"No," I countered, "I don't see that children *owe* anything to their parents – beyond the doubtful gift of birth. I don't say, either, that they shouldn't do anything for them. That's a different matter altogether. But it seems to me that since the parents are responsible for the child's existence, they owe everything to him. Now, if it were the other way around, and the child were responsible for the parents' existence, then certainly I would say that he owes them a great deal."

I went on for some time in this logical strain, and for once the Old Man did not interrupt me; but throughout my exposition of these complacent views he just sat there staring at me in absolute silence, biting pieces off his fingernails with his new teeth, deliberately spitting them out straight at me one after the other like delayed-action bullets. No words could have so stingingly conveyed his rejection of my thought and his contempt for the thinker. Never in my life had I felt relaxed or even comfortable while sitting in the same room with him. Now I was agonized and appalled by this glimpse I had just had into the unplumbable bitterness of the man's mind, and my feeling was that at the moment I could not even remain in the house with him for another second, thinking as I was of how his inwardly boiling rage against some of the others was still more intense than what he had shown against me, of how he must feel himself to be surrounded by antagonisms like a ring of spears prodding him toward the final abyss, and yet was stubbornly holding on to life up to the very last vengeful moment. With my mind in a whirl of horror I got up and made for the back door, only to find that icy hail was pelting down over the Heights in a thunderous density. I rushed off to my room and took up my *Portable Spinoza*.

The stagnant situation in the house was getting me down so frequently that, in spite of the physical comfort and the leisure of being at home, I was beginning to think of taking off again. Mom and Dad simply could not leave each other in peace for as much as ten minutes at a time, and consequently nobody else in the house could get any peace. I had to admit that in this regard Mom was the chief disturber, for the Old Man might have sat there on his couch by the window all day, his still-powerful hands crossed over his genitals, head falling forward limply, and his wispy white hair tangled all over his head, if Mom had not kept after him. Instead of talking he was in the habit of making a constant and monotonous sibilant sound that was neither whistling nor humming nor singing. It exasperated Mom beyond all measure.

"What in the world is you always *sifflin'* like that for?" she frequently demanded of him.

"Aw, leave me alone for *five* minutes, will you? You won't rest y'self, nor you won't let nobody else rest. Always got a bumblebee up yer arse, you have."

Or else they were forever at odds over the car, which the Old Man wanted to leave where it was about six days a week but which Mom, if she could get around at all, wanted to be out in seven days if she could get anybody to drive her. Her daily campaign to get out of the house usually started after her breafast. "My, it's a fine day!" She would fire this first shot at no one in particular; then about dinner time she always came out with a remark about how nice a day it was for a little run. Finally at two o'clock: "Come on, Dad. Let's go out for a drive. I feels like some fresh air, and it's a sin to stick in the house on a fine day like this. Besides, I got one or two little things I wants to get at the supermarket."

That last bit generally put the Old Man off the whole idea because, though he had not a thing in the world to do, he got into an itching temper if he had to wait as much as fifteen minutes for her in the car. The notion of going into the store with her and helping her with the shopping never occurred to him. Their usual compromise in this dispute, which took hours each day to settle, was to go out for an hour or so on Wednesday and Saturday afternoons if the weather was not too bad or driving conditions not dangerous.

They were indeed a sad pair, two old people chafing and cursing with boredom when there was nothing going on at Racer's, and forever raging against the burden of time they had to drag on from one long, stale Sunday to another. At times there did come a moment of civility between them, but to find it was like a mining operation where you have to turn over a ton of earth in order to produce one ounce of precious metal. At other times I became convinced that Mom's mind as well as her body was breaking down under the strain of (or as a result of) her year of solitary confinement with the Old Man and all this mere waiting for death. Not only was her former rough and hard-hitting humour disappearing, but she could not now take the least little joke against herself or any of her actions.

Often we all had to pass things off and pretend not to have noticed anything strange. Once, during a rare card game, she held up the nine of diamonds, somebody having just played the eight, and asked with wandering eye and a total want of confidence in herself: "Do that beat that?"

Worst of all was her tendency to reveal things said to her in confidence, or as a private joke, and under her promise of their not going further. "Juju says you're like a monument," she blurted out at the Old Man one day when all three of us were at the dinner table. After several trying experiences like this, I learned to be wary of what I told her, but then her reaction was to begin telling me what other members of the family were saying or had said in the past about me and my way of life.

Racer, it seemed, was my chief critic. "He says you ought to have your arse kicked," she informed me with a laugh. "You with all your learning, and not a copper to your name. He says you ought to be *made* to work steady like everyone else, and no foolishness about it." It seemed almost that her only purpose in life was to stir up trouble, any excitement at all to relieve the vacuous flurry of her thoughts and the crushing monotony of her whole life. Combined with the poisonous effluvia that emanated all day from the Old Man's mind, like the black bile continually burping up from his stomach, her antics were almost too much for even a quiet, well-wishing son to bear.

In morbid moments I suspected that the Old Man, whom from my childhood onward I had always secretly believed to be half mad, had within a year driven Mom to a similar condition and very nearly precipitated her into the grave. She was most moving and pitiable of all when in rare moments of stillness she now looked out on the world and even on her own children with the remote and timeless gaze of one who has been brushed by the wings of death. Death alone could lift the yoke from her neck or from Dad's and put a merciful end to all those years which they had endured together in harness but never in harmony, urged forward in time by the momentum of their hapless union and its biological consequences.

What finally decided me to leave was the approach of Mom and Dad's golden wedding anniversary. Christmas at home was bad enough, with all its humbug and pretence and calculated gift-giving, and above all the problem of what if anything to give the Old Man as a present just to keep him quiet – with its explosive card games, drunkenness, gluttony, new-born hates and feuds, childish resentments of fancied slights between one family group and another. All that was hard to swallow, certainly; but the idea of *celebrating* the fifty years of war between two of the most ill-matched people in the world, of rejoicing in something that by the laws of man should never have taken place at all, and by the laws of humanity should never have been continued – all that was simply too much for my stomach to take. I resolved on escape in the early spring before the anniversary was close and my reason for flight too painfully obvious. This time Mom was too far gone in melancholy to make any effort at stopping me, merely casting herself on my mercy and at last accepting my decision with a kind of dumb despair.

And then on the Saturday night before I was due to leave, the Old Man died suddenly of a heart attack.

CHAPTER

8

SAUL

Appropriately enough, he died during a game of cards while slamming the jack of trumps down on Mom's ace. It was all over in a minute or two. With his arm still upraised he gave a convulsive gasp, the card fluttered quietly down from his hand, and he slumped forward on the table with no other sign of a mortal seizure beyond a slight foam at the lips and that sudden frightening remoteness in his entire look and posture. There was no time for any parting words — no last complaint or curse before the darkness came down over his dark spirit forever. Even when the doctor came and confirmed his death, we could hardly believe he was gone at last.

My departure was now postponed indefinitely, and Fudge arrived home on the following Sunday vowing that by some mistake he had not received Mom's previous and premature telegram about Dad's dying condition until the news had also reached him that there was no immediate danger. In any case, Mom was more than eager to forgive him this or any other fault. She implicitly believed his story, and from the first moment he was back in the house began to peck at him with all her old carnivorous urgency. The very afternoon he arrived I overheard her offering to help him with the maintenance payments to Jean (out of her forthcoming old-age pension) if only he would promise to stay home now and try to stay sober as well. From Fudge's look and manner. I gathered that he might very well be persuaded to stay home.

It was the month of March, and the first question that now arose was whether Dad was to be buried at this time or if he was to have the usual church service and then be kept until spring when the frost would be out of the ground and burial much easier. Mom did say at one point: "I feels like I'd like to keep un for a little while, now he's gone," but she herself was quite incapable of deciding anything, being prostrate with relief; and so we called a family conference, headed by Ank, and with almost no discussion at all settled for immediate burial, even though that would be considerably more expensive in every way.

Hilda and Racer agreed to share the extra expense between them. Mom insisted on paying the basic funeral expenses out of the estate, which we knew was all hers according to the will, but I fancied a certain parsimony in her approach to the matter now that her life-long provider was gone. Perhaps this attitude was indirect proof of her feeling that from now on she might have to look out for herself no matter how many children she had. Futhermore, she immediately announced that she would never leave her own home (her gaol as she had always called it), and in this decision I already saw her plan to keep Fudge in the house with her permanently, since by common agreement among us it was established that she must not be trusted hereafter to live in safety all by herself.

On the day of the funeral, as we all stood around the grave, I covertly studied the family faces and wondered what thoughts were passing behind the walls of their eyes. Ank looked as fierce and sombre as if he were having his picture taken; Hilda was equally hard to judge because she was totally preoccupied with supporting and comforting Mom; and Racer, fortified by neat whiskey against the cold, looked only a little more browned-off with everything than he usually did. Crawfie stood with an enormous handkerchief billowing whitely in one hand, but he had a face so long and solemn by nature that it would have taken a cataclysm of emotion to make his feelings apparent. And as for Fudge, he stood to one side twisting and squirming and fretting just as he had done in childhood when any sort of occasion that roused or called for emotion came suddenly upon him.

I myself could make no pretence to any real grief. My inmost thought concerning the Old Man was a wonder at the miracle of his surviving so long and not being launched into hell by one of his sons ahead of his time. And the moment when I first looked down on him in his coffin my chief thought was of the physical smallness of a man in death, after the eviscerators got through with him.

During the days that followed his passing, I had particular cause to consider my true feelings about him because I, as the one with the most education in the family, had been deputed by Mom to compose an inscription for the tombstone that she insisted must go up over his grave. All my cogitations over this task began with the same query: How was it that in all these years in this town our father had come to be known in the mill as an honest, hard-working man; on Humber Heights as a decent, God-fearing neighbour; and inside his own home as an unmitigated son of a bitch? The mystery of his rebarbative nature was as deep as the mystery of life itself, yet if only for my own personal satisfaction I had to find some reason, some clue to account for his profound unhappiness within himself and the way he had injected misery into those closest to him like some vicious, inalienable disease.

How came it that a man who had been right about so many things, especially where his family was concerned, could be so blind to the one thing needful in the hearts of all his kin? In my mental thrashing about, I inevitably compared him with Mom in his relationship to us children. She too had faults like mountains, but when you had climbed over them and come down into the soft and pleasant valley of her real nature you found always that she held open to you the door of human kindness and communication. In his puzzling rage against all life, the Old Man slammed that door in your face.

There lay the fundamental difference between them. Even Mom's follies and crimes in relation to Fudge were explicable when I considered them against the background of the arctic void which the Old Man created around himself and sent through Mom a chill of dismay, and might have frozen her into death if in those later years she had not had Fudge close by to warm her with his presence and keep flowing the wellspring of her all too human kindness.

I could not escape the thought that the Old Man's perversity had been deliberate and gratuitous. He had gone down to oblivion convinced that his wife and all his children scorned him because he could not even write his own name, but I knew from my own experience and from talking to Hilda and the others that this was a distortion of the truth. True, we despised him. That had to be admitted in common honesty; the point was, however, that our scorn was our revenge for never having had a soft word from him in the tender days of our childhood, and again our revenge for the blighting fear he had instilled into our young minds and bodies.

How to put any of the truth within the narrow space of a tombstone? It could not be done, or if done in brief, could not be made public in that way. So for many days and nights I considered what word was appropriate to write above our father's grave, something that might even suggest the true bitterness of his life and the ultimate tragic loneliness of his death. I could find no more than this:

SAUL STONE
1892–1963

He had no middle name, and the starkness of those two monosyllables with their dates, to tell merely for what period of time this human identity had trodden this earth, seemed to symbolize in itself the terrible meagreness and coldness of his life. Less tragic the whole picture might have been if the venom that flowed in his veins had died with him; but it passed on as a dark legacy to each one of his sons and came out in various forms of abnormality which stunted our growth as human beings, gave us a terror of all responsibility, and cut us off from the life-saving to-and-fro of emotional warmth.

In Ank, it came out chiefly as an insensitivity amounting to brutishness; in Racer, as a secretly rooted conviction of life's futility, no matter what success was achieved; in Crawfie, as callousness that cried out a whip, so inhuman it appeared to be; and in Fudge (through the instrumentality of Mom), as a pathological immaturity well past his time of manhood. Nor had I escaped, since from youth I knew myself to be infected with a secret coldness and a savage misanthropy that grew with the years like a galloping cancer. None of the other boys could bear life at all without the drug and the periodical forgetfulness of the booze, and my own confirmed addiction after my stomach failed me was to the printed word or the flickering dream-world of the movies.

All these undeniable facts brought me no closer to an explanation of Dad's fate, of all the wasted opportunities for human tenderness in his life, and all the hate that had twisted and tormented him for as long as we his children could remember. I concluded that no explanation would ever come to satisfy my mind, and yet in the course of my searching I did seem to find one clue that made the mystery less deep, if no less terrible, than when I had begun to consider it. This clue I found after many more hours of reflection on the palpable blight that Dad had cast over the lives of all his sons. Might it not reasonably be, I asked myself, that he in turn had been blighted and desiccated and warped by the conditions of his own early years?

From there my mind travelled back to all I had heard of the horror of his ancestry in Ireland and his own childhood and youth in Raggedy Cove, Conception Bay. I thought of the frightful circumstances under which he had been born a semi-orphan, and of how harsh and bitter must have been his fight for the right just to go on living. Many grim tales I had heard and read of life in our island home over those years. Our father's daily companions and his great unresting enemies had been hunger and insecurity, which perhaps had left neither to him nor those close to him any inclination or indeed any strength for the indulgence of the softer emotions; it was grimness and battle all the way through his early life on the east coast of this island and Labrador, where each day's food must be won from a capricious ocean or a niggardly cold and rocky soil. It was mostly a famine and rarely a feast for anyone then living in the Raggedy Coves of our crazy coastline. Not until our father had been some years in the economic haven of Milltown was he ever liberated from this fret and fear of a screaming stomach. And then it was too late.

Was there any truth in my idea that by some strange process of diffusion this physical misery and the implacable hardness it gave him somehow passed into his moral and emotional and spiritual nature as well? Did it leave in his mind and heart a substratum of fear that made him invincibly shy of revealing himself or exposing himself so that he might receive still more hurt in the human relationships of daily life?

Poverty, and its Siamese twin ignorance, must have caused him endless humiliations of spirit long before he was a man, and bred in him that profound modesty which is such a distinguishing mark of our people as a whole that it amounts to an island-wide inferiority complex. Emotional constriction – and from such causes – has always been a well-known feature of Newfoundland life. It was as though all the hardship and hunger our fathers collectively endured had materialized in the form of a spectre which dogged them through all their days and was forever warning them to put no trust in this life nor in anyone connected with it or with them for as long as life endured.

I hoped there was some truth in my idea, for then I could

see a brighter side to the picture. To the extent that economic causes explained Dad's tragedy, I could feel certain that it would never occur again, since the day was long past when isolation and its attendant horrors was our island's chief curse, and men in obscure bays and coves had to exist on a dole of six cents a day if no fish came to their grounds in a particular year.

We as Newfoundlanders were no longer the stepchildren of a distant and once-rapacious Empire. We were now brothers to one-half of a mighty nearby continent, and that one great fact alone insured us for the foreseeable future against privation and the lonely death-in-life, both humanly and economically, that so many of our forefathers had known.

All this could be of no benefit to Dad, and it could be of little benefit to any of his sons. For them too the damage was done, and the relative prosperity of recent years made no essential difference. Home had bred them, and Milltown possessed them; there they remained, strangers to their own blood and faithful to nothing but the bottle. Each of them had passed through his own loneliness to the edge of desolation. It seemed that in childhood they had been inoculated with a virus which broke out later in the form of an almost complete paralysis of the human being. Neither Ank, Racer, Crawfie, nor Fudge could shake free of the strange fatal lethargy which the spewing forth of a father's indiscriminate hate had cast over the will of each one of them.

And I? Once more, seeing that Fudge was now restored to Mom's arms and probably for good, thus leaving her as contented as she could ever hope to be during the remainder of her life – once more I said goodbye to Milltown and all its works. I thanked God for Hilda, but I was bent on going for good. So for the last time I took the westbound express and struck out blindly across the world in my urgent and frantic and hopeless hunt for love.

THE NEW CANADIAN LIBRARY

- n 1. OVER PRAIRIE TRAILS / Frederick Philip Grove
- n 2. SUCH IS MY BELOVED / Morley Callaghan
- n 3. LITERARY LAPSES / Stephen Leacock
- n 4. AS FOR ME AND MY HOUSE / Sinclair Ross
- n 5. THE TIN FLUTE / Gabrielle Roy
- n 6. THE CLOCKMAKER / Thomas Chandler Haliburton
- n 7. THE LAST BARRIER AND OTHER STORIES / Charles G. D. Roberts
- n 8. BAROMETER RISING / Hugh MacLennan
- n 9. AT THE TIDE'S TURN AND OTHER STORIES / Thomas H. Raddall
- n10. ARCADIAN ADVENTURES WITH THE IDLE RICH / Stephen Leacock
- n11. HABITANT POEMS / William Henry Drummond
- n12. THIRTY ACRES / Ringuet
- n13. EARTH AND HIGH HEAVEN / Gwethalyn Graham
- n14. THE MAN FROM GLENGARRY / Ralph Connor
- n15. SUNSHINE SKETCHES OF A LITTLE TOWN / Stephen Leacock
- n16. THE STEPSURE LETTERS / Thomas McCulloch
- n17. MORE JOY IN HEAVEN / Morley Callaghan
- n18. WILD GEESE / Martha Ostenso
- n19. THE MASTER OF THE MILL / Frederick Philip Grove
- n20. THE IMPERIALIST / Sara Jeannette Duncan
- n21. DELIGHT / Mazo de la Roche
- n22. THE SECOND SCROLL / A. M. Klein
- n23. THE MOUNTAIN AND THE VALLEY / Ernest Buckler
- n24. THE RICH MAN / Henry Kreisel
- n25. WHERE NESTS THE WATER HEN / Gabrielle Roy
- n26. THE TOWN BELOW / Roger Lemelin
- n27. THE HISTORY OF EMILY MONTAGUE / Frances Brooke
- n28. MY DISCOVERY OF ENGLAND / Stephen Leacock
- n29. SWAMP ANGEL / Ethel Wilson
- n30. EACH MAN'S SON / Hugh MacLennan
- n31. ROUGHING IT IN THE BUSH / Susanna Moodie
- n32. WHITE NARCISSUS / Raymond Knister
- n33. THEY SHALL INHERIT THE EARTH / Morley Callaghan
- n34. TURVEY / Earle Birney
- n35. NONSENSE NOVELS / Stephen Leacock
- n36. GRAIN / R. J. C. Stead
- n37. LAST OF THE CURLEWS / Fred Bodsworth
- n38. THE NYMPH AND THE LAMP / Thomas H. Raddall
- n39. JUDITH HEARNE / Brian Moore
- n40. THE CASHIER / Gabrielle Roy
- n41. UNDER THE RIBS OF DEATH / John Marlyn
- n42. WOODSMEN OF THE WEST / M. Allerdale Grainger
- n43. MOONBEAMS FROM THE LARGER LUNACY / Stephen Leacock
- n44. SARAH BINKS / Paul Hiebert
- n45. SON OF A SMALLER HERO / Mordecai Richler
- n46. WINTER STUDIES AND SUMMER RAMBLES / Anna Jameson
- n47. REMEMBER ME / Edward Meade
- n48. FRENZIED FICTION / Stephen Leacock
- n49. FRUITS OF THE EARTH / Frederick Philip Grove
- n50. SETTLERS OF THE MARSH / Frederick Philip Grove

- n51. THE BACKWOODS OF CANADA / Catharine Parr Traill
- n52. MUSIC AT THE CLOSE / Edward McCourt
- n53. MY REMARKABLE UNCLE / Stephen Leacock
- n54. THE DOUBLE HOOK / Sheila Watson
- n55. TIGER DUNLOP'S UPPER CANADA / William Dunlop
- n56. STREET OF RICHES / Gabrielle Roy
- n57. SHORT CIRCUITS / Stephen Leacock
- n58. WACOUSTA / John Richardson
- n59. THE STONE ANGEL / Margaret Laurence
- n60. FURTHER FOOLISHNESS / Stephen Leacock
- n61. MARCHBANKS' ALMANACK / Robertson Davies
- n62. THE LAMP AT NOON AND OTHER STORIES / Sinclair Ross
- n63. THE HARBOUR MASTER / Theodore Goodridge Roberts
- n64. THE CANADIAN SETTLER'S GUIDE / Catharine Parr Traill
- n65. THE GOLDEN DOG / William Kirby
- n66. THE APPRENTICESHIP OF DUDDY KRAVITZ / Mordecai Richler
- n67. BEHIND THE BEYOND / Stephen Leacock
- n68. A STRANGE MANUSCRIPT FOUND IN A COPPER CYLINDER / James De Mille
- n69. LAST LEAVES / Stephen Leacock
- n70. THE TOMORROW-TAMER / Margaret Laurence
- n71. ODYSSEUS EVER RETURNING / George Woodcock
- n72. THE CURÉ OF ST. PHILIPPE / Francis William Grey
- n73. THE FAVOURITE GAME / Leonard Cohen
- n74. WINNOWED WISDOM / Stephen Leacock
- n75. THE SEATS OF THE MIGHTY / Gilbert Parker
- n76. A SEARCH FOR AMERICA / Frederick Philip Grove
- n77. THE BETRAYAL / Henry Kreisel
- n78. MAD SHADOWS / Marie-Claire Blais
- n79. THE INCOMPARABLE ATUK / Mordecai Richler
- n80. THE LUCK OF GINGER COFFEY / Brian Moore
- n81. JOHN SUTHERLAND: ESSAYS, CONTROVERSIES AND POEMS / Miriam Waddington
- n82. PEACE SHALL DESTROY MANY / Rudy Henry Wiebe
- n83. A VOICE FROM THE ATTIC / Robertson Davies
- n84. PROCHAIN EPISODE / Hubert Aquin
- n85. ROGER SUDDEN / Thomas H. Raddall
- n86. MIST ON THE RIVER / Hubert Evans
- n87. THE FIRE-DWELLERS / Margaret Laurence
- n88. THE DESERTER / Douglas LePan
- n89. ANTOINETTE DE MIRECOURT / Rosanna Leprohon
- n90. ALLEGRO / Felix Leclerc
- n91. THE END OF THE WORLD AND OTHER STORIES / Mavis Gallant
- n92. IN THE VILLAGE OF VIGER AND OTHER STORIES / Duncan Campbell Scott
- n93. THE EDIBLE WOMAN / Margaret Atwood
- n94. IN SEARCH OF MYSELF / Frederick Philip Grove
- n95. FEAST OF STEPHEN / Robertson Davies
- n96. A BIRD IN THE HOUSE / Margaret Laurence
- n97. THE WOODEN SWORD / Edward McCourt
- n98. PRIDE'S FANCY / Thomas Raddall
- n99. OX BELLS AND FIREFLIES / Ernest Buckler
- n100. ABOVE GROUND / Jack Ludwig
- n101. NEW PRIEST IN CONCEPTION BAY / Robert Traill Spence Lowell
- n102. THE FLYING YEARS / Frederick Niven
- n103. WIND WITHOUT RAIN / Selwyn Dewdney
- n104. TETE BLANCHE / Marie-Claire Blais

n105. TAY JOHN / Howard O'Hagan
n106. CANADIANS OF OLD / Charles G. D. Roberts
n107. HEADWATERS OF CANADIAN LITERATURE / Andrew MacMechan
n108. THE BLUE MOUNTAINS OF CHINA / Rudy Wiebe
n109. THE HIDDEN MOUNTAIN / Gabrielle Roy
n110. THE HEART OF THE ANCIENT WOOD / Charles G. D. Roberts
n111. JEST OF GOD / Margaret Laurence
n112. SELF CONDEMNED / Wyndham Lewis
n113. DUST OVER THE CITY / André Langevin
n114. OUR DAILY BREAD / Frederick Philip Grove
n115. THE CANADIAN NOVEL IN THE TWENTIETH CENTURY / edited by George Woodcock
n116. THE VIKING HEART / Laura Goodman Salverson
n117. DOWN THE LONG TABLE / Earle Birney
n118. GLENGARRY SCHOOL DAYS / Ralph Connor
n119. THE PLOUFFE FAMILY / Roger Lemelin
n120. WINDFLOWER / Gabrielle Roy
n121. THE DISINHERITED / Matt Cohen
n122. THE TEMPTATIONS OF BIG BEAR / Rudy Wiebe
n123. PANDORA / Sylvia Fraser
n124. HOUSE OF HATE / Percy Janes
n125. A CANDLE TO LIGHT THE SUN / Patricia Blondal
n126. THIS SIDE JORDAN / Margaret Laurence
n127. THE RED FEATHERS / T. G. Roberts
n128. I AM MARY DUNNE / Brian Moore
n129. THE ROAD PAST ALTAMONT / Gabrielle Roy
n130. KNIFE ON THE TABLE / Jacques Godbout
n131. THE MANAWAKA WORLD OF MARGARET LAURENCE / Clara Thomas

o 2. MASKS OF FICTION: CANADIAN CRITICS ON CANADIAN PROSE / edited by A. J. M. Smith
o 3. MASKS OF POETRY: CANADIAN CRITICS ON CANADIAN VERSE / edited by A. J. M. Smith

POETS OF CANADA:

o 1. VOL. I: POETS OF THE CONFEDERATION / edited by Malcolm Ross
o 4. VOL. III: POETRY OF MIDCENTURY / edited by Milton Wilson
o 5. VOL. II: POETS BETWEEN THE WARS / edited by Milton Wilson
o 6. THE POEMS OF EARLE BIRNEY
o 7. VOL. IV: POETS OF CONTEMPORARY CANADA / edited by Eli Mandel
o 8. VOL. V: NINETEENTH-CENTURY NARRATIVE POEMS / edited by David Sinclair
o 9. SELECTED POEMS OF BLISS CARMAN / edited by John Robert Sorfleet

CANADIAN WRITERS

w 1. MARSHALL MCLUHAN / Dennis Duffy
w 2. E. J. PRATT / Milton Wilson
w 3. MARGARET LAURENCE / Clara Thomas
w 4. FREDERICK PHILIP GROVE / Ronald Sutherland

- w 5. LEONARD COHEN / Michael Ondaatje
- w 6. MORDECAI RICHLER / George Woodcock
- w 7. STEPHEN LEACOCK / Robertson Davis
- w 8. HUGH MACLENNAN / Alec Lucas
- w 9. EARLE BIRNEY / Richard Robillard
- w10. NORTHROP FRYE / Ronald Bates
- w11. MALCOLM LOWRY / William H. New
- w12. JAMES REANEY / Ross G. Woodman
- w13. GEORGE WOODCOCK / Peter Hughes
- **w14. FARLEY MOWAT / Alec Lucas**
- **w15. ERNEST BUCKLER / Alan Young**